Into the
Night Sky

ALSO BY CAROLINE FINNERTY

The Last Goodbye

In a Moment

Into the Night Sky

Caroline Finnerty

WARD
RIVER
PRESS

This novel is entirely a work of fiction. The names, characters and incidents portrayed in it are the work of the author's imagination. Any resemblance to actual persons, living or dead, events or localities is entirely coincidental.

Published 2015
by Ward River Press
123 Grange Hill, Baldoyle
Dublin 13, Ireland
www.wardriverpress.com

A catalogue record for this book is available from the British Library.

1

ISBN 978-1-78199-957-8

Printed and bound by CPI Group (UK) Ltd, Croydon, CR0 4YY
Author cover photo Peter Evers of Penry Photography

www.wardriverpress.com

ABOUT THE AUTHOR

Caroline Finnerty lives on the banks of the Grand Canal in the County Kildare countryside with her husband, three children and their dog. *Into the Night Sky* is her third novel.

You can learn more about Caroline on her website www.carolinefinnerty.ie or on Facebook www.facebook.com/carolinefinnertybooks or on Twitter where she goes as @cfinnertywriter

For Simon,
My love, always.

He stands in the evening stillness and breathes in deeply. The air is cold – it hits his lungs hard and sharp, tasting like wood smoke from the chimneys channelling their smoke upwards in diagonal lines. He exhales and watches his breath cloud out into the air in front of him. The grass is already white-tipped and everything looks bleached under the moonlight. It feels as though he is intruding into nature's time – the time when she wishes to be left alone in the magic of night before the demands of a new day take over. Somewhere in the middle distance he can hear the dry snap of a twig breaking. He takes hold of the letter in his gloved hand and brings the paper up close to his face to read afresh the words he wrote just minutes before while sitting at the kitchen table. Their kitchen table. He studies his own handwriting for a minute. Already the words seem to be losing their familiarity – they don't say everything that he wanted to say, like something got lost between his head and the paper.

He folds the letter in half and picks up the white paper lantern. He secures the letter on a hook inside the top of the lantern which he then sets down while he roots for the box of matches in his pocket, finds it and takes one out. It makes a dry, scraping sound as he pulls it back along the rough red strip until "Shsssssisshh", the flame hisses to life and the smell of sulphur enters his nostrils. He has always liked that smell. He brings the match to meet the lighting strip of the lantern and watches as it catches fire instantly and starts to glow a warm orange. It's the same colour as when you look up at the sun with your eyes closed on a fine summer's day and you can see the blood inside your lids.

He holds the lantern steady with both hands, keeping it with him until the moment that he is ready to let go and then he releases it and it starts its ascent upwards, carrying his words with it. He looks on as it wobbles back and forth while it tries to find its first feet on the air and he worries that it might not make it up there after all. He watches anxiously but it holds its own and continues upwards until it is level with the slate rooftops of the nearby houses. It gets braver still and climbs above the yellow chimneypots, ready to go on its way, into the night sky.

Chapter 1

Something bad is going to happen. She can feel it. The feeling is suffocating. Stifling. What if she has stopped breathing? What if the duvet is covering her face? What if she accidentally rolls on top of her and smothers her?

Ella Wilde bolts upright in the bed and reaches out to place a hand on her daughter Maisie's small body to check yet again if she is still breathing. She feels the gentle rise and fall of her chest and, reassured, she lies back down. But the voice starts up again. *Now! Quickly, you really need to check her now! Something bad is going to happen.* She can't shake it off. It is coming from the very kernel of her being. It is ten past four in the morning and this has been happening all night long. On and on it goes. She sits up again and reaches over to do the same thing and of course Maisie is still breathing, as she knew she would be. Logically she knows that at five months old Maisie is past the risk age for cot death but still the thought torments her. She tries to switch off and sleep, but then a niggling doubt perched on the ever-present gnawing feeling of dread starts again. *Check her now,* the voice says, *she might have stopped now* – and she has to check her because she knows that the one time she doesn't check, is the time that something will happen.

The clock reads six and she decides to get up and go upstairs to the kitchen of their converted Martello tower house, letting her husband Dan and Maisie sleep on in the bed. Outside the window the sun is starting to come up, lighting the sky in shades of orange and red. The sea glimmers silver. She can feel her heart thumping against her ribcage and she doesn't know why.

A while later Dan comes up the stairs with the baby in his arms. He hands her over to Ella and sets about making her a bottle.

"You're up early."

"I couldn't sleep."

"I've noticed that you haven't been sleeping well at all lately."

"I think I'm going mad," she blurts out. "I can't sleep. I lie awake all night long staring at the ceiling."

"Why?" he says, pushing two slices of bread down into the toaster while he waits for the bottle to heat.

"I don't know what is wrong with me."

"You're just tired."

"It's more than that. I'm exhausted all the time. I just can't seem to get it together at all. It's like the smallest of tasks stresses me out completely and sends me into a tizzy."

"Well, you're under a lot of pressure at work."

"But this is different –"

"How do you mean?"

"I just can't explain it."

"Look, once you have a decent night's sleep you'll be grand."

"Do you really think so?" She feels the pressure of tears build at the corners of her eyes but she blinks them back quickly.

"Yeah, of course I do."

He is laughing now and she knows he doesn't get it. He isn't taking her seriously, he doesn't understand how awful things have been for her lately and she doesn't seem to be able to articulate it to make him understand. The problem is, she thinks wryly, that she's not sure if she even understands it herself.

Later she straps Maisie into her car seat and climbs into the driver's seat. She's not sure where she's going to go but all she knows is that she can't face staring at the stone walls of her kitchen all day. Dan is taking their two older children, Celeste and Dot, to their swimming lessons so it's just her and Maisie alone together for the afternoon. She is about to turn the key in the ignition when the doubts start up again. *What if she's not strapped in properly? What if the straps are too loose?* She doesn't trust that she has done it properly so she has to get back out and check it again. This has been happening a lot lately. Her mind constantly questions itself.

She drives down the steep incline from Land's End Rock. The sea is twinkling on her left and yellow flowered gorse bushes and green scrub cover the rocks on her right. Her heart is thumping inside her chest, as it has been all night. She can't shake off the feeling of dread, like a hole in the pit of her stomach, that something awful is going to happen.

She drives through the pretty fishing village with its pastel-coloured shop fronts and down by the coast. She crosses over the tracks of the DART line and then through grim, geometrically planned housing estates.

Soon she finds herself on the dual carriageway. The blinding whiteness of the low-burning winter sun makes it hard to see the road before her. She is in the right-hand lane as cars whizz past in the lane on her left. She can see a driver come up close behind her in her rear-view mirror. He flashes his lights but she doesn't move. He does it again. She ignores him, so he moves into the left lane and draws level with her. When she looks over at him, she sees that his whole face is contorted in anger. His index finger is stabbing at the air in front of him as he gestures at her to get out of the overtaking lane. She doesn't need to hear him to tell that he is shouting. She turns away from him and studies the crash barrier running along the central median instead. Its smooth concrete form is glistening in the morning sunlight. She wonders, if she drove into it right now, would she cross over to the other side of it or would it just bounce her back onto her own? She hates these thoughts; they just arrive in her mind, plant themselves there like wild seeds, and take over until she has to use all her strength to push them out again. They keep coming lately and they frighten her.

Eventually the man gives up and drives on past her.

A while later she sees a sign for the exit for the city centre and, pulling erratically across two lanes of traffic, she decides that this is where she will go.

Her tyres screech off the painted surface of the underground car park. Finding a space, she silences the engine. She gets out and sounds echo around like in a swimming pool. Gingerly she lifts Maisie's car seat out and clips it onto the buggy frame, saying silent thank-you's when she doesn't wake.

Outside she pushes Maisie along, aware as always of the double takes that her presence attracts. "Is that Ella Wilde?" she can hear them whisper. She lowers her head and keeps on walking. She sees a mother bending over her baby to kiss it in its buggy. Everything about the woman's actions seems effortless. Why can't she be like that? Why doesn't it come to her that easily? She knows she is staring but she just can't help it. She wants to go up and ask her how she does it. She wants to know what the difference is between her and this woman – what is she doing wrong? Suddenly out of nowhere she feels tears roll down her cheeks. All around her are women capable of meeting their children's needs but she feels so overwhelmed by the basics. The woman rights herself and notices Ella looking at her. She flashes her a smile but Ella turns away and quickly pushes the buggy inside a shop.

She takes the lift to the upper level where the designer clothes are. Exiting the lift, she stops in front of a black silk dress with a plunging neckline and runs her fingers over the cool material.

A beautifully made-up girl, with fuchsia-pink lipstick, comes over and smiles at her, showing off perfect white teeth. Her heels leave tiny dents in the plush carpet as she walks. Ella feels ashamed of herself, but her immediate reaction is jealousy. She is jealous of her beauty. Jealous of the time she must have spent over her blow-dried hair that morning. Jealous of her smile. Her youth. Ella didn't even brush her hair leaving the house, let alone put on make-up. Except for in work, she can't remember the last time she even wore make-up.

"Can I help you there at all?"

She can almost see the girl's mind working hard, trying to figure out where she recognises her from.

"I'm just having a look, thank you." She forces herself to smile back at the girl. She knows what will come next: 'I hope you don't mind me asking but you're not Ella Wilde, are you?' She turns and wheels the buggy away before she has to go through the usual exchange. She doesn't have the energy for it.

"Okay, well, I'll be just over here if you need help – just shout," the girl calls after Ella before walking off again in her stilettos.

Ella fingers a wool skirt with scalloped beading before walking along to where high-heeled shoes and buttery-soft leather bags adorn the walls. She takes down a suede bag with a plaited leather handle. It's the palest blue in colour – if it was on a paint chart the colour would be called 'dewy morning'. Checking the label, she sees it is by an up-and-coming Irish designer. She recalls reading something about him in one of the magazines that came with the Sunday papers last week. She looks around and sees the sales assistant is chatting with another girl at the counter. She unzips the bag and looks inside at the silk lining before sticking her hand inside to check the pockets. Taking out the price tag she sees that it costs nine hundred and eighty euro. She knows she can afford to walk up to the checkout now and pay for it but instead she feels that buzz of adrenalin shoot around her body. The same one that she can never say no to. Her eyes scan the floor around her from left to right and back again. The sales assistants are looking in the opposite direction, still engrossed in their conversation. In one fluid movement she stuffs the bag into the bottom of the buggy underneath a blanket.

Her heart is racing so loudly she can almost hear her blood as it is pumped through her veins. She is sure that they must be able to hear it too. She quickly pushes the buggy back over towards the lift and presses the button to call it, willing it to hurry up. She is convinced she can hear someone coming up behind her, but when she turns around she finds it's just her imagination playing tricks. No one seems to have noticed her. The lift arrives and she shoves the buggy inside but has to wait for what feels like an eternity until the doors close. Her heart is thumping wildly. She can feel the tension in her shoulders. Sweat is building under her arms and she knows her face is red. Finally they draw closed and she dares to breathe again. Palms sweaty, she presses the button and they glide downwards to the ground floor.

She sees Maisie has just woken and is now beaming up at her with the widest gummy smile, like she knows what they have just done. Ella smiles back at her, feeling a surge of love for her child. The lift announces their arrival at the ground floor, the doors separate and they walk out.

"Excuse me!"

Someone is calling her. She pretends not to hear them and pushes the buggy forward. She is near the door.

"Excuse me, madam! Excuse me!" The voice is insistent.

She keeps going forward, like a rugby player determined to get the try. She needs to get across the line.

"Excuse me." The voice is almost beside her.

She is almost at the door now. Her stomach is somersaulting. In just three steps she will be at the door. *Three . . . two . . . almost there . . . one . . .*

She feels a tap on her shoulder. She stops the buggy and turns to face the security guard. He is an inoffensive-looking middle-aged man, dressed in a suit.

"I'm sorry to bother you, love, but is this yours?" He is holding her calfskin leather glove in his hand. "I think you dropped it as you came out of the lift a moment ago?"

She can't remember ever feeling more relieved in her life. "Oh sorry – I was miles away there." She takes the glove from him. "Thank you, thank you so much."

"No problem, madam. I hope you have a lovely day."

"You too!" She steps outside onto Grafton Street and walks hurriedly up the street. It is not until she rounds the corner onto Duke Street that she dares to stop. She stands on the cobblelock and breathes in the cool air until she starts to calm down.

Chapter 2

Conor Fahy sees the three boys on the path outside his shop as he approaches it and immediately his heart rate quickens. *They're just kids*, he tells himself. *Don't let them get to you.*

"Excuse me, please." He tries to go around the tracksuit-wearing boys who are standing blocking the doorway to his shop. Whenever he moves right they move right, whenever he moves left they move left. "Come on, get out of the way," he says, losing patience.

"That's no way to speak to the people who were minding your shop for you, mister!" the tallest of the three, a freckly child with slitted eyes, says to him.

He guesses they are aged somewhere between eight and ten.

"Yeah, you were! Come on, clear off."

"No – you've got to pay us, mister," the slitty-eyed child says. The smallest of the trio says, "A tenner – you owe us a tenner."

"Get out of here."

He gently pushes them out of the way but the middle one throws himself on the ground. "Aw, me arm, you hurted me arm!" He rolls back and forth across the path in mock agony. "He hurted me arm!" he shouts to a bewildered man walking past them on the path.

"You better watch yourself, mister – that's going to cost

you! That's no way to treat a youngfella who was watching your shop for yeh!" the oldest of the three says ominously.

Conor steps over the writhing boy and goes inside his shop, ready to start another day.

After he checks his emails, he goes out the back to open up the boxes that arrived yesterday from the wholesaler. He splits one open, running his blade down the brown tape. He reads the back covers of the books inside briefly. There is the new Linwood Barclay and a debut set amongst the Inuit people of Greenland, which has become a word-of-mouth sensation. He carries them out and makes a display in the window. He's relieved to see that there's no sign of the three terrorists. They must have finally got bored. The sun is glinting off the glass, showing up the hardened bits of cement that were splattered on there during the construction but were never cleaned off properly by the builders.

Sometimes he hates this place. Really, *really* hates it. He hates everything that it represents – the dreams that were never fulfilled, and the debt that is a noose around his neck. He could have stayed in his old job. Not just for the security of it – he had actually enjoyed it. He'd had a decent salary, a pension and health insurance. Now he has none of that and, instead, all the benefits have been replaced with constant worry.

He had opened Haymarket Books six years ago when things were booming. Having worked as a bookseller for many years, the romantic in him had loved the thought of running his own store, recommending the books of his choice to his customers, building up relationships with them so that they always trusted his suggestions. But six months after opening, the articulated lorry of the Celtic Tiger had screeched to an abrupt halt and Conor now lay amongst the wreckage. He had soon discovered that the reality of owning his own bookshop was a lot less rosy than what he had envisioned. What *had* he been thinking by opening up a store in this location? But the developers had promised that it was an up-and-coming area and was to be the new hub of the city

11

centre – *"the new cultural heart of Dublin"* they had quoted on their glossy brochures which were full of beautiful, laughing people sipping coffee-to-go from cardboard cups and clutching armfuls of glossy shopping bags.

And he had fallen for it.

Now, five years later, the apartments above his shop and the units on either side of him still lie empty and he is stuck in a twenty-five-year lease, with an exorbitant upwards-only rent clause that he just can't get out of. The US software company that used to have its telesales up the street from him had recently moved the jobs to the lower-cost labour market of India and now that empty building is just another one joining its neighbours in lying idle on Haymarket Street.

Conor goes home that evening and finds bills lying in wait for him on the doormat as they always are. He knows they are bills because they come regularly now, always by registered post with the words *'strictly private and confidential'* or *'urgent'* stamped in red ink across the top of the envelopes. He doesn't need to open them to know what they say. His mortgage has bounced again and his arrears are creeping up, like a mountain he will never be able to scale. If he doesn't pay his gas bill this month they will disconnect him. He has never been in financial difficulty in his life before, not even as a student. He was always able to pay his own way but now the debts are closing in around his neck. They're coming at him from every direction and just when he thinks he's about to get his head above water again, some other bill comes and demands its payment too. When he goes to work the demands are waiting for him there, and when he comes home they are there too. He stares around at the IKEA kitchen presses, and for the hundredth time that day wishes she was here. He wishes he could reach out to her, draw her close and tell her how much he misses her. He would hold her tightly in his arms and tell her how hard it is without her. How awful every day has been without her.

Chapter 3

Fifteen Years Earlier
Goa, India

They leave their hostel and step out onto the dusty road. The heat hits them like a wall as it does every time they go outside – even in the evenings it is still intense. They stop to browse in the street market. Rails of T-shirts surround tables crowded with cigarette lighters, souvenirs, beach bags, trinkets and carved animal statues. Vibrant colours shout at them – reds, blues, greens and yellows all vying for their attention. Cattle wander nosily between the stalls. The engine of a passing motorbike rips through the air; the dust rises in its wake.

Her clear blue eyes are immediately drawn towards the colourful paper lanterns that hang along the top fringes of each stall.

"Ah, papierlaternen!" Her eyes are wide with excitement. "How do you say it in English?"

And he thinks this is what she must have looked like as a child. Innocent. Excited. "Paper lanterns, you mean?"

"I love these!"

Her skin is golden from the sun and he can see the hairs on her arms have been bleached white. Frayed and worn friendship bracelets climb her slender wrists. She is wearing a faded purple vest and silk skirt with a repeating orange-and-black Aztec pattern. The straps of her turquoise bikini are tied up around her neck.

13

"We do these on St Martin's Day back home. All the children carry lanterns on the street and sing songs. We have to buy one!"

"Okay," he agrees because he can never say no to her.

They buy the lantern and take it down to the beach and light it. They watch as it rises up and floats out over the calm sea.

"It is so pretty, isn't it?" she says.

"Beautiful."

They are both sitting on the sand, she in the space between his legs. Her head rests against his chest and rises every time his chest inhales. The dying sunlight is still warm on their skin. They are the only ones on the beach at this time of the evening. Fishing boats lie beached on the shore, ready and waiting to bring home tomorrow's haul. The majestic palm trees crouch over, some boughs almost parallel with the sand. They whisper their secrets in the gentle breeze.

"Do you think we'll still be sitting like this together when we're seventy-five?"

"Uh-huh."

"What about eighty-seven?"

"Uh-huh."

"Ninety-two?" She turns around to face him.

"Hopefully – if you'll be able to push my wheelchair over this sand," he says, grinning at her.

Her leather sandals lie kicked off beside his. The sea roars loud in their ears.

The fire-red sun moves lower until it is almost level with the horizon and in minutes it is gone. The sun always sets quickly here. Soon dusk gives way to night and the beach is cloaked in darkness. He sifts the sand through his fingertips and feels the fine grains fall through them as though his hands are the egg timer of life.

Time moves forward.

Chapter 4

The next morning Ella is woken by Maisie crying at two o'clock. It pierces through her head and once inside seems to hit off everything that is in there, through matter and bone. A grunting Dan finally throws back the duvet and gets up and brings Maisie into their bed. She snuggles in beside Ella and falls back asleep but Ella is left wide awake, thinking. She can't stop thinking about what she did yesterday in the department store. She is disgusted with herself – she feels sick whenever she thinks about it. It has been so long since she has done it that she thought she had left it behind her. Why has it resurfaced again now? What is wrong with her? Why is she doing this? It is as if she doesn't know herself any more. She can practically afford to buy anything she wants to, so why is she caught up in this shoplifting and stealing nightmare?

Her heart is racing in her chest like it does every morning when the rest of the family are fast asleep and her mind is wide awake, full of hatred and self-loathing. But the thing is, that even though she hates what she has done, she knows that she will do it again. She is powerless against it and that is what frightens her most.

She gets out of bed and makes herself a black coffee. She looks around at the circular walls of her kitchen. She had loved this house when they'd bought it. It was one of a number of defence towers built by the British along the Irish coastline in the nineteenth century to help defend against possible Napoleonic invasion. She and Dan had spent a lot of time and money converting it into a home, using a specialist conservation architect from the UK who had overseen similar projects over there. Ella had worked closely with the interior designer to ensure the decor reflected her and Dan's personalities. They were privileged to be among the small number of people across the world that could say they lived in a Martello tower, but now she felt as though the solid stone walls imprisoned her. Except for the kitchen on the top floor with its three-hundred-and-sixty-degree windows and views over the bay and the headland, the thickness of the walls in the rest of the house kept out the light and made the place feel cool and damp, having been built originally for protection rather than with modern needs in mind.

"I was wondering where you'd got to," Dan says, coming into the kitchen where Ella is seated in an armchair sipping her third mug of coffee.

"I couldn't sleep."

"Again? Are you sure you're okay?" He starts measuring out scoops of formula and levelling them with a knife before tipping them into the bottle. "Do you think that maybe you should have a word with your doctor? She might give you sleeping pills or something?" Dan is a fixer. He wants to have a reason why Ella is behaving like this and to fix it for her.

"Nah, it's probably just that the mornings are getting brighter and I'm finding it hard to sleep in –"

"Okay, well, when the girls get up, how about I take the three of them off for a little while to give you a break, yeah?"

She forces herself to smile at him because that's what he wants to see. "That'd be lovely, thanks, Dan."

"You make sure you go and treat yourself, do you hear me?

Take as long as you need."

"Sure, thanks, darling."

After Dan has taken the three girls off, Ella gets into her jeep and drives into town. The tide is out, exposing the long sandy strand, as she travels along the Clontarf road. The heavy rain from the night before has washed the sky clean and the day looks bright and new. She can see Bull Island in the distance. She goes past Fairview Park and soon she is in the city centre. She finds a parking space near St Stephen's Green. She strolls through the green on the diagonal and decides to sit on a bench in the morning sunshine. She closes her eyes and lets the heat of the spring sun warm her cheeks. It feels good.

She goes into a large department store, the same one she was in yesterday and feels the eyes on her as she walks. She walks around the home wares section, running her fingers over sheets with an expensive thread count and polished silver candelabras. The crisp smell of a pomegranate-and-fig candle fills the air. She used to love interiors but somewhere over the last few months she has lost the love of it. It all seems so futile now. Pointless, the lot of it. She catches sight of herself in a mirror. The reflection shows a tired woman with skin which is lined and grey. She hates what she sees. She picks up a leather-bound notebook.

"It's fabulous, isn't it?" The sales assistant has come up beside her. "It only came in yesterday."

"It's lovely."

"I hate asking – but myself and Emily, the girl over there, were just wondering if you are Ella Wilde?"

Ella looks over to see another young girl looking over at them anxiously. "I am."

The girl smiles. "I knew it was you!" she says triumphantly. "I wasn't sure and Emily said it wasn't you but I knew I was right!" The girl seems genuinely thrilled to meet her. "My mam and dad watch your show every night," she starts to gush.

"Glad to hear it."

"Well, I suppose I'd better leave you to get on with your shopping or my manager will kill me but if you need any help just shout."

"Great, thanks for your help –" she reads the girl's name badge, "Sandra."

Sandra beams at her and leaves.

She meanders down to the jewellery section and looks down at the glass display cases.

"Can I help you there, madam?" the man behind the counter says.

"Yes, I was wondering if I could try on that watch there, please?"

"Certainly." He opens the case with a key and takes the watch out, displaying it on the glass in front of Ella.

It has a platinum band and the clock face has diamonds studded around the mother-of-pearl face. She puts it on her wrist, holding it out to admire it. "It's beautiful."

"This is the latest model – it has a dual time-zone display for people who do a lot of travelling, a five-piece link metal bracelet and of course the signature fluted bezel."

She fingers the watch delicately, then removes it.

"Would you like to see more watches?"

"Hmmmh, a watch or bracelet, something to treat myself with." She laughs. It sounds fake and high-pitched to her ear.

"Well, we all need to treat ourselves now and again, don't we?" He takes out a tray of diamond bracelets, glittering and sparkling. "Maybe one of these?" He lifts one out and places it on her wrist. "This one is from our vintage collection."

"It's stunning."

A young couple come in. Ella can tell by their excited giddiness and affection towards each other that they have just got engaged. He rubs his hand up and down along her arm excitedly before reaching for her hand below the counter. She remembers when she and Dan used to be like that, couldn't keep their hands off one another, but now she can't even remember the last time they have had sex. Definitely not since Maisie was born anyway.

"Excuse me for one second while I call my colleague to come and serve them." He goes over to the phone and lifts it.

While he has his back to her she grabs her handbag off the floor and walks quickly through the make-up hall as uniformed girls try to get her to stop and sample their perfumes. She keeps looking straight ahead. She can hear the voice calling after her but she won't turn around. The shocked faces of the make-up girls mirror what is happening behind her but she keeps walking forward. The voice is getting louder. She is nearly there. Finally she goes through the doors and steps out into the fresh air of Grafton Street.

"I'm sorry, madam, but I believe you are still wearing the bracelet that you were trying on." The man from the jewellery counter positions himself in front of her so she cannot go forward. He is flanked by two security guards.

"Oh God, am I? I – I – I'm so sorry – I forgot to take it off! I just remembered I was supposed to be meeting my husband and . . . God, this is embarrassing . . . I can't believe I forgot I was wearing it! Here, sorry . . . " She starts to undo the clasp but her fingers are awkward and clumsy and she can't seem to get a hold on it.

"Would you mind accompanying us back inside, please?" one of the guards asks.

"But I can't, I'm supposed to be meeting my husband."

"Well, perhaps you could ring him and tell him what has happened," says the guard.

"But, here, you can have it back –" She has finally managed to open it and she is thrusting the thing at him. "I wasn't trying to steal it!"

"I'm afraid we will still need you to accompany us."

"But why? I didn't do anything wrong!"

"You left the store with a very valuable piece of jewellery on your person which you didn't pay for. Store procedure means we have to investigate that."

"But it was just a mistake – you've got it all wrong! Wait until my solicitor hears about this!"

"This way, madam – we don't want to make a scene now, do we?"

"No."

Reluctantly she allows them to lead her into the store and down to the back. They swipe their way in through a door and down a white walled corridor that is far removed from the plush front-of-house of the store. They lead her into a small room with security cameras, a desk and two chairs. She notices on the monitor a black-and-white image of the jewellery room she was just in.

They gesture for her to sit down.

"The Gardaí are on their way."

"You've called the Gardaí?" The feeling of dread makes its way over her body. She can feel her hands start to tremble. "But I haven't done anything wrong!"

"You walked out of the shop with a bracelet worth almost thirty-five-thousand euro on your wrist."

"But I told you – it was a mistake – I just forgot to take it off."

"We have you on camera here yesterday. You walked out of the door with a very expensive handbag. It wasn't noticed initially and it was only when we went back over our CCTV that we saw what had happened. We will be handing it over to the Gardaí this time."

The male and female Gardaí who show up try not to look surprised at who she is. They escort her out through the rear entrance of the store, which is usually used by delivery drivers. They have a squad car waiting for her and she is taken to Pearse Street Garda Station.

"But they have it all wrong!" she protests.

"Look, we have to follow up – you were outside the shop with a thirty-five-thousand-euro bracelet," the female Garda who escorted her to the station is saying. "It doesn't matter who you are. You'd be amazed at the people that we pick up for shoplifting – all ages, colours and demographics."

"What's going to happen now?"

"Well, that depends on the store and on whether they want to prosecute or not."

"Oh God!" Ella says, holding her head in her hands. "It'll be everywhere – you can't – I'll never work again." Suddenly she is tired. The tears start and she is worried that they will never stop. She feels the wetness of her tears in the palms of her hands. She is starting to lose the will to fight. The Garda places a cup of tea in front of her and, even though she doesn't normally drink tea, she finds herself drinking it anyway and enjoying its milky sugariness.

"Why did you do it, Ella?" the Garda asks softly.

"I – I – I – just don't know – I haven't been coping well lately . . . Everything has been sliding and getting on top of me. I don't know why I did it – it's not about the money. I could afford to buy it if I really wanted to but I don't know . . . something just comes over me and I have to let it out and it just happens. And I hate myself for it, I hate myself so much."

The Garda is nodding and hands her a tissue. "Here."

"Thanks," Ella says, blowing her nose into it. "I'm such a pathetic mess."

"Look, I've seen a lot of shoplifting cases in my time as a member of An Garda Síochána and I think what has happened today is different to most of the petty shoplifting cases that come before us where someone steals something because it is something that they want, but can't afford to buy. Sometimes there is something going on behind the surface, something a lot deeper that is trying to get out, and it manifests itself in the form of shoplifting. It can often be a cry for help and I think in your case this might be so. I think you need to talk to someone, Ella."

Ella shakes her head determinedly.

"Okay, well, you'll receive a summons for the district court in the post shortly and for now you are free to go on bail."

"But what's going to happen in court?"

"I can't say what the outcome is going to be but shoplifting is a crime punishable by a fine and/or imprisonment. The store say they have evidence of you stealing on camera at another date, which doesn't help matters. You are free to go for now and you should receive the summons in the next few weeks."

A shaky Ella goes to stand up.

"Is there anyone you want to call – you mentioned your husband?"

"Oh God, I can't – I don't want him to bring the kids here."

"Well, I'd really prefer if you had someone with you, Ella. I can call him for you if you like – it might be easier if I tell him?"

She nods. "Okay," she says in a whisper.

Chapter 5

Dan is walking down the strand with the children. The two older girls are clambering over rocks while he pushes Maisie's buggy along on the flat sand below them. Every now and again they stall in a ridge and he has to manoeuvre the buggy around it. It's a nice day, he thinks. The wind is chilly but the sun sits in a periwinkle-blue sky. He feels his phone vibrate in his pocket and, after fishing it out, holds it up between his shoulder and ear as he walks.

"Is that Dan Devlin?" the woman on the other end asks.

"It is."

"This is Garda Bernice Moore calling from Pearse Street Garda Station."

"How can I help you?" He stops walking with the buggy and turns his back to the wind.

"I have your wife here – Ella Wilde."

His first reaction is panic. "My wife? Is she okay?"

"Don't worry, she's okay, but she is in a spot of difficulty and she has asked for you to come down to the station to accompany her home."

"What's happened? Is everything all right?"

"I'd rather you came to the station first and then we can explain everything."

"Sure, okay, I'm about thirty minutes away. I'll be there as soon as I can."

He can see the worry on the small faces of Celeste and Dot as they follow the Garda through the warren of offices down towards the back of the station. Maisie, in his arms, seems to be the only one not perturbed by the situation they find themselves in.

The female Garda who is escorting them stops outside a room and tells Dan, "She's in here," then turns to the children and says, "Would you girls like to follow me up here? I think we have a few biscuits in the canteen that you might like."

Dan nods wordlessly and hands Maisie over to her. He watches momentarily as they follow after the Garda while he takes a deep breath, then pushes open the door leading into the small room where Ella is being questioned.

"What's happened?" Dan asks as soon as he sees her. Her eyes are red-rimmed and she is shaking uncontrollably on the plastic chair.

"Ella has been arrested for attempted shoplifting," Bernice says softly.

"Well, you've got that all wrong for a start! There is no way Ella would shoplift!" He turns to Ella to back him up.

"Unfortunately, I know it might come as a shock to you but she has admitted to the crime. We are releasing her on bail so she is free to go now but she is in a very distressed state and I would rather she had some company leaving the station."

Ella looks up at him and he immediately knows that it is true.

"Ella, are you okay?"

She nods. She is almost unrecognisable from the woman in their kitchen earlier on that same morning. The woman that is his wife. There is a vacancy in her eyes.

"Okay, let's get you out of here, yeah?"

"I'll be in touch, Ella, as soon as I have further details," says the Garda.

She nods and follows Dan to collect the children and then outside to where he has parked the jeep. Having spent the last hour in a small windowless room, the sun blinds her eyes. She climbs up into the passenger side and Dan starts the engine. She stares out at the scenery, which flickers in silhouettes past the window. They drive home the rest of the way in silence. Even the children for once are quiet.

They wait for the electric gates to part and then drive in and pull up in the driveway.

Dan lets them into the house and they climb the stairs to the living room with Dan carrying Maisie in her car seat. Still nobody speaks. Ella sits down on the sofa. She is shivering violently now. Her teeth are rattling against each other. Dan gets a blanket from their bedroom downstairs and puts it around her shoulders and makes her a strong cup of coffee before going back up to the kitchen to fix the girls something to eat.

"So are you going to tell me what the hell is going on?" he says, sitting down on the ottoman in front of her later that evening after he has put the girls to bed. "I mean, why would you shoplift?"

"It was a mistake – I never meant to take it."

"Well, then, why do they have you on camera stealing a bag there yesterday, Ella? What is going on? I don't get it – I just cannot understand why you would feel the need to steal? It's not as if we're short of cash!" His voice is raised and she can hear the contempt in it.

"I'm sorry," she sobs. "I hate myself for doing it."

"But I just don't get it! Why would you do such a thing? What the hell is wrong with you?"

"I don't know – I can't understand it myself."

"You don't know – is that all you're giving me here? Come on, Ella, even you must see that that's a bit of a weak explanation! I really expected you to tell me that they'd got it

25

all wrong or at the very least that you had a plausible explanation – I don't know – maybe you were carrying out some research as part of an assignment for work or something – but the fact that you can offer me *no* reason for what you did is just too much for me to get my head around. And then me having to bring the kids into a Garda station – they were afraid of their lives, Ella! Celeste asked me when I was tucking her up in bed if you were going to gaol!"

"I'm so sorry, Dan – I never meant for you all to be brought into this." She starts to sob.

"Oh, sorry if we all gatecrashed on your solo run there, Ella! Well, why the hell then were you going around acting like a one-woman Bonnie and Clyde! And what happens next? I mean Celeste had a fairly valid point – are you going to wind up in prison? Am I going to have to be bringing the kids to visit you in gaol next?"

"Please, Dan, stop!"

"What, Ella? You don't like hearing this? Well, why didn't you think of your children before you started going around lining your pockets? I can't believe you've brought all this onto our doorstep for no reason other than . . . you see, that's the problem here . . . " He stands up and draws his hands down over his face. "I don't even have a fucking reason! Jesus Christ, Ella, what have you done?"

When she wakes the next morning she looks around the living room. She is still wearing the same clothes as yesterday. They feel crumpled and grubby against her skin. It takes a while for her to remember what had happened the previous day. Then it hits her like a train slicing through the countryside. Her head is thumping like it would after a wild night out except there was no alcohol involved yesterday. She looks up at the clock on the wall and sees it is almost eleven o'clock – she can't remember the last time that she slept in for this long.

She sits up and listens but there is no sound coming from

the rest of the tower. It is eerily quiet. She gets up and climbs the stairs to the kitchen. She notices Dan's car isn't in the drive – he must have taken the three children out somewhere. She pops two paracetamol, then fills a glass with water and sits down at the breakfast bar. The Sunday papers are sitting waiting for her on the kitchen table. Her face is on the front page of three of them. **'TV Presenter Arrested for Theft of 35,000 Bracelet.'** Another says **'Ella's Wilde Rampage'** and then goes on to say that she clearly feels that her six-figure salary isn't enough.

She turns them all face down on the counter-top.

Her phone starts ringing then. The first call she fields is from her dad, followed then by her sister Andrea and of course they both assume it was a mistake and rally to her defence. She loves them for that but she has to tell them that it's true and then she has to go through the same disbelief and the 'but whys' that she went through with Dan.

The next phone call is from Malcolm, her boss at the station. He doesn't waste time getting straight to the point.

"Ella, I saw the papers. Do you mind telling me what the hell is going on?"

"I'm sorry, Malcolm – I'm really sorry . . ."

"So it's true then? For God's sake, I assumed you were going to tell me it was a set-up or something!"

"It was a mistake, Malcolm, I – I – I didn't mean for it to happen . . . "

"A mistake – how can you say that?" his voice booms. "It says here, and I quote, *'Ms Wilde was also caught on the store's CCTV camera taking a designer handbag in recent days.'* What am I meant to do now? I can hardly have you fronting a show which grills politicians who falsify expense claims in the Dáil, or puts it up to the fat-cats heading Government quangos that they're being overpaid! This won't sit well with the viewers, Ella. I've worked in television for a long time and I can tell you that they're not going to like this at all."

Ella can almost imagine him pointing a finger into the empty air beside him.

"We're a state-owned broadcaster, Ella – the tax-payers pay our salaries! How do you think this will look to them? Our show fights the fight of the common people –we uphold moral values and disdain theft, fraud and greed."

"I know but I never meant for it to happen –"

"I've spoken with the board and we've made a decision. We can't have you back, Ella, I'm afraid. It's not going to wash with the public and the whole show could go under if we had you back – you do understand that, don't you? Something like this is contagious and we have to limit it – do you understand what I'm saying?"

"But you can't let me go just like that – I haven't even been convicted yet. I've worked there for almost twenty years – you can't just throw me over like that!"

"You know just as well as I do that when you're in the public eye fronting a TV show you have a responsibility to uphold – it's the first thing you learn when you get a job like that."

"So that's it, is that what you're saying?"

"I'm sorry, Ella, I really am, but the shareholders won't tolerate it. *The Evening Review* is the station's flagship show and if our presenters don't have integrity then our show doesn't have integrity."

The blood is coursing loudly in her ears, her throat feels like it is closing tighter. She hangs up before she has to hear him say anything else.

Malcolm's words are left ringing in her ears like music after a bad nightclub. She feels totally panicked. This cannot be happening. It can't be. Her job is everything to her, it's the only job she has ever known, and without it she's nothing.

"Ella, it's Conor." His voice comes in over the intercom. "Can you let me in?"

She gets off the chair and lifts the handset to buzz him in

through the gates. Then she takes the stairs down to the hallway and when she opens the door he is standing there.

He throws his arms around her and draws her into a strong embrace. "I saw the papers – are you okay?" he says, holding her by the elbows and bending his knees so that his eyes are level with hers.

"No, Conor, no, I'm not." Her voice breaks into tears and he wraps her in his arms again.

He follows her upstairs and takes a seat while she makes the coffee.

"What happened?"

"The same as you read in the paper – I walked out of the shop with a €35,000 bracelet on my wrist. And the bag the day before."

"Did you just forget to pay or something?"

She shakes her head. "I wish that were true, Conor," she takes a deep breath, "but I did it. I deliberately took them."

He looks at her in amazement. "But I don't get it – why would you do that?"

"I don't know, Conor, I don't know why I did it."

"Is there something else going on? You and Dan aren't having money problems, are you?"

"No, not at all."

"But then why would you steal something?" he asks, bemused.

"I can't explain it – it's like I got this urge and I couldn't help myself – it overcame me and I had to do it. Does that make any sense?"

"Not really, if I'm totally honest with you."

"I know, it doesn't really make much sense to me either." She wipes her eyes with a tissue. "Since Maisie was born I haven't been feeling like myself. I'm not sleeping at night and I don't know but I just feel really anxious all the time. I keep worrying about things that will probably never happen."

"Why do you think that is?" he asks softly.

"I don't know. I just don't know." And she doesn't know. It's all she can think about, yet she can't put into words exactly how she is feeling. "I think I'm just tired." She flops down into a chair beside him. "Malcolm called. The shareholders want me gone, I've lost my job."

"Oh God, Ella, I'm really sorry."

Chapter 6

Ella wakes before the alarm even has a chance to sound. She waits for it to go and then she pounces on it with her hand, feeling a hollow victory. Her head is fuzzy with tiredness, like it is covered in a layer of felt and she can't see out properly through the fibres. She got out of bed seven times to check on Maisie during the night and each time the baby had been sleeping peacefully, but the worries of cot-death continue to torment her. The bed is empty on his side. He slept in the spare room again last night. He hasn't slept beside her since she was arrested. Taking a deep breath, she pulls back the duvet and gets out of bed.

The tower is chilly this morning and she wraps her robe tightly around her, belting it twice. With quick steps, she searches out the rugs that are draped across the cold flagstones as she makes her way into the bathroom. She pulls down her pyjama bottoms and sits on to the toilet seat.

He comes blustering through the door a minute later and stands in front of the sink. She notices that he is already dressed for work. Without looking at her, he grabs the toothpaste and tries to pump out some of the gel. It is stuck and she hears him grow frustrated. He has to push the bottom of the container upwards to squeeze the last of it onto his brush.

31

"We need more toothpaste!" he growls back at her.

"I'll get some in the supermarket later," she says, making a mental note to buy some.

He starts brushing his teeth and her eyes watch his even strokes hypnotically as he moves his brush up and down. When she is finished, she walks to the sink to wash her hands. He steps to the right to let her in while at the same time spitting out his toothpaste into the sink beside her. He sticks the brush under the flow of water before giving his teeth another quick brush before a final spit.

She turns to him and takes a deep breath inwards, "Dan, I –"

But he isn't listening and then he wordlessly rushes out the door. She hears the *thump, thump, thump* of his feet on the stairs, the *thump* of the hall door as he pulls it closed, followed by the *thump* of his car door. The engine starts and when she goes to look out the porthole-shaped window, she can see him making his way down the winding drive. *Here we go*, she thinks, *another day*. And the familiar knot of anxiety in her stomach winds itself tighter.

As she climbs the circular staircase upwards towards their kitchen, she can feel the weight of her body with every step. Yet again she finds herself wishing that they lived in a normal house. The circular walls and vaulted ceilings seem to be moving in closer towards her today, squashing her in between them. Sometimes she wishes they lived in a square house, with straight lines and angles, a house that wasn't upside down, where you walked in and didn't have to climb up twenty-six steps to reach the kitchen.

The girls are still sleeping – she has another hour before she'll need to call them. She makes herself a coffee, savouring the stillness of the kitchen. She sits up at the breakfast bar and, clasping the mug in her hands, looks out the window at the strange calm of the greeny-grey sea below her. It looks ominous today, like a giant bath calling to her, trying to lure her in.

When she is finished she puts her mug down and takes the

circular staircase back down to the bottom of the tower. She creeps out into the hallway and softly opens and closes the old wooden front door so as not to wake everyone. She carefully makes her way down the old stone staircase that leads to the cove. It was the steps that led her to buy their house. She loved how they connected the house to the water. She can almost feel the gravitational pull of the tides, pulling her towards the water, back to where we all come from. Where it all began and could end too. She walks over the loose pebbles and stones underfoot. The wind fights against her, it pushes her back. It whips strips of her hair against her face and takes her breath with it. The blade-like grass on the headland, dotted with the pretty yellow of trailing tormentil flowers, stands strong and tall from centuries of evolution. She climbs up onto her favourite rock, finding the groove she likes best. Vapour trails rip through the pewter sky like wounds. She watches a red-beaked oystercatcher as it picks its steps across the sand, searching out cockles. A gull swoops down and squawks just over her head. And then Ella screams. She screams loud but the wind is always louder than her.

On Monday morning Mrs Frawley lets herself in with her key and climbs the stairs up to the tower where Ella is sitting at the long kitchen table in her dressing gown and slippers. Celeste and Dot run to hug the woman who has been minding them since they were newborn infants.

Ella can see the disappointment in the older woman's eyes before she even begins to speak.

"I know you've probably seen the papers . . ."

"Yes, I have. Girls, why don't you two run down and put on your uniforms?"

They do as she instructs.

"So it's true then?" she says after they are gone.

She doesn't go to sit down and Ella finds herself tensing up in response.

"I'm sorry, Mrs Frawley, I really am . . ."

"Was it a mistake? Was that it? Did you just forget to pay?"

Ella says nothing. She has no words inside her that can explain the force within her that caused her to do what she has done. She shakes her head.

"I haven't slept a wink all night. I just can't stop thinking about it all. Ella, what were you thinking? I just don't understand why you would do such a thing." There are tears in her eyes. "You weren't raised that way."

The woman's disappointment in her is obvious and it makes Ella want to crawl into the ground and hide with embarrassment.

"I'm sorry, Mrs Frawley. I know I've let you and everyone else down. I feel terrible."

"It's yourself you have let down, Ella. So what happens next?"

"I'll get a summons for the district court soon. I'm meeting my solicitor later on."

Mrs Frawley nods. "That's wise, Ella. So I take it you're not going in to the studio today then?"

"Actually," she pauses, "I've been fired. Malcolm called to say they can't have me back in case I taint the show." There is a bitter edge to her voice.

"Oh no, Ella! I'm truly sorry to hear that – I know how much your work meant to you." She stops to clear her throat before continuing. "Look, Ella, I've wanted to talk to you about something for a while, but I think now is probably the right time . . ."

"What is it?"

"I'm sorry, Ella, I wish the timing was better but I can't stay on working for you any more."

"What?"

"I think it's time that I retired."

"*Retired?* But why?"

34

"Well, for a start, now that you have no job there isn't room for the two of us in the house."

"I won't get under your feet, you don't need to worry about that. You can still go about your own routines and your way of doing things – I won't interfere."

"But that's not it, Ella."

"You can't, Mrs Frawley – please, whatever it is – if you need more money – whatever you want, please, I'll do it."

"Oh Ella," she laughs. "It's not anything like that."

"But what about the girls? You're like a grandmother to them!"

"They'll understand and I'll obviously come and visit them."

"Please, Mrs Frawley, don't go – don't do this to me."

"I know this is hard on you but I think it could actually be a good thing for you. You need to try and look at this as an opportunity to spend more time with the children. They need you, Ella, especially now. They need their mother. I will stay on until the end of the week but Friday will be my last day."

She then walks down the stairs and helps the girls finish getting ready for school. As Ella stands there in her kitchen, she feels as though her world is crumbling and she is moving further down into a void of unknowns. All of her constants, the things that she thought she could rely on in her life, like Dan and Mrs Frawley and her job, are just slipping away from her.

"Mrs Frawley is leaving us," she tells Dan when he comes home from work that night.

He drops his bag and looks at her. "And so the fallout continues," he says sardonically. "Well, in all fairness, can you really blame her? She must be disgusted by what you did."

Then he turns and walks out of the room.

Chapter 7

Rachel McLoughlin hears the door shut downstairs and she bolts upwards in the bed. Her heart hammers against her ribcage. There are footsteps on the stairs now, getting ever closer. She grabs her phone in her hand, ready to ring the Gardaí. The footsteps cross the landing and then the door to her bedroom opens and he is standing there.

Marcus is standing in her doorway.

"You scared the shit out of me! What are you doing here? You're meant to be in Tokyo!" She sits up against the headboard and switches on her lamp.

"Well, Frankfurt actually. I had an overnight stopover there before my connection back to Dublin but I saw there was a flight to London that was boarding so I managed to get on it and I knew from there I could get to Dublin easily enough and be with you faster. I couldn't face sitting in a hotel room on my own for another night. I needed to be with you." He climbs up onto the bed beside her and gives her a lingering kiss on the lips.

Her eyes work their way up his face, over his jawline bristly with dark stubble, his broad, easy grin and then finally they settle on his smiling hazel-green eyes. When she'd first met him, she'd thought that they were the same age. He looks a good ten years younger than his forty-three years – maybe because of the way that he dresses. His sideburns, recently peppered with flecks of grey, are the only thing that give his age away.

"So how did the meeting go?"

He had been in Tokyo on a buying trip for his clothing company, *Salo*.

"It went well. I should know next week but I don't think I managed to insult anyone by getting the etiquette wrong. Here, I bought you this . . ." He goes and unzips the side of his suitcase and takes out an object wrapped in sheets of newspaper. Coming back to the bed, he hands it to her.

She unwraps it to find a small battered-looking Japanese Geisha doll.

"I picked it up on a street stall – it was either that or a *Hello Kitty* schoolbag so I made an executive decision."

Rachel laughs and takes the doll and looks at her heavily painted face and the ruby-red flowers of her kimono. Her eyebrows are slanted downwards so she appears to be frowning at them.

"It's hideous, isn't it?" Marcus is saying.

Rachel stands the doll up on the bedside table so that she is leaning against her alarm clock and then she reaches forward to kiss him, feeling the familiar outline of his lips against her own. "I'm glad you're here."

"God, I've really missed you. I know it's only been three days but I needed to feel your arms around me," he murmurs into her long dark hair.

His hand starts moving up inside the silk fabric of her nightdress and her skin comes alive under his fingertips. He starts to pull it down at the front, exposing her breasts. He straightens up for a moment and pulls his sweater off over his head before tossing it onto the floor.

"That doll is freaking me out." He grabs it and hurtles it across the room where it bangs against the wardrobe door.

"Hey, that was my present!" she says in mock anger, before leaning in to meet his lips again and running her fingers over the contours of his chest, feeling the strands of wiry chest hair before moving down further to unbuckle his belt.

He tugs off his jeans and then is on top of her again. He slips inside her and soon they are moving together as one.

When she wakes up the next day and opens her eyes, Marcus is looking at her with a big grin on his face. She sees her underwear and nightdress lying on the floor from where he had thrown them last night.

"Well, this beats waking up in a hotel room in Frankfurt, that's for sure." He leans in and kisses her on the forehead. "Good morning, my love."

Soon they are making love again until they are interrupted by her phone ringing. She groans and wishes she were the kind of person who could just ignore it but instead reaches a hand out to check who it is. The name of Ursula, her team leader, lights up on the screen. Her stomach sinks and she hits answer.

"Rachel, hi. Sorry to ring you so early, I hope I didn't wake you?"

"No, I was already up." She sighs, pulling back the duvet to get out of bed.

"Oh good – I have an emergency for you, I'm afraid – three children, we think ages four, two and one – found at home alone by a neighbour. No sign of any parents and it's not known how long they've been on their own. A neighbour heard crying through the wall all night long and when she went in to investigate she found them all in a terrible state. She called the Gardaí who are there now. They're all quite distressed. The neighbour is with them at the moment but they need a social worker to go over there ASAP."

Rachel cradles the phone between her shoulder and ear and goes downstairs to the kitchen to grab a pen and paper to scribble down the details as Ursula calls them out to her. She writes down the address and then hangs up. Then she makes another phone call to cancel the two meetings she had scheduled for that morning before going back upstairs.

Marcus is sitting up in bed, playfully pouting. "Aren't you coming back to bed?" he asks.

"I'm sorry, darling, but I have to run – it's an emergency."

"Damn! Well, why don't I make us breakfast while you get ready for work?" he says, getting out of the bed.

"I'm sorry, I won't have time."

"So after me flying around the world to see you, you're kicking me out, Ms McLoughlin – is that what you're trying to tell me?"

"'Fraid so!"

"Okay – well, at least I know where I stand." He comes over and draws her close. "I suppose I'd better run anyway – I've loads to catch up on."

"Will I see you later?"

"I'm going to the cinema with Eli and Alexandra – you're welcome to join us?"

"Ach, no, you three go ahead without me. I know I'll probably be too exhausted to sit through a movie."

"Okay – well, I'll call you later – love you."

"I love you too."

She showers and gets into a fitted woollen dress with court shoes. She runs a brush through her hair before taking the lift down to the underground car park and getting into her car. She puts the address that Ursula gave her into her sat nav and reverses out of her space.

As she drives through the rush-hour traffic her mind wanders. She knows she will arrive at this house to find neglected children, probably hungry and living in squalor. Maybe their mother will arrive back, or maybe she won't. From seeing too many similar cases she knows that, unless the mother has a really good reason for leaving them alone, the children might end up being put into care temporarily. The odds are already stacked against them and they are still so young.

Sometimes she thinks she is mad to do this job. It has a habit of seeping in underneath her skin and staying with her long after her working day is done. It used to get in on her, it used to really, really upset her. No matter how good she is at her job or how on top of it she tries to be, there will always be more children out there going through the same thing. When she was in school and wanted to be a social worker, she had such ideals and dreams – all the usual aspirations and hopes of a teenager who thinks '*I will be the one to change things*'. She had really thought that she could change the world. But she couldn't. She had learnt that lesson early on. When she first started doing this job there were days when she would come home from work and cry just from the sheer frustration of seeing nothing change. Or because of the infuriating bureaucracy she had to deal with day in day out. But what was almost worse than all of that were the cynical people populating the top ranks who just didn't seem to care enough to fight for the children any more. She swore she would never let herself become like them, no matter how frustrated she got.

Eventually the voice on her sat-nav tells her to take the next right. She indicates and turns into the housing estate of the address that she has been given. It looks just like every other middle-class suburban estate. It's not the kind of place where you would expect to see this sort of thing – then again Rachel has been doing this job long enough to know that it always happens where you least expect it. It's not just a working-class problem – it's an every-class problem. She follows the curving road along until she pulls up outside the house. Except for the long grass in the front garden it is the same as all the other houses on the road. There is nothing to indicate what might be happening behind its walls.

She turns off the engine and takes a deep breath. Right so, she thinks, here we go.

Chapter 8

That evening Rachel climbs the concrete steps leading up to her duplex, puts her key in the door and lets herself into her home. She notices that more cracks have appeared on the cardboard-like walls just inside the door. They spread out like veins. She is afraid to slam a door in case a new one appears on the wall afterwards. Although she won't admit it to anyone, sometimes she finds this place depressing. It was a quickly built Celtic Tiger job, lacking design or decent materials. The bathroom-ware was never sealed properly and Rachel has to angle the shower a certain way or it will leak down to the apartment beneath her. Two of the kitchen presses have come off their hinges already. All her neighbours are the same – young professionals like herself stuck in these boxes. She had slept out overnight in her car to try and get a footing on the property ladder and gratefully took whatever was left by the time she had reached the top of the queue. Then there were all the add-ons – fifteen thousand for a parking space, five grand extra for a south-facing balcony. She shudders at the total cost of what is now worth less than half of her hard-earned money. There are half-finished units in the block opposite hers with shell-like windows and exposed steel girders sitting there in a limbo state for six years now.

Rachel had wanted to buy her own place for ages. She had kept on watching as prices rose and one by one her friends all bit the bullet and became mortgage-holders. When she had eventually managed to save up enough for a deposit and finally did take the plunge, the housing market had collapsed six months later.

She opens the press and pulls down the remainder of a bottle of red that she had opened the night before. She needs it after the day she has had. She spent the day in a grotty kitchen with the upset children who didn't have English as a first language. There were dirty tear-tracks down their faces and they kept saying things that she just didn't understand. Eventually they had managed to get an interpreter in to talk to them which helped to calm them down a bit. Then their mother had arrived back, dazed and not fully with it, but she had got aggressive when Rachel told her who she was and tried to get a scissors from the drawer but clumsily fell over and banged her head against a kitchen cabinet, giving herself a large gash above her left eye. So then an ambulance was called, an emergency care order put in place and the three crying, exhausted and frightened children were handed over into state care. And Rachel knew from seeing so many similar cases, so many children crying out for the basics, that this was going to be the start of a long and arduous path for these three young children. This was going to be the defining moment in their lives. Already not even out of nappies and this was the watershed – everything from now on would come back to this moment. They might get lucky, they might not and this was the bit she found the hardest.

She goes out to the living room and plonks down in front of *Grey's Anatomy* on the TV. Every time she tries to forget, images of the children with skin the colour of caramel come into her head. She can't forget those dark-brown, almost black, almond-shaped eyes peeping out at her. She can't stop thinking about how sad and lost they looked in this world even though they had only been here for such a short time already.

She finishes the first glass and welcomes the mellow fuzziness that descends upon her as she sits back into her sofa. When that is gone she finds herself filling her glass with the remaining wine. She might as well finish it now, she thinks.

When Rachel gets up the next morning, her head is pounding. She had finished the open bottle and uncorked another one afterwards. There is a thumping pain behind the sockets of her eyes. She knew she shouldn't have opened the second bottle. But even with all that wine, she didn't sleep well at all, and the faces of the three children had haunted her dreams.

She has such a full day ahead of her today. She needs to check on the children from yesterday and then she needs to source potential foster families for another case involving young children that has recently been assigned to her. She has made a few calls to families that she knows and has worked with before, but it's proving to be difficult because there are five of them. She will try her best to keep them all together but she knows even before she has begun that it's going to be next to impossible.

Chapter 9

The morning is quiet; it's been quiet a lot lately. The bell over the door goes and he jumps up from the chair when he sees the door opening and the three boys back again. They are standing just inside his doorstep looking in at him, just waiting to get a reaction. His heart starts racing again.

"Get out now and close the door after you!" he shouts at them.

"Who's going to make us?" says the oldest and they grin at him.

"I am!"

He walks over and, one by one, lifts each of them over the threshold of his door and onto the path outside before pulling the door closed. They stand outside and stare in at him through the glass, begging him to react.

Suddenly he snaps. He opens the door. "*Get away from my shop!*" he roars. "*Get away from my shop now!*"

They step backwards on to the path.

"Go on – go – or I'm calling the Guards!"

"It's public property, mister – we're just standing on the path."

He goes over again and shuts the door closed on them. How is he ever meant to get a customer through the door if this lot keep intimidating whatever few he has? The Guards never take him seriously – they keep telling him that "They're only young fellas" and that they've bigger problems to be dealing with.

It's one of those days where he really misses Leni. Of course, he misses her every day but some days it seems to ache a lot more – it sears through his skin and cuts right down to the bone. He longs to be able to tell her about what is worrying him and to share the load with her. She always knew what he should do or what to say to him to help him stop worrying. She would say in her funny Irish-German accent "Cop yourself on, Conor" and then they would both laugh at that.

He is about to turn from the door when he sees Ella's black jeep pull up outside. She waves at him through the glass before climbing down and lifting Maisie's car seat out from the back. The three boys move out of her way on the path.

"What's going on with them?" she asks as soon as she is inside the shop.

"They've nothing better to do except cause trouble for me. They'll be gone in a while. I wasn't expecting to see you this morning?"

"I wasn't in the mood for going home and staring at the walls until it's time to pick the girls up again."

He can see that she hasn't brushed her hair   there is a halo of frizz around her head. "Want a cuppa?"

"Yeah, go on then."

"Do you want a bun?"

"No, I'm not really that hungry . . . "

He goes out the back and throws teabags into mugs while he is waiting for the kettle to boil. He carries them back out the front to where Ella is unzipping Maisie from her snowsuit.

"Here, want a hold of your goddaughter?" She is holding her out to him.

He takes her, pulls out one of the chairs from the reading

nook and sits down with her. Ella uses her palms to lever herself up to sit on the counter and then clasps the mug of tea between her hands.

A rosy-cheeked Maisie uses her two feet to push up against his lap.

"She's getting so big."

"She is."

A trail of dribble runs down the baby's chin and lands on his jeans. He reaches for a tissue to wipe it up.

"Is she teething?" he asks.

"I don't know," she sighs. "She has me awake all night anyway."

"The poor little thing." He sticks his finger in her mouth and lets her chomp down on it.

"Eh . . . where's my sympathy?" she asks.

"Aw, poor Ella!"

She forces a laugh.

Thud. The sound hits off the glass window of the shop front.

"What the hell was that?" Ella asks. She looks towards the window as the thuds are repeated. There are large muddy circles appearing like waves on the glass. "Jesus, are they playing football against your glass?"

"Yep." He exhales heavily, walks over to the door and pulls it open. "Right, that's it! Clear off right now or I'm calling the Guards!" he roars out at them.

They ignore him and the thuds continue. *Thud. Thud. Thud. Thud.*

"Do they normally do this?" she asks when he comes back in.

Thud. Thud. Thud. She watches the glass shake with each impact.

He sighs. "They're a nightmare lately – they're constantly hanging around outside the shop. I know they're just doing it to get a reaction from me. I should just try and ignore them . . . but it's so hard when they're destroying my livelihood."

46

"Shouldn't they be at school or something?"

He looks at her like she's mad. "Never mind them – they'll get bored in a while."

"Little shits!"

"Look, they're moving off already . . ."

The boys take off down the street, bouncing their ball from one to the other.

"So, anyway, forget about them," Conor says. "How are you doing? How are you finding it all?"

"Yeah, it's okay – I'm trying to get used to it." *Slowly.*

She smiles at him from underneath the fringe that has grown so long he doesn't know how she can stand having it hanging in her front of her eyes all the time.

"So you're all right?"

"Yeah. Good and bad days." Her voice wobbles. She doesn't tell him that the bad days far outnumber the good, the guilt that is like a parasite constantly eating its way through her body. "I just don't know what to do with myself, Conor. It's such a shock not going out the door to work every day."

"It's just a readjustment."

"Yeah." She sighs heavily.

"Have you tried speaking to someone?"

"How do you mean?"

"Well, to a doctor or a therapist or someone . . . you still haven't even addressed the issue of why you did it in the first place."

"Leave it, Conor," she warns. She can't look at him because she is afraid she won't be able to hold it together.

"Fine." He sighs heavily and then shrugs in surrender. Every time he tries to bring it up with her that she is ignoring the bigger issue she grows defensive and he hasn't pushed her on it.

She looks out the window at the white van that has pulled up beside her jeep. "Shit, the clampers!"

She hops down off the counter and runs outside the door.

She manages to stop them just before they put the yellow clamp on her wheel. She puts money in the meter and comes back into the shop.

"I keep telling you – you need to start paying for parking!" he says.

"I forgot!"

"You always forget." He pauses. "Look, Ella, it'll all blow over soon." His tone is softer now.

"Do you think? Because it doesn't seem to be getting any better." She puts her head in her hands. "I don't think I can take much more of it, Conor." Her voice is trembling.

"Hey, it's going to be okay," he says, shocked by her admission. "You just have to ride it out. Come on, it's all going to be okay – you've got to be strong, yeah?" He lifts Maisie up in his left arm and comes over to rub Ella's shoulder with his free hand.

"I'm trying," she whispers. "I really am."

Chapter 10

The microwave always gives three beeps when it is done. Conor opens the door and removes the cling film from the other half of last night's shepherd's pie. He takes the plate into the sitting room and flicks on the TV. He has a pile of paperwork beside him that he is supposed to be catching up on but he can't bring himself to do it.

He can't wait for winter to be over and for spring to come again. He always finds the dark evenings hard when you can't go anywhere or do anything. The evenings seem to stretch out endlessly when he is alone. He has been going to bed earlier and earlier to read, just to pass the time.

He watches a documentary about life in the trenches in World War One and, when he looks up at the clock, it is nearly nine o'clock. Nine is a reasonable time to go to bed, he thinks. Any earlier would just be pathetic.

It is just after nine o'clock when Ella finally has the three children in bed. Celeste has fallen asleep sitting up reading under the lamplight in her bedroom. Ella pulls up the blanket over her eldest daughter's chest and switches off the light. Bone-tired, she lets her weight sink into the semicircle-shaped purple velvet sofa. She'd had it custom-designed to fit along the circular walls of the room but she can never get comfortable on it. She fixes the cushions behind her back and tucks her feet up underneath her. Sipping her chilled Sancerre, she watches a woman screaming at a man in *EastEnders* but it makes her uncomfortable so she changes over to a cookery show. She always said that when she had more time she would watch shows like this and finally learn how to cook properly from scratch, using fresh ingredients. She watches the chef chopping lemongrass but her concentration dips after a few minutes so she flicks over. She sees an ad for *The Evening Review*. She looks at the presenter brought in to replace her, barely out of college and after landing a job that thousands would kill for. A job that Ella had worked her way up the ladder for years to reach. She feels anger rise inside her towards this girl, who is still in the prime of her youth. She has everything that Ella once had. She picks up the remote and changes back to *EastEnders*.

Dan still isn't home. She isn't sure if he is genuinely working late or just staying late to avoid her. It is almost ten when she hears the door open downstairs. He climbs the spiral staircase and enters the living room. She picks up the remote and lowers the volume on the TV.

"How was your day?" she asks.

"Fine." He won't look her in the eye.

She hates him being like this with her. She wants to get up off the sofa and go over to him. She wants for him to put his arms around her. She wants to tell him exactly how she is feeling and for him to tell her that it will all be okay. She wants to take it all back. She wishes she could undo it all and start over.

"There's dinner in the kitchen."

"Thanks." He exhales loudly and climbs the stairs up to the top floor.

After he is gone she gets up off the sofa and goes downstairs to run herself a bath. She flicks on the lights, which the brochure promised would give the room a spa-like feel. As the water thunders into the tub, she undresses. Walking over the heated tiles, she catches sight of her body in the mirror. Usually she would look away from her own reflection but this time she stops and places a palm on either side of her stomach. She stretches the skin, slack like an elephant's, outwards until it is taut. She turns to the side and sucks it in, until she can hold it in no longer. Then she exhales and lets it all out again. She lowers the lights and adds some bath oil to the water. She climbs in and sinks into it so that, from her shoulders down, her body is submerged. Closing her eyes, she pulls her head under, letting the water rush in and fill her ears until it drowns out everything else. She stays like that until she has to take a breath and comes back up. The back of her head rests against the rim of the tub, while her bottom lip curls onto the surface of the water.

When she gets out, she sits on the edge of the tub and dries herself off. She can hear the muffled sound of the television travelling down from upstairs. The stone walls of the tower always bounce sound around.

She is exhausted: it feels like each one of her bones is too heavy for her body. She goes to check on Maisie, placing a hand on her chest to make sure she is still breathing. She is reassured by the even beat of her chest rising and falling, Then she gets into her pyjamas and climbs into bed. She turns off her lamp and waits for sleep to come.

What feels like minutes later she can hear crying somewhere in the distance. She peels her eyes open to check her alarm clock: it's ten past five. Dan isn't beside her – he must have gone into the spare room again last night. She lies there still hoping that the crying will stop. But it doesn't, instead it gets louder with every scream. Finally she pulls back the goose-feather duvet, gets out of bed and makes the journey across the cold floor to the cot at the foot of their bed to lift Maisie.

The baby bucks against her, arching backwards so that Ella really has to use her strength to stop her from tumbling out of her arms. "Shush, it's okay, it's okay," she whispers.

The house is freezing cold and she knows that Dan forgot to set the heating to come on before he went to bed. She reaches blindly for her dressing gown and creeps out of the bedroom with the baby.

The stone floors are icy-cold underfoot as she walks. She climbs the staircase to the kitchen and switches on the light, casting a yellow glow around the room. She sees Maisie is red-cheeked and snotty-nosed from her hysterical crying. She walks around the room with Maisie lying against her shoulder but the baby grows even more fractious. She can't do this; she is just no good at it. She feels helpless and doesn't know what to do to calm the baby down. She never knows the right thing to do.

She puts her on the changing table while she changes her sodden nappy. Maisie keeps on crying.

A sleepy Dot comes into the kitchen. Ella quickly wipes away her tears with the back of her hand.

"Maisie woke me up, Mummy!" Dot complains. "Teacher says that we need to get a good night's sleep to help our concen-stration."

"It's con-cen-*tra*tion."

She makes a bottle for Maisie and puts it in the microwave to heat up. She picks up a wineglass that Dan must have left on the kitchen table after she had gone to bed last night, and puts it in the dishwasher. Dot is already pulling boxes of cereal out of the press for her breakfast. Ella makes her breakfast and they all go down to the living room, Maisie at last quiet. Ella flicks on the TV and finds the kids' channels which seem to broadcast children's programmes all night long. She switches on a cartoon and props Maisie up against cushions on the sofa beside her sister who is eating her cereal.

She hears Dan getting up just before seven. He comes up

the stairs into the living room and Dot runs into his arms. He lifts her up and swings her around the room. "Hello, my little Dotty-Dot!"

She is giggling. "It's Princess Dotty-Dot, remember, Daddy?"

"Oh sorry, I'm so silly – I meant Princess Dotty-Dot."

Maisie starts chuckling when she sees her sister being spun around.

Dan goes back to packing up his laptop into its case and winding the plug around the power pack. "Have you seen my keys?"

Ella lifts a cardigan belonging to one of the girls, picks the keys up from underneath and hands them to him. "Are you not having breakfast?"

"No, I've got to fly – session is due to start at seven thirty this morning."

Later that morning Ella sits in the doctor's waiting room for Maisie's vaccines. A card had arrived in the post the week before, reminding her that they were overdue, and yet again she thought about how much Mrs Frawley had seamlessly taken care of in her time working for them. She can't help staring at all the other mothers seated around the room, watching how they interact with their babies. They make it look effortless; they are not stressing like her. If their baby cries, they soothe it and it stops. Ella's jaw is tense from hoping that Maisie won't wake. If she starts crying here, she knows she won't be able to make her quiet again.

She sees the other patients' eyes as they slowly realise where they recognise her from. She looks down at the grey marl tiles on the floor and follows the swirling pattern with her eyes. She really hopes that she is called soon. She looks up at the leaflet-holder on the wall. All the fliers start with questions. They all compete as they try to register their symptoms with the people populating the waiting room. *Are you? Have you? Do you?* The questions talk to her. They are the only things that ask how she is feeling.

After a few minutes the doctor sticks her head around the door and calls in her next patient. Ella marvels at how the woman carries her baby, her changing bag and steers her two-year-old son into the room at the same time without any panic. *It's not meant to be this hard*, Ella keeps repeating. *What is wrong with me?* she wonders for the umpteenth time. What is so wrong with her that she is almost devoid of all natural maternal instinct and can't attend to the most basic needs of her own children?

At last the nurse comes out and calls Ella into the room. Ella eyes the needle, which lies at the side of the cardboard tray, waiting to pierce through her baby's pudgy skin. She sees its pointed sharpness and knows it will wake her. She wants to run with her there and then, but instead she does as the nurse tells her and takes a seat at the end of the desk while the nurse busies herself with filling out Maisie's vaccination card.

"It's nice to finally meet you, Ella," the nurse says.

Ella's ears automatically pick out the word 'finally'.

"I think it was your childminder that I met the last time?" the nurse continues.

Ella nods. "Yeah, you would have met Mrs Frawley then."

"You must have gone back to work early?"

"Yes, I had to go back when she was only a month old."

"Wow, that must have been tough! Well, it's nice to finally meet Maisie's mum."

Ella is grateful that she doesn't mention the newspaper headlines.

"So how are you getting on, Ella? You're probably a dab hand at it by this stage – Maisie is your third child, right?"

"She cries a lot."

The nurse looks at Ella first and then at Maisie who is still sleeping soundly in her car seat.

"She's a baby – they all do that unfortunately!" She laughs.

"You've probably just forgotten since the other two."

She doesn't remember it being like that with the other two.

"I keep thinking that she's going to stop breathing or something."

"I think most parents will admit to worrying about it at some stage but as long she's sleeping on her back and not wrapped up too warmly, she should be fine."

"So it's normal then?" she asks.

"Completely," the nurse smiles.

"I just feel useless though." The words are out before she knows it.

The nurse puts down the vaccination card. "But did you feel like this with the other two?"

"Well, I can't remember, I . . . em . . . I . . . wasn't around that much when they were small if I'm honest."

"Oh."

Ella can hear the judgement in her voice.

"Look, I think all mothers feel like that at some stage," the nurse says, "even when they've had babies before."

"But why don't people ever talk about it? It's just so . . . so . . . massive."

The nurse peers at her over the rims of her steel-framed glasses. "Okay, why don't you lift her out and strip her down to her vest – it's two jabs today, I'm afraid."

"But she'll cry!"

The nurse laughs. "I vaccinate over twenty babies a day – believe me, I know she will cry!"

Ella bends down, unstraps Maisie and delicately unzips her from her padded snowsuit. Maisie startles and her brown eyes pop open.

"Hello, beautiful," the nurse says and takes her hand.

This woman, this strange woman, seems more confident than Ella is with her own daughter. "You're not going to like me, no, you're not," she coos. She instructs Ella on the best way to hold her. "Right, are you ready then?"

Ella closes her eyes and waits to hear Maisie's roar. Finally it comes, a desperate *waaah, waaah,* before she starts screaming.

"It's okay, little one, it's okay," Ella says over and over again.

"All right, Ella – if you turn her this way, we'll do the same again on the other side."

She reluctantly does what she is told. And this time Maisie roars and Ella wants to cry with her.

"Don't worry, we're all done. Now, if she develops a temperature or is irritable give her some Calpol. Of course, if at any stage you're worried, give the surgery a call. Here's a card with our number."

Ella manages to calm Maisie down and get her back into her snowsuit. She is just about to go out the door when the nurse stops her. "Why don't you and Maisie go along to the mother and baby group? There's one on in the Parish Hall every Friday morning."

"Oh, I don't think I'm a mother-and-baby-group kind of person," she says, dismissing her quickly. It sounds like her very worst nightmare.

The nurse looks at her as if she's trying to assess her. "Really?"

"It's just not my scene," she adds with a tone of defensiveness.

"Well, if you say so, but it can be an invaluable way of meeting other people in the area or even just to have a cup of tea and a chat with mothers going through the same thing as you. Maybe you shouldn't rule it out without giving it a go."

"Okay, I might . . . "

But she has no intention of going anywhere near it. Listening to other mothers worrying about how many poos their baby does in a day or how to introduce lumpy food to their baby's diet. She's not like them. No way.

Chapter 11

They are a thoroughly modern family, the Traynors, or should that be the *Traynor-Corless-McWilliamses*? It sounded like a firm of solicitors when you said it like that. Rachel and Marcus were on their way over to the house of his ex-wife, Jules Corless, the mother of his two grown-up children Eli and Alexandra. Jules had recently had a third child with her new husband Brian McWilliams and they were having a barbecue to celebrate the child's christening.

It is just after seven when their taxi pulls up on the tree-lined avenue in front of Jules' and Brian's house. They get out, Marcus takes her hand in his and they walk up the path towards the door.

"Rachel, come on in – it's so good to see you again!" Jules says, opening the door and taking her warmly into her arms.

"What about me?" Marcus asks, leaning in to give her a kiss on the cheek.

"And you, of course! Come on through to the garden – Brian is just lighting the charcoal." She stops and places her hand on Rachel's elbow. "And don't worry, we have special veggie sausages just for you, Rachel."

In the early days, when she had first met Marcus it used to freak her out, the level of comfortableness and good relations between them all. Any divorced couples that she knew were acrimoniously divorced – they hated each other with a lingering bitterness. But Marcus and Jules still liked each other and, more than that, Marcus counted Jules as one of his best friends. Rachel used to feel intimidated by it, if she is really honest, and whenever she talked to her best friend Shirley about the closeness of his relationship with his ex-wife, Shirley would scrunch up her face in suspicion: "Isn't it a bit weird though? You don't think there's anything still going on there, do you?" Rachel had worried about it for a while, treating Jules with a wary coolness every time they saw each other. She had eventually spilled out her feelings to Marcus, confessing how strange she found it all, and he had seemed genuinely upset. He had never thought for a second that she would find the whole thing unsettling. He had assured her that they just had a great friendship and he was very proud of how they had managed to maintain their relationship after the divorce because their two children would never know the tug of sparing one parent's feelings over the other's or the stress of trying to keep them apart at family occasions.

"But if you get on so well, why did you and Jules break up then?" she remembered asking him.

"Because we are essentially two very different people. We started out as friends in university – then we got together and soon after she was pregnant. We were so young and naïve – we were only eighteen. When I look at Eli now, I can't imagine him being responsible for a baby and he's nearly six years older than I was at the time! Our parents were keen for us to get married, so we did, and then we had Alex. But sometimes when you're with someone from such a young age you don't even know yourself properly and it was only as we got older that we both got to know ourselves and realised that our relationship was essentially what it started out as: friendship. We had drifted apart and were more like brother and sister than husband and wife. We'll always love and care for each other, but some people are meant to be just friends and me and Jules were that." He had pulled her up on top of him then. "But you and me, we're meant to be lovers *and friends,* and that's the best bit."

They are all sitting down around the table now while Brian flips meat on the griddle. The smell of the lilac tree scents the air. The sun is just starting to set in a pinky orange sky.

"So how are you finding it all?" Rachel asks as Jules fills her glass with chilled white wine.

"I'm good. I don't remember being this tired with the other two, though, but that would be my age – 'elderly gravida' is what they described me as in the hospital – but look," she is nodding over to where Eli is cradling his infant brother on his knee, "he's the best thing to ever happen to our family. He's cemented us all together."

Jules had told Rachel the story about how she didn't realise that she was pregnant until she was ten weeks gone. She had put her absent period and emotional state down to the start of the menopause and so at the age of forty-three with a twenty-four-year-old son and a twenty-two-year-old daughter it had certainly come as a surprise.

Rachel gets up to fill her plate with salad. She looks over at Marcus who is now lifting the baby from Eli's arms. She watches for a moment as he strokes his head, then he puts his fingers inside the curl of the child's fingers and he grips on tightly. She feels her chest tighten and her breathing seems to stop. It feels like someone is searing a hot rock of coal through her heart. The longing feels so acute, so painful. She badly wants this for them. So badly.

"What about you, Rachel?" Jules says, coming up beside her and following her line of vision over to Marcus. "Do you think that you and Marcus will ever have children together?"

"Hmmh, I'd like to, I really would, but I don't think Marcus is quite there yet," she says wistfully. "I'm not sure if he's ever going to be there, to be honest." She combs her fingers back through her hair. She feels uncomfortable talking about this with his ex-wife. It feels disloyal to him somehow.

"He'll come round. Marcus loves you very much – I can see that. What you two have together is different from what we had. If he knows how much it means to you then I'm sure he'll realise that it would be really good for both of you."

Rachel really wants to believe what this woman is saying. All she wants is for Marcus to turn around to tell her that he has changed his mind and is ready to start a new journey into parenthood with her, but she also knows him well enough to realise that that isn't going to happen.

Jules continues around the garden, filling up the wineglasses of her friends and relations, while Rachel makes her way over to sit down beside Marcus. Dusk starts to fall as the sun sets in an intense orange glow. She lets her weight sink into the chair; for some reason her whole body feels heavier now than when they had first come in. The candles on the table in front of them flicker in the gentle evening breeze. He gently places the baby into her arms and they each know what the other is thinking. She traces her finger along the clockwise whorl of hair on top of the baby's head. They feel the weight of sadness descend upon them yet again.

When they leave the barbecue, they flag a passing taxi down on the street outside. They sit into the back seat and Rachel rests her head on his shoulder. Street lights flick past the window outside. The taxi brings them to his place: a two-up, two-down red-brick house on the South Circular Road.

They let themselves inside and he makes them both their favourite nightcap of a Bailey's coffee and sits down onto the sofa beside her.

"You're very quiet," he says eventually. "Are you okay?"

"I'm good, just tired." She lies back into his arms and he strokes her hair. "Just . . . Jules asked me if you and I are ever planning on having children." She knows she is throwing it out there to test him; she knows this but she can't help it. She needs to discuss it again. She is so desperate to resolve this issue between them.

"Oh . . . I see . . . And what did you say to her?"

"I just said that I was hoping that you'd come round to the idea."

"But I won't, Rachel, you know that, don't you?" He turns to look at her and takes her hands in his.

"I know," she whispers, "but it's hard. You know how important it is to me to have children. I see Jules with wee Leo, who you were great with by the way – and I wish we had that or could have that, not even right now, but I need to know that it's in our future."

"I'm sorry, Rach, but it's the just the one thing that I can't give you."

"But I feel it every day – it is physically calling to me, and I know that sounds clichéd but I really have to listen to it. When I see a mother with a baby, my stomach somersaults inside because the yearning is so strong – do you get it Marcus? It's that strong!"

"Aw, Rach, I know, but it's just not something I want. I'm sorry, I wish that I did, but it's not an option for me. I have Eli and Alex and I adore them but that's it for me. They're adults now, they're both in college and they're starting to establish a little bit of independence away from me and Jules, and I love the freedom that you and I have now. I love how we can take off for a weekend or go out for dinner whenever we feel like it. It's not that easy with babies. I hate the thought of having to go all the way back through that again. I look at Jules with her newborn and I can't help but think it'd be my worst nightmare going back there again. I can't go back to the sleepless nights, nappies and sterilising everything. I know it's different for me because I already have children but I can't go back there. I know that's not fair on you. I'm sorry I can't be what you want me to be."

It's the familiar pang of sadness that has been coming a lot lately because she knows that sooner or later they will have to finish what they have together. Their relationship will have to come to an end because there is nowhere for them to go any more. They have come to a fork in their road and either she has to make the decision to forgo having children or else he needs to change his mind about not having more. She has given it so much thought. She has tried to imagine her life without children in it – she pictures herself as a fifty-year-old and Marcus ten years older than that again, childfree and careless as they go about life, but it isn't what she wants for her future. Whenever she thinks about them like that, it doesn't fill her with warmth. There is something missing from the picture.

But they both know that neither of them is going to change their mind – they've been over it time and time again. They've fought, they've gone without talking, they've cried about it, but ultimately they both know that sooner or later they are going to have to go their separate ways.

Chapter 12

Ella gets up, puts on her dressing gown and goes down to the cove to smoke a cigarette. She hasn't smoked in years but in the last few weeks she has found herself going back to them. When she is finished she takes the butt and puts it into the dustbin before going back inside to wake the girls for school. She opens each of their doors to rouse them before climbing the stone staircase to the top of the tower to get breakfast ready. A few minutes later and there is still no sign of either of the girls. She looks up at the clock.

"Come on, girls, wake up, we're going to be late again!" she shouts down from the balcony, looking down through the centre of the spiral staircase to the bottom of the Martello tower where the bedrooms are.

Dot bounces up the stairs a few minutes later and Ella can hear Celeste trudging heavily behind her. They sit down at the table and Celeste eats her Cheerios behind a makeshift wall of cereal boxes.

Ella starts buttering bread to make their lunches and opens every cupboard door in sequence, searching for missing lunchbox lids. Then giving up as the effort defeats her, she decides to put their lunches into plastic supermarket bags. Once again she finds herself wondering how Mrs Frawley had made minding her children seem effortless over the years. While the girls are eating, she goes back down to wake Maisie. Her baby is fast asleep on her tummy with her bum raised high in the air. She rests her hand on her warm body to feel the reassuring rise and fall of daughter's back. It seems a shame to wake her now that she is finally sleeping, having been awake most of the night, but they have to go. As soon as Ella lifts her, Maisie starts to cry. She puts her into her snowsuit, trying her best to be delicate as she inserts flailing limbs through the narrow holes.

Outside she straps the baby into her car seat and ushers the girls into the jeep. She gets into the front seat and, when she sees the time on the clock, she knows they will definitely be late. Again. The engine roars to life and she waits for the electric gates to open.

Maisie's cries are ringing through the air.

"*Stop crying, Maisie!*" Celeste roars at her. "Can't you do something to make her stop, Mum?"

"Mum, Maisie is really annoying!" Dot complains.

Ella's head just hears noises coming at her from every angle, like arrows – they keep coming and piercing through her skull: the baby screaming and the two girls shouting at her to make her stop screaming. She wonders, if she pressed the accelerator really hard and closed her eyes, what would happen? Where would she end up? There is a perilous drop to the sea below – but as soon as the thought enters her head, it leaves again just as fast.

Ella pulls up at the school and sees the group of mothers look in the direction of her jeep. She lets the girls out and leaves Maisie where she is. Celeste, upon spotting her best friend Gilly, runs straight over and hugs her. Ella walks after her with Dot's small hand inside her own. She feels eyes on her with each step. Her heart rate quickens. She takes a deep breath when she reaches Gilly's mum Gail.

"Hi, Gail – cold this morning, isn't it?"

Celeste and Gilly are chattering excitedly beside them.

"Oh, hi, Ella." Gail looks around her at the other mothers. "Yes, it's a chilly one all right." She moves to walk past Ella to go to the rest of the group who are standing at the wall.

Ella forces herself to continue. "Was Gilly able to do her maths homework yesterday? Only Celeste found it hard."

"Well, she struggled a bit on question four but we got there in the end." Her tone is polite but her eyes keep darting over to the group of women who are watching their conversation intently.

"Look, would you like to grab a coffee?" Ella blurts out, cringing inside at having to put herself out there like this. At exposing how pathetic she is in front of these women. She watches Gail as her brain tries rapidly to think up an excuse to get away from her.

"Oh, sorry, I can't this morning." Again her eyes look over to the other women. "I've already arranged to meet the ladies over there – sorry, Ella." She plasters a smile on her face.

"Oh, of course . . . well . . . I mean any morning is good with me now that I'm not in work . . . you know . . . I've more time for things like that." She feels like she is a little girl again, desperately trying to make friends in the schoolyard.

"Sure, Ella, yeah, we'll arrange something. Okay, well, I'd better go then – I don't want to keep the girls waiting."

"Okay, great – well, we'll do something soon then, I guess?"

"Sure."

She is left standing there as Gail makes her way over to the women. She can see them talking and then all the heads turn to look at her at the same time. She forces a smile on her face and walks back to the car.

Conor is walking down the street. The easterly wind is howling up the Liffey and he ducks his face down to shelter from it. He watches the battle between wind and water as the wind tries to force the river backwards against its natural flow. He passes under the bridge at Tara Street Station as weary commuters spill out from the DART. He stops to put some coins into a cup held out by a homeless man sitting under the bridge on a square of cardboard, his legs covered with a filthy sleeping bag. He feels sorry for the city's homeless population in weather like this.

His phone rings in his pocket and he scrabbles to take it out. It is Ella.

"What are you doing?"

"Just on my way to open up. Why?"

She sighs. "I'm the pariah of the school gate!"

"What's happened?" He rounds the corner onto Haymarket Street.

"Well, it seems –"

"*Shit!*" He can see a gaping hole in the window of his shop in the distance. He starts to run towards it.

"What is it?" says Ella. "What's wrong?"

"It's the window – they've smashed the fucking window in!"

"Oh no! I'll be right over."

After he hangs up, he stands outside his shop, the pavement littered with shards of glass. Crumbs of glass stick under the soles of his shoes. He looks inside and sees a concrete breeze block standing upended beside the knocked-over window display of books. Pages of the books are flapping in the wind as if trying to decide which side they want to fall on. He unlocks the door and goes inside. More glass greets him there. He runs his hands down over his face and lashes out to kick a book on the floor, "*Fuck!*" His whole body is trembling with rage. He doesn't have an alarm any more – he had to get rid of it because he couldn't afford to pay the monthly monitoring charge. He does a quick check around but thankfully nothing seems to be missing. Then he rings the Gardaí again. This time they say they'll send someone out to have a look.

While he is waiting for them to arrive, he googles 'Dublin Glaziers' and sets about getting a company to come out and repair the window. He feels sick when they quote him figures over the phone but he has no other option. He goes out the back and finds some cardboard boxes from yesterday's delivery to cover up the hole. He takes a brush and starts sweeping up the glass shards. After he has done the inside of the shop, he goes out to do the path.

He sees the same three boys standing further up the street, watching him.

"What happened to your window, mister?" the smallest one shouts over.

"You bloody well know what happened it!" he roars back at them.

"Well, it wasn't us!"

"Yeah, and it's just a coincidence that you guys cause trouble here every day?"

"You better watch what you're saying, mister – we didn't break your fucking window!"

They turn and walk away and, as they do, the oldest boy turns back to look at him over his shoulder through narrowed eyes. It gives Conor the shivers.

He begins to sweep up the glass from the pavement.

Ella's jeep pulls up by the kerb a few minutes later.

She jumps out and then lifts out Maisie who has finally fallen asleep in her car seat. Placing Maisie at her feet, she stands on the path beside him, surveying the damage.

"You're going to have to sort this out, Conor – they've gone too far this time!"

"The Guards are on their way."

"Have you got someone to come and replace it?"

"Yeah, I have a guy calling soon, but I just don't have that kind of money lying around. I've already had to ask the landlord to wait another week for the rent."

"Don't worry – I can pay for it."

"I can't ask you to cover the cost of a shop window, Ella!"

"Look, you can pay me back again when things are a bit easier for you – or your insurance might even cover it."

He rests the brush against the timber shop front.

"I don't know how much longer I can keep it going, Ella. My customers are dwindling and the rent is killing me."

"The recession is crippling everyone but, if you can ride it out, you've got the bones of a really good business here."

"Look around you – it's just a street of empty units and apartments – I'm so far off the beaten track."

"But what about the offices up the road? Surely they bring in some footfall during the week?"

"Hardly any. Come on, let's go inside." He sighs heavily.

They go into the shop and Ella goes out the back and puts the kettle on. She comes back with two mugs and places one down beside him. The bell rings and a customer enters. She is an older lady who lives in the terrace of houses behind the shop.

"What happened to your window, love?"

"Some gangsters threw a block through it."

"That's desperate – and you've such a lovely little shop in here. It's great to see someone trying to make a go of it instead of all the empty shops one after the other."

"Thank you." He is about to add a sarcastic comment about how he is glad that he is making the streets look nice for everyone else even though he is drowning in a sea of debt, but he stops himself just in time. That would be a sure way of getting rid of whatever customers he has left.

"Those builders ruined this street, so they did! They forced out all the small businesses that were here since I was a young one. Then they built all these fancy shops – and all of them empty bar your own! Anyway I could be here all day giving out about that shower – I'm looking for a book on how to get a baby to sleep properly –"

"Aren't we all!" Ella sighs, wearily nodding at Maisie who

is still sleeping soundly, catching up on the sleep she missed the night before.

The woman smiles. "She's a lovely little thing. How old is she?"

"Five months."

"My daughter had a baby three weeks ago and they're not getting a minute's sleep. I said I'd call in here and see if you've anything that might help her. She's desperate at this stage, so she is."

"I feel her pain," says Ella.

Conor leads the woman over to the shelves where the parenting books are. He shows her a few of his popular titles and she reads the back covers for a few minutes before choosing one. Conor takes for it at the till.

She nods at the window. "There's no call for carry-on like that. This place is getting worse, full of scumbags now, but when I was growing up it was a lovely place, full of decent honest folk."

"Ah, I suppose it's like everywhere – a few troublemakers give a place a bad name."

She nods. "Well, I hope you get it sorted."

Maisie wakes up soon after the customer leaves and Ella takes her up in her arms. "Come here, little one."

Maisie looks around, her sleepy eyes adjusting to the light.

"Hello, Maisie," Conor says. "Did you have a good sleep?"

"Of course she did! Wasn't she making up for the hours she lost since ten past five this morning! You don't know how lucky you are getting a full night's sleep every night."

"Yeah . . . maybe." His face darkens.

"Hey, don't worry, we'll get your window fixed soon. Did you ever manage to get a book club going?"

"Yeah, I've a few names now so I've one starting soon, I hope."

"You see! All that will help, I bet you. And I can help you to design a few posters. What do you reckon?"

"God, listen to you, you should go into consultancy."

"Yeah, well, you never know, now that I'm unemployed . . . "

"I just feel like everything that I've worked so hard for is slipping away from me." His voice wobbles. "I'm killing myself working seven days a week and for what? I've nothing to show for it." He wishes Leni was here. She would know what to do. She would tell him to stop feeling sorry for himself and to get his act together but he just can't seem to do it.

"Here, c'mon." She reaches up and puts her arm on his shoulder. "'*Even the darkest night will end and the sun will rise,*'" she says softly.

"*Les Mis?*"

She nods. "Well done."

"Well, it would want to start rising pretty soon!"

Chapter 13

A few days later Conor is working through a stack of paperwork when the door opens. He stands up to greet the customer but instead he is confronted with a small boy of around six or seven years of age. He isn't one of the usual three but he has that same look about him. He is wearing a knock-off of a Nike hoody with the slogan '*Just Do It*' emblazoned across the front, his tracksuit bottoms are too short and Conor can see an inch of bare skin above his white ankle socks. He is wearing round glasses and his sandy hair is falling down over his eyes.

Not another one, Conor thinks. He feels the rage build inside him. He can't cope with any more of the brazen children around here. They seem to be getting younger and younger and are afraid of nothing.

The boy strolls into the shop as though he is any ordinary customer.

"Eh no, you don't," Conor says, walking towards him and putting his arm out to stop him. "Get out of my shop."

The boy looks taken aback and stops dead.

Conor puts his hands on the boy's shoulders and turns him back around to face the door. "Go on, go – I've had enough of you lot causing trouble."

"Sorry – I only wanted to look at the books, mister."

Close-up, Conor notices that chestnut-brown freckles are sprinkled across the bridge of his nose.

"Well, you've looked, so you can go now."

The boy turns and looks him in the eye before walking out of the shop. Conor feels the tension wind tighter as he stands at the window and watches the small silhouette with the sunken shoulders as he walks off down the street.

The phone rings on the desk beside him, interrupting his thoughts.

"Conor, it's Robert Gordon here."

His heart sinks. Robert Gordon is his landlord. "Hi, Robert."

"I just checked the account there, Conor, and the rent hasn't hit again this month?"

"I'm sorry, Robert, I just don't have it – can you hang on another couple of days and I'll see what I can do?"

"Look, this is happening every month now, Conor. I know you have your troubles and business is tough at the moment but it's tough on all of us. I'm getting it in the neck from the bank because now my mortgage payment on the property will bounce. They won't give me so much as an inch – they're gone so nervous that they'll move in on me if it's late again."

"But I just don't have it – if I had the money I'd pay it –"

"Well, I can hardly go back to my bank and tell them that!"

"Look, the rent is killing me, Robert, and my window was smashed in a few days ago – is there anything that you can do for me on it?"

"I've told you before, Conor, it's just barely covering the mortgage – I'm not making a penny on it. I would help you if I could, but I can't afford to take the hit either. I don't like reminding you but you were the one who signed your name on the lease . . . "

"Don't I know it," Conor says wearily.

He hangs up on him and holds his head in his hands. He doesn't know what he is going to do. He sold his car a few months back. He didn't really use it anyway but it had been nice to have there if he ever wanted to go somewhere. He couldn't afford to run it any more, so it had to go. Selling it had helped to keep him afloat for a while. When Leni was here they were never flush but one of them was always able to cover the bills if the other was having a bad month. Now he is on his own, trying to survive and keep a roof over his head on a business that is losing money. He has nothing left. Nothing.

Chapter 14

Three Years Earlier

They stand looking around the concrete shell. Copper and white plastic pipes stick up randomly from the dusty grey floor.

"It's hard to imagine what it's going to look like," he says, looking at the shop front that has yet to be glazed and instead is just boarded up with wood.

"Nonsense, that's what your imagination is for! Close your eyes." Her words echo and bounce around the four walls.

He looks at her. "I can't."

"Go on, do it!" she orders.

So he does as he is told and closes his eyes.

"Now," she says, "just imagine that behind you will be your desk with some shelves, on your right you'll have some lovely dark-wood floor-to-ceiling shelves and the same on your left. Maybe you'll have the children's section here and then comfy chairs so people can sit down and read too. Then exactly where you are standing now there will be freestanding shelves – you know, with self-help books, maybe travel books too. Now can you see it clearly in your mind?"

He opens his eyes again and lets them adjust to the light. She comes up and puts her arms around him. Her blonde hair is pulled up messily into a loose bun. He likes when it's like that as he can see the contours of her face properly – its Germanic angles, the fullness of her lips, the small crater in her forehead left behind from when she had chicken-pox at the age of eight.

"I just know it will be amazing. Have you decided on the name yet?"

"Well, I was thinking since we're on Haymarket Street – what about 'Haymarket Books'?"

"I like it – it's better than 'Conor's Bookshop' like you were going to call it," she laughs. "I'm so proud of you, Conor. Leaving your job to follow your dream like this."

"Well, it was your idea that I should give it a go."

"But, still, you have done all of this yourself. Just think – in a few weeks all this will be transformed into the best bookshop in Dublin."

"In Ireland!"

"Of course, in Ireland," she laughs.

He pulls her closer towards him. "I hope it all works out now," he says anxiously.

Although he is excited, the worries of failure, the twenty-five-year lease, the figures and targets that he needs to meet just to break even and then the loan repayments too, have been keeping him awake at night. He worries about his inexperience in the industry – yes, he loves books and has worked as a bookseller, but is that enough? He is not a risk-taker by nature and, if it wasn't for Leni's unwavering belief in him, he probably wouldn't even be doing this. Everything he has – their entire future – is staked on this working out.

"It will. I know it will. You will be great, Conor." She rubs his arm. "Come, let's get food. I'm hungry."

Chapter 15

The Nespresso machine hisses while Shirley busies herself making two mugs of coffee.

"I need this after last night."

"Bad night with Tiernan?" Rachel asks.

"I saw every hour on the clock. I think he's teething."

"Ach, the poor wee man!"

Rachel is over at her friend Shirley's house. They have been best friends since just after Rachel moved to Dublin from the North and they had shared a house together in Sandymount.

"So how're things with Marcus?" Shirley asks, setting the mugs down on top of coasters on the table.

"I just don't know what I'm going to do, Shirl." Rachel clasps her two hands around her mug. "What we have together is perfect – it's so great – I've never met anyone like him before . . . when we're together, it feels amazing – I've never felt so happy!"

"I sense a 'but' coming?"

"But he can't give me what I want so I don't think I have any choice other than to break up with him . . . but it's a really, really hard decision to make . . . "

"You just need to go cold turkey – cut him out of your life today and stop making excuses. Delete his number right now.

Throw out the belongings that he still has lying around in your place. It's like ripping off a plaster – you need to do it fast and in one go. It'll be a sharp pain for a moment but it'll hurt less in the long run. You're peeling it back bit by bit and we all know it's more painful that way – but the end result is all the same."

"I wish it was that easy, Shirley. We've been together for three years – that's a long time. It's a big chunk of someone's life."

"Life expectancy is increasing. I heard this thing on the radio the other day, saying that it's quite likely that we're all going to live to the age of one hundred. So, if you think about it, three years is only three percent of your life – not really that big a deal in the grand scheme of things, Rachel, sorry!"

"You are such an accountant!"

"No, I'm a realist."

"Sometimes I wonder would it really be that bad, a life without children? For all I know even if he was willing to have a child with me, we mightn't be able to and I could have thrown away a great relationship for nothing."

"Yes, but on the flipside of that, if you *are* able to have children, you want to have them and he doesn't."

"I know, I know, you're right," she sighs. "Shirley, for once could you not be just a comforting shoulder to moan on?" she laughs.

"Nope! Look, sorry if I'm being flippant. I know this is hard on you but the way I see it is that neither of you is going to change your mind so I think you need to stop prolonging the inevitable."

The door opens and Hugh comes into the kitchen. "Hi, Rachel, how are you today?"

"I'm great, thanks, Hugh. You wife here is being her usual searingly honest self."

He bends over and gives Shirley a kiss on the cheek. He always does this whenever he enters a room that she is in, even if he last saw her only fifteen minutes ago. "What are you saying now, love?"

"I'm just saying it as it is."

He looks at Rachel, his eyes widened in pretend fear. "Tiernan is still sound asleep anyway. I just checked on him there."

"Thanks, darling."

"I updated the feeding chart too – it was twenty-five minutes at three fifteen, wasn't it?"

"Yes, that was it."

He laughs. "My brain is gone to pot since Tiernan arrived!" He smiles indulgently at both of them but Rachel knows that the smile is for Shirley really.

Shirley and Hugh are the kind of couple that play board games together and don't cheat. They hold hands when they go for a walk. They are always so complimentary to each other, exchanging little knowing smiles. It seems impossible to Rachel to imagine them having sex though. She wonders if Hugh keeps stopping every few minutes to make sure Shirley is all right – she imagines him saying 'Are you sure now, darling? I don't want to hurt you'. When they had announced they were having a baby, Rachel had to accept that they probably had had sex (just the one time) although she hadn't ruled out artificial insemination. Of course Hugh had held Shirley's hand during the antenatal classes and educated himself in labour techniques to minimise pain. They had both practised hypnobirthing mantras. He had made her a playlist for labour full of powerful songs or slow, inspiring ones in case she had got disheartened at any point and then another playlist with calming womb sounds to be played for when the baby was just about to be born to ease the transition into the world. They had chosen a home birth and had researched it extensively but when little Tiernan had decided to do his first poo (*meconium* – Hugh had explained to her) inside his mother, it had ended up with an emergency Caesarean in the maternity hospital anyway.

When Baby Tiernan arrived, instead of feeling the strain like most new parents, they grew even closer together. Even though Shirley was breastfeeding they did the night feeds 'together' so Hugh didn't miss valuable bonding time – "Feeding time is when they bond, you know!" he had said seriously to Rachel. Even their families got on and this year, Shirley and Hugh and both sets of parents were all going to the Dordogne region in France on holiday with Tiernan.

Rachel had always thought that someday she and Marcus would be like that together, that they would be the couple being consumed with birth plans and having their life dictated by feeding schedules, but she now knows that they probably never will be. She is starting to obsess about it. She was visiting an infant as part of a case in work earlier in the week and when the baby had started cooing up at her from her wicker basket, she had felt her eyes fill with tears. She had brushed it off with the baby's mother as a pollen allergy, but she knows that she can't keep on going like this, it is affecting her so badly. She can't look at a mother with a baby without feeling her stomach churning until the point where she almost feels nauseated and then the ever-present ache sets in in her heart as she thinks about her and Marcus.

"Will I make you a fresh cup of tea?" Hugh asks. "You two look like you've lots to talk about."

"That would be lovely, honey." Shirley smiles up at him and Rachel feels her heart break a little bit more.

Chapter 16

The rain is spilling down the windowpanes of the shop. He watches as rivulets run down the glass. It is miserable outside and the streets are empty. He hasn't had a customer in all morning. No one in his or her right mind would venture out in weather like this. The bell sounds and when he looks up again, he sees the boy from yesterday standing there looking at him. He isn't wearing a coat. He is soaked through and rain drips off him down onto the floor.

"Eh . . . can I help you there?" Conor asks.

"Are you okay? You look very sad, mister."

"I'm fine. Now what are you doing here again? I thought I told you yesterday to get lost?"

"But I just want to look at your books."

"Well, now you've looked. Go on – get out of here."

The boy ignores him and walks over to the shelves where the children's books are. He lifts down a farmyard picture book that has animals hiding underneath flaps. He starts to flick through it, lifting the flaps as he turns the pages.

Conor follows over and stands beside him. "Do you mind? You're going to destroy those books with your wet fingers!"

"I'm only having a look," he says, putting it back up on the shelf.

"I told you already – I've enough of you lot causing trouble."

"What's this one?" the boy asks, ignoring him and taking down another one.

"*Horrid Henry.*"

"Can I read that?"

"No, you can't!" he says, taking the book from his hand and putting it back up in the same place on the shelf. "This is a bookshop not a library – I'm in the business of selling books."

"But you can sell it when I'm finished with it," the boy suggests, like it is a perfectly reasonable solution.

Conor sees that he isn't being cheeky. "Where's your mother? You're too young to be out on the streets on your own, especially in this weather."

"I'm nearly eight!" He seems insulted.

He doesn't look it – there are six-year-olds taller than him. Conor notices that one of his shoelaces, dirty and sodden from trailing the ground, is open.

"You'd better tie that in case you trip up," he says, pointing down at the lace.

The boy looks down at it and shrugs his shoulders. "What's your name?" he asks.

"Conor."

"I'm Jack."

"Hi, Jack."

"You've lots of books, Conor."

"Well, that's because it's a bookshop, Jack."

"Have you ever counted them all up?"

"What, to find out how many I have? No, I can't say I've ever done that."

"Want to do it now?" His eyes are wide and eager.

"Eh, no, I'll pass on that offer, thanks."

"Okay, well, maybe another time. I know, why don't we play hide the book? I'll take a book and hide it in between all the other books and you have to find it?"

"Sounds great but I'm kinda busy right now."

"Oh right." He pauses for a minute. "You don't look busy. You have no one in your shop."

"I'm doing paperwork."

"What's your favourite book of all the ones in here?"

"Oh God, I don't know . . . I couldn't choose just one." He is exasperated. "Now come on, you have to go – I've work to do."

"Is that why you're sad all the time?"

"I'm not sad."

"Well, you look sad – you always seem sad whenever I look at you through the window."

"I didn't know I had an audience!"

"We could read together if you want? Teacher says I'm a great reader."

"I'm sure you are but that's enough now – come on, off you go. I've got a business to run." He turns him around and marches him over towards the door.

They stand on the step; the rain is still teeming down, making ripples in the puddles on the road outside. He doesn't have the heart to let him out in it.

"Hang on, wait a sec –" He turns, goes behind the counter and grabs an umbrella that a customer had left behind one day. "Here, you'd better take this with you." He hands it to the boy and helps him to put it up.

"I'll give it back to you."

"Don't worry about it, hold onto it."

"Bye, mister." Jack is waving at him from under the umbrella. The rain is rolling off it and falling into the puddles around his feet.

"Bye, Jack."

Ella pulls back the heavy wooden door and sees her sister Andrea standing there with her two daughters, sheltering underneath an umbrella.

"I wasn't expecting to see you?"

"Well, I had to pick up something in the village so I said we'd come up for a cuppa to see how you're doing?"

They climb the spiral stairs up to the kitchen. Andrea sits down at the kitchen table and straightaway Dot climbs up on to her knee, while Celeste goes over to play with her curly hair. She likes pushing her fingers up through the curls and pushing them up together into a tight coil and then letting them spring back out again. The girls love Andrea. Andrea's two girls are sitting up beside them at the table, feeding beads onto thread to make friendship bracelets with a kit that Andrea brought over with her.

"Where's little Maisie?"

"She's in the nursery having a nap."

"Every time I call over she's asleep – she's a dream baby, isn't she?"

"Well, you should have heard her screaming the house down earlier on," Celeste says.

"She's a baby, Celeste!" Andrea says, laughing.

"Well, Celeste has a point. She cries a lot – just not much when you're here."

She gets up to make the coffee but then they can hear Maisie start to cry on the monitor. *Make the coffee or attend to Maisie, make the coffee or go to Maisie?* This is the problem: she can't seem to make the simplest of decisions. Everything is fazing her when she knows logically it shouldn't be a big deal.

"You make the coffee and I'll get her," Andrea offers, getting up off the chair and going downstairs.

"Thanks," Ella says, relieved.

The girls follow after her. They always follow her around.

Ella takes her time making the coffee, savouring the unusual moment of quiet in the kitchen until Andrea comes back up the stairs with a sleepy Maisie cuddling in towards her neck. She watches her sister with her baby and not for the

83

first time thinks Andrea has a natural ability that she just doesn't possess.

"She's such a cutie, Ella." Andrea sits back down at the table and cuddles Maisie closely.

"You were always like that with babies," Ella says.

"Like what?"

"The way you just know how to hold her and calm her." Ella looks down at the floor and she sighs. "I think when the maternal genes were being given out, you got them all and I got whatever dregs were left over! Sometimes I can't believe that we're sisters!"

"Well, I'm hardly The Baby Whisperer! Sure all they are is tiny little people!"

"But they're so delicate and fragile – I'm so afraid that I'll do something wrong and harm her."

"Ella – she's your third child – the way you go on you'd think she was your first! You're not going to kill her – it's normal to be a bit anxious. I've probably forgotten what it's like to have a tiny baby. It seems like ages ago since mine were this small." She smiles lovingly at the child who is beaming back at her.

"I know – you'd think I'd have got my act together by now." She sighs heavily. "I'm useless at the whole thing."

"No, you're not. Do you know what I think it is?"

"What?"

"That job was your life – being at home all day, it's a huge change for you."

"Tell me about it," she says wryly.

"Stop being so hard on yourself – you'll be fine. Some mothers want to, or need to work, and then there are some like me that want to be with their babies. It doesn't mean my style of motherhood is any better than yours."

They can hear the girls' shrieks of laughter bounce off the stone walls and travel up through the tower from where they are playing downstairs.

"But it is – I hardly know my own children! I just seem to be so bad at this motherhood thing. I don't have a natural instinct like you have. And Celeste is being very distant."

"Really? She's probably just missing Mrs Frawley – she'll be okay, I promise."

"Do you really think so?"

"Of course she will! You've had a difficult couple of weeks but you'll get there – look, everything happens for a reason. I know losing your job has hit you hard – you gave your life to that show. Sure you were back to work after six weeks for all of them! But maybe you should try seeing it as an opportunity to spend more time with your children. Every cloud and all that?"

"I know, you're right. I'm trying to see it like that, I really am. You know, I didn't have a choice. If I'd taken any longer out I would have been replaced. That's the way it is in TV: if you have a job you need to hold onto it with both hands because there are a hundred other younger, prettier girls just waiting for the chance."

"You've had a difficult few months – it's going to take a bit of getting used to – but I guarantee you will look back on this time and won't regret it. You'll find your feet – I promise. And if it's really not your thing being at home with the kids then you can always look for another job."

"Are you mad? My name is like a dirty word on Irish TV right now."

"It'll all blow over – in a few more weeks no-one will remember any of this."

"Hmmh . . . maybe in the year 2047 after the whole fiasco has died down."

"But it was a mistake for God's sake! You are being treated so unfairly!"

Andrea keeps referring to it as a mistake, even though they both know that the reason the store is bringing it to court is because she had taken another item the day before, but

Andrea can't bear to accept the truth about her younger sister.

They fall silent for a minute before Andrea speaks again. "Oh, while I think of it, I'm going to ask Dad over for dinner on Sunday – that's if you're around."

"He might be off doing something with his lady friend." Ella laughs.

"Yeah, he seems to really like her, doesn't he?"

"He does. Of course I tried asking him about her but he said they were only friends. I don't believe him though."

"Well, I'm glad, good for him. At least someone's relationship is going well."

"Are things okay with yourself and Dan?"

"Well, he's still very angry with me – and I understand that. He's working all hours of the day at the minute – I think he's trying to avoid me to be honest."

"Well, it's important that he knows how you're feeling. You need to tell him how difficult you're finding it at the moment."

"That's difficult when he isn't even talking to me."

"He's a good man, Ella, but this has been a big shock to him. He'll come round, just give him time."

Chapter 17

"*Woah, woah, wooooooaaaaaaaaaaaaaaaaaaaaaaah . . .*"

Conor hears the crash against his shop front. He runs out to see what the commotion is. He sees the three boys are busy pushing each other up and down the street in an abandoned shopping trolley from Rafferty's supermarket. One gets inside it, then the other two run with it down the street for a bit before letting it go and watch it careering down the path in front of them.

He goes back inside and shuts the door on them. Soon after the door opens again and Conor's heart jumps, but when he looks up it is Jack.

The boy walks over and puts the umbrella on the counter in front of Conor. "I just wanted to give you your brolly back, mister."

"You could have held on to it," he says, putting it behind the till. "I've loads of them."

"Me ma always says that if you borrow something you have to give it back."

"That's good advice. Speaking of your ma – where is she?"

"At home in bed."

"I see. So she doesn't know you're out roaming the streets then?"

"I'm not!" He is defensive. "I only came here to see you."

He is wearing the same tracksuit bottoms that he'd been wearing before and a black T-shirt with the fluorescent green face of an alien on it. It's four degrees outside.

"I guess I should feel honoured so. Should you not be at home doing your homework or something?"

"I do it after me dinner. We usedta always go to the homework club. Ma was like a teacher but she wasn't really – she just made sure everyone was doing their sums or she would sometimes have to help them with their reading. She never gave out or anything but now she's too tired to do it any more so we just go straight home. Wanna hear a joke?"

"Okay."

"Why does Ireland keep getting bigger?"

"I don't know – why does Ireland keep getting bigger?"

"Because it keeps *dublin'* and *dublin'*. Do you get it? Dublin and *doublin'*?"

"That's a good one, Jack."

"Want to hear it again?

"I think you really nailed it that time."

"Can I look at the books?"

"Go on," he sighs heavily.

He bends his head to start typing up an email. He looks up now and again to check that the boy isn't causing trouble or fleecing him. But he's sitting down on the floor with a book on his knees and his back resting against the shelves, reading. Conor can't see the cover from here but the boy seems to be engrossed in whatever it is so he leaves him alone and gets on with his work.

A customer comes into the shop and goes over to the travel section. "I'm looking for a book on Egypt. I'm going there on my holidays in a few weeks."

Conor comes out from behind the till and goes over to help her.

She looks at the boy and smiles. "Must be a good book," she says to Conor.

"Must be."

She takes a book down from the shelf and leafs through it before selecting another one and doing the same. Eventually she settles on one. "This one seems to be good," she says. "I'll take it."

They walk over to the till and Conor rings up her purchase and puts it in a paper bag. "It's a cold one out there today, isn't it?"

"It is. That wind would cut you in two! Thanks a million."

The customer goes on her way again and finally Jack gets up and comes back over to him.

"What are you reading?" Conor asks.

"It's about a boy who is sent to live with his aunt because his brother is sick and he might catch the disease and he's so bored there cos there are no other children so he goes exploring in the garden at night."

"Show me." Conor looks at the cover. "Ah, *Tom's Midnight Garden*! I loved that as a boy."

"You read it too?"

"A long time ago now."

"What, like fifty years or something?"

"Eh no, probably more like thirty."

"Oh," Jack says, sounding disappointed.

Conor goes back to the counter and Jack follows him.

"Who's that?" He nods at the photo frame beside the till.

"That's my girlfriend Leni."

"Leni – that's a weird name for a girl!"

"She's German." He still can't bring himself to talk about her in the past tense.

"Why is she wearing those funny red trousers?"

"They're not funny trousers – we were in Thailand – they're called fisherman pants. Everybody wears them over there."

"Well, they look funny to me! Where's Thailand anyway?"

"Asia."

"Where's A-sha?"

"A-she- a. Hang on a sec." He goes over to the shelves and takes down a children's atlas. He opens it up on the world. "Here's Ireland, here's England – we're in Europe – and all the way over here, this is Thailand – and all this landmass here," he circles the page with his finger, "is called Asia."

"What were you doing there?"

"We were travelling around. We went through all these countries. India, Burma or some people call it Myanmar – Cambodia, Laos, Vietnam." He points out their coloured shapes to Jack.

"But where did you live?"

"We stayed in hostels and hotels and even in a tent at times."

"Cool! How did you go there?"

"Well, we went by plane."

"I've never been on a plane," Jack says wistfully.

"You're still young, you've lots of time yet."

"Seán Brady went on a plane one time and he did a wee and it went all the way down the toilet and onto the people below but they thought it was rain – they didn't know it was his wee!"

"Really?"

"Yeah, it was gross. Maybe I'll ask Ma if I can go on a plane when I go home. I better go – she might be awake and she'll be looking for me."

"Yeah, you probably should go then."

"See ya, mister, thanks for letting me read your book."

"No worries – oh, and Jack?"

"Yeah?"

"Call me Conor, will you?"

Chapter 18

Rachel is in Marcus's place. They have just finished the meal that he has cooked for her and are relaxing over a bottle of wine on the sofa. He has lowered the lights and candles flicker softly around the room. She has finally decided to address the issue with him once and for all. After talking it through with Shirley she knows that she can't keep putting off the inevitable. It isn't fair to either of them. They both know that they are at a watershed in their relationship, they have been for a while now, and Rachel needs to make the choice about whether a life with Marcus but without children is a possibility for her . . . or else, a life without Marcus.

"You know what I want to talk to you about, don't you?" she says eventually after taking an age to work up the courage to say the words.

He nods. "I feel like I'm eating my last meal on death row." He smiles a sad smile.

"I always thought you'd come round, y'know? People make those kinds of grand statements all the time and they change their mind. When I first met Shirley, for example, she swore that she was going to be a career woman, that kids would hinder that, but then after being married for all of three months she announces she is pregnant and casts aside all of her previously held ideals."

He sighs. "I know some people probably think I'm being too stubborn on this issue and that I should just do whatever it takes to make you happy – sure there are men fathering children every day of the week and they're not even aware of it! But I don't think it would be fair to bring a child into the world if I don't want it. Would you like to be conceived because your father was just doing it to hold onto the woman he loved? It's not the right reason to have a baby with you and that's why I can't do it. I wish I could, darling."

"Damn you and your morals!" She smiles bitter-sweetly at him. "I can't even argue back with you because you're right – that's the bloody frustrating part of it all."

"The last thing I want is for you to wake up one day and resent me and we're sitting across the kitchen table from each other eating our cornflakes and you're seething because you're thinking about everything that I took from you. That would be awful, and then we'd just be miserable. I love you and I want you to be happy, that's why I don't want to deny you the opportunity of experiencing what I have with Eli and Alex."

"You're perfect – we're perfect together – but I've always wanted children and I can't see myself without them. I'm sorry, Marcus, but it's all I've been thinking about lately and I don't think I can accept that part of you. I really wish I could."

It is a tiresome battle of wills and they never seem to be able to get past it and she knows that they never will get past it.

"So what are we going to do now?" he asks.

"The only thing we can do."

They both fall silent, knowing that the inevitable has now come upon them. There can be no more ignoring the huge divide between them; the time has come to go their separate ways.

"Just lie here with me, please, just for tonight," he whispers to her, stroking her face delicately. "Let's face it in the morning."

Chapter 19

"I'm making myself a sandwich – do you want one?"

Jack nods eagerly. "I'm starving."

"You're always starving!"

Conor goes out the back and takes down the bread and starts making two of his usual ham-and-cheese sandwiches and brings them out the front.

"Thanks, mister," Jack says as he takes his one and starts to devour it. He moves across the edge of the white bread in half-moon-shaped bites.

"I keep telling you to call me Conor – 'mister' makes me feel like I'm ancient." He takes a bite of his own sandwich.

"You are ancient."

"I'm only thirty-five."

"Ma is only thirty-two and she's old so you're *really* ancient!"

"You really know how to make a man feel good, don't you?"

"Yep," he says, biting off a bit of the crust. "It's my birthday next week."

"Wow – so you'll be the big eight then?"

"Yep. Ma says I was meant to be born in January but she was waiting and waiting for me to come outta her tummy.

And then on the very first day of February I was born. Ma said I was hanging on because it wouldn't have suited me to be born in January – it's too cold and dreary for me because I'm so sunny and bright."

"That's one way of describing you! So what are you going to get for your birthday?"

"I really want to get the new Real Madrid jersey with Ronaldo 7 on the back but Ma says they change jerseys more often than she changes her knickerses and they cost a lot of money so she mightn't have enough to buy me it."

"Yeah, well, she's right – it's probably best not to get your hopes up."

"Okay. So what are we going to do today?"

"Well, I'm not sure about you but I've got work to do."

"Well, you don't look that busy to me." He looks around the shop which is empty as usual. Conor hasn't had a customer in almost two hours.

"I have paperwork to do."

"Well, can I read more of *Tom's Midnight Garden* while you're doing your paperwork?"

"Go on then."

He goes to his usual spot, slumped on the floor, and reads.

A man comes in with a little girl and approaches Conor.

"I bought the Steve Jobs one you recommended before and I really liked it so I was hoping you could recommend something else for me?"

"Sure."

"This is a really good book, mister," Jack says.

The man and girl hadn't noticed him sitting on the floor and look down at him and smile.

"It's about a boy who has to go and live with his aunt and uncle in a really boring old house and he has no one to play with and when everyone goes to sleep a garden appears when he goes through the back door but it's not there in the daytime – it only comes when everyone else is in bed."

"What is it called?"

"*Tom's Midnight Garden.*"

"You might like that one, Tess – what do you reckon? Want to give it a try?"

She nods shyly.

"We'll take that anyway," the man says to Conor. "That's a great salesperson you've got there!"

Conor nods and smiles.

"So what do you recommend for me?" the customer asks.

"How about sports autobiogs? This Andre Agassi one is great even for non-sports fans."

"Sure I'll give it a try so."

Conor rings up the purchases and the father and daughter leave the shop with their books, hand in hand.

"I'll have to give you a job in here soon!" Conor says to Jack.

"Really? I could be your helper. I could read all the books and then tell everyone to buy them!"

"Simple really, isn't it?"

Jack nods at him eagerly and Conor reaches out to rub his hair.

"Did you get much homework?" She looks into her rear-view mirror at the girls in the back seat.

"It's Friday, Mum – Mrs Johnson never gives us homework on a Friday."

"Sorry, I forgot. That's good though. What about you, Dot?"

"Flashcards."

"What time will Dad be home?" Celeste asks.

"I'm not sure."

"I haven't seen him since Sunday."

"Really?"

"Yeah."

"Well, he's been working really hard at the moment. They have a lot of clients booked in."

"He used to say the same thing to me about you."

"He did?"

"Yeah, you were always at the station, remember?"

"I know, love, but I'm here now. Hey – why don't we go and get something to eat in the café, huh? As a Friday treat?"

They park at the harbour and she takes in the panorama of pretty fishing boats, white yachts contrasted against the buildings painted in pastel colours.

They go in and grab seats. The girls have what they always have – chocolate cake for Celeste and herself with ice cream on the side and the cheese board for Dot.

"You're going to turn into a block of cheese if you eat any more of it, Dot Devlin!" Ella says.

Dot giggles and swings her legs, crossed at the ankles, underneath her chair.

Maisie is drinking her bottle in her buggy so at least she is quiet. They sit back and wait for their food. It's nice, Ella thinks. The kids are in good form and for once Maisie isn't crying.

An older lady is looking over at her. It makes her feel uneasy. She turns back to the girls.

"I can't believe my baby is almost eight."

"Stop, Mum, I'm not your baby!"

"Oh, you know what I mean – you will always be my baby."

"Do you want to have a party?"

"No."

"Oh, why not?"

"Well, no one will come."

"Of course they will – we'll invite the class like last time."

"I'm telling you they won't come. There's no point. Everyone hates me."

"Celeste, why would you say that?"

"They do – no one wants to play with me."

"But what about Gilly?"

"Her mum told her not to play with me any more."

Ella tries her best to keep the emotion out of her voice. "But . . . but why would she do that?" The words sting her. She knows why. It's one thing treating her like that but not her daughter.

Celeste shrugs. "I don't know, Mum," she says sadly.

"Aren't you Ella Wilde?" the woman who had been staring over at her for the last ten minutes says on her way out the door.

"Yes, I am."

"Well, shame on you! You're being paid a six-figure salary out of *my* money and it still isn't enough for you – that's pure, scandalous greed in my book!" she hisses and tiny drops of spittle fly from her mouth and land on Ella.

Celeste and Dot are listening to the exchange with horrified faces.

"Look, I'm sorry but I'm just here with my kids and –"

"You should be ashamed of yourself! With you meant to be a role model for the people of Ireland!" she says scornfully.

"Mummy, what is that lady saying?" Dot says.

"It's okay, love. Come on, girls, put on your coats."

"But what about my cake?" Celeste says in protest.

"Come on, Celeste, we have to go."

"That's not fair! You said we were getting cake!"

"I said *come on*!" Her voice is raised.

The woman's eyes are burning into her.

She gets the buggy and steers the children out through the door. Once outside she pushes the buggy over towards the low harbour wall and stares at the oil forming abstract patterns on the water. Pinks, blues and greens trail lazily across the surface.

That afternoon Ella is lying down in her bedroom and the sound of American canned laughter filters down to her from where Celeste and Dot are watching TV upstairs. An overtired Maisie is in the nursery having a nap. Ella has been crying for two hours now and she just can't seem to stop the tears. They just keep streaming down her face and her skin is raw and sore. She can't keep this going any more. It's as if she doesn't know herself any more. She is a mess. A failure and a mess. Soon she can hear Maisie's cry start up on the monitor. She pulls herself up and goes into the nursery.

"Shush, little one, it's okay, it's all going to be okay," she repeats as she lifts her up.

Maisie's small body clings against her mother's as she gasps breathy tears. Ella tries rubbing her back in case she has wind but Maisie arches against her so she walks around the room with her. But the baby grows hysterical. Her body is rigid and her face is puce from exerting herself with tears.

"I'm sorry, baby, I'm so sorry that I never know what to do with you," Ella whispers into her milky neck. She can't do this, she is just no good at it. Tears start to stream down her face again and fall in wet droplets on her daughter's silky hair. She feels helpless and doesn't know what to do to calm the baby down. She never knows the right thing to do.

She puts the baby in her cot and, trembling, goes back into her bedroom. She can hear Maisie screaming through the walls and whatever primitive force or small amount of maternal instinct that she has pulls her to go back to her, but she doesn't trust herself to pick her up. She is paralysed from helping her own daughter.

She decides to ring Dan. She needs him to help her. She is ready to tell him everything – how hard she has been finding it lately, how she can't cope and she doesn't understand why. How she finds herself crying all day long, every day, and the tears never seem to find an end. She's ready to tell him about all of it. She dials his number and her heart is racing, *thump, thump, thump*. While it rings she practises what she's going to say to him. She is going to tell him exactly how she is feeling, once and for all.

"Ella?"

She can't get the words out. They are a fragmented mess inside her head and she doesn't know how to put them together.

"Ella, are you there?" he says impatiently.

"I . . . I can't do it – I'm sorry – I need you to help me."

"Sorry, Ella, but is this urgent? I'm up the walls here." He starts to have a conversation with somebody in the background – she hears him say, "Get him back in again – we need to redo that layer."

I can't cope. I want you to help me. But she doesn't say any of these things and instead says, "It's nothing . . . I'll see you later."

She hangs up and lies down. She can feel yet more tears fall down her face. She needs help.

Chapter 20

Two weeks have gone by and Rachel and Marcus haven't contacted each other. She finds the evenings are the worst. She was meant to go to the gym tonight but she couldn't face it. She can't seem to face anything at the moment. When she was with Marcus, they might get a takeaway or go to the cinema together but since they broke up she finds the time so long. She knows she could give Shirley a call but, since she has had Tiernan, understandably she doesn't have the same freedom to go places any more and Rachel doesn't want to burden her. She has lots of friends at home in Antrim but it's only now she realises that in Dublin she just has Marcus and Shirley and now they are both out of action.

She is frighteningly lonely. She has resisted the urge to ring him several times a day and, in the evenings, when she is at her most vulnerable, she has purposely put her phone in another room to stop herself from picking it up and texting him. It has been so hard to make that break.

It is her birthday tomorrow and there is something about her birthday that always makes her feel a little bit sad, a little bit vulnerable. Even when she and Marcus were very happy together, she never really liked her birthday. She is not sure if it's a getting-older thing or not but it always makes her take stock of her life to date. It's a day where she has always found herself turn the magnifying glass of self-inspection inwards, where the flaws and things that she isn't happy about in her life look bigger.

On her last birthday Marcus had woken her up with breakfast in bed and on the side of the tray was an envelope. When she opened it up, she realised that it was the first clue of a treasure hunt that he had planned out for her.

"Lions and tigers and bears oh my,
We'll be watching the animals you and I,
Like a wide-eyed child with an eager grin,
Hop in the car and I'll take you for a spin."

She had guessed it was the zoo and after she'd finished the breakfast, they had gone there. Then the next clue had led to the Guinness storehouse.

"Where the drink is dark and vats are deep,
I hope the smell of hops won't send you to sleep,
As we zoom to the top, to take in the view,
We'll clink our glasses to me and you."

Finally, just as dusk was descending on the city, they'd ended up in a lovely gastro pub on the waterfront in Howth, sitting by the fire cuddled up in a snug, eating seafood. It had been the perfect day.

It is so hard to accept that all of the good times that they'd had together are over, and not because they don't love each other – in fact, she knows there are few couples who could be more in love than they are – but it's a case of 'right person, wrong time'.

It is always when she is feeling a little low that memories creep up on her and remind her of the fun that they used to have. They'd had a lot of good times together and that's what makes the break-up so hard to accept.

There are flowers waiting for her on her desk when she gets in to the office the next morning.

"Who are these from?" she asks her colleagues but they just tell her that a courier delivered them shortly before she got in. She takes out the card from its envelope. It reads: *'Happy birthday, my love, missing you every day.'*

She finds herself looking up at the ceiling because that is the only way she can fight back the tears. She takes a few breaths to compose herself before sitting down at her desk and turning on her computer and going about her work.

She goes to an appointment with a juvenile liaison officer and then she has a court hearing to attend in the afternoon.

On her way home that evening she knows that she definitely needs wine. She knows she is drinking too much but today it's her birthday, so she pulls into the filling station a few minutes from her house. She goes into the shop and buys a bottle of Pinot Grigio and a vegetarian lasagne ready meal.

She arrives home and puts her handbag down on the breakfast bar. She opens the wine, pours herself a generous glass and drinks it fast. She doesn't bother with the ready meal and after a while the wine makes her feel pleasantly light-headed and the hunger has gone. Exactly how she wants to feel.

A while later the intercom goes and she hears Shirley's voice sing "Happy Birthday" down the line to her.

"Thanks," Rachel mumbles, buzzing her in.

"I'm taking you out for some birthday drinks tonight!" Shirley announces as soon as Rachel opens the door to her. She is wearing a patterned wrap dress and court shoes and Rachel notices that she has got her hair done.

"Do you mind if we don't, Shirl – I'm not really feeling up to celebrating."

"Nonsense!" Shirley says with a wave of her hand, in her uniquely bossy way. "You need to stop this and pull yourself together – moping around here in this apartment won't do you any good!"

"It's a duplex," Rachel says defensively. Shirley is forever calling it an apartment and it grates on her nerves. Just because Shirley and Hugh had enough money squirreled away to buy their four-bedroomed house years before the crash.

"Okay, 'duplex' then – stop being so pedantic." Shirley softens. "Come on, Rach, there was a reason why you two broke up."

"I know but it's just really, really sad and my birthday always makes me feel a bit teary." She can't stop thinking of the song, "It's My Party and I'll Cry If I Want To" by Lesley Gore. It's been worming its way through her head all day long.

"Now go on into your room and get changed – we're going out."

When Rachel reappears Shirley tells her that her shoes are too high and she will break her neck in them so she makes her wear a pair of her work shoes which are lower and more sensible and that makes her feel even more pathetic. They go to a dimly lit wine bar on Suffolk Street but Shirley isn't drinking because she will be feeding Tiernan during the night – "But you go on – don't let me stop you," she says.

So Rachel orders a sixty-eight-euro bottle of Barolo, not because she knows a lot about wine but because it is one of the most expensive ones on the list and she feels like she deserves it.

"Jesus, don't hold back!" Shirley says.

"I'm not."

"So how are you doing?"

"I'm just really sad, y'know?"

"Oh, of course you are, darling. It's going to take time."

Rachel takes a tissue from her bag and dabs at her eyes. The kindness from Shirley has brought the tears close to the surface. "God, I can't believe I am going to cry here."

"You're such an embarrassment." Shirley is smiling at her. She sniffles. "He sent me flowers today."

Shirley nods. "Thoughtful. So that's it – he's not going to change his mind?"

"Nope," Rachel says in a whisper. "That's it. I suppose a small part of me had secretly hoped that the break-up would be enough to make him change his mind but deep down I know that that is never going to happen."

After half an hour Shirley declares that she has to go 'pump' because Hugh has sent her a photo of Tiernan dressed for bed and it made her milk come in when she looked at it.

"But where's your pump?"

"I have a manual one in here." She pats the side of her leather tote, giving Rachel a wink.

Rachel studies her bag wondering where this 'pump' is. She is half expecting to see something resembling a bicycle pump sticking out over the top or something. She pours herself a second glass while Shirley is gone and drinks it down.

She notices a man and woman arguing two tables up from her. The man slams down money for the bill on the table before leaving the mortified woman on her own. It makes her sad. She tries to flash a sympathetic look at the woman but she won't make eye contact and instead gets up straight away and follows after him.

"Such a waste," Shirley tuts as she sits back down at the table again.

"What is?"

"The milk – I spend all that time eating well and drinking enough water to give Ballygowan supply issues, to make enough milk for Tiernan, and then I stand pumping it in a dingy toilet and pouring it down the sink."

"The glamour of motherhood, eh?" Rachel wonders if she will ever get the chance to experience it. She had always taken it for granted that children would be in her future but now, after everything that has happened with Marcus, she isn't so sure. What if she never meets anybody else? Or what if she does and she discovers that she can't have children? And then at the age of thirty-three there is the well-worn cliché of her biological clock ticking loudly to contend with. Time isn't on her side.

Rachel has just finished the bottle and is feeling nicely drunk. She is about to order another when Shirley says that she had better go home in time to do Tiernan's 'dream feed' at eleven o'clock.

"I'm sorry – you don't mind, do you?"

"No, no, of course not – I've had enough anyway."

"I'd say you'll feel it tomorrow."

Shirley drops her off outside her flat. She walks across the car park and climbs the stairs to her duplex. She watches the headlights of Shirley's car in the darkness as she turns around to head back to her little family.

Chapter 21

Conor is standing outside on the path, checking that his new window display looks all right, when he sees Jack coming along on a bike, using the tips of his toes to slow himself down. He has to use all his strength to stop the bike and for a second it looks as though he won't be able to. Finally its front wheel stops dead, right between Conor's legs.

"Sorry, me brakes aren't working, mister."

"I can see that . . . hi, Jack. Nice bike. And please stop calling me 'mister'!"

Jack leans the bike up against the shop front and they go inside.

"Where are you coming from?"

"I was in the chemist with me da – he's getting his Fairy Liquid – I was bored so I said I'd come and visit you."

"Well, thanks, I guess. But why's he buying Fairy Liquid in a chemist's?"

"It's green stuff that Mr O'Shea gives Da to drink every day. He gets really thirsty if he doesn't have it."

Conor hasn't a clue what he is talking about. "Won't your dad be looking for you?"

He shrugs his shoulders.

"Maybe not then," Conor says. "I was just about to get a

sandwich – do you want one?"

"I'm starving."

Conor butters bread and assembles a ham-and-cheese sandwich for himself and one for Jack. He watches as the boy devours it.

"Do you want another one?"

He nods. "Yes, please."

Conor sets about making another sandwich.

"Can I have a drink too? I'm really thirsty. I asked Da if I could have some of his green stuff because I was really thirsty too but then Mr O'Shea in the chemist's went mad, saying I could never, ever drink it. Ever. So I asked him 'Not even if there was no water left in the whole wide world?' which I think would be kinda hard because there's all the rivers and lakes and the oceans. Even the Liffey has a lot of water and that's not the world's longest river, Teacher says it's the Nile, but I wouldn't drink the water in the Liffey because it looks all brown and slimy and gross. But Teacher was telling us about the Ice Age yesterday so that could happen again and all the water would turn to ice and I'd have to ice-skate to school. But Mr O'Shea looked really mad then so I didn't say anything else." He takes a deep breath. "So can I have a glass of water?"

"Sure." Conor fills him a glass from the tap. "Where's your mam today?"

"In bed."

"Again?"

Jack takes another bite of his sandwich and nods. "She sleeps a lot."

"Yeah, I can see that . . ." Conor says. "Doesn't your mother worry about where you are?"

Jack shrugs his shoulders. "She thinks I'm out playing with me friends."

"Well, why aren't you?"

"Because they're always doing silly things like playing

knick-knacks on Mrs Morton. I don't think it's nice and then she comes out and says 'Do you lot think I came down in the last shower or wha'? I know it was yous!' and then I go all red. Anyway I like reading *Tom's Midnight Garden* and your sandwiches are all right too. I wonder if Mrs Morton was around at the same time as Hattie?"

"You mean in the Victorian era? Oh, I don't think she's that old, Jack."

"Are you sure? Because she is so old, like really, really old. She smells old and she wears shorts for her knickerses – I know because I've seen them over the wall hanging on her washing line – ma says they're called 'bloomers' and everyone wore them in the olden days."

Conor has to bite his tongue to stop laughing. They go back out to the front.

A man comes in and buys the latest Jeffrey Deaver.

"He only bought one book," Jack says.

"I know. I sold it to him."

"But there's hundreds of books in here!"

"Thousands actually."

"What happens if no one buys all your books?"

"I pack up my belongings and see if there are any park benches going spare."

"Huh?" says Jack through a mouthful of sandwich.

"Oh, never mind."

"Teacher says that reading books is like exercise for your brain."

"Well, she's right."

"So can I read a bit more of the book about the boy in the garden because I want to have the muscliest brain in the whole class?"

"Go on then." He sighs but he doesn't mind. "I would hate to stand in the way of you gaining a muscly brain."

Jack sits down in his usual position on the floor, with his back resting against the shelves and his knees drawn up in front of him. Conor busies himself with his usual jobs. He finds himself staring across the shop at Jack, at his youthful face engrossed in the book.

"Hey, what the fuck are you doing in here?"

Conor looks up to find a thin, wiry man standing in the doorway. His hair is dark and his face peppered with stubborn black stubble. He is looking at Jack, demanding an answer.

"I'm only reading a book, Da," Jack says.

"Well, you can't just run off without telling me where you're going!"

"I was bored!" Jack shrugs.

"I'm after being up and down the street looking for you."

"Sorry – he just came in a few minutes ago," Conor says, but the man just glares at him.

"How did you know I was here?" Jack asks.

"I saw your bleedin' bike outside the window, didn't I? C'mon, put the book away – your ma's going to kill me if you're late home!"

"Right, I'm coming, da," Jack says, getting up. "See you, mister – thanks for letting me read the book again."

"No worries, Jack, see you soon."

Jack's dad stands on the floor for a minute and stares at Conor through narrowed eyes.

Conor finds himself looking away and searching out the floor.

Then the man steers Jack out the door.

Chapter 22

Ella gets the girls up and ready and the school-run battle starts again. Soon she is parked outside the school alongside the other four-wheel drives, each one bigger and roomier than the last. As they near the school, she can see the other mothers are already getting back into their cars, having been on time for the school run. They are all standing there laughing. A thought flits through her mind that they are laughing at her but then she thinks she is probably being paranoid. She pulls up into the car park, turns off her engine and hops down to let the girls out.

"Want a hand?" She reaches up to help Dot down and then holds a hand out to Celeste.

"I don't need your help," the older girl says as she pushes her away.

She unstraps Maisie and puts her on her hip. She inhales a scent that is a mixture of sea salt from the wind coming off the bay and the skin on Maisie's neck.

It is then that she notices that Dot is wearing her ballet slippers instead of her winter boots.

"Where are your boots?" She can hear the despair in her own voice.

"I didn't want to wear them today. I like my ballet shoes better, Mummy."

The thin-soled salmon-pink slippers look wildly wrong with the navy-and-green tartan uniform. And it's so cold out.

But she can't face this battle so she doesn't. "Right, come on, we'd better hurry on!" She leads the girls towards the school gate. She kisses them goodbye and makes her way back to the jeep. She straps Maisie back in and the baby starts to cry once more. Wearily she turns on the engine and starts to drive but even the heavy noise of her diesel SUV can't drown Maisie out. She is getting louder and when Ella looks behind her in the rear-view mirror, she sees her small red face is angry and wet from tears. She turns up the radio. If she concentrates really hard on what the presenter is saying, she can almost block out the crying.

She feels so alone. She realises that except for a phone call from the alarm company and the lady on the check-out in Tesco yesterday, she hasn't had a conversation with an adult person for two days now. No one seems to understand what it's like. She can't tell anyone about this feeling because she knows herself she sounds crazy and irrational.

The words of the nurse who did Maisie's vaccinations ring in her head. Maybe she is right. She decides she will give it a go. At least there will be people that she can talk to. It cannot be any worse than how she is feeling right now. She takes a right turn and finds herself driving into the church car park.

She takes a deep breath, swallows hard and pulls open the heavy oak door of the parish hall. She can feel all eyes on her and she blows upwards to take her fringe out of her eyes.

"I'm here for the mother and baby group," she says to the women gathered inside the door.

"Oh, hi!" they all say.

As she unwraps her scarf from around her neck, she counts eleven women and seventeen babies. She can't ever remember feeling this nervous before. Even presenting on live TV wasn't as nerve-racking at this. She can see some of them trying to work out where they recognise her from.

"Are you Ella Wilde?" one of them finally says. Her eyes are narrowed, her brow creased downwards. It is followed by a look of distaste.

"Yes," she nods. "I am."

This is met with silence.

Ella walks away from her and sits down on the edge of a blanket spread out on the floor, like the other mothers are doing.

"Okay, well, why don't I start the music?" one woman in a paisley-patterned dress says. She gets up and presses play on a portable CD player and the hall fills with plingy xylophone music knocking out 'The Wheels on the Bus'.

They all chorus *"The wheels on the bus go round and round, round and round, round and round . . ."*

The other mothers start doing the actions. They are tooting pretend horns and pulling down on imaginary bells using ropes made of air. Now they are flicking their fingers, doing flashing lights. She can't do it. She feels ridiculously self-conscious. They are all watching her, expecting her to join in with them.

"The children on the bus go u-up and down, u-up and down, u-up and down . . ."

They are starting to stand up so she makes a half-hearted attempt to stand up too, but by the time she is up, they all sit back down again. She can't remember ever hearing this many verses. On and on they go. The older babies are dancing and Maisie sits on her knee, batting her little hands. Then the track changes to *'Mary Had a Little Lamb'* and thankfully there don't seem to be any actions for this one but they're all singing along.

Finally the CD comes to an end and the mothers get up and walk over to a table where there is a kettle and some mugs and a packet of Chocolate Digestives. The toddlers are dashing around the room while the smaller babies play with the toys surrounding them on the blanket. She props Maisie up against some cushions and follows the others over to the table. The women seemed to have grouped into a circle with their backs to her. She looks at them from the outside. They are all dressed how a mother should dress, she thinks. Like if you opened a catalogue from Marks and Spencer's, these women would be in it. Wrap dresses with thick tights and smart cardigans. Tunic tops are layered over jeans and ankle boots. Ella looks down at her Converse, faded jeans and sweatshirt and feels like a scruffy teenager beside them. She grabbed the first things she found in her wardrobe that morning. She doesn't have the energy to make an effort with her appearance these days.

"So do you live nearby?" one of the mothers who was late in and has also been left outside the impenetrable circle, asks.

She has a friendly smiling face and sometimes Ella wishes that she had a face like this. Open and innocent. She obviously doesn't recognise her.

"Yeah, up on Land's End Rock."

"Oh lovely – you're really living on the edge there!" she jokes and Ella obliges her with a smile. "We're in The Cedars. Is she your first?" She points to Maisie who is chewing down on a rattle in her mouth.

"She's my third actually. My other two are ages five and eight."

"Oh wow."

"What about you – is he your first?"

"Yes, he is – we were trying for a very long time to have a baby but he was worth the wait." She smiles over in her son's direction where he is trying to crawl, pushing backwards on his tummy until he ends up at the wall.

"He's gorgeous," Ella says because she isn't sure what else to say.

"Thanks. Sorry, I didn't get your name?"

"Ella," she says. "Ella Devlin." Devlin is her married name.

"I'm Ger, Ger Rowan." She reaches out to shake Ella's hand but is met by a biscuit.

Ella shifts her biscuit into the same hand as the mug and shakes her hand back. "Nice to meet you, Ger."

"Are you going back to work soon?" Ger asks.

"Eh no . . . not for the next while anyway."

"I suppose it's hard with three of them – I'm not going back either – well, I'm hoping to freelance a bit from home, so fingers crossed it all works out."

"Good for you."

"It's hard, isn't it?"

"It is – you'd think on my third I'd be an expert." She laughs nervously.

"No, I mean coming to these things." Ger nods her head at the women behind them.

"Oh yeah." She feels stupid. Then she whispers, "They're hardly rolling out the red carpet of motherhood solidarity, are they?"

Ger laughs. "I feel like I'm back in the school playground again. Remember, when you had to ask people to play with you? Well, that's what it's like here!"

Ella laughs too. Someone is tapping on her shoulder. It's the woman in the paisley dress again, "Isn't that your baby?" she says in an accusing tone.

Ella's eyes follow the woman's pointing finger and she sees that Maisie has fallen over from the position where Ella had propped her up with cushions on the floor. She is crying.

She rushes over and picks her up.

Soon after, the mums start to disband and go to wash their cups and pack up their babies under layers of coats, hats and blankets.

"Home time," Ger smiles. "Will I see you next week?" She struggles to bend her son's arm inside the sleeve of his jacket.

"Yeah, sure."

And she feels awful for lying to her because she has been so

114

nice to her but there is no way she will be coming back here. Later that evening she and Dan are sitting in the living room. He has the remote and is flicking idly through the TV stations. The children are finally in bed. Her shoulders are knotted with tension and she tries to massage them by reaching her hand over her shoulder. He finally settles on a rugby match.

"Please don't ignore me, Dan. This is horrible. I'm finding the tension between us unbearable."

"Well, in all fairness, none of the rest of us are exactly having a laugh about it!"

"I just want to talk to you."

"We are talking!"

"I'm just finding it so hard."

"What do you expect, Ella? And what about everyone else? It's not just you that is suffering the fall-out here – the shockwaves go much wider than that. You've dragged our whole family into this mess. I know the guys in work are talking about it too but no one has the balls to dare say it to my face. Celeste told me that Gilly's mum told her that she was not allowed to play with her any more? Do you realise now what you've done?"

"I know, she told me that too," she whispers.

She wonders if she should tell him. Maybe now is the time to have it out in the open, once and for all after all these years. She can stop carrying the weight of it around with her.

His eyes are on her and she takes a deep breath in and counts *one . . . two . . .* if she tells him, she can finally share the load with someone . . . *three . . .*

She knows that if she tells him about it, things will never be the same between them again. She takes a deep breath and gets ready to say the words that she hasn't been able to say before. "I –"

"*Yessssssssssss!* Go on lads, that's the play!" he roars. The team have scored a try and he jumps off the seat, pulling a clenched fist down through the air.

Chapter 23

"Guess what?" Jack has come running in through the door.

"What?"

"You have to guess!"

"You got no homework today?"

"No!"

"Okay, you found fifty euro on the street."

"No."

"I could actually be here all day, Jack – do you want to give me a clue?"

"Da was waiting for me in the kitchen with Ma after school yesterday. I thought I was going to be in trouble because Da told Ma that I was here instead of outside playing with me friends."

"And?"

"He had tickets to the Ireland versus Portugal match last night for my birthday!"

"No way! Cool!" Conor is genuinely impressed. He had heard people on the radio trying to source tickets but they were rarer than hen's teeth apparently.

"Ma wasn't happy and got really cross with Da and said he needs to ask her first and I thought she was going to say no but then me Auntie Libby called over – she's ma's sister and she told Ma to let me go because it was my birthday. So she said 'Go on, but make sure you get changed outta that uniform first!'"

"Well, did you enjoy it?"

"It was brilliant. I know I'm not meant to say it because Ireland lost but I love Ronaldo even more now. He slided across the pitch and tipped the ball into the back of the net and then he ran around like this." He pulls his T-shirt up over his head and starts running around the shop and crashes into a stand of Mills & Boon paperbacks. "Oh sorry, Conor," he says, beginning to pick up the fallen books. "Then afterwards Da said he knew where the team were getting on their bus so we went and waited at the gate and waited and waited and it was starting to get dark and I said I wanted to go because I don't really like the dark and Da said we should hang on for another five minutes and I said I just wanted to go home but then the bus came! The driver didn't want to stop but Da stood in the middle of the road and waved at him so he had to stop or else he was going to run him over. I thought he might run him over actually because he looked a bit mad. Then he put down his window and talked to Da for a minute and I don't know what he said but they let me on the bus and I got all their autographs. Look at this . . ." He takes out a carefully folded sheet of A4 paper from the back pocket of his jeans with names jotted hastily in slants across it.

"Wow, that's amazing! You'll have to get that framed. Fair play to your dad and all the players. It might be worth a lot of money in years to come."

Jack beams proudly. "That's what Ma said. She said I have to mind it and if she finds it squished up into a ball in my pocket after coming out of the wash, she'll go through me for a shortcut – but there's no way I'll let that happen – it's my most precious thing ever. Then on the way home to celebrate we went for a McDonald's. I love the chips there and the burgers too but I always throw away the gherkin." He scrunches up his face in disgust.

"Well, it sounds like you had a great time, huh?"

"I did. Da is all right sometimes."

"How's your ma?"

"She's sleeping more than ever and she's even still sleepy when she wakes up. Libby made my dinner last night. She made fish – not like fish fingers, it was a proper fish from the sea. The whole house was stinking – you should have smelt it! I wouldn't eat it so she laughed and said I was the exact same as Ma when she was little girl because she hated fish too."

"I see. And you're okay? You would tell me if you were upset or worried, wouldn't you?"

"Yeah, I'm fine – sure haven't I all the autographs of the whole Irish team? You should've seen all the boys in school – they all wanted to see it but I wouldn't let anyone touch it in case they damaged it. They said Da was the coolest da and then Teacher taught us the song 'Olé, Olé, Olé, Olé'."

Chapter 24

"I love that song!" Ella and Conor are seated in a coffee shop on George's Street after finishing a quick Sunday brunch before he has to open up the shop, Maisie asleep in her car-seat.

He listens for a minute to hear it over the din in the coffee shop. "Remember when she played in the Student's Union and you couldn't get a ticket so I ended up letting you in through the fire escape but then we both got thrown out?"

"Yep. Sorry about that." She places her mug of coffee down on the table. "That was the night of 'the kiss' actually."

"Was it? God, you've a good memory!"

She nods. "We went back to mine after and we shared a bottle of vodka with no mixer while we waited for everyone else to come home and it just happened."

"Eh, I think you'll find that you insisted that we kiss to see if our relationship was really as platonic as we both thought."

She laughs "Well, the girls said I had to test it – and guess what, it was."

"I was a little bit offended actually –"

"Why?"

"Because you didn't fall madly in love with me and my dashing tortoiseshell glasses afterwards."

"Me too," she sighs, "but it was like kissing my brother –

it was just all wrong. And the glasses were terrible. They made you look like Roy Orbison."

"That wasn't the look I was going for."

"At least we established there and then that we're better off as friends and there was definitely no chemistry between us."

"You had just started seeing that guy, the rugby jock – what was his name again?"

"Henno?"

"That's it – I'll never forget it when he introduced himself to me with a handshake that would break rocks. He hated me."

"He did actually but he was a loser."

The waitress comes over and clears off their plates.

"So how's the shop going? Any more trouble from those youngsters?" she asks.

"Oh, they're still there hanging around."

"Well, I hope they haven't broken any more windows since!"

"No, thank God. Look, thanks again for that loan . . . " He is blushing. "I'll get you back as soon as I can – I had the landlord on so I had to pay up the rent."

"Honestly, Conor, there's no rush – whenever you can afford it."

"What happens if I can never afford it?"

"What do you mean?"

"Well, I'm worried about the business – I don't know from month to month if I'm going to be able to keep my head above water and I hate it."

"You'll get there. Every business is finding it tough right now. It's the recession, everyone's in the same boat."

"Anyway, enough about that – I don't want to get depressed. How've you been? Are things getting any better for you?"

"I'm doing okay, I'm just trying to get on with things as best I can. Celeste is being a nightmare – she hates me."

"She's only eight."

"That's what worries me! If she's like this now, what will she be like when she's a teenager?"

"Well, why do you think she's like that?"

"I have a lot of options to choose from – option A: I think she's giving me a guilt trip because I wasn't really there for the first eight years of her life. Andrea reckons it's option B: that she misses Mrs Frawley. Or maybe it's option C: because some of the girls in her class have been warned to stay away from her because of me."

"How do you know that?"

"She told me – the other mothers have warned their daughters not to play with her."

"They can't do that – they're only children. Poor Celeste. That's not on – that's a form of bullying."

"I know, you're right." She sighs. "When is it going to end, Conor?"

"What?"

"The dirty looks from people who don't even know me, everywhere I go?"

"Really?"

She nods. "The mothers at the school gate and at the mother and baby group. I was in a coffee shop with the girls the other day when a woman came over and said I was a horrible person and that I deserved everything I got."

"She did not!" He is shocked.

Ella nods.

"Did the girls hear her?"

"Yes – they were right there. They didn't know what was going on. Whatever about attacking me, when it comes to my children it's a different matter."

"I didn't know it was that bad, Ella."

She sighs. "Look, I just have to get over it. I got myself into this mess, eh? I'm sorry for being so self-absorbed when I know things are hard for you as well – what I'm going through doesn't hold a candle to what you've been through."

"Have you tried looking for other work?"

She shakes her head. "I rang Malcolm at the station to see if there was any chance of going back but no one wants to know me in there any more." She sighs heavily. "So I'm trying to look on the positives – it's a chance to make up for the time I've missed with the girls, y'know?"

"Well, that's good, isn't it?"

"It is, but it's hard, Conor – I'm finding the adjustment very hard." She feels her voice waver and she tells herself not to cry.

"You'll be okay. I know you, Ella, you're tough. Who was it that said 'If you aren't in over your head, then how do you know how tall you are?'"

"TS Eliot."

"You should have been on the quiz team. I still don't know why you weren't picked."

"Because they brought Hilda Morrison in at the last minute – I was shafted, remember? God, I seem to have a history of this sort of stuff."

"Yeah, I remember. I still don't understand it though – you beat her in the try-outs."

She looks down at the floor and focuses on a crack in the honey-wood floorboards where a two-cent coin is wedged on its side. "It was years ago, Conor."

"And Eric Keogh was mad about you too. Surely having the Team Captain on side was a sure way of getting on?"

Stop it, stop it right now.

"Maybe he was pissed off because you wouldn't shag him?" he continues.

"Stop it, Conor – that's enough!" Her tone is uncharacteristically sharp.

"Hey, sorry, I'm only joking!" He puts his two hands up in the air. He is taken aback by her extreme reaction. "Ella, I'm sorry –"

"Yeah, it's fine."

"I didn't mean to upset you –"

"I said it's fine. I need to head on home anyway. We're meeting Dad for dinner later."

"Ella, please –"

But the cloud has descended down around her and the chink into the Ella that he knows has closed shut again.

"Can you just leave it? It's fine, honestly."

"Right . . . well, I'd better head on anyway – it's almost time to open up."

Chapter 25

When Conor wakes the next morning, the first thing that hits him when he opens his eyes is Ella's anger with him the day before. He gets out of bed, picks up the phone and dials her number but it rings out. It goes straight to voicemail. He hears her singsongy voice:

"Hi, it's Ella – please leave a message."

It's been so long since her voice has sounded like this. Upbeat and fun.

"Ella . . . it's me . . . look, I'm sorry about yesterday . . . I didn't mean to upset you . . . maybe give me a call when you get this, yeah?"

He hangs up and runs his hands down over his face. The last thing he wants to do is fight with her, the only person he really has left in his life.

Later on, he is working on his display when he sees Jack outside the glass. The boy comes into the store and steps up onto the window display platform with him.

"This is cool!"

A woman with yellow-blonde hair and a pinched face walks by and stares at them both. Jack waves eagerly at her and she half-heartedly waves back, her arm not quite reaching its full potential.

"Feels like we're in a zoo, doesn't it?" Conor says.

Jack starts pretending to be a monkey. He dances up and down the platform with his arms curled under. Then stands dead still, obviously pretending to be a mannequin.

"You were in school today?" Conor asks, gesturing to the grey school uniform he is wearing.

"Yeah, but Ma forgot to pick me up so I came here. She usually waits for me at the gate and we walk home then."

"What? You mean your mother left you waiting outside the school?"

Jack's face grows serious. "She might have been asleep or something though."

"Maybe you should go home to your own house in case she's looking for you now? Maybe something happened to make her late?"

"I waited for *aaaaaaggggggges*. Everyone was gone home, even the teachers. Mrs Flood – she's the one with the massive nose and Seán Higgins calls her Concorde because her nose is so pointy – well, she's the principal and she told me to go on home, that my ma was probably just running late and I'd meet her along on the way –" he pauses to push his glasses up on the bridge of his nose, "but I didn't see her, so then I came in here because I want to know what happens next with Hattie and Tom."

"Well, I'm not so sure . . . maybe you should go home, Jack."

Jack's face is crestfallen; his brown eyes look impossibly sad. "Please, can I just read one more chapter?"

"Ah Jack, I don't want your dad getting on to me again."

"Don't worry – he's probably in the pub."

"How do you know?"

"Because that's what Ma always says – 'If you're looking for Da, you're guaranteed to find him in the pub'. Ma always says 'If work was in bed, Da would sleep on the floor'. I'm not sure what it means but she says it means that Da is lazy but one time when Mrs Morton bought too many things in the shop, Da helped her to carry them all home and her bags were really heavy so he's not that lazy. I think she really likes cakes a lot because she had three different cakes and a Swiss Roll too in her bag."

"Okay . . . well, maybe you can just read one chapter but then you have to go home, all right?"

Jack runs over and sits in his usual spot, his back sloped against the shelves.

"Do you want a chair?" Conor asks, wondering at the same time if he is mad offering to make the child more comfortable – he'll never get rid of him then.

"Nah, I like it like this."

"Okay."

"Do you want a Giant Jawbreaker?" He fishes a bag full of neon-orange sweets out of the pocket of his trousers.

"No, thanks, Jack, I'll pass. Careful your teeth don't fall out with those yokes."

Jack pokes his head up out of the book a while later. "What's this word?"

"Spell it out to me."

"Q-U-A-R-A-N-T-I-N-E?"

"Huh?" Conor loses track of the letters as Jack calls them out. "Let me see." He comes over and peers over Jack's shoulder to where his finger is underlining the word on the page. "Oh, that's *quarantine*."

"What does it mean?"

"It's when someone is sick and they have to stay away from other people so that they don't catch it."

"Oh." He grows silent for a minute. "Should Ma be in quarantine?"

"Why – is she sick?"

"Yeah, she was getting sick this morning before I went to school and then she said that she felt terrible and would I mind if she didn't walk me to school this morning."

"Oh, I see – well, it depends on what is wrong with her then.

126

Some illnesses are contagious but not too serious like when you have a cold so you wouldn't need to be quarantined then."

"I'm not sure what's wrong with Ma." He looks sad. "She's been sick lots of times this week."

"Well, I'm sure she'll be right as rain again soon, huh?"

"Yeah . . . I hope so. I don't like it at all when she's sick."

"You're a good kid, Jack, do you know that?"

"Why?"

"You just are."

Rachel is in the canteen getting a coffee and while it is being made she quickly scans the front page of the newspaper that is beside the till. Her eyes immediately pick out his name amongst the thousands of other words on the page. She reaches out, picks it up and holds it out straight between her two hands. The headline reads '**Marcus Traynor to Acquire Francine Label**'. Francine's is a French clothing group, which Marcus had been looking to buy for a long time.

"That'll be two eighty, love – did you want sugar with that?"

"What?" She looks up to where the woman is holding up two sachets of sugar, waiting for her to make her mind up. "Oh sorry . . . no, thanks."

She goes into the bathroom and locks herself into a cubicle, sits on the closed lid and cries it all out. She is happy for him but she wishes she could be with him to celebrate – this is a big deal for the company that he founded. It is his first foray into Europe. Little triggers like this send her backwards again. She stops when she hears someone come in to use the toilet beside her. She waits until they leave the cubicle, wash their hands, use the hand dryer, before the footsteps make their way back out again. She takes a bundle of cardboard-like 2-ply toilet paper and uses it to blow her nose and then comes out and looks at herself in the mirror. Her face is red and sticky from tears and her mascara is smudged underneath her eyes. She gets some more tissue from the holder and tries to fix her make-up as best she can. She tidies her hair and then, taking a deep breath, goes back to her desk.

The only good thing from today is that miraculously she thinks she might have a foster family for the five children. She is to meet them at five o'clock so she needs to get herself together before then.

It is after eight when she is driving down the back of her housing estate to where the developers decided to hide all the cheap box-design, flat-roofed duplexes. She picked up a takeaway on her way because there is nothing that reinforces her status of being alone in this world more than cooking for one. She gets out of the car and climbs up the steps to the duplex, passing an intimidating gang of hooded teenagers. She feels their eyes follow her as she walks. She quickens her steps until she reaches her door. Putting the key in the lock, she opens it, closes it behind her and shuts out the world.

She is exhausted. She takes down the bottle half full of wine from the press and twists and pulls the cork that she had squeezed back into the top of the bottle the night before. It releases with a *pop* and she lets the full-bodied Rioja fill up her glass. Even the sound of the wine filling her glass is soothing. Usually Wednesday is her no-wine day. Herself and Shirley used to have a joke where they figured that because they didn't drink on Wednesdays, they weren't alcoholics – Monday was okay because Monday was Monday, Tuesday you had to finish off Monday's bottle or it would go off. Then no wine on Wednesday. Thursday was okay because it was nearly the weekend and then Friday, Saturday and Sunday *were* the weekend. That was a long time ago now, long before Shirley moved in with Hugh and got settled, but Rachel feels that her life hasn't moved on from that stage.

She curls her legs up underneath her and eats her tofu dish straight from its plastic container because she can't be bothered to get a plate.

Chapter 26

As Ella waits inside her jeep, her stomach is somersaulting. She can see them all gathered around the gates. She feels sick. The dread gets worse every day. While the rest of them stand around talking, she now waits until the children start appearing at the schoolyard before she gets out.

The bell sounds and soon the yard is filled with children running towards their parents. She swallows hard, turns off the engine and climbs down. She goes around the back and takes Maisie out of her seat and carries her on her hip. They turn to look at her but turn away quickly again in case they make eye contact with her. She's not sure if it's in her imagination but the conversations seem to stop whenever she gets close to them. They all have their backs to her. Maisie starts to stretch in her arms and get angsty.

Finally she sees Dot, with the two bobbles on her red knitted hat bobbing up and down as she runs.

"Mummy!" She wraps her two arms around her mother's legs and Ella bends as much as she can with Maisie in her arms to put her free arm around her. She sees some of Celeste's classmates showing their artwork to their parents. The yard starts to empty as children make their way back to their cars with their parents. She looks up again to see if

Celeste is coming but there is no sign of her. Eventually she sees her coming through the door – she is the last to leave the building and takes her time crossing the now almost empty schoolyard. Ella knows instantly that something is wrong.

"Hi, love," she says when Celeste reaches the gate.

Silence.

"What is it? What's wrong with you?" she asks.

They walk back to the jeep where Dot chats happily about what princess clothes she should change into when she gets home. "Should I wear my blue sparkly necklace or the ladybird one?"

"I think the blue one would be nice with your purple ball gown."

"Yes, you're right, Mummy. Good choice."

Celeste stares out through the window. They climb the hill running along the cliff, the sunlight flashing white on the surface of the water. They go through their gates and pull up outside the tower. They all go inside and climb the stairs to the kitchen. Celeste still hasn't spoken to her.

"Do you want something to eat?" Ella asks the girls.

"Can I have a toasted brie sandwich?" Dot asks.

"Sure." She laughs. "I should have guessed that's what you'd ask for. What do you want, Celeste?"

No answer.

"Celeste, I asked you a question."

"It's all your fault!" she bursts out. "Everyone hates me."

"Did something happen in school today – is that what this is all about?"

"Everyone was invited to Gilly's birthday party – everyone except me, Mum." Her voice breaks and she starts to cry.

"Oh, love, I'm sorry." She tries to put her arms around her daughter to calm her down. "Don't worry, I'm . . . I'm . . . sure it was just a mistake."

"No, it wasn't, it's because of you! She doesn't want me at her party because you're my mother. It's all your fault!"

"Please, Celeste, I'll talk to your teacher – we'll sort it out – don't worry." She tries to hug her. "I bet her mum just forgot to send in yours."

"Get off me!" She pulls away from her. "You're so embarrassing – all the other girls' mums wear nice, trendy clothes and you just wear old jeans and jumpers with tatty runners and your hair is always messy. You *never* look nice!" She is now screaming, her eyes are watery with tears and her face is red.

"Celeste, I –"

"I hate you, Mum! I want Mrs Frawley back!"

Ella stands and watches her daughter run down the stairs to her bedroom. She knows that Celeste is feeling angry and humiliated and she should probably go after her and draw her into a hug but she can't bring herself to do it so instead she sits down at the table.

"Mum?" It's Dot this time.

"Yeah?"

"Maybe Celeste is right – you do look a bit scruffy. Do you want me to give you a makeover? I can make you look just like a princess?"

"Sounds good, Dotty."

"Okay, hang on until I get my equipment – you'll be the prettiest mummy-princess in the whole wild world, just wait and see!"

It is after nine o'clock when Dan comes in that evening. The children are already in bed. Ella serves him up a plate of reheated chilli and lets her weight sink into a chair beside him while he eats.

His phone vibrates on the table. He picks it up and starts scrolling down through the message.

"Celeste and I had a huge argument today – well, she fought with me."

"What's happened now?" His eyes are still on his phone.

"Well, apparently it's Gilly's birthday party and the whole class have been invited except her."

He places his phone back down on the table and looks up at her. "But I thought they were best friends? This has gone too far – that's bullying. You're going to have to do something about it!"

"Like what?"

"Well, talk to her mother and tell her that it's not on and she should be ashamed of herself excluding an eight-year-old child like that!"

"But it'll just make it all worse if I have a go at her – she'll really get her back up then!"

"Well, you have to do something – it's your fault that this is happening."

"Do you think I enjoy seeing my daughter going through this? I'm just trying to get to the bottom of this problem, Dan."

"Well, I'm just saying that everything was fine with Celeste until you started going around robbing shops!"

"Well, thanks very much, Dan! Nice to see that our marriage is built on such a bedrock of support."

"I'm sorry, Ella. I'm just saying it the way it is."

"You mean the way Gilly's mother sees it?"

"What do you want me to say? You have to deal with it, Ella! Stop sitting around moping and thinking 'poor me'! You need to nip this in the bud before the kids are affected any more. You got yourself into this mess, you're going to have to get yourself out of it."

"Fuck you, Dan!"

She grabs her handbag and takes the staircase two steps at a time until she is down the three flights. It is at times like this that this places feels exactly what the original stonemasons who built it had intended it to be: a defensive tower. Even she can appreciate the irony whenever she reads the story of Rapunzel for Dot at bedtime. She reaches the archway of the front door, opens it and slams it shut behind her. She gets into her jeep and drives quickly until she is at the electric gates. She waits for them to part for what seems like an age. She jerkily pulls off again and drives down the hill in the darkness.

Everywhere is still; there is no moon out tonight, only the fuzzy sodium glow of the city across the bay. She pulls over, gets out and stands in the orangey darkness. Silent tears run down her face – she can taste their saltiness in her mouth. Car lights glide along on the road beneath her. In the distance she can see Dublin Port and the Ringsend chimney stacks. An airplane is coming in over the Irish Sea before angling on the diagonal in the direction of the airport. Cars whir past her on the road. *Zum, zum, zum,* they repeat.

There are so many options – there is the water below – or the cars on the road beside her. There is a train station nearby. So many options. She could end all of this now but she knows she'd never have the bottle to do it. Instead she gets back into her jeep and drives.

The red light of a mini-petrol-pump lights up on her dash. She drives for a while before she sees a petrol station in the distance. She indicates, pulls into the forecourt and fills up. Then she goes inside to pay. She walks up and down the aisles. She stops for a minute in front of the cleaning products and picks up a bottle of hand soap. She reads the back and then looks around. No one is watching her and in one quick, birdlike movement, she stuffs the bottle into her bag. Her heart is racing and she is waiting for someone to pounce but it doesn't happen. Then she goes towards the fridge and picks up a litre of milk because she remembers that they are running low. Going up to the counter to pay, she hands the milk to the Indian guy behind the counter for him to scan.

"Pump two as well, please."

He presses a button on his touch screen. "That'll be 94.39 please."

She takes her wallet from underneath the hand soap and takes out her card to pay. She looks up amongst the shelves stocked with car-windscreen washes and blister packs of paracetamol and sees a grainy black-and-white CCTV monitor, which is fixed on the spot where she just was.

"Anything else?" He is looking straight at her. His deep-brown eyes are looking directly into hers.

She starts to panic. Is this a trick? If she says no will they say they saw her put the hand soap in her bag? "No, thank you," she answers. Her heart is racing.

"We have to ask that," he whispers conspiratorially. "The manager makes us say it to all the customers to try and increase sales."

"Oh yeah, of course." She laughs but it is a bit too high. "Are you on all night?"

"Yes, I do seven to seven, so long night ahead."

"Oh no – well, I hope the time flies for you."

"Me too! Goodnight."

She stuffs her wallet back into her bag and, as she walks back towards her jeep, the adrenalin is like a drug coursing through her body, being pumped around by her racing heart.

"Where did you go to last night?" he says as she gets out of bed the next morning. His fingers move up along his shirt, buttoning as he talks.

She walks around him and goes into the bathroom. "Just leave it, Dan," she says through gritted teeth before slamming the door closed on him.

"You're just angry because you know I'm right, Ella!" he shouts back at her through the wood. "That's what this is all about – the truth hurts!"

She hears him slamming the front door and hears the *beep-beep* of his car door unlocking before he starts making his way down the driveway.

She sits on the side of the bathtub and cries. She keeps thinking about what she did in the petrol station last night and it makes her feel sick. She hates herself, hates what she is capable of. She hates the way she does it but what she hates even more is that she can't stop herself. She feels powerless against these urges. It is disgusting, she is disgusting. What if she had been caught? She's already in enough trouble without adding something like that into the mix. She gets into the shower and turns the water temperature up high so that her skin starts to pinken. She scrubs it with the loofah over and over again until it hurts. She wishes she could take off her own skin. Just peel it off like a snake and cast it aside.

She steps out of the shower and puts on her dressing gown.

Dot's small head peeps around the door. "Mummy, what's wrong? Why was Daddy shouting at you?" Her small face is creased with worry. "Why are you crying again?"

"I'm not – I'm okay, Dot, love." She wipes the tears away quickly with the back of her hand.

"You cry too much, Mum. Is it because my room is messy again because I promise I'll try really, really hard to keep it tidy so you won't cry any more."

"Oh, Dot, love, no – it's not that at all, I promise. It's nothing to do with you. I'm just feeling a bit sad today, that's all."

"But you're always sad, Mum. Is it because Celeste doesn't like you?"

"Of course she likes me, Dot!"

Dot shakes her head from side to side. "No, she doesn't, Mum – she's always telling me how much she hates you," she says solemnly. "But it's okay because I like you and I think Maisie does too but she can't talk yet so I'm not really sure about her."

Ella can't help but laugh at that. "Come here to me, you." She pulls her in close and breathes in the scent of her hair and the warm skin of her neck. "How could I be sad when I've got you in my life, Dot Devlin?"

"Let's go upstairs and get some breakfast."

She knows that she needs to get herself together. She feels she is sinking further and further beneath her layer of felt – it is almost enveloping her completely.

Chapter 27

Today is a bad day. He always knew that today would be difficult but, now that it's here, it's bloody awful. It is acute and hits him from every direction. Every time he sees the date on an email or invoice or on the top right-hand corner of the computer screen, it is a reminder of everything that has gone so horribly wrong in the last year.

He picks up the phone on the desk and dials her parents' number in Germany. Sometimes he needs to feel closer to her and this is the only way he knows. These are her ties.

It rings for a long time.

He imagines the phone ringing around the wooden house nestled deep in the shadows of the Black Forest. He pictures her hurrying over the wooden floorboards with its colourful scatter rugs to answer it.

"Hallo?" She sounds breathless.

"Hallo, Bettina – it's Conor."

"*Ach, hallo, Conor. Wie gehts? Alles gut?*"

They have this half English/German exchange whenever he rings.

"*Ja, ja, und du?*"

"*Oh ja, alles gut hier.*"

"And *Rolf ist* good *auch?*"

"Ja, War ein bisschen krank letzte Woche, aber jetzt gehts ihm besser."

"Ah, gut. Wie ist das Wetter?"

"Wir haben viel Schnee seit letzter Woche."

"Es ist sehr kalt hier aber keine Schnee."

It is their usual polite exchange about the difference in the weather between where he is in Ireland and she is in Germany. He wonders if she knows the significance of the date.

"Wie gehts mit der Buchhandlung?"

"Okay, aber ein bisschen ruhig." She always asks him about the shop and he always says the same thing, that it's a bit quiet. For once it would be nice to tell her that he is busy.

"Diese Dinge brauchen Zeit. Hab Geduld."

That is exactly what Leni would have said, that he needs to give it time and to have patience. *"Ja – du bist richtig,"* he sighs because it is easier to agree but he is all out of patience.

A customer comes in then. He watches her as she glances around at the shelves.

"Komm doch mal nach Bayern auf Besuch."

She has been trying to get him to come over to stay with them for months now.

"Ja, ich muss aber es ist sehr hart die Zeit bekommen." He always blames it on being too busy but the truth is he can't face going there without Leni. He knows there would be too many memories waiting to trip him up. *"Also, ich geh besser. Ich habe einen Kunden."*

"Na dann . . . bis später, Conor."

"Bis später, Grußen nach Ralf."

He hangs up and goes to help the customer who has come in. She is dressed in a suit and heels and he hopes she has come in from the offices down the street. He had asked to put posters up in their canteen the week before to advertise the shop.

"I'm looking for a Valentine's gift for my husband." She seems embarrassed.

He remembers the date and that means that next week is

Valentine's Day and yet his shop is devoid of red paper hearts on string and a window full of love notes like the other bookshops have.

"I know it's over-commercialised hype," she adds quickly.

"Well, sometimes it's nice to make a special effort for one day, isn't it?" He thinks for a minute before bringing her over to the non-fiction section and taking down a book of old-fashioned love letters. "These are really beautiful."

She looks at him uncertainly. "I'm not sure if he's a love-letter kind of guy," she says, laughing.

"Really? They're beautiful – have a read of some and see what you think."

He leaves her alone while she flicks through them. He bought the same book for Leni before and she had loved it. They had sat up in bed for hours together with her sitting in between his legs with her head resting back against his chest. She had read them out loud to him. Sometimes she would stop and turn around to ask him what a particular word meant. One after the other they had read them, mainly stories of people separated by war. Often old-fashioned and stoic expressions of love in a different era.

"Why does no one write these any more? Everyone just sends emails or text messages nowadays," she had said wistfully. "They don't even go to the trouble of spelling the words properly any more – it's all shorthand. It's not right."

So he had written her love letters after that. Sometimes he would hide them in places around the house for her to find, or he would post them to her in work, sealed with wax. She had loved getting them. He wonders where they are now. Probably with the rest of her stuff that he still isn't able to face sorting out.

He looks back down at his paperwork. Last month's sales figure is staring off the page at him. It is down again on the same time last year. He taps some figures into his calculator but the percentage drop is frightening and he almost wishes that he hadn't.

He looks back over to the customer who is now putting the book back up on the shelf. She gives him an apologetic half-smile and then walks quickly out the door.

It's hard not to take it personally, but on today of all days it gets to him. He moves away from the computer, picks up a book and fires it at the shelves. He watches as it flies along through the air as if weightless before careering against the shelves and plunging to the floor. It falls back on its spine with pages wavering between falling left and right. When he looks up he see the three lads are back and their three faces are pressed against the window, staring in at him, laughing. But today he almost feels like laughing hysterically with them. He goes over and picks up the book again and unfolds the corner of the cover that got bent in the fall. He puts it in its rightful place back on the shelf.

He rings Ella again and this time she answers.

"I'm sorry for what I said. I didn't mean to upset you."

"Don't worry about it. Sorry I didn't get to ring you back – the kids were a nightmare and by the time I sat down it just went out of my head."

"Are you okay?"

"Yeah, I'm fine . . . I was just having a bad day . . ."

"Would you mind if I called over? I don't think I could face being on my own tonight."

"Sure, of course, Conor."

Even though it's not yet five o'clock, it is already dark. It feels as though the long winter evenings have been here forever. He decides to close the shop early. There has been no one in the shop in the last two hours anyway. He takes the DART and then walks along the coast road in the darkness to Ella's house. The lights in the arc of Dublin Bay twinkle in the distance. He eventually reaches the gate to the Martello tower. He presses the buzzer. It bleeps and he waits for it to be answered. After a few minutes, he presses it again and finally he hears her voice.

"Conor?" She sounds weary.

"Hi there."

"Hang on and I'll let you in."

Eventually the gates open and he walks up the driveway towards the house.

"I could have picked you up from the station," she chides when she opens the door to him.

"The walk did me good. Look, I just want to say I'm sorry again about joking about the quiz team the other day – I didn't realise I was overstepping the mark."

"Don't worry about it. I know you didn't mean any harm."

"Conor, why haven't you been over to see us?" Dot comes down the stairs with her hands on her hips.

"Hi, Dot, I'm sorry, I was really busy."

"Well, Mummy was sad."

Ella looks down at her daughter. "I'm okay, Dot."

"Well, why are you always crying then?"

She feels her stomach sink. She wishes she'd been able to hide it from the children.

"Are you okay, Ella?" He notices she is wearing her grey jersey pyjamas.

"Sorry, I never bothered getting dressed today," she says.

"But didn't you have to pick up the girls from school?"

"I put a coat on."

She has lost more weight over the few weeks. Her fringe has now grown down over her eyes. He follows her upstairs and through the living room where he sees Celeste lying the length of the sofa watching TV.

"Hi, Celeste."

"Hi, Conor," she mutters.

He follows Ella up to the kitchen on the top level. Maisie is in her highchair. There are pots bubbling on the stove.

"Will you stay for dinner?"

"I'd like that thanks," he says and adds quickly, "if it's not too much trouble."

"We're just having pasta."

"Sounds great."

He sits down at the table and Ella continues feeding Maisie some bright orange purée.

Every surface is taken over with children's paraphernalia – school books, tiny plastic Barbie shoes and children's artwork all compete for space. The red shiny Formica presses are covered in pink butterfly stickers.

"The girls have been busy." He gestures to the presses.

"To think that this place was once sought after by interiors magazines looking to do a feature on it!" she says.

When Maisie has eaten all of her food, Ella wipes her face and unstraps her.

She comes to sit down at the table with Maisie on her knee.

"Can I take her?" he asks.

"Sure."

He lifts the sleepy form over the table and sits her on his knee. She sits back against his chest and he can feel her little heart thumping below his palm. He puts his index finger inside her pudgy hand. Her mouth is forming little O shapes and small gurgles come out.

He turns to Ella. "Leni would have been due today."

Chapter 28

Eight Months Earlier

She is late. Two days now. She stops into the Tesco Metro on the way home. She finds the aisle where the pregnancy tests are and looks at the rectangular boxes on the shelves. She is bombarded with different types – own brand compete against some which claim to be 99% accurate from the day of a missed period – but then, when she looks at the shelf underneath, there are others that are sensitive from six days before and she is torn. She picks them up and reads the backs of the boxes. She decides on the one that is accurate from the early stages and she feels as though everyone is staring at her as she walks through the aisle, even though she knows they are probably preoccupied with sniffing shampoos or burying boxes of tampons under the groceries in their own baskets.

She cycles home with the bag in the basket and rushes upstairs to their bathroom. She takes the pregnancy test out of its foil wrapper. She knows she should wait for him but she can't. Patience isn't her strength. She unfolds the instructions to make sure she has them right in her head. She holds the test under her urine then puts the cap back on and leaves it on the side of the bathtub, making sure it is level like the instructions have told her to do. The three-minute wait is interminable. Three minutes can change your life. She gets up and starts tidying shampoo bottles and hair-gel containers on the shelves, but keeps stopping to see if the test is done. Finally she sees the second pink line. She is pregnant. They are pregnant. Two will become Three.

Then her mind starts racing with thoughts. What will he say? Can they afford this?

She hears his key in the door soon after. He climbs the stairs and they meet in the bedroom. He takes her in his arms. She pulls back and thrusts the pregnancy test into his hands. He looks confused for a minute and then it dawns on him. He is going to be a father. He wraps his arms around her and lifts her into the air. He swings her around until they both feel slightly dizzy and have to sit down on the edge of the bed.

"That night after Ryan's?" he asks.

She nods. "I think so."

"Wow." He is stunned.

"It is good, yes?" Her forehead creases in worry. The chicken-pox scar between her eyes folds in on itself.

He turns to reassure her. "Yes, it is – it's a shock but a good shock."

"You don't think it will be too much with the shop and everything?"

"No, this is good. Really, really good." A slow grin spreads across his face as the realisation starts to sink in.

She sits back with a stunned smile on her face. "I have to ring Mutti to tell her."

"Already! Don't you want to wait until we get it confirmed in the doctor's?"

"But I have to tell her, I'm so excited." She is already off the bed and pulling out her laptop to bring up Skype.

"Okay." He laughs. "Let's call her."

Chapter 29

"Oh my God, I'm so sorry, Conor!" Ella's hands fly to her mouth. "I didn't know she was pregnant!"

"Nobody did – we hadn't told anyone – well, except for her parents." He smiles at the memory.

"So she was pregnant when she was . . . y'know?" She can't bring herself to say the word.

"Yeah . . . she was."

"How far along was she?"

"Two months. We wanted to wait until after the first trimester before we started to tell people."

"God, I'm so sorry, Conor – I can't believe it." She is stunned. She gets up and stands at the sink and looks out into the evening darkness that has descended over Dublin Bay. She can see the lights of Dún Laoghaire twinkling far in the distance before her. "I didn't even know you were trying."

"Well, we weren't, not really. It came as a bit of a surprise, to be honest." Then he adds quickly, "But a good one."

He looks around her kitchen, which is full of fond memories. He can almost hear the laughter echoing off the stone walls again. Late-night dinner parties with lots of wine, Dan and Ella regaling them with funny stories. Leni would sometimes miss the punch line to a joke because of the language barrier so he would have to explain it to her and then she would throw her head back and laugh too a little bit later than everyone else. The kids' christenings, the birthday parties. They had even spent Christmas here two years ago when the snow had been so bad that the flight to Germany they were meant to be on was cancelled and Ella had insisted that they come to hers. She had underestimated the time on the turkey and they had eaten a plate of vegetables followed by the turkey on its own nearly two hours later.

Maisie is now pushing upwards with her feet on his knees.

Dot comes up the stairs wearing peacock-blue suede high heels and a full-length evening dress belonging to Ella, which she has to lift with every step she takes. She is also wearing her pink bicycle helmet on her head.

She wobbles on the heels as she reaches the top and Ella jumps up to steady her. "Be careful in those things, for God's sake!"

"How do I look?" Dot asks, attempting a wobbly twirl in front of Conor.

"You look beautiful – you're way better-looking than that Rapunzel one!"

"Thank you, Conor." She bows to him. "Will you marry me when I'm twenty-seven?"

"Absolutely. I'm waiting for you, Dot Devlin – you know you're the only girl for me."

She flashes him a smile and turns to go back down the stairs again.

"Take those heels off before you go anywhere!" Ella says.

After the sound of Dot's footsteps fade on the stairs, Ella turns back to Conor. "Why didn't you tell me about the pregnancy?"

"I couldn't say it – you were pregnant with Maisie at the time and I couldn't do it to you."

"Oh Conor, you should have though – I feel really bad about you carrying that grief along with losing your partner. God, it's just awful." She reaches over and takes his hand.

"Do you know what gets me?" he says.

"What?"

"That I could be passing him every day on the street and I wouldn't know that it was he who robbed me of the two people I loved most in the world – he took away my whole future and he's just out there now living his life but I don't get to live mine. It's so . . . so . . . hard."

"I'm sorry, Conor." She squeezes his hand tightly. "Want to go out and get pissed tonight? I can get Andrea to come over to mind the kids until Dan get home?"

"Nah, think I'd just prefer to be alone, if that's okay?"

"Sure, well, give me a shout if you need someone to get paralytic drunk with."

"Thanks for the offer."

There is a hissing from the cooker and she gets up to see the water has almost boiled off the pasta. It has started to fragment. Hardly *al dente* but it would have to do. She drains it in a colander and stirs in the sauce before serving it into bowls. She shouts down to the girls who come back up the stairs, Dot still in her bicycle helmet/ball gown regalia.

They sit in around the table, lunging for Parmesan and forks.

"Eh . . . do you want to leave some Parmesan for the rest of us?" Ella says to Dot who is spooning snowy mounds of cheese onto her plate.

Conor uses his right hand to spear some pasta onto his fork – he has his left arm around Maisie who is still on his knee. She is holding a teething ring between her fingers and lifting it towards her mouth.

"Are you sure you don't want me to put her in her high chair?" Ella asks Conor.

"No, I like holding her actually."

She smiles sadly at him. She feels the pressure of tears building behind her eyes and she forces herself to look up at the timber beams which span her kitchen ceiling. He would have been holding his own newborn in his hands today if things had been different.

"Is Dan going to be home soon?" he asks.

"No, he's working late all week on the new *Four from Saskatchewan* album."

"Cool!" He starts tapping out their last single, which was full of ukuleles and banjos. They are one of these new folk/rock bands.

Celeste puts her fork down and glares down the table at him. He stops tapping.

"Celeste, honey, have you had enough?" Ella asks her.

She doesn't answer.

"Celeste, I'm speaking to you."

Still no answer.

After they've finished, Ella tells Celeste to finish her homework. The child stares back at her.

Conor stands up and hands Maisie over to her. "I should probably be heading on – you probably need to get them into bed."

"Will you be okay?"

"Yeah, of course."

"I mean about Leni, y'know . . . and the baby and everything."

He shrugs. "I'll be fine honestly."

"I'll give you a lift to the station."

"No, the walk will do me good. I could do with the fresh air to clear the head."

He stands outside the Martello tower in the darkness. He breathes in the evening air and can taste the sea-salt on his tongue.

"It's just another day," he tells himself. "Time moves forward. *'Tomorrow, and tomorrow, and tomorrow, Creeps in this petty pace from day to day . . .'*"

Later that evening he sits down at the kitchen table and pours out his feelings on to paper like he has been doing since she died. It's the only thing that helps.

My Darling Leni,

Today has been a hard one. They're all hard but today was pretty bad. I didn't think I would get through it to be honest but then I thought of you and I knew that that wasn't what you would want for me. So that's why I'm doing this instead – you always loved lanterns.

Today should have been different for us – we should have been holding our baby in our arms or maybe counting down the days if you went overdue. You see what really gets me is that people lie. They lie all the time – blatant lies – they tell me that it will get easier but it never does. Never. I know it's just because they don't know what else to say to me – what can you say to the man who has lost his world? That's why they feel like they have to say something full of positivity and hope – but I'm not five years old. All I ever wanted from life was for us to be together – that was it – but it seems that even that was too much to ask.

Wherever you are out there, sleep well, my love.

My love, always,

Conor

Then he steps out into his back garden and puts the letter inside a lantern before lighting it and sending it up into the night sky.

Chapter 30

The small freckly face with the gap-toothed grin comes through the door and Conor can't help smiling when he sees him. His visits are now a daily occurrence and, rather than seeing them as an irritation like he used to, Conor has found himself actually looking forward to them.

"Hey, Jack, how've you been?"

"Hey, Conor. What are you doing?" This is the first time the boy has called him by his name instead of the usual 'mister'.

"Working. How about you?"

"I said I'd better give you a hand – it's not fair on you having to do all the work by yourself."

Conor smiles at him. "Or maybe you just want a sandwich?" He has now started to make sure that the mini-fridge out the back is stocked with ham and cheese so that he can always make Jack a sandwich.

"Well, okay, if you're offering. Can I use your crapper? I'm burstin'!"

"Excuse me?"

Jack starts to laugh. "That's what Da always calls it – a crapper."

"It's kind of disgusting."

"Yeah, that's what Ma says too."

"Go on," he sighs.

While Jack is in the toilet he realises this is the part of the day that he looks forward to most. His visits from Jack are the only thing keeping him going at the moment. They get him through the day and he doesn't dread the four walls of his shop quite as much as he has been for the last few months. His chats with Jack take his mind off his problems and worries. Through Jack, he gets to enjoy the innocence of childhood once again.

"What happened to you yesterday? I was wondering where you got to?" Conor asks as he cuts the bread.

"Me and Ma never woke up so I missed school! I usually wake up first – Ma says that I must have been a bird in another life because I'm always up with the lark and then I go in and wake Ma and give her a cup of tea, but yesterday I didn't wake early and neither did Ma and when I went into her room and she looked at the clock, she said, 'Oh my God, Jack, it's after ten o'clock! You're late for school!' So I thought I was going to be in big trouble with Teacher but Ma said, 'Why don't we have a day on the couch with our quilts and watch TV?'. So we watched a film from the olden days about a girl and she had no ma and da so she had to mind herself and feed herself and buy all the things herself but her dad gave her a suitcase full of golden coins so she was rich and she had a horse in her house."

"Pippi Longstocking?"

"Yeah, that was it. The horse was walking around inside in her sitting room but lucky her ceilings were high and he didn't bang his head. A horse would never fit inside my house. Ma says you couldn't swing a cat in our kitchen so you definitely couldn't fit a horse in there. Then we watched a show about cooking and Ma said, 'All that effort and then it's eaten in about two minutes flat', then Ma had a little sleep on the couch so I watched *Ben 10* and Four Arms is my favourite because he can crush anything even stuff that is super strong. Then Ma woke up so it was her turn to choose something to watch so she picked Judge Judy who was shouting at a man and then Ma said Judge Judy annoys her sometimes though because she doesn't listen to the people and it's important to listen, isn't it, Conor?"

"It is, Jack –"

"Yeah, that's what Ma says too. Then that woman Rachel came to the house and she asked Ma why I wasn't in school and Ma said, 'Ah, everyone deserves a day off now and again, don't they, Jack?' and then she messed up my hair. I thought Rachel was going to be mad with me but she said nothing. I think she's a bit scared of Ma. Ma doesn't like Rachel at all. I know she doesn't because she never asks her if she wants a cup of tea when she comes in. And Ma says that you should always ask people if they would like a cup of tea when they visit your house. Ma calls her the 'prissy one' – 'Oh, here comes the prissy one again,' she says and she rolls her eyes and then I laugh. Rachel's hair is all bouncy like she has loads of springs stuck onto her head and her face is a bit orange. Ma says she must be up half the night getting ready for work. She wears suits and high heels and the other day she was coming out of our door and she forgot we had a step and she fell down and knocked all her papers everywhere and I started laughing and Ma said that I shouldn't laugh when someone falls because it's not nice, but when Rachel was gone she laughed too and we both laughed so hard that Ma said that if she didn't stop laughing some of her wee was going to come out so we had to stop. And then that made me laugh even more because I never heard of a ma wetting her knickers before, only little girls, and then I imagined if she couldn't stop laughing and the whole kitchen was filled with wee and it turned into a river and burst through the door into the hall and went all the way down the street and everyone was covered in Ma's wee! And then it would come in the door here and wet all your books and I'd be in a boat sailing on the wee river trying to tell you 'Watch out, Conor, Ma's wee is coming, run for your life!'" Jack starts laughing again.

"That's some imagination you've got there."

"That's what Ma always says." He grins. "Here, want to hear another joke?"

"Go for it."

"Why are pirates grumpy?"

"I don't know."

"Because they *arrrrrrrggh*. Get it?"

Conor ruffles his hair. "I'd better make that sandwich, matey. Get it?"

Jack smiles. "Yeah, I was wondering when you were going to do it. I'm starving!"

"You're always starving."

"Can I read some more of *Tom's Midnight Garden*. I'm on chapter fifteen now."

"You're a fast reader."

"What happens when I finish the book?" He looks worried.

"I guess we'll have to find you something else to read then, won't we?"

"Ah, that's okay then because I was afraid to read it too quickly and then I wouldn't be able to come to your shop any more."

"There's always a book here for you, Jack."

Jack smiles up at him before running over and sitting on the floor in his usual spot and Conor goes out the back and starts layering ham and cheese between slices of white bread. He used to eat brown himself because Leni said it was healthier for him but Jack doesn't like brown so he buys white now.

That afternoon Rachel makes her way past walls graffitied with IRA slogans and a green strewn with plastic bags where fattened seagulls and big beady-eyed crows scavenge for food.

She pulls up outside 9 St Dominic's Terrace, the home of Jack White. She knows that Tina and Jack hate her visits. The tension is obvious but she tries to pretend that she doesn't notice it.

She raps the knocker and waits for Tina to answer.

A pale-faced Tina pulls back the door and wordlessly lets her in. Rachel follows her down the laminated floor of the hallway, which smells like last night's dinner, and into the small kitchen.

"How're you doing this week, Tina?"

"Grand."

"And where's wee Jack?" She looks around the room with its cluttered worktops, where a two-litre bottle of Coke sits on the counter with the lid missing.

"He's only a young fella – he has to be allowed go out and play with his friends sometimes."

"Oh, I had hoped to have a chat with him today, but no worries," Rachel says as breezily as she can. Her head is still thumping.

"You've a bit of lipstick on your teeth."

"Do I? Oh, sorry . . ." She rubs her forefinger against her teeth. Is she imagining it or does Tina seem to be smirking? "Thanks," she mumbles. "Right," she says, taking out her notebook. "Would you mind if I ask you a few questions – I'll keep it short." Because she has worked with the family previously as Jack was identified as a vulnerable baby when he was born, she has been requested by the courts to prepare a Section 20 report to make a recommendation as to who she feels is the best choice to become Jack's guardian after Tina passes away. She has to interview Tina about her preferences for Jack's care but, because the woman is terminally ill, she has to do it in stages so as not to tire her out.

Tina sighs. "Well, this is all a waste of time – there's no need for you – I've already told everyone me sister Libby is the best person."

"I know you're frustrated with the process, Tina, but I'm only doing as the judge ordered. It's my job is to take all the information on board about Jack and the people in his life and make an impartial decision."

"Well, let's hope you make the right one then," Tina says sharply, looking down at the floor.

Rachel knows that it must be hard for Tina to accept what is happening to her, that she won't be around to see her son grow up, and having to discuss what happens to him after she dies.

"Okay, maybe today you can tell me some more about your relationship with Jack's father John-Paul?"

"I've told you before, we were together on and off since I was fourteen. He gave me my first joint and then everything else. We were always breaking up and then he'd have managed to score a bit of gear and I couldn't say no so we'd be back together again. Then I found out I was having Jack when I was twenty-three and that was it for me. I'd had enough of shooting up in squats, being out of it for days on end. I wanted things to be different for my baby so I got myself on a withdrawal programme but John-Paul didn't and, Jesus, if it was bad enough listening to him when I was on the gear, it was ten times worse off it. Anyways we broke up for a while and then Jack was born and he was mad about him, he really was, so we gave it another go for Jack's sake but he was still up to all sorts. One day I found a bag of gear in the buggy – imagine if Jack had picked it up and swallowed some? So I threw John-Paul out and he went off the rails. Then he came back when Jack was three and said he was off everything and I believed him and I took him back. We were grand for a while but, instead of doing drugs, he was drinking like a fish and he's an angry man on the drink so I threw him out again and I've never looked back." She sighs impatiently. "You know all of this anyway."

"It's been a long time since I last worked with you, Tina,

and I need to make sure I have the facts right. Just to double-check with you – John-Paul never sought to become a guardian of Jack before?"

"No, thank God. He came up here the other day telling me I had to make him a guardian, that it was the law. He must think I'm awful thick but there's no way I'll be helping him to become Jack's guardian. No way. You have to do everything, Rachel – everything that you can to stop that happening. John-Paul loves Jack, I know that, but he can barely take care of himself, let alone Jack. He says he's off the gear but I don't know and he lives in that pub – I'm surprised they don't start charging him rent for his stool in there. But it's his temper that scares me the most. I put up with it for long enough but Jack is soft – he wouldn't be able for that at all. He'd lose his life. There is no way you can let him have him. Promise me, Rachel, you have to promise me that you won't let him have him!" She leans forward and squeezes Rachel's hand, pressing her fingers hard into hers until it hurts and her hand is left with white finger marks. "That's the only thing I'm asking you – don't let John-Paul get custody. You have to promise me, Rachel."

"Just to be clear, Tina, I make a recommendation based on my interviews but please remember that at the end of the day the decision rests with the courts – I can only make a recommendation. Sometimes they take it on board, sometimes they don't. I'm sorry but I can't promise anything."

"Well, there is no way – literally over my dead body – will I let John-Paul have custody of him."

Rachel cringes at her ironic choice of words. "So what other people could I talk to, to get a feel for things?"

"I don't know. Me da has Alzheimer's – he's in a home – me ma is dead and Jack's other grandparents on his da's side are dead too. I know you'll be talking to Libby anyway. Did you try his teacher?"

"I did. I met with her earlier in the week and she spoke very highly of him. She said that he's a very bright and capable little boy and a joy to have in the classroom."

"Well, I don't know where he gets it from – it's not from me or his da."

Rachel can tell she is being modest as there is pride on her face.

"Well, if what his teacher said is anything to go by, you have done a great job with him."

"Thanks, Rachel."

It is a rare moment of truce between the two women.

They fall silent until Rachel speaks again. "So have you told him yet?"

"No."

Rachel thinks she can hear a wobble in Tina's usually defensive tone.

"Not yet."

"Okay, well, it might be an idea to start mentioning it to him soon, so he has time to get used to it. I need to be able to talk to him about what his preferences are but at the moment he isn't even aware that you are terminally ill."

"How is an eight-year-old ever going to get used to losing his mother?"

"I know you can never prepare a child for something like that but I think it would be for the best if he knew – just so it's not a complete shock . . . y'know . . . when the time comes."

"But that's not fair on a young fella – sure how is he meant to decide something like that?"

"But you have to remember, Tina, if Jack also tells me that he doesn't want to live with his father then it strengthens your case in court. The court put a lot of weight on the child's testimony – it's not like years ago where no-one consulted with the children in these cases – nowadays it's all about listening to the child."

"I see."

"Talk to him, Tina – he needs to know, it's the best way."

"Right."

"How are you feeling today?" Rachel asks, changing the subject. She knows that Tina is in quite a bit of pain – she can see it etched in the lines on her face. She tries to bear this in mind whenever Tina is proving difficult.

"Awful. The nurse was here earlier with some more tablets for me but they're not worth a shite."

"I'm sorry they're no good," she says sympathetically.

"Six weeks they reckon – six weeks is all I've left in this damn place." She looks around the room.

"I'm so sorry, Tina – I truly am."

"I did so many bad things when I was younger – drugs and drink – I'd be outta it for days on end – if there was ever a time I deserved to die that was it but then I got clean, you know? As soon as I knew about Jack growing inside me, I didn't touch that stuff any more. That was it, Jack was my priority then." She pauses. "Someone's having a laugh somewhere."

"It's very cruel, I have to say. Life isn't fair."

"I just wish I could go knowing that he's going to be okay, you know?"

"Well, that's where I can help. I promise you I'll do my very best for you and for him. It's my job to find the next best guardian for Jack – after his mother of course."

Tina nods.

"Okay, well, I'll head on then. I've some things to catch up on in the office but I'll be back next week to see how you're getting on – you might try and have Jack here too, yeah?"

"I'll do my best." But she doesn't sound very convincing.

"Talk to Jack, won't you, Tina?"

"Watch yourself on the way out – we don't want you tripping over that step again."

When Rachel gets home that evening she is exhausted. Her visits to Tina White and the constant resistance that she is met with are taking their toll on her. She lets the weight of her body sink into the sofa.

Evening times are the worst. That's the time when she feels the pain of Marcus's absence from her life the most. She is so fed up with everything. It all feels so pointless and empty. After the break-up, she has been left with a huge void and she can't tell anyone that this is how she is feeling. Her parents would only worry if she told them. She is sick of pretending that she is happy whenever she sees her friends at home in Antrim. They think she is living the glamorous lifestyle portrayed by *Sex and the City*. They regularly say they're jealous of her husband-less, childfree lifestyle, being able to lie-in at weekends and go away at the drop of a hat. If she tells them she is going away for the weekend, they will reply with 'You've a great life. Isn't it well for you – easy knowing you've no kids'. They almost make her feel guilty about it. They think she is living the dream but it hurts her when they say that because she would trade places with any one of them in the morning. Shirley is the only person who knows about the break-up. She hasn't been able to face telling anybody else yet. Even though she knows things are definitely over between them, the finality of that step seems almost too much to bear at this stage.

Chapter 31

Today Ella has an appointment with Celeste's teacher after school. She's going to do what Dan has told her do. She is determined to sort this out once and for all.

She has arranged for Andrea to come to the school with her to take the girls home and, after she sees them off, she takes a deep breath and pushes open the door to the classroom. She is dreading this. She feels her heart begin to start up again with that mixture of anxiousness and love that always comes with Celeste.

She walks towards the front of the classroom where Ms Woods is sitting at her desk, through low-level chairs and desks painted in glossy fire-engine-red paint. Handmade posters with multiplication tables line the walls. She looks around at the shelves heavy with toys and abacuses, artwork with cotton wool, the knitted teddies that they did last term. They brought them home for the parents to help stuff and sew them. She remembers the stuffing kept coming out through the holes as she tried to stitch it. She had failed so dismally that Mrs Frawley had to step in and save the day. As usual.

She has never met Ms Woods, Celeste's teacher, before. She knows that she should have – she should have met her daughter's teacher – but she had always sent Dan along to the parent-teacher meetings. Of course Mrs Frawley would have met her when she was bringing Celeste or collecting her from school. Ella is acutely aware of how uninvolved she has been in her daughter's education before now.

Ms Woods is looking at her, ready and waiting for her to say something.

The familiar tightness starts in her chest and makes its way up her throat. She worries that the words won't come out.

"I – I am Ella Wilde – Devlin – I'm Celeste's mother."

"I know who you are." She pushes over a neat pile of copybooks to the right.

Of course she does, Ella thinks.

"Take a seat."

Ella sits down on the hard plastic chair.

"What can I do for you?" Ms Woods pushes up her glasses onto the bridge of her nose.

"Well, it's about Celeste . . ." Ella pauses. "I think she's being excluded by some of the other girls –"

"And what makes you think that?"

"Well, there have been a few . . ." she pauses, searching for the right word, "incidents."

"Incidents? Like what?"

"Well, she has said that some of the girls won't play with her at break times. And there is a birthday party on next week that she wasn't invited to."

"Now I'm sure you understand that I can't interfere in who does and does not get invited to a birthday party. You can't expect her to be invited to *every* party now, surely?"

"Of course not but I think it's deliberate – I think that one set of parents in particular is excluding her on purpose . . . "

"And why would they do that?"

"I . . . eh . . . I think it might be because of me actually . . . "

"Oh, I see – you feel the other parents don't want their daughters associating with Celeste because of . . . em . . . the incident . . . ?"

Ella nods and looks down at the vinyl floor covering.

"Well, to be honest from what you've told me today, it doesn't sound like bullying to me – in fact, it sounds like perfectly normal behaviour for eight-year-old girls – one minute they're best pals, the next they're worst enemies – I have a class of twenty-eight of them so I should know!"

Ella feels stupid then, like she's imagining a problem that doesn't exist and is wasting this woman's time. Yet again she feels frustration because she hasn't been able to articulate what it is that she wants to say, except now she is letting Celeste down.

"Okay, well, if you think everything is okay, then I'll leave it and hope things improve with Celeste. Thanks for staying back to meet with me." She picks up her bag, the grey suede slouchy one with the fringing, and gets up off the chair.

"I'm telling you they'll be best friends again next week – that's what they're like at that age."

Ella nods. "Well, let's hope so." But she doesn't feel convinced. She walks a zigzag line between the desks to get to the door. She reaches the door handle, opens it and walks out of the classroom.

Conor checks the clock. It's 4.15. Usually Jack is here by now.

He checks the clock again: 4.25. He starts to wonder where Jack is and then tells himself that he is being silly. He's probably off doing something with his mother. He goes back to doing his VAT return. He finally managed to pay the rent, two weeks late, and it's a weight off his mind.

Finally the door opens.

"Hey, Jack, I didn't think you were coming today."

"Rachel came and was asking me loads of questions so I couldn't go anywhere. I had to wait for her to go and then Ma was in a bad mood so I said I was going out to play."

"Who's Rachel?"

"Y'know, the prissy one?"

161

But Conor doesn't know. He keeps hearing Jack talking about her and he guesses that she is an official of some kind but he doesn't know why or what for and neither does Jack it seems. He doesn't want to probe but trying to piece Jack's chaotic life together and keep up with its cast of people is difficult.

"And now Ma's in a bad mood."

"Why is your ma in a bad mood?"

"She's always in a bad mood whenever Rachel comes. She said she wishes people would just listen to her and that this one would stop poking her nose into our business and leave us alone. She always makes Ma all angry and that's why I don't like her. She whispers if I'm there and they always talk for *aagggges* and then they go quiet whenever I go near them. Ma says she's wrecked tired when she's finished with her because she keeps asking her stupid questions and writing down the answers in her notebook like Inspector bloody Clouseau."

"Well, sometimes we all have to do things we don't want to do – look at me, I have to do this VAT return even though I don't want to."

"Well, it's not fair." He crosses his arms stubbornly.

"Life's not fair, Jack." Conor decides to change the subject. "So did you get the results of your maths test back?"

Jack nods. "I got eight out of ten."

"Well done! If you keep going like that I might start getting you to do this for me –" He points at his paperwork.

Jack smiles. "I could do loads of work for you and then you could pay me and I could use the money to buy things like books and Giant Jawbreakers. I'd buy something nice for Ma too because she seems a bit sad all the time now so maybe some perfume might cheer her up. I grew her a daffodil plant in school for Mother's Day and I gave it to her and she started to cry and I wasn't sure if she hated the daffodil or not. Mine didn't grow as big as Kev Higgins's or Franky Ward's. So I didn't know if she was happy or sad because it was too small and then she started laughing, saying that of course she was happy but a bit sad too, so I was confused. How can you be happy and sad at the same?"

"Well, people are funny, you know? Sometimes when something makes us really, really happy we cry."

"Well, that's just weird. I never cry when I'm happy, not even when Santa got me an Xbox with Minecraft for Christmas last year. That was the best present ever!"

"Yeah, you're right, people are weird."

"You don't think Ma was sad about the daffodil so? I know ma's like chocolates and those smelly bubble-bath things that make the house all stinky but I didn't have enough money to buy any of those – maybe if I had a job though I could buy her something nice."

"How about making her a cup of tea or doing a job for her? I'm sure that would make her happy."

"Yeah, maybe. Why don't you have any kids, Conor?"

"Well . . . I . . . "

"Do you not like them?"

"Of course I do! I nearly did but it . . . just didn't happen."

"Why?"

"Like I said, sometimes life isn't fair."

"Why?"

"Because my girlfriend died."

"Were you sad?"

He nods. "Yeah, I was – very sad. I still am to be honest."

"Well, that's a pity because I think you'd be an okay dad."

"Only okay?"

"Well, good then, I suppose."

"Thanks, Jack, that really does mean a lot, thank you."

"I better go. I'm meant to be getting milk in the shop for our tea and I don't want Ma to start crying again."

Chapter 32

Ella stands on the pier, looking out at the pretty fishing boats bobbing gently in the harbour. The sunlight is bright and the colourful buildings behind her look like one of those colour-enhanced John Hinde picture postcards showing Ireland at its very best. The wind whips the end of her scarf up into her face and she pushes it down again.

The girls run ahead of her into the playground and she follows behind with Maisie wrapped up in her buggy.

Inside the playground, she sits down on a bench and watches the girls running across the bouncy surface in chaotic directions.

A man comes in a while later and sits down on the bench beside her. His two boys run over and commandeer the pirate ship.

"Nice day, isn't it?"

"Spring has sprung," she says dryly.

"About time. It's been a long winter."

She nods. "It sure has."

He has a kind face. His eyes are darkest brown so you can't see his pupils. He is slightly round about the middle but he is attractive. He bends forward and starts rooting in the rucksack at his feet. He comes back up with a packet of ginger nuts. "Want a biscuit?" he asks, offering the packet to her.

Her automatic response is to say no. She doesn't have the energy to get dragged into a conversation with a stranger but she finds herself taking it from him anyway and biting into its sugary hardness.

"Don't tell my wife this – but I never leave the house without a packet of these." He taps the side of packet with his forefinger.

"Bribery?" she asks.

He nods. "Absolutely, works every time!"

"Don't worry – your secret is safe with me. You have to cut yourself some slack when you can, don't you?"

Since she has been at home she is seeing a lot more dads collecting children from school or doing the daytime activities like ballet drop-offs, playground runs. It reminds her of those old wartime movies where the men returned home from war with injuries and had to mind the children while the women went out to work to provide for their families.

"I recognise you from somewhere," he says, using his thumbs to push up another biscuit from the packet.

"Really?" She tries to sound surprised but she doesn't pull it off. She would never have made an actress. Two weeks in Dramasoc had told her that.

"You're yer' one off the telly!" he says through a mouthful of ginger nut. "You were caught running off with that watch, or maybe it was a bracelet – the really dear one."

She is waiting for what will surely come next.

"How've you been? You got a right doin'."

She turns to look at him, wondering if she has heard him right or if he is taking the piss out of her but his brown eyes seem genuine. He is the first person to ask how she has been since that fateful day.

"I'm . . . I'm . . . em . . . okay, y'know."

"I'm an alcoholic," he says out of nowhere. "Recovering, I should add – I've been dry for four years now, since just after

Jake over there was born." He points with a ginger nut between his thumb and forefinger to the smaller of the boys who is swinging from the monkey bars with his two arms. "But I couldn't do it to Laura any more – that's the wife. I couldn't keep putting her through that. She had a toddler to look after and then the baby, and I was a bigger trouble to her than either of the boys. I would vanish on benders for days at a time and wouldn't answer my phone. Sure the day of Jake's christening, I sloped off to the pub for a swift one but it wasn't until my brother-in-law hauled me out of there at six o'clock that I realised I had missed the whole thing – I missed my own son's christening, the whole bloody thing, and poor Laura had to tell the priest that I got called in to work. She was mortified. When I finally showed my face, she was in bits. God, I knew, of all the things I'd done to her, this was the very worst of them – that was my rock bottom. That was when I realised that I couldn't do that to her any more and if I was to have any chance of holding onto my family, I had to change. And I did. I went into a treatment program and got dried out but then I was made redundant six months ago – I'm a plasterer by trade. I think Laura was awful worried that I'd go back on the drink again but, thank God, I didn't. I was tempted – believe me I had some dark days but I could never go back to that place again no matter how bad it gets. It's hard being without a job though – I've always worked even at my worst. I was always the first on the site at eight o'clock every morning. I was always able to provide for my family."

"It'll pick up soon."

"Here's hoping. I'm trying to see the positives in it. At least I'm getting to spend time with the boys. I never did that before and I must say I'm actually enjoying it. You lost your job too, didn't you? I read it in the paper."

She nods. That is one thing she has never been able to get used to: strangers knowing details about her life. The older one of his boys is screaming as he zip-lines across in front of them.

She watches Dot climbing a rope wall, determined that she will get to the top even though it's designed for kids a lot older than her.

"I'll be up in court soon."

"How do you think it will go?"

"I don't know – it depends on the judge on the day. My solicitor says that the best I can hope for is a fine but I could get a sentence too if they want to make an example of me."

He nods.

"I just wish I could turn back the clock," she says.

"Who are you telling? But you can't change the past – the future is the only thing that we have control over – that's one thing we learn in our meetings – I go to AA every week. We can't undo the hurt that we did to others – believe me, if I could go back and not do those terrible things to Laura I would but I can't do that so I'm going to spend the rest of my life making it up to her."

"Sounds like she's a lucky woman."

"I'm the lucky one. I wouldn't be here today if it wasn't for that woman. Look, you're probably at rock bottom yourself right now, but it has happened and you can't change that. You have to take the experience and use it to learn from. What I mean is – why did you decide to walk out of that shop with that thing still on your wrist? Were there other things going on at the time that you weren't happy about? Something must have happened to make you do something that you wouldn't ordinarily do."

She looks down at red-and-green-coloured surface. "Maybe," she sighs. "Maybe . . . "

"Stop beating yourself up – it could have been an awful lot worse – at least nobody got hurt."

But they did.

He continues. "Look, you're paying for your mistake now so it's time to forgive yourself."

But she knows she will never be able to forgive herself. Ever.

She stands up off the bench and holds the girls' coats out for them.

"Celeste, Dot, come on, time to go now. Maisie needs her bottle."

She turns to the man. "Thanks for the biscuit."

"Anytime."

She pushes the buggy out of the playground.

Chapter 33

Rachel pulls up outside the address that she was given for her appointment with Jack's father, John-Paul. She knocks on the door of the terraced house but there is no answer. She peers in the window through grey lacy net curtains but it seems there is no one home. She is just about to get into her car when she sees him coming up the street towards her.

"Sorry I'm late," he says, drawing level with her.

The first thing she notices is how angular his face is. It is hard and bony. Cheekbones jut out over jawbones; his nose veers off to the left. Dark stubble dots his jaw line.

"Hi, John-Paul. I'm Rachel McLoughlin, nice to meet you."

They shake hands. There is a faint smell of spirits off his breath.

"Come on in."

She notices that his teeth are badly discoloured and black deposits sit in the grooves between them. He opens the door and shows her into a dull room. There is a settee and a TV but not much else.

She sits down on the settee. "Okay, so, as you know, I'm the social worker appointed by the court to carry out the Section 20 report about who should have guardianship of

169

Jack after Tina passes away and I wanted to talk to you, as Jack's father, for a little while to get your view on things. But first I just want to make sure that you understand the reasons for this report being carried out?"

"Yeah, it's because Tina, me ex, is dying and she wants me son to live with her sister instead of with his da where he belongs."

"Right, and as part of this assessment I will need to take notes, if that's okay with you?"

"Grand."

"I also have to make you aware that the report will be seen by the legal teams in the case too."

"I've nothing to hide."

"Okay, great. We'll get started so and if you're unsure of anything at any time just stop me, okay?"

He nods.

"How often would you see Jack?"

"Every few days. I'd see him more only his ma doesn't like me going over there and she doesn't let Jack stay here on his own either."

"And why do you think that is?"

"I dunno." He shrugs his shoulders. "She's been mad with me since we broke up."

"When did you and Tina break up and what were the reasons for that break-up?"

"When Tina was pregnant we broke up for a while but then when I saw me son I knew I had to give it another go, but then she started flipping out over every little thing and I couldn't handle it to be honest. It was doing me head in."

"And why do you think it is that Tina doesn't want Jack to live with you?"

"Tina doesn't like me, that's what this is all about. But I've been off the gear for three years now, I'm a different man than when I was with her."

"How long have you been living at this address?"

"Three years."

"Where were you before that?"

"Well, I lived with Tina when we were together and then I stayed in me mates' houses – just till I got me own gaff, you know?"

"Do you work?"

"I'm looking for a job but there's nothing out there at the minute."

"When did you leave school?"

"After me Inter."

"Why was that?"

"I hated school, so I did. All the rules and the teachers giving it loads all the time – it just wasn't for me."

"Now I know from looking back through previous reports, and you already mentioned it, that you do have a history of substance abuse."

"Yeah, but like I said I've been clean for three years now."

"Are you enrolled in any treatment programme?"

"I get me phy every day in the chemist."

"You mean methadone, yeah?"

He nods.

"And which chemist is that?"

"O'Shea's."

"I know it – there on Haymarket Street."

He nods.

"Okay and how about alcohol?"

"I like a few pints the same as the next fella."

"Have you a criminal record?"

"One time Tina called the Guards on me because I was roaring and shouting when I was drunk but I never hurt anyone. I broke into a car one time and robbed a woman's handbag but that was when I was off me head. But I wouldn't do anything like that now," he adds quickly.

"And what do you think is the best for Jack? If you had to tell the judge."

171

"He's my son and he should be with his da. A child belongs with their parents and if his ma is dead then he should be with me. I don't see why her sister should get him! I'm his da, I have rights!"

"Well, it's up to the judge then to make a decision based on the information in my report. I can only make a recommendation and –"

"But I'm his *da*!"

"It doesn't matter, because legally you never applied to become a guardian."

"But I don't need to be a guardian to me own son."

"Unfortunately this is the way the law works in relation to unmarried parents."

"This country is a fucking joke! He's me son!"

She delves some more into his relationship with both Tina and Jack before she decides that she has enough information for her report.

"Okay, well, thanks so much, John-Paul. I really appreciate you answering those questions for me. As you know I have a few people to speak with before I finish my report."

She says goodbye to him and gets into her car. She drives back to the office to write up her notes from her interview with him while they are still fresh in her mind. She still needs to meet Tina's sister Libby, who at the moment looks likely to be the best candidate for guardianship of Jack but that could all change when she actually meets her.

Ella stares at the letter envelope in front of her, knowing what it contains. She tears the brown envelope along its gummed part and unfolds the letter inside. It is the court summons and it is dated for June 4th next. She feels her chest tighten and her breathing starts to quicken. She picks up the phone to ring Conor. She feels awful unburdening her problems on him when he has been through so much himself lately.

"Hi – it's me. Can you –" she gulps, "can you talk for a minute?"

"Hi there, everything okay?" He sounds distracted like he is trying to do something in the shop and talk to her at the same time.

"Yeah, I'm just . . ." She takes a deep breath. "The court summons has just arrived."

He exhales. "Oh no, Ella, I'm sorry. How are you feeling about it?"

"I'm just finding it so hard." He can hear the tremble in her voice that threatens to break at any minute. The shop bell goes and a load of tourists come into the shop. He is torn between going to help them and listening to Ella – but Ella sounds like she needs him more right now.

She swallows. "It's just difficult, y'know?"

"Excuse me – we are looking for a tourist guide to Dublin?"

"Of course it is . . . one minute . . ."

There is the sound of the phone dropping and muffling. She hears him talking to the customers before he picks the phone back up again.

"Sorry, are you still there?"

"Yeah."

"Look, can I ring you back later? I just need to ring this through."

"Yeah, sure, no worries. I was –"

"Sorry, I have to go – why don't we meet for a drink later, yeah?"

Conor shuts up the shop and walks over the cobblestones to the pub on Fade Street where he has arranged to meet Ella. He orders a pint and sits into a snug to wait for her.

Her head appears around the corner a few minutes later. "Sorry I'm late. Dan was late home. Again."

"No worries, I'm only just in before you anyway."

She goes up to the bar and orders a glass of wine, before sliding into the seat beside him.

"Is everything okay?" Conor asks.

She flips over a paper coaster between her forefinger and thumb before taking a sip from her Chianti. "You know . . . the same. It's dated June 4th."

"Well, fingers crossed it won't be as bad as you think. Hopefully the judge will go easy on you as you're pleading guilty."

"I don't know . . . my solicitor has warned me that they might try to make an example of me because it's bound to be a high-profile case – to raise awareness of the penalties for shoplifting. But it's the media I'm most scared about."

"Well, I'll be with you every step of the way, you know that. And you have Dan."

"Dan!" She laughs a hollow laugh. "Dan who thinks I should just suck it up and stop feeling sorry for myself?"

"He didn't say that?"

"He can't understand why I'm taking it so badly. He just doesn't get how much this has ruined my life."

"Well, you did have a huge upheaval – the incident itself, then losing your job, then Mrs Frawley packing up. You need to talk to him about this and tell him exactly how you're feeling."

"Do you know what, Conor?" She turns to look at him. "I just don't think I have the energy to fight for our marriage."

"I can't understand why you would let it drag on and just don't try and talk to him. If you love him, which I know you do, then stop wasting time and try to get things back on track between you again." If losing Leni has taught him anything it is that life is too precious to fight with the people we love.

"But I've tried, Conor, honest to God I've tried so many times but he just doesn't get it. At this stage it just seems so far out of reach!"

"Are things really that bad between you?"

"I just don't know how to get him to listen to me – to what I'm trying to say. I just feel so alone right now. He just doesn't understand what I'm going through. I think I'm starting to hate him, Conor – I never thought I use that word about my own husband but that's how I feel right now."

Chapter 34

The bell tinkles and before Conor can even look up he hears "*Aaaaaaaaarrggggh!*" and a red-faced Jack is standing in the middle of his shop. His eyes are glazed with tears.

"What's going on?" Conor asks, closing his notebook shut. "Shouldn't you be at school?"

"We have a half-day and Rachel is in our house again. I hate her. She was going on and on with her questions and then she sat on a packet of Giant Jawbreakers that I had left open on the couch and they all melted and there was all green and red stuck to her skirt and she was all uppity saying she'd have to get it dry-cleaned and I was so mad with her because they were my sweets and I *love* Giant Jawbreakers even though Ma says they'll break my jaws one of these days but I don't think they will because I've eaten hundreds and thousands of them and it hasn't happened yet. Then Ma said I had to say sorry to her even though it wasn't my fault that she sat there – I didn't tell her to sit down! So I ran out the door and came here."

"Okay, calm down, Jack."

"It's not fair! I hate her."

"Who? Rachel?"

He nods. "I hate the way she keeps coming to our house

and tries to talk to me and makes Ma all cross and puts her in a bad mood. Me and Ma are much better when she's not there. I don't like it when Ma gets cross with me. Rachel ruins everything!"

The anger gives way to tears.

"Hey, come on, Jack! I bet if you go home now your ma will have forgotten all about it." He puts an arm around his shoulders.

"No, she won't! She'll still be mad and cross with me for running off when Rachel was there. She always says I have to be on my best behaviour when she's in our house – she says it's important that I show her what a good lad I am – but I just got so angry today that I couldn't do it."

"Calm down, Jack – look, maybe you should go home in case your ma is worried – come back tomorrow when she has calmed down."

"No." He shakes his head stubbornly.

"Okay, I'll cut you a deal – why don't you take the book home with you and give your ma a big hug and tell her you're sorry for running off on her, all right?"

"No, I don't want to bring it home," Jack answers stubbornly. "I like coming here to read it."

"All right. You can read a few pages but then you've got to go on home, okay?"

"Maybe."

"Jack?" he says sternly.

"Okay."

"All right, you sit down over there and I'll make you something to eat, deal?"

"Okay," he says sulkily.

After Jack has gone home, Conor is doing some dusting in the shop when the door opens and the boys are standing on the step.

"Paedo," one of them says.

"Excuse me?"

"You're a paedo – everyone knows it. We see you here with Jack White every day. If you don't give us money we're going to tell everyone that you made us go into your shop and were feeling us too."

Conor's shoulders tense with rage. He can feel the blood coursing through his ears and making its way up along his face. He walks over to the eldest, grabs him by the collar of his jumper and lifts him off the floor so that his face is just millimetres from his own. His two friends start to back away towards the door and when they get there, open it and run.

"Come back, lads, come back! Wait!" the boy he is lifting calls. "Keith – Ronan – wait!"

"What's your name?" Conor says as he steps outside and lowers him down onto the path, still keeping a hold of his collar.

"Jordan," he says shakily.

"What?" Conor says again.

"Jordan," he says louder this time.

"Now, Jordan, I'm warning you – this is the last time I'm going to say it. I want you and your little friends to leave me and my shop alone, do you hear me?"

The boy nods quickly.

"I can't hear you – I said are you going to leave me and my shop alone?"

"Yes." His voice is trembling.

"Good. I'm going to let you go now and you're going to walk out of this shop and run after your little friends and I'm never going to see any of the three of you again. Do you understand me?"

He nods eagerly.

Conor lowers him back down and releases his grip from his jumper. The boy scarpers towards the door and runs out into the street.

After they have gone it takes Conor a long time to calm

down. His heart is still beating too fast. He instantly starts to wonder if he has gone too far. Will they go home and tell their parents? He could have started another battle entirely. He should have just ignored them. This could get a whole lot worse.

Rachel drives along the driveway, hearing the sound of the gravel crunch underneath her tyres. Mature oak trees and sycamores shade the drive. Paddocks are on either side and the land rolls on for miles around her. Eventually the house comes into view. Jack wasn't exaggerating when he said Libby lived in a mansion. It looks as though it is a new build but designed to look older. You have to stare really hard at the walls to tell if it's old or not. She steps out onto the stones and the freshness of the country air fills her lungs. She climbs the steps leading to the front door, pushes the bell and waits.

When Libby opens the door, Rachel sees the similarities between herself and Tina. They have the same bluish-green eye-colour with specks of hazel and they both have identical snub noses, but it is obvious that the woman standing in front of her has led a very different life to her younger sister. She doesn't have that telltale weathered look in her face and, whereas she has only ever seen Tina wearing tracksuit bottoms and hoodys, her sister's clothes appear to be far more carefully chosen. She greets Rachel and leads her down a black-and-white chequered hallway with neatly lined wellies and a coat stand. Rachel follows her through to the sunroom at the back of the house. Beams flood into the room, showing tiny dust particles dancing in the light. She looks out to the lawn where she can see a sunken trampoline and a tree house in the garden before the grass slopes off down towards a coniferous forest.

"Thanks for meeting with me, Libby. You have a really lovely home. It's so peaceful and quiet out here compared to the hustle and bustle of Dublin."

"Oh, thank you. You found us okay then? It's a bit remote out this way," she says nervously.

"Your directions were spot on," Rachel responds.

Rachel looks around the room before walking over to a wall of family photos in matching silver frames. There are pictures of smiling children sitting on Santa's knee, a family picture taken at a beach somewhere, another of the three boys with pink-tinged cheeks playing in the snow.

"That one there is Jack," Libby says, coming up behind her and pointing to one of a pink-faced newborn with a disgruntled look on his face. "I took it just minutes after he was born. I was with Tina in the delivery room. After Tina, I was the next person to hold him."

"It's a lovely picture."

"Sit down. Can I get you something to drink?"

"I'm all right, thanks."

"How about juice or water even?"

"I'm fine, thanks."

"Well, I have some apple tart if you'd like something to eat? I won't lie, I didn't bake it myself but it's from the bakery in town – they always do good ones."

"Honestly, I'm actually grand, thanks."

"Sorry – I'm not trying to be annoying, I'm just not used to this, y'know? I'm a bit anxious if the truth be told."

"Don't worry, you have nothing to be worried about, Libby. I just want to ask you a few questions to get a feel for you and your family and your relationship with Jack. There are no trick questions – just answer the questions as honestly as you can and we'll be fine."

"Right, I'll do my best." She takes a deep breath.

"Shall we get started so?"

Libby nods.

"Okay, to start with I just want to find out a bit about your own family. What ages are your boys?"

"Well, Stephen is thirteen, Martin is ten and Eoghan is nine – there are seven months between him and Jack."

"And do the boys see much of Jack?"

"Oh yeah, they all get on so well. We call over there a lot or sometimes Tina and Jack come to stay with us for a few days – you know, during the school holidays or at Christmas time. We're very close."

"Okay, so how long have you been living at this address?"

"Oh God, since just after Stephen was born – so twelve years now."

"And your children all attend the local school?"

"Yes, well, the two younger boys are in primary school and Stephen has just started in secondary this year."

"How do you find the school?"

"Great. It's a small country school – there's only one class in each year. My three have been very happy there."

"Okay, and do you work?"

"I do a bit of flower arranging part-time. Well, it's more a hobby than a job but if someone I know is getting married I'll do their flowers or if someone needs flowers for another occasion, y'know?"

"And do you work from home or do you have a premises?"

"I have a shed down the garden that I use."

"And your husband, what does he do?"

"He has his own business – they supply specialist equipment for hospitals."

"Does he travel much?"

"No, not usually – he's normally home every day."

"And how does he feel about potentially having custody of Jack?"

"Well, he's completely on board – he loves Jack – we all do. He wants it to happen as much as I do."

"And, financially, how would having another child to care for impact on your family?"

"We've talked about it and it's fine. I don't mean to sound crass, but we can afford it."

Rachel notices Libby is blushing. She looks down at her notepad and writes something.

"Have your sons ever had any behavioural problems or anything that I should know about?"

"Nothing outside the normal things with kids – Eoghan did go through a period of bedwetting there about two years ago but it turns out he was being bullied by an older boy at his football training. We addressed it with the trainer and the other boy's parents and he's been fine ever since."

"Why do you think Jack should live with you and your family?"

"Because I love him. My family are like Jack's extended family. He has been part of our lives literally since the day he was born. Tina is my sister and I love her dearly and Jack is an extension of that love. I can give him so much. I'll never replace Tina, I wouldn't want to, but I can certainly give him enough love and care and a happy family home and I think that's worth something."

"What would you think if John-Paul was awarded guardianship?"

"It would be wrong." Her faces reddens. "He has been in and out of that boy's life. There's nothing stable about him. He can't even look after himself, let alone Jack. I can't let that happen, I couldn't do that to Tina. It's bad enough having to watch your little sister battle terminal cancer – it's really, really hard," she pauses for a moment, "but if John-Paul was awarded custody of that boy, it would break my heart altogether." Her voice is trembling.

"Very well, Libby – thanks for allowing me to come here today and for answering my questions. The only thing you need to be aware of is that my report is only a recommendation – some judges don't even bother to read them and just make up their own minds on the evidence presented to them, so please keep that in mind, okay? We won't know until the day of the hearing itself what the outcome is going to be."

"Well, any judge worth his or her salt can see that John-

Paul isn't any good for Jack. I don't want him out of the boy's life because it's important that he knows who his dad is, but on a day-to-day basis Jack needs stability and I can give him that. It's breaking my heart every time I think about what's coming down the tracks for him, so can you imagine how poor Tina is feeling? At least if she knows that he's going to be properly looked after, after she's gone, it'd be something. That's all I want, to be able to do right by my sister."

Rachel nods. "I understand this must be so hard for you, Libby – that's why I want you to know that I'm going to do my very best to make sure that we get the very best outcome for Jack."

Chapter 35

Conor puts down the phone to his wholesaler. He is stocking up on the latest word-of-mouth sensation, a new Scandi psychological thriller translated as *The Lighthouse Keeper*, which is set to be huge. They were talking about it on the radio that morning and already he has sold four of the five copies that he has in stock. He could really use a blockbuster right now. They're an easy sell. They bring people who don't usually buy books back into bookshops.

The bell tinkles as the door opens. Conor looks up and sees Jack.

"Hey, Jack!"

He has got taller in the last few weeks and the gap of bare skin between where his tracksuit bottoms stop and his runners begin has got wider. He seems to have forgotten his socks. "What's happening?"

"It's Tuesday," Jack announces wearily as if he has the weight of the world on his shoulders.

"And?"

"Well, Rachel always comes on a Tuesday now, so that's why I told Ma I was going outside to play – in case she comes again today."

"Who is this Rachel you're forever moaning about?"

"You know – the prissy one!" he says somewhat impatiently.

"Yeah, I know, but why does she come to your house? Is she a friend of your ma's or something?"

"Nooooo – Ma hates her – even more than me! I don't know who she is." He shrugs his shoulders. "Ma is always in bad form after she calls in to us. Ma is in bad form a lot lately. When I went home yesterday she was crying again. Sometimes I see her crying and I ask 'What's wrong, Ma?' And she says 'Oh, it's nothing, love', but I say 'Well, you only cry if there's something wrong'. So yesterday I asked her and she said 'I've just got a pain in me tummy' and then I said that it must be really sore because one time I had a really bad pain in my tummy – it was really, *really* bad – but I didn't cry, so hers must have been even sorer. She says what is she going to do without me but I told her that she's being really silly because I'm not going away anywhere, I see her every day. I only go to school and here but I didn't say that bit because she doesn't know that I come here. Then she smiled and told me to get her a tissue so she could dry her eyes and I asked her if the pain in her tummy was gone then and she said that it was."

As Conor lets the boy talk, he tries to piece together the jigsaw of Jack White's life for the last few weeks but it doesn't make sense to him. Conor knows that the boy loves his mother and would do anything for her and from what he can tell she loves him too, except for the fact that she seems to sleep a lot. And then there is this Rachel person – who is she and what does she want with Jack's mother?

"Well, hopefully she's all right now."

"I just wish everything was back to the way it usedta be. Before Ma was sad and sleepy all the time. When Ma picked me up from school and then we went to the homework club together, then home for our tea and Rachel never came."

"I'm sure it will be all be back to normal soon, Jack."

He looks up at him, wide-eyed and serious. "I went to the church on my way here and I tried to light a candle but then

Mrs Keely the sacristan came out and saw me and told me to get out and stop causing trouble – but I wasn't messing, cross my heart and hope to die. She said that young fellas today are pure brazen and that I should be ashamed of myself causing trouble in the house of the Lord but I just wanted to light a candle to pray for Ma to be happy again. That's what Ma always does when she says something is worrying her – she lights a candle in the church. So now my prayer won't come true."

"Never mind all that – it's the thought that counts, isn't it?" He puts his arm around his shoulders and rubs his arm. "Why don't you read some more of *Tom's Midnight Garden* while I make you a sandwich if you want?"

He runs over to his usual spot on the floor and takes the book off the shelf. Conor comes out a minute later with the white bread sandwich.

Jack takes a bite and says, "Ma is always giving out to me because I run away out the door without eating anything after school but I like your sandwiches better – Ma always makes me eat brown bread – she says it's better for me."

Conor feels guilty then for undoing whatever dietary goodness his mother was trying to instil in him.

"Leni always made me eat brown too," he sighs. "But I have to agree with you, white tastes way nicer."

Ella silences the engine. She gets out of the jeep, steps out into the quiet cul-de-sac and walks towards Mrs Frawley's house. Then she has second thoughts about coming here – she should really just turn around and go back home again – but something pulls her towards the front door. She wants to sit on the stiff-backed chairs in Mrs Frawley's good front room with its perfectly straight cushions and china on display in the glass cabinet. She wants to sit in that room with Mrs Frawley. They have always called her Mrs Frawley even though, as far as Ella knows, she has never been married.

She presses the bell and waits. She doesn't know what she is going to say to her. It feels as though she is waiting for ages for her to answer. She checks her watch and it is almost five. Mrs Frawley has probably gone out for her daily walk. Just as she is turning around to head back towards her jeep, she hears a voice calling her from the door.

"Ella, love, is that you? What are you doing here?"

She turns around to see Mrs Frawley standing on the step in her usual uniform of a high-necked pullover and skirt.

"I didn't know where else to go."

"I see. Well, you had better come inside so."

Ella follows her wordlessly into the house.

"Shall I make us a pot of tea?"

Ella nods. She goes into Mrs Frawley's sitting room and sits down on the wingback chair. The room is chilly. Unlike Ella, Mrs Frawley never seems to feel the cold. Even in the depths of winter she would always have the windows in the tower open to have the sea air blasting in. Ella finds herself looking around the orderly room. It is meticulously tidy as everything associated with Mrs Frawley always is. She notices that she has changed the carpet since she was here last.

A few minutes later Mrs Frawley comes back in with a tray and a china teapot painted with yellow primroses and matching teacups. "Where are the girls?" she asks.

"Andrea has them."

"I see. I'm sorry I've nothing sweet to offer you but I wasn't expecting visitors today."

She places the tray down on the coffee table and sits on the centre of the sofa. She starts to pour the tea in a steady arc into a cup, which she then hands to Ella.

She pours for herself and they sit sipping the tea.

"So how are they doing?" she says eventually.

"They're good." Ella pauses. "They miss you though."

Mrs Frawley half smiles. "I was going to come to visit, when things settle down again in a few weeks."

"Please come back." The words are out before she can help it.

"Now, Ella, I told you before – it's for the best. You will thank me for this one day, I promise you."

"But I can't cope, I just can't do it."

"Do what, love?"

"I can't do the whole mother thing."

The older woman laughs. "It's too late now, my dear – you have three little people relying on you."

"I'm no good at it . . . "

"Ella, you know very well that that is one phrase I will *not* allow you to use!"

"Sorry," she says, suitably chastened.

"You're doing fine, dear."

"But I'm not – you don't see me every day. Maisie cries all the time, Celeste hates me – Dot I can just about handle. Just about. I'm a disaster. I can't do it. Please, Mrs Frawley, please come back to us – if not for me, for the children's sake?"

"You know I can't do that, dear."

"But why not?"

"It would never have worked out with the two of us there and, besides, my time had come anyway. I think at this stage of my life I'd quite like to embark on a new adventure."

"Like what?" Ella is aghast. This is Mrs Frawley – she doesn't do adventures.

"I don't know, that's the fun of it all. When I first came to your house to look after yourself and Andrea, you were two very lost little girls, God bless you, but I was only supposed to be doing the job for a few weeks as a favour to a friend of your dad's. But when I met your father and got to know him, when the few weeks were up I just couldn't walk out on him and leave him in the lurch. So I stayed on with your family. Initially it was only supposed to be for a few months but as you know I ended up staying there, until first Andrea and then you went off to university. Then when you had Celeste and you were working on *The Evening Review* and you asked me to come and work for you, I really wasn't sure. I mean it was a different thing raising you and your sister but to start again with your offspring, well, I think I would have liked a new challenge at that stage of my life. But, with all due respect to you, you were in a bad way and I knew you were under a lot of pressure and I couldn't say no to you. It reminded me of the way you used to always get around me to have a treat after dinner even though you had acted up during the day and I swore you weren't getting any treats for your bold behaviour."

Ella smiles.

"Celeste reminds me a lot of you at that age, you know."

"Really?"

"She does. She's a bright girl but she's headstrong and she certainly won't make being her parent easy – but her spirit and tenacity will get her far, just like her mother."

"She really misses you."

"And I miss her too but it's about time I retired. I've been meaning to do it for a long time but then when you lost your job, the time felt right."

Ella has never been able to put an age on her. She guesses she was in her twenties when she came to work for her father back when Ella was four and Andrea was six, so she calculates that she must be somewhere in the region of between sixty and seventy years of age now. She looks good though – she maintains her trim figure by walking. When she worked for Ella she pushed the buggy up the steep hills of the headland every day, come hail, rain or shine.

"Ella, you have had a difficult few weeks but I didn't make my decision lightly. It was my time to go – you do understand that, don't you, dear?"

Ella nods but she doesn't.

"I know this is hard on you right now but it will get better, trust me. I've known you since you were four years old and I like to think that I've got to know you quite well over the years." She is smiling kindly. "I think you will look back on this and thank me. Just you wait and see. As I always say, everything happens for a reason."

"But there is no reason. My life is over!"

"Don't you think you are being a bit dramatic?"

"But it feels that way."

"Ella, my love, excuse me if I sound unkind now . . . yes, you did a stupid thing but you need to put everything into perspective – it's not the end of the world. So what? You lost your job but you have so many good things in your life. Your children are beautiful and healthy, thank goodness, and you have a lovely husband. Financially you have no worries either. I'm not criticising you but did you ever stop in all those years of striving to get to the top and just take the time to take stock and appreciate that? A lot of people would gladly trade places with you in the morning."

"No, but –"

"Well, then, when life throws an upheaval in your path you have to try to turn it around into an opportunity. At the moment you have the chance to spend some time with the girls, and there will be other jobs down the line, I'm sure of it."

"I think that there is something wrong with me."

"How do you mean?"

"That I'm not maternal or something. That it is genetic . . . I don't know . . . I feel like I'm going to mess everything up and that I'm going to turn out like my own mother . . . I'm so scared that history is going to repeat itself and that I'm going to let down my kids as well."

"No, you most certainly are not, because you won't let that happen! You are not your mother!" Mrs Frawley says sternly. "I don't like speaking ill of a person that I have never met but she made her choice and, frankly, as the person who had the pleasure of *trying* to step into her shoes and *trying* to raise you and Andrea into two young ladies, while your father earned a living, I think I am entitled to speak my mind. In my opinion she made a pretty poor choice in leaving her family for a man who by all accounts didn't treat her very well in the end and certainly not half as well as your father did. I'm not sure if it's my place to say that and I'm certainly not trying to take credit for how you've turned out, because you have a marvellous father, but I do allow myself a small bit of pride whenever I see you and Andrea and I can't help thinking of how much your mother missed out on."

Ella is stunned. This is the first time she has ever heard Mrs Frawley discuss her mother. She usually refuses to be drawn on the subject. As a teenager Ella went through a period of wanting to know more about why she had left them, where she was now and if she had ever been in contact since. She knew that the topic was off limits with her father. Her gentle, good-natured father had been so heart-broken and destroyed by her mother's desertion, he had never really got over it. So she used to annoy Mrs Frawley instead. She would think up elaborate ways of trying to extract more information from her and try to trick her into telling her things about the past by pretending her dad had told her something and hoping that Mrs Frawley would take the bait – but the woman to her credit never divulged.

Ella has two memories of her mother. The first is standing in a supermarket queue with her when she was wearing her royal-blue woollen coat. Even then she was aware that her mother had stood out from all the other women in the shop with their grey and black coats. She was like a painted character forced to live in a monochrome world. Another lady had come up to them and said "She looks just like you" and she remembers her mother had smiled down at her and squeezed her hand tightly. The other memory is sitting in their garden on a sweltering summer's day. It had to have been the heat wave of '76. She remembers picking blades of grass and

191

handing them to her mother who would tear them down the middle until they were split in two pieces before handing them back to her again. But she isn't sure if she can even rely on those memories. Can she trust them? Perhaps they were snatched images from photos she had seen and they had somehow bled together into a fuzzy muddle her mind.

Sometimes she scans the faces of women in the streets and wonders if they are her mother. She looks at middle-aged women with similar-shaped grey-green eyes like hers. Sometimes she stares at them so much that they give her a funny look in return and she is forced to look away quickly. It always seems strange to Ella that Andrea has no interest in learning where their mother is – she had closed that chapter of her life on the day she left them – but Ella has always felt it is a gaping hole in her life.

"Do you know where she is now?" Ella can't help herself from asking.

"I don't, Ella dear, but you should just leave it in the past now. There is no point in raking over old ground. Speaking of your dad, how is he?" She is obviously keen to change the subject.

"He's good. He has recently met a lady in the golf club and, although he never says as much, I think they might be more than just friends."

"Well, it would be nice indeed if he found a companion at his age. Your father is a good man, generous to a fault and so very kind."

"Yeah, I'm happy for him."

"Look, you will get through this and come out the other side of it because you are strong."

"Do you really think so?"

"Of course I do."

"You should go off home now, my dear – I'm sure Dan is getting worried about you."

Ella stands up. "Will you call up to see the girls soon?"

"I'd like that."

She walks Ella to the door.

Ella stands down off the step and turns back around. "Mrs Frawley?"

"Yes, dear?"

"Are you really proud of me – even with the shoplifting and everything?"

"Of course I am, Ella. Yes, you and I have had a few run-ins over the years and I still am quite upset by what has happened but I am so proud of you today. Very proud."

"Thanks, Mrs Frawley, and thank you for everything that you've done for me over the years. I probably didn't tell you enough how much I appreciated it but I really do."

"You're very welcome."

"Okay, well, I'd better get going. Goodbye."

"Goodbye, Ella."

Chapter 36

Rachel is sitting at the kitchen table at 9 St Dominic's Terrace.

"So did you get a chance to talk to him yet?"

"I can't do it."

"So you didn't tell him then?"

"That's what I'm after saying, amn't I?"

"Well, he needs to be told, Tina. I thought we both agreed that it was for the best?"

"I can't have that conversation with him. I just can't do it."

"That's okay, I understand it's hard, but we do need to tell him, Tina. Would it be any easier if I was to talk to him for you instead?"

She nods. "If that's the way it has to be, then yeah."

"Okay, well, if I stop by on Tuesday can you try to have him here for me?"

"I'll try my best."

"How did you get on with Libby the other day?"

"We had a good chat. Look, Tina, I really can't be talking to you about it. I have to try and remain impartial."

The other woman remains quiet.

"What's wrong, Tina?"

"It's not meant to be like this. Why should I have to make plans for someone else to raise my boy because I won't be here to do it?"

"It's shit." Rachel's hands fly towards her mouth as she realises what she has said out loud.

Tina looks up at her, open-mouthed.

"I'm sorry, I know I probably shouldn't say that but there is no other way of saying it. What you're going through right now – what you have to think about for Jack's future – it's shit. It's not fair. No parent should have to do that . . . I . . . eh . . . I just wanted to say that."

"That's life, isn't it?" Tina mumbles.

"Look, I should probably head on but I'll see you Tuesday. Look after yourself."

"Bye . . . oh, and Rachel?"

"Yes?"

"Thanks."

Rachel is driving out of St Dominic's Terrace and she feels exhausted. The conversation with Tina is weighing heavily on her mind. She sees so much wrong in this world from doing this job but then every once in a while she'll come across someone like Tina White who restores her faith in human nature again. The odds were stacked against Jack from the moment he was conceived but, because Tina was determined to sort herself out, she enrolled in a treatment programme and transformed her life for the sake of her unborn baby. Unfortunately Rachel doesn't always see people turn their lives around like this and that's what makes the situation with Tina and Jack so unbearably sad.

She stops when a football bounces across the grey concrete ripples of the road and a boy about Jack's age runs across the road after it. She waits for him to fish it out from underneath a car before driving on again. She comes up to traffic lights and while she is stopped she reaches back with her left hand to rub the knots out of her shoulder. Dusk is falling; the long darkness of winter finally seems to be lifting. Finally. As she looks around the street she sees John-Paul standing outside

195

the pub. There are iron bars covering the windows and letters are missing from the sign over the door. He is standing chatting to a few other men. He draws hard on a cigarette so his whole face is pinched up into hundreds of tiny lines and then he exhales mini smoke circles. He doesn't see her and she watches him for a few moments until the lights turn green.

She goes home and, instead of making dinner, she pours herself a glass of red. She fills up the glass more than she should, until it is just slightly below the lip. She picks up the phone and rings Shirley but gets her singsong message: *'Hi, this is Shirley. If I don't answer, it's probably because I'm knee-deep in some baby poo.'* Then she gives a little laugh. *'Please leave a message and I'll call you back.'*

She hangs up without leaving a message. It's lashing down outside, the rain is running down her windows. She stares in a trance at the drips running to join other drips to form small rivers, joining bigger ones to stream down the window. She rings her mother next. She feels an acute longing to be with her parents, the like of which she hasn't felt since she first moved to Dublin and had spent months feeling homesick. She would give anything to be sitting in their kitchen right now, beside the Aga with its neatly folded piles of clothes on top that her mother would have left there to 'air'. She wants to be back at home, she wants to be five years old again where none of the trappings and responsibilities of adulthood can get her. The negative equity, the broken heart, the work pressures – they are non-existent when you are five. To be five years old again and your only worry is whether you have enough money to buy apple drops *and* a bar of chocolate.

She tells her she's coming home at the weekend. She's made up her mind to go up home and tell them about the break-up. The thought of looking at their disappointed and concerned faces after she tells them is awful though. They will probably say something like 'We just want you to be happy, love' and that will be all it would take for her to fall to pieces. That is the problem – their kindness will be the very worst bit.

"Is Marcus coming too, love?" her mother asks.

"No, not this time, Mam."

She knows her mother, as a devout Catholic, was never too keen on Marcus. She was from a different era where a separated man, let alone a divorced one, was a tainted man. Every time Rachel went home her mother would try to initiate a conversation with her about where the relationship was going but Rachel, not wanting to confront what she knew her mother was thinking, would swiftly change the subject. She hadn't wanted to tell her about Marcus's decision not to have any more children – she felt it would further cement the negative image her mother had of him, so she had never discussed their problems with her.

They talk about Rachel's job, her washing line which was blown over in the high winds the night before, Rachel's younger sister Imogen who is due to give birth to her first child imminently. The fact that her dad's car had passed its MOT.

Rachel doesn't tell her about Marcus. She looks out at the lights coming from the other apartment blocks beside her and wonders if there is anyone else as lonely as she is behind their yellow brickwork walls.

Chapter 37

Ella comes in the door of Haymarket Books with a screaming Maisie in her arms. She has a woolly hat pulled down over her unruly hair and she's wearing thick black army boots and her parka jacket. Conor tries not to look too shocked by her appearance but she has completely let herself go over the last few weeks. She was always so groomed. He knows it was because she had hair and make-up people at the station every day but this is another level. There is no chance of her being recognised like this, that's for sure.

She is jigging Maisie up and down on her hip, trying to soothe her, and he can tell that she is stressed.

"She's been crying the whole car journey over here."

"Hey, calm down, give her here to me." He takes her and unzips her from her snowsuit. "What is it, little Maisie, huh?" Her small face is red and wet. She is catching her breath between tears. "Come on now, you're okay."

"I've fed her, I've changed her, I've cuddled her but she still screams!"

"Well, maybe she's in pain somewhere."

He puts Maisie between his knees and tilts her chest against the inside of his thigh and rubs her back in firm, circular motions. She starts to calm down, soothed by the repetitious movement of his palm.

"There, there, little one, it's all right."

"Where did you learn that?"

"I saw Leni doing it before with her niece."

"She would have been such a good mother." She sighs and flops down on a chair beside him. "She was so good with kids."

"She was."

Suddenly Maisie gives a huge burp, releasing some trapped wind.

"There we go – feeling better?" He looks at the little face whose lids are drooping closed in tiredness.

"You'll have Supernanny asking you for tips next. I'm just so rubbish at the whole thing – I'm only realising now how much Mrs Frawley did for me all those years. She practically raised my children and I never thanked her properly for it. I mean, I gave her a generous pay check every week and lovely presents for her birthday or Christmas – in fact, I showered her with gifts, but I never truly appreciated how much she did for us – I never said a proper thank-you, you know?"

"There's no way she'll come back to work for you?"

She shakes her head. "I went to visit her recently. She said she had been meaning to retire for a while anyway but that me losing my job had made her mind up for her. She said it would be good for me to spend some time with the kids without her being there too but I'll never find anyone like Mrs Frawley again – she was like a grandmother to the kids. Celeste and Dot miss her terribly. I think that's why Celeste is so angry with me – because it's all my fault that Mrs Frawley doesn't mind them any more."

"Are things any better with Dan?"

She shakes her head. "I've tried talking to him but he just doesn't get it. He just keeps saying that it's all my own fault – which I know it is. When the summons came he just shrugged his shoulders and said, 'Well, you knew it was going to come at some stage'. Whenever I tell him that I'm finding things hard, he just says that I got myself into this mess in the first place. But I've never felt like this before – I go to bed and I can't sleep – I spend the whole night just staring up at the ceiling or fretting that Maisie will stop breathing and then during the day all I want to do is climb back into my bed to sleep until the day is over. I spend every day feeling afraid of what's coming. I feel sick in the pit of my stomach every time she cries. I just can't seem to do anything right. Sometimes it feels as though this whole thing is happening to somebody else and I'm just going through the motions of day-to-day life."

"You need to speak to someone."

"What do you mean?"

"Maybe have a word with your doctor."

"Maybe," she sighs. "But I can't face it. I just feel so tired and weary. Like everything, even coming here to see you was such a huge effort."

"I'm worried about you – you haven't been yourself at all lately. I mean, first the shoplifting and I know losing your job has been hard on you, but I'm really starting to worry about you, Ella."

"Don't worry, I'm not about to jump off Howth Head . . . yet."

"That's not even funny, Ella."

"Sorry." She is contrite. "So how are you doing . . . with everything?" She's clearly trying to change the subject.

"In some ways it feels like the longest few months of my life but in another way it still feels as raw as yesterday. He or she would have been a month old now."

"Conor, I –" She starts feeding the loose chain of her watch around her wrist, feeling awkward at the mention of the baby. She feels guilty because she has her baby and he doesn't have his. She has Maisie and she still isn't able to be a proper mother to her. Conor would have made a good father. He would have been a natural, glad to get stuck in and help Leni out.

"Look, Conor, I'm sorry – I'm sure it must be hard to watch me with her and think that he or she would be doing all the things now that Maisie is doing."

"I don't want you to feel bad, Ella – you're the only person I can talk to about it. I need to be able to talk about it, you know. I've been robbed of everything. The two-year-old banging his or her head off the wall, the five-year-old nervously entering their classroom for the first time. I've missed all of that."

"I know you have. It's not one bit fair."

Chapter 38

Dublin 2011

He comes up to the gate and watches as one by one her students file out the door for the last time. She bends down to hug each child in turn as they go past her. Their parents are giving her cards, gifts and flowers. She chats easily with them. She has grown close to them over the last year of teaching their children. He waits until she has waved them all goodbye before coming over.

"Are you okay?"

"I will miss them a lot."

"You always say that."

"But it's true – I always do. I get to know them and love them over a year and then they grow up and leave me."

She is pouting, her bottom lip turned out. He has always loved her lips – the feel of the downward cleft of her bottom lip against his, the full sensation of them against his own.

He follows her back into the classroom and sits down on a chair many sizes too small for him. She starts to laugh. "You look like the Big Friendly Giant in that – here, have mine, I'll take that one."

It is a colourful room full of orderly wooden toys that stack together and slot into one another neatly. Six neat tables and matching small chairs. Children's artwork hangs around

*the walls. She opened this Montessori school two years after
she left her job in finance to retrain as a Montessori teacher.
She has always loved children. He has seen her when they are
eating a feast of lunch in the garden of her parents' house.
Leni would prefer to sit at the children's picnic table with her
many nieces and nephews instead of sitting with the adults.
She is one of those people who seem equally at ease with
children as they are with grown-ups.*

*"Well, how about I treat you to lunch? The stock has
started to arrive. Can you believe, I'll be in my own bookshop
– my very own bookshop, smelling all papery and inky? What
if mine doesn't have that smell or what if it smells all wrong?
What if it still smells of the wooden sawdust or the plastic
wrapping from the books?"*

*"You worry too much, Conor – you need to take a deep
breath. You are trusting your dreams so it is natural to be
nervous. It will all be okay. Maybe you should light a lantern
too!"*

*They are going, as they always do, on the last day of the
Montessori term to light a paper lantern to wish the children
happy and bright futures and send it out over the sea. It's a
tradition Leni has had since her first class graduated.*

*"Ah, c'mon, Leni, you know I always feel stupid doing
those things."*

*"It's good for you. It forces you to recognise what is
worrying you and set it free." She comes over and messes his
hair. "Come on, Mr Sceptical – even if you don't believe in it,
it can't do you any harm."*

"I suppose not," he grumbles.

Chapter 39

The phone is ringing but it's in her dream. It is loud and obnoxious and calls her away from the deep recesses of sleep. Eventually she realises that it is her phone on the table beside her bed. She scrambles a hand across the top of it and hits answer.

She hears his voice. First comes its soothing tone, and then a few moments later, the familiar heavy sadness sets in. "Rach, it's me."

"Marcus?" She sits up straight in the bed.

"I'm sitting here in a hotel room in Singapore, I've just got into my hotel room after seventeen hours of travelling, the kitchen is closed and I've missed the cut-off time for room service. I'm tired, hungry and emotional and I'm just fed up. I'm fed up with it all. I'm missing you, Rachel, so badly. I want to be with you always, I want so badly for us to be together."

"But, Marcus, you know why we can't be! If you tell me you've changed your mind then I'm yours, I'm there – you know that!" Her tone is both weary and frustrated.

"I know, Rach," his voice breaks. "I know, I wish I could – sometimes I let my heart go and say *'Just do it – you want her, you love her – do what it takes to have her in your arms*

204

every day' but then my head jumps in and tells me why I can't. I'm sorry, I shouldn't even be calling you."

"Marcus, we've been through this, it's killing me. I want this no more than you do but it's not my decision. I wish more than anything we could be together as well but not having children is a deal-breaker for me, you know that." There is unmistakable anger in her voice but she can't help it. This isn't her choice. She feels tears of sadness fall down her face. Hearing his voice like that, vulnerable and needy, has upset her but he knows why she had to break up with him. He hadn't left her with any other choice.

"I know – you're right – I do know that and it's not fair that I'm ringing you now. I'm being a selfish pratt and I'm thinking of myself first. I'm sorry, I shouldn't have called you. I'm no good for you. You need to find somebody else, somebody who can give you the happiness that you deserve. I love you, look after yourself, Rach."

The next day Rachel is seated in the restaurant where she has arranged to meet Shirley for lunch. She comes in a few minutes after her, pushing Tiernan in his buggy. She is dressed in her Tod's loafers, camel trousers cut-off at the ankle, pale-blue shirt and a navy blazer. It is the daytime uniform of so many of the young mothers around here.

She can't believe how much Tiernan has grown. She takes him up in her arms and lets him nestle back against her while they read the menu. She breathes him in. He is warm and soft and smells of apricot oil.

"I can't believe how big he's after getting."

"He is, isn't he?" Shirley beams.

"So how was your breastfeeding club? I can't believe they have clubs for that sort of thing."

"Yeah, I've replaced nightclubs with breastfeeding clubs."

"I presume it's not quite strobe lights, smoke machines and drum 'n' bass while women sit around breastfeeding?"

"No, not quite. It's just a chance for new mothers to chat and get advice on the questions that we have – it's really good actually. I've met lots of new friends who understand what it's like – you know, the sleep deprivation, the feeding worries and all of that."

Sometimes when Shirley mentions her other new-mum friends, Rachel feels a bolt of jealousy flood through her – she can't help it. Sometimes she feels like she is being left behind. Rachel knows that she and Shirley will move on and meet new friends at different stages of their lives but she worries that since she had Tiernan the differences between them are too great and that their friendship will drift away and come to its natural end.

"Oh God, listen to me – I'm being insensitive, aren't I?"

"No, you're not – not at all. I'm glad for you – I've never seen you look happier."

"Thanks, Rachel. Tiernan is literally the best thing to ever happen to me."

"Well, he is pretty gorgeous." Rachel has never seen her friend so happy. It makes her feel the heartache of her and Marcus's situation even more.

"So how've you been doing?" Shirley says, closing the menu and putting it down on the table.

"I'm okay." She doesn't tell her about last night's phone call. She knows it will just anger Shirley.

"Really?"

"So have you, ladies, decided what you would like to order?" A white-aproned waiter comes over with a pen in one hand and his notebook flipped open in the other.

"Hmmmh . . . I think I'm going to go for the calamari – I would choose the chilli beef salad but I'm afraid Tiernan won't like the way it makes my milk taste . . . so, yeah, I'll go for the calamari, please."

"And you?" He turns to Rachel.

"I think I'll have the goat's cheese tartlet, please."

"Great, thanks, ladies." He takes their menus from them and goes off to another table.

Tiernan is batting his little arms and smiling up at Rachel. She cuddles him against her. "He is just precious. I just feel so sad right now."

"I'm so sorry you feel like that – but you have me. I know I have Tiernan now and we don't get to see each other like we used to but I miss you too."

"But you have all your new Earth Mother buddies."

"Come on, Rachel, you're my best friend. Don't get me wrong – those girls are great but sometimes I want to talk about something other than babies, you know. I did have a life before this little man came along and I'm still the same person that I was then." She reaches across the table for Rachel's hand. "I'll always have time for you, you know that, don't you?"

"I know."

That weekend Rachel drives home to Antrim. She tells her mam and dad everything about her and Marcus. They just listen and only interrupt to fill her mug with more tea. They don't say things like they never liked him anyway or we told you it would all end in tears. When she pulls back the duvet of her childhood bed that night where her mam had left in a hot water bottle to warm up the sheets for her, she feels surprisingly all right. She wishes she had confided in them earlier. It is good to have it all out in the open and not have the burden of trying to put on a brave face on their relationship. To simply be here, embraced in the welcoming arms of her home is exactly what she needs right now.

Chapter 40

"So this is where you are!" John-Paul's voice roars into the shop. "Your ma's been on the phone roaring at me again to know if you're with me – I had to leave my pint after me and everything to go looking for you again. What are you playin' at, Jack, running off all the time?"

"Ma forgot to pick me up from school!" he protests.

"Well, you know where the house is! You could have gone home! Now your ma is up the walls because she thinks something has happened to you. You know what your ma is like when she starts banging on, Jack. She's chewing me ear the whole time. I don't need the hassle! I can't even have a quiet pint any more without your ma ringing me up – like it's all my fault. I thought that Rachel one told you that you weren't to come back here again?"

He turns then to Conor.

"I'm starting to think you're bribing him in the door – what do you use? Smarties, is it? What is it with you hanging out with young fellas?"

"Now hang on there a minute – I don't know what you're getting at but I don't ask Jack to come here – he comes of his own accord." Conor is starting to get nervous. There is look about Jack's dad that warns he could just snap at any minute.

"I'm watching you – don't you think that I don't know what you're at!"

His finger is millimetres from Conor's face. Conor can smell the alcohol on his breath – he moves backwards.

John-Paul stands and stares at Conor for a minute, his eyes narrowed.

"Come on, Jack – outta here. Now!" He grabs his shoulder roughly and pushes him towards the door.

"I'm coming, Da."

Conor watches them go out the door. He goes out and stands on the doorstep and watches them walking up the street. Jack trails behind John-Paul. His shoulders are sunken and he's dragging his feet along the pavement. The boy turns around. Conor forces a smile on his face but Jack doesn't smile back at him.

Rachel is just coming out Tina's gate when she sees John-Paul coming up the path towards her. Jack storms past her and goes straight into the house without a word.

"Rachel – hang on there a minute, love – I want to talk to you about something."

She waits for him to come up beside her on the path.

"What is it, John-Paul? I'm already running late for my next appointment."

"Tina told me you found Jack hanging out in the bookshop down on Haymarket Street the other day. I just wanted to tell you that I've found him in there a few times meself and I don't trust that fella. There's something weird about him hanging around with a young boy like that and a few of the young fellas around here are saying he's a pervert. Fellas like that need to have their bits chopped off, the dirty scumbag!" His purple-rimmed eyes are ablaze.

"Right, okay. Thanks for letting me know, John-Paul." She opens the car and sits into it. She goes to pull the door shut but John-Paul is still holding onto it. He rests his folded arms on the frame.

"There's too many of those sorts around, y'know, always looking out for young fellas to be taking advantage of. You should keep an eye on him, y'know?"

"All right, I'll look into it."

"Okay, I'm just heading in to see Jack for a while."

Rachel knows he is trying to make a point. "Well, that's good, I'm glad to hear it. Look, I'd better go. See you, John-Paul."

The next day at the usual time Conor hears the usual screech of a bike outside his shop. When he goes over to the window to look, he sees it is Jack in his grey tracksuit bottoms that are too short for him. He opens the door.

"Hiya, Jack. You're going to have to get those brakes fixed – that thing is lethal! Was everything all right when you went home yesterday?"

"Oh yeah, Ma didn't wake up – that's why she forgot to pick me up."

"I see. Is she okay, your mother?"

"Yeah, why?"

"Oh, I was just wondering."

"I'm sorry Da wasn't very nice to you yesterday. Sometimes he gets mad and shouts a lot. When he lived with us, Ma used to tell him to get out of the house whenever he'd start his roaring and carrying on. That's why he doesn't live with us any more because Ma was sick of telling him to be quiet so one night she told him to get out of the house and now every day she says 'Isn't the peace and quiet grand, Jack?' and she's right because me and Ma are a good team. When she's resting in bed I make her a cup of tea and put it on her locker and she says 'Jack, you're a darlin', an absolute darlin' and then she gets up and sometimes we do tidying up or else sometimes she says 'I'm too tired – let's take a day off from the cleaning today, love'. I'm her big strong boy. I mind her when she's tired or sad. I make her tea when she's in bed in the mornings and I help carry in the briquettes and stack them in the fireplace but she won't let me light them yet. She says it's too dangerous but maybe when I'm nine she'll let me."

"Sounds like you're the man of the house, Jack. Your ma is a lucky lady to have a fella like you taking care of her."

He smiles and his little cheeks start to pinken. Conor notices his chest is plumped out a little.

"Well, I better go, Ma will be looking for me."

"All right, Jack, I'll see you soon, I suppose."

Just as Jack is going out the door the bell tinkles and a glamorous woman with a lot of dark, glossy waves billowing around her shoulders, is standing in the shop. She is wearing a skirt suit and she has a string of pearls around her neck.

"What are you doing here?" Jack says, blushing furiously.

"Eh . . . can I help you there at all?" Conor asks, looking from one to the other.

"I was just looking for Jack." She turns to him. "You were meant to be in the house today, wee man – why did you run off like that?"

"How did you find me here?" he says stubbornly.

"Well, I was on my way home but I saw your bike outside so I said I'd see if you were in here."

"Well, you shoulda kept on driving!"

"Jack!" Conor says and then turns to the woman. "Sorry but do you mind me asking who are you?"

"I'm Rachel, Rachel McLoughlin," She offers him a slender manicured hand. "I'm a social worker."

So this is the famous Rachel. "I'm Conor Fahy – Jack has mentioned you before."

"Oh?"

"No, he just said you sometimes call to see him."

"I see." She turns to Jack. "I need to talk to you, wee man." She bends down to his level. "What do you say we go back home and have a chat, huh?"

"I don't want to!"

"Well, maybe we could ask your mum to give you something nice when we get back there, how about that?"

"I'm not a baby – that's not going to make me go."

"Ach, wee man, I know you're not a baby," she cajoles.

"And I don't like you calling me 'wee man' either!"

"Okay, I promise not to call you 'wee man' again but I really do need to talk to you, Jack."

"Jack, maybe you should head on home with Rachel. You can call back tomorrow, yeah?"

"It's not fair – why won't you just leave me and Ma alone!" He storms out of the shop.

"Thanks," she mumbles. "I'd better go, while I have him." She follows him out the door, trying to keep up with him in her heels. "I'll meet you back at the house, Jack!" She shouts after him as he gets up on his bike and cycles off down Haymarket Street. She gets back into her car to follow him.

When Rachel arrives back at the house, there is no sign of Jack. She waits in the kitchen until he finally comes through the door.

"You took your time. You must have done the Tour de France on the way back and all," she says jokily.

"I told you, I don't want to talk to you!"

Tina is sitting at the kitchen table with her head in her hands. "Where did you go to, Jack? I told you Rachel was coming to talk to you today. You have to stop running off on me like that."

"He was in the bookshop – you know, the wee one up on Haymarket Street," Rachel says.

"Jack? In a bookshop?" She turns to Jack. "What were you doing in there?"

"I like going there. Conor is my friend."

"Who the hell is Conor?"

"He seems to be the owner," Rachel says.

"How often are you going there?"

"I go most days after I come home from school."

"Well, this is the first I knew of it! I thought you were out playing with your friends!" Tina goes to get up from the table but the pain slices through her so she stays where she is. "What are you doing there?"

"Conor lets me read his books and help out in the shop."

"So let me get this straight – you're hanging out in a bookshop every day with a man and I don't even know? What are you playing at, Jack?"

"At least Conor gives me sandwiches and lets me read his books. You're always asleep or too tired to play with me!" His little face is red with rage and he looks close to tears.

"Okay, calm down, everyone," Rachel says, stepping in to diffuse the situation. "Tina, you look tired – why don't you go and have a lie-down for a little while, while I have a chat with Jack, okay?"

Tina does as she is told and gingerly gets up from the table and goes out the door. They hear her footprints, laboured and slow, as she climbs the stairs and then finally a door closes.

The time has come to tell Jack. Rachel has been thinking about it all week, worrying how he is going to react and the best way to tell him. There is no 'best way', she has decided.

She takes a deep breath. "Jack, I know you don't want to talk to me but it's important."

"Now you've got Ma all mad with me."

"She's not mad really, Jack – you worried her, that's all. You need to tell her where you're going from now on, deal?"

"I guess so."

"Look, Jack, there is something I want to talk to you about. Something important."

He is kicking the backs of his heels against the legs of the chair. He won't meet her eyes.

"Jack, pet, you do know that your ma is very sick, don't you?"

His feet stop swinging and he goes very still. He nods

slowly and then starts to speak almost in a whisper. "Ma doesn't know I hear her but sometimes I do hear her getting sick in the toilet because it's beside my bedroom and Ma says the walls are made from paper."

"Your ma has cancer, Jack. Do you know what that is?"

He starts to talk. "Kinda – me granda had it and it's like having lots and lots of bad bugs inside your body and you need lots of medicine to fight them but the medicine makes you very sick and tired."

"That's the best way I've ever heard it described, Jack. You could teach the doctors a thing or two, huh?"

He smiles his gappy smile at her.

"With your ma, Jack, the doctors have given her lots of medicine which is why you've seen her being sick and tired but it hasn't worked. The medicine hasn't made her better. Do you understand, Jack?"

"Can't they just give her a new one? One time when I had a cough and Dr Maguire gave me medicine and it didn't work so Ma had to bring me back again to get a different one and the new one worked."

She nods. "It's kind of the same except the doctors have no more medicine for your ma, Jack." She takes a deep breath. "It's very hard for me to tell you this, Jack, but the doctors don't think your ma is ever going to get better."

Silence.

"Your ma is dying, Jack. I'm so sorry." She reaches out to hold his hand but he pulls it away from her. "Do you understand what that means, wee man?"

She tries to read his face but it remains expressionless.

All he can hear is a loud buzzing noise inside his ears like there are a million bees buzzing around in there, swarming around him and he can't get away from them. They are chasing him around and around in circles. He feels very hot and there are black and yellow stripes everywhere. They are on the wall, on the floor; everywhere he looks they are there in front him. They are on Rachel's face and she looks like the biggest bee of all.

"Jack, Jack – are you okay? You're gone very pale. Jack?" She is trying to get his attention but he is just staring into space. "Jack?" She jumps up and grabs a tea towel from where it hangs beside the sink. She runs it under cold water, squeezes it and holds it up against his forehead, which is clammy with sweat. "Are you feeling okay, pet?"

"I want you to go now."

"Jack, love, I know this is hard for you and it's a lot for you to take in but I'm going to be right here with you – I'll help you through it as best I can, wee man –"

"I told you I don't like it when you call me that."

"I'm sorry Jack – I –"

"Please go now." His voice is small. The fight has left him.

"Okay, Jack, if you want me to go, I'll go. I just want to go up and tell your ma first though so she knows I'm gone. She has my number – if you ever want to talk about things some more give me a call and I'll come right over, okay? And, Jack, I really am so, so, sorry."

Rachel pulls out onto the road and she can feel the weight of tears building behind her eyes. *Do not cry. Don't you dare cry.* She isn't concentrating on where she is going, she is just driving on autopilot around the city-centre streets because she can't think straight. She drives down a one-way street the wrong way and only realises when another driver flashes his lights at her. She pulls over and finally gives in to tears. They stream down her cheeks and she doesn't even attempt to wipe them away.

"Stop being so stupid!" she tells herself, banging her palm against the steering wheel. "This is your job – you have to toughen up." But that was one of the hardest things that she has ever had to do. It had been awful seeing Jack like that. Like his entire world had just ended, which in fairness it had.

She wonders yet again if she is mad doing this job? There

were easier ways to make a living – she could get a job working in an office, maybe doing something with spreadsheets, data entry or answering phones. Every day as a social worker was a battle where you were often facing the most dysfunctional and saddest situations in society and sometimes it was overwhelming to think of how little one person could do. She'd had to accept a long time ago that she couldn't change the world. They had been taught in college that this was their job and just like any job. You have to leave your work behind you at the end of the day . . . but on a day like today it was very hard to do that.

She would ring Tina tonight to see how Jack was doing. The next few weeks were going to be very tough on him.

Chapter 41

Jack runs out of the kitchen, runs out the gate of 9 St Dominic's Terrace and keeps on running – past the funeral parlour with its net curtains, past the butcher's, past the street stalls with boxes of Daz washing powder stacked high. The swarm of bees are chasing him down the street, round the corner past the chemist's, the butcher's and Rafferty's. He can't lose them. They are so loud, like a vortex of yellow and black swirling through his head. He keeps going until he is outside Conor's bookshop on Haymarket Street. His whole body is trembling when he comes in through the door.

"What is it, Jack, what's happened to you? Here, sit down – you look like you're about to collapse." Conor sits Jack on to the chair and bends down on his hunkers in front of him. "What is it, Jack?"

"Ma is going to die. Rachel told me."

"What do you mean, Jack?"

"Rachel told me that Ma is very sick and that she's going to die soon because she has bad bugs inside in her body and the doctors have no more medicine left for her. I asked Ma if Rachel was lying because I don't like her, but Ma said that it's true and she's very sick and that's why she is in bed all the time and forgetting to pick me up from school and make my dinner."

"Oh Jack, I'm so sorry, mate." He puts his arms around him and Jack puts his forehead against his neck and he can feel the wetness of his tears. Suddenly Jack's story all clicks into place.

"I don't want Ma to die – who's going to look after me?"

"Hey, you've got your da –"

"But I don't want to live with him. He doesn't know anything the way Ma does. His dinners are gross – he lets the beans touch off the sausages. And he's always getting mad."

"Look, Jack, I don't know what to say but I'm sure Rachel and your ma have a plan."

"I'm so scared! I love Ma – she's the best ma in the world. I don't want her to die."

"It's going to be okay, Jack, it's all going to be okay."

And Conor feels awful for lying to him. People said the same thing to him after Leni died but things are still awful. Just like he finds now, they just didn't know what else to say.

Ella stares around the stone walls of her living room. The sea is crashing wildly outside. The winds have been so high for the last few days and she watches the spray from the waves as it rushes up into the air, clashes off the windows in a hiss before running down her circular windows. Everyone else is in bed – Dan and the children are all tucked up behind the bedroom walls but she is not. She wishes like them she could be cocooned in the safety of sleep but it doesn't come so easily to her these days. Most nights she lies awake twisting and turning and getting in and out of bed to check on Maisie until the early hours before eventually falling asleep after six but then her alarm goes an hour later because it's time to do the school run. And this is how her life has been, surviving on the bare skeleton of sleep that her body allows her to have and then living like an exhausted wreck all day.

She decides to text Conor. She punches out "**Are you awake by any chance?**"

Her phone rings almost instantly.

"Can't sleep either, huh?" his voice says on the other end.

"I keep thinking that the house is going to blow out into the sea."

"Well, I reckon, considering the fact that it's survived two-hundred-odd years clinging onto the shoreline, you might just be okay. Here, I have one for you – what is the name given to the cold and dry wind in southern France that blows down from the north along the Rhône towards the Mediterranean Sea?"

"The Mistral. Come on, you'll have to do better than that – you're losing your edge – even Celeste would have got that one!"

"Really, too easy? I thought it was a good one."

"Better luck next time. So what has you awake?"

"If I said *everything* would you accuse me of being melodramatic?"

"Not at all, go right ahead," she says.

"Okay, well then, *everything*."

"Sounds pretty much the same as me."

"I don't think I told you but there's this boy who comes into the shop – Jack is his name – anyway he helps take my mind off things."

"A boy? Who comes into your shop?"

"He's a local kid – he just seems to have taken a shine to my shop for some reason and stops by after school every day."

"So you've got this kid who comes in to hang out with you in your shop? That just sounds weird."

"No, honestly, he's great – he eats a sandwich, reads a few pages of a book and goes home for his tea."

"Jesus, you're like a home for waifs and strays."

"Hardly. Well, anyway, it turns out that his mother is dying of cancer – she hasn't got long left either."

"Oh no, that's awful. What age is he?"

"He's just turned eight."

"Well, that is fucking shit – excuse my language – but it is. The poor kid."

"I can't stop thinking about it – I know the whole thing is strange – this random child just turns up in my shop day after day but I've got to know him and he's a good kid. His dad seems to be shady enough so I'm not sure what's going to happen to him now . . ."

"God, that's terrible. It really makes you think, doesn't it?"

They are silent for a while, and then Conor says, "So how've you been?"

"Okay, just trying to get on with things – take each day as it comes."

"Are people still giving you a hard time?"

"Yeah, I thought it would have all died down by now but Radio 1 did a whole show on shoplifting today and of course rolled my case out. I listened to the whole thing and people who don't know me and have never met me rang in to say what a horrible person I was and that they were glad they no longer had to look at my face on their screens every night. Everyone seems to have an opinion on me."

"You should have just turned it off."

"I know," she sighs. "I guess I'm a sucker for torturing myself. Then in the paper today there was a report about the increase in crime this year and they used my photo beside it. They just keep turning the screw. I think I have to face the fact that this is never going to leave me – I'm stuck with this forever. I'm now the poster girl for theft – if you've got a story about shoplifting, stick a photo of Ella Wilde in beside it."

"God, they're really getting mileage out of it. It's going to be rough for a while – you were the presenter of *The Evening Review*, for God's sake – you broke stories of politicians and high-profile people who had been caught drink driving. I think that's why they're being so vicious now – because you were the last person they would have expected to do something like that." He pauses for a minute. "So how's Celeste getting on in school? Is it any better for her?"

"She's still getting the cold shoulder. She hasn't been invited on any play dates or birthday parties since it happened. I think she's embarrassed. She won't talk to me about it. I tried to talk to her teacher but she didn't help at all – she more or less told me that I'm overreacting – I felt she wasn't willing to try and help the situation."

"Poor kid."

"I know and the worst thing is that it's all my fault."

Chapter 42

"What colour is for sad?"

"How do you mean?"

"Rachel keeps trying to talk to me about Ma being sick and all, but I don't want to talk. She wants me to draw a picture of my feelings and my family. She says I can put them in different colours like blue could be sad and red could be happy but I hate the colour red, so she said blue could be happy then and orange could be sad so I asked her what colour being afraid was and she said maybe purple and I said that that's a girl colour so she said what about brown but I don't like brown either so she said never mind, we could try it again another day."

"I'm not really sure, to be honest, which colour is for sad. I think it can be whatever colour you want it to be."

"Ma said my Auntie Libby is coming to live with us for a while."

"And do you like her?"

"Yeah, she's nice, she's always making cakes. Ma calls her Delia Smith when she bakes but I don't know who that is. She has three boys but they're not coming because they have to go to school and they live far away in the country in a big huge house and they even have cows in their garden! And our house only has three bedrooms so they wouldn't all fit unless Ma bought bunk beds for us all. That would be cool. I'd have to have the top one because it's my bedroom."

"Obviously."

"What happens when we die, Conor – where do we go to?"

Conor stops what he is doing and looks up at Jack.

"How come you want to know?"

"I want to know where Ma is going to be."

"Well, it's a big question. No-one knows for sure but some people think we go to heaven."

"Is heaven in the sky?"

"Well, some people think it is but some people believe that heaven is everywhere – that it is all around us."

"What, like the dead people are walking beside us? That's weird!"

"Kind of. You might not be able to see a person but they'll always be there."

"But how do you know they are?"

"Well, it's hard to explain. I guess you just have to believe that they are."

Jack is staring at him sceptically.

"Okay, let me show you what I mean," says Conor. "Come out the back with me for a minute."

Jack follows him behind the till and through the doorway leading out to the back. They walk past the exposed concrete block work and a network of copper-and-white plastic pipes that the builders had promised him they would paint but they never did. They walk past the small sink and the shelf with his paperwork files, into the stockroom.

"What are we doing in here?" Jack says, staring around at the wooden shelves full of cardboard boxes of books.

"I want to show you something. Okay. So you can see me now, can't you?"

"Uh-huh."

He walks over and trips the light switch so the stockroom is instantly cloaked in darkness.

"Okay, can you see me now?"

"No."

"But you know that I'm still here, don't you?"

"Yeah."

"Well, I think that's what it's like when we die – we can't see the person or even talk to them but we know that they're still there with us."

Jack starts laughing. "I'm a zombie." He puts his two arms out to try and feel where Conor is. "I'm going to get you!" He bumps into a cardboard box and starts to laugh.

Suddenly there is a female voice, calling Jack's name. "Jack? Jack? Are you in here?"

"Oh no, it's Rachel," Jack says quickly.

Conor fumbles along the rough concrete wall in the darkness for the light switch but he can't seem to find it. Finally his fingers come upon it and he flicks the switch to see Rachel standing at the stockroom door with her arms folded.

"What's going on in here?" She is looking at him warily.

"Sorry, I was just trying to show Jack something –"

"But you were in complete darkness – you couldn't possibly show him anything in the dark!"

"I know but I was trying to show him –"

"What? What were you trying to show him?"

He realises what she is thinking. "God no, I wasn't – no way – I wasn't doing anything like that – I would never do that – this isn't what it looks like -"

"And what does it look like?" Rachel asks.

Shit. "Well . . . em . . . Jack told me about his mother and I was just trying to show him what happens, y'know, when people . . ." he lowers his voice to a whisper, "die."

"I really don't think that that is any of your business. I'm not sure what is going on here but come on, Jack, we have to go. Your ma is looking for you."

Outside the shop, Rachel turns to Jack.

"You're not to go back there, Jack, do you understand?"

"I don't have to do what you tell me – you're not me ma!"

"I know that but I'm asking you not to go there and I know your ma will be in agreement with me."

"Why can't I?" he protests. "I like Conor and I like reading his books."

"You just can't, okay? It's not appropriate for an eight-year-old boy to be hanging around with a grown man."

"Why?"

"Look, Jack pet, you just have to take my word for it. I don't want to see you back there again – it's for your own good."

"I hate you! Ever since you came to our house things have been bad. It's all your fault!"

"I know you are going through a difficult time right now, Jack, and you might not see it like this, but my job is to try to help you."

"No, it's not! You just ruin everything!" he screams at her and storms off ahead of her.

Rachel is running in her heels trying to keep up with his pace but, every time she gets near him, he takes off again. "Slow down, Jack." She is just about level with him and he sprints off ahead of her again. "Jack, come back here! Jack!" She keeps going as fast as she can in her heels.

"Where were you?" Tina asks when Jack comes through the door. "You've a face on you that would turn milk sour. Don't tell me you were down in that bookshop again?"

"Uh-huh," says Rachel breathlessly as she comes in the door behind him. "You were right – that's where I found him."

"What has you going into that place, Jack?"

"I told him not to go back there," Rachel says. "I'm not sure I trust that man very much."

"Conor is my friend – he's the only one who understands. I hate you!" he says, staring Rachel straight in the eye.

Jack goes up the stairs to his room.

"I don't like Jack going down to that place – God only knows what that fella's up to," Tina says when they are on their own.

"I would have to agree with you, Tina, I don't think it's appropriate. I'm going to check with the Guards to see if they've ever come across him before. I had a word with Jack anyway so hopefully that will be the end of the matter. So how's he been doing this week?"

"As you can see yourself, he's up and down. He was very upset after."

"Did you try and talk to him about who he would like to live with afterwards?"

"No, I didn't. Not yet, he's not in the right place yet."

"Okay, well, it's probably best to do it soon, yeah? It's very important that we have Jack's point of view taken into consideration as well."

"I know," she sighs. "I know."

Chapter 43

Switching on the computer, Conor looks around, running his eyes over his dark-wood shelves heaving with books that never seem to move. The bargain bins are where most of his sales seem to be coming from lately. He opens his diary to see what he needs to do today and scans down through the list. First off he needs to box up some returns to send them back to the wholesaler. He also needs to send an apologetic email to a children's author that he had asked to come along to do a reading instore on Saturday, except no children had turned up. The author had been very understanding and apologised to *him* for not being enough of a draw but he had been so embarrassed. It seemed like everything he did in an attempt to drum up business ultimately proved unsuccessful.

After he is finished the returns, the bell rings and he looks up from where he is writing up some new 'recommended reading' shelf-talkers. It has been a while since the three terrorists have set foot near him or his shop. He hasn't even seen them hanging around on the street outside. Can he dare hope that he has finally managed to scare them off?

The door opens and it is Mrs Morton, a little old lady who lives in the terrace behind the shop. She always wears a brown rain mac and a paisley-patterned headscarf knotted beneath her chin. She usually comes in once a week for a chat and sometimes, if she has money left over from her pension, she buys herself a book as a treat.

"Good morning, Conor, how are you today?" She makes her way unsteadily over to the till.

"I'm good, thanks, Mrs Morton, how are you keeping yourself?"

"I'm okay, dear. I was in with Doctor Maguire earlier on with my chest again." She leans in over the counter to him.

"Have you still not managed to shake off that infection?"

"Well, hopefully, the prescription that he gave me will help fight it off now."

"I hope so too – that's a nasty one you got."

"I was doing some baking and I said I'd drop you in a few, love."

"Ah, you shouldn't have!"

"Sure who's going to be eating them now, aren't all of mine gone? I keep meaning to make less because they just go to waste these days but I guess old habits die hard," she says sadly.

"How are Donal and the kids getting on?" Donal, her only child, his wife and their three children, like a lot of Irish families, had recently had to emigrate to Melbourne, Australia, in search of work. The newspapers often ran features on families just like them under the headline 'Generation Emigration'.

"They're getting on all right. Donal has found a job now, thank God. I was very worried about them there for a while. And the kids are settling well into their new school so that's a relief, but I miss them a lot. My eldest grandson, Nathan, he gave me his old computer and set me up with that Skype thing before they left. He showed me how to use it and all, but I can't be doing that at my age. It will never make up for having them across the road from me."

"No, I suppose it must be very hard on you."

"That shower in the Dáil have a lot to answer for. They ruined this country, so they did! Splitting up families, sending them to the other side of the world to work. We're almost gone back to the famine days again, so we are!"

"It's not easy, is it? This came in the other day and I thought you might like it so I kept a copy aside for you." He hands her a romance novel.

"Ah, God bless you, Conor, but I haven't collected my pension yet this week."

"Nonsense, don't worry about that. Have a read and sure you can drop it back to me whenever you're finished with it."

"Are you sure?"

"Absolutely."

"You'll never get this shop to survive if you keep giving me free books, y'know!" she chides.

"Ah, but you're one of my best customers, Mrs M."

"Well, thank you, dear, you're too good. I love the romances. I'll look forward to starting this with a nice cup of tea later."

"Don't mention it."

"Was that young Jack White I saw coming out of here the other day?"

"It probably was – he often comes in for a while after school to read the books."

"Ah, bless him. He's a clever lad by all accounts. His mother is very sick though, God love him. She hasn't long left. That cancer is a terrible thing – that's what took my Vincent from me! You'd think they'd have a cure for it at this stage. If only all the mothers around here were like Tina White. She may have been wild when she was younger but she has done a great job with him. She used to be mad for the drink and the drugs, but then when she found out she was pregnant, she copped herself on and got clean. When Jack was born she got a job in the community centre running a mother and toddler group. It was perfect because she could bring Jack with her.

Then, when Jack started school, she set up a breakfast club for the local kids to make sure they never went to school hungry and an after-school club to help them do their homework. She loves that boy more than life itself and he idolises her. That's what makes this all so sad because as soon as she knew she was expecting him, she did her best for him. It's such a shame what is coming down the tracks for them though." She leans in and puts her aged hand with its brown liver spots over his on the counter. It feels cold and frail on his. "But as you and I know only too well, Conor, life isn't fair."

"No, it's not."

"So how are you doing yourself?"

"I'm okay. I'm trying to keep busy, y'know?"

"I do, love. Unfortunately I know it only too well. When my Vincent passed on everyone was telling me that it would get easier in time but it's a lie because he's twenty-two years dead this June and it hasn't. I think you just learn to accept it a bit more."

He nods. "I think you're probably right. Thanks, Mrs M."

When she is finished she says her goodbyes and he watches as her petite figure leaves the shop.

Chapter 44

Two weeks later Rachel takes a deep breath and dials Marcus's number. He answers on the third ring.

"Rachel? How are you?" She can hear the excited shock in his voice.

"Alex called."

"Oh no," he groans. "I didn't think she'd do that."

"You knew she was going to?"

"Yeah, she said she wanted you to come to her graduation but you don't have to go – you can just make up an excuse," he says quickly.

"Really? Does she know that we've broken up?"

"Yes, but I think it's part of her grand scheme to get us back together. I think she's worried about me, to be honest. It's fairly pathetic when your twenty-two-year-old daughter feels the need to sort out your love life, isn't it?"

"Well, if it's important to her, then I'd like to go."

"Are you sure?"

"Yeah, I want to."

"Okay, well, do you want me to pick you up?"

"Well, maybe I should just meet you there, y'know . . . "

"Of course . . . "

"It's for the best, Marcus."

That Saturday she pauses at the formidable circular columns fronting the Aula Maxima, where Alex has told her that the graduation ceremony is being held, and takes a deep breath. She makes her way in along the rows of seating and eventually spots Marcus and Jules waving her over. Her heart flips over in her chest when she sees him again. She feels that same acute sadness, the one she felt for weeks after they broke up, flood through her again. She takes a deep breath to gather herself before walking over to them. She slots into a seat beside Eli and greets everyone. They chat briefly until a hush falls on the hall as the robed procession of academic staff take their seats at the front of the room. One by one students are clapped and cheered as they are presented with their scrolls. When it is Alex's turn, Rachel claps as loudly as the rest of her family do.

After the ceremony they head for lunch to the restaurant that Jules has booked for them. She is longing to be near to him but instead Alex sits down beside her at the table and she doesn't have the heart to move. Marcus ends up seated at the other end of the table beside Brian. They catch each other's eye several times over the course of the meal and the same feelings for him stir up inside her once again. The baby starts to get tetchy soon after dessert so Jules and Brian head off as soon as the bill is settled. Eli and Alex are heading out with their friends, leaving Marcus and Rachel alone together. They finish off the wine before walking outside onto the street.

"Thanks for coming, Rach, I know it probably wasn't easy being here today but it meant a lot to Alex – to me as well actually. It's been lovely to have you here."

She loves how the sun falls on his face and lights it up, she loves how his sandy hair is always slightly tousled but it's his smile that always draws her in. Wide and warm, when he smiles it spreads up into his hazel eyes with their bright flecks of green. She's missed it.

"Well, I had a lovely day. I suppose I'd, eh . . . better . . . go."

"Do you have to? Don't go yet – please – I've barely talked to you all day. How about we go for a drink for old time's sake?"

She knows she should just say no – she can hear Shirley's sensible voice telling her 'Don't do it, Rachel, don't do it. Just rip off that plaster for once and for all. It'll be a sharp pain for a moment but it'll hurt less in the long run'. She should get into her car and end this now but instead she finds herself saying "Why not?"

"So how've you been?" she asks after they sit down into the cosy snug.

"Okay . . . yeah . . . keeping busy. I finally managed to buy Francine's."

"I saw that you were buying it in the paper. Congratulations! Marcus Traynor goes international!"

"So how have you been?"

"I'm good . . . y'know . . . lots of caseloads on at the moment."

"That's what I love about you, Rach – you're such a good-bones. You're always so busy caring about everyone else . . . I've really missed you."

"I've missed you too."

Suddenly he leans forward and his mouth covers hers. She wants him so badly. Now. The urgency is overwhelming. They get up from the table, leaving their drinks behind and go out into the brightness of the daylight. Marcus flags a taxi and they both jump inside. He goes to give his address but she interjects and tells the taxi to go to her place – she lives closer. The air between them is charged with tension – it is palpable. They practically race out of the car and up the steps of her duplex. She opens the door and closes it quickly behind them.

It is all so familiar as his tongue explores her mouth. His hand is moving over her bust, before it makes its way downwards and under the hem of her dress. She can feel his erection pressing against her. She knows exactly what comes next. She knows she shouldn't do it but she can't help it. The worst thing she could possibly do is invite him back into her life again but she can't face being on her own tonight. Just for tonight she longs for the touch of someone familiar, someone who will hold her in his arms and take care of her. On a day like today she longs for the familiarity of someone who knows her. She needs to feel his fingertips on her body, breathe in his scent, which is a mixture of aftershave and manliness, taste the saltiness of the light perspiration on his skin. She doesn't care about everything else that has gone on between them – for tonight she just wants intimacy with someone. One hand is moving through her hair, caressing the sensitive skin at the base of her neck. He starts kissing along her décolletage and down along the mound of her breasts. Tingles race through her body. He unzips her dress and it falls around her feet on the floor. "These are new." He looks admiringly at the midnight-blue satin lingerie with black lace trim. He is pushing down her bra straps and unfastening the clasp at the back to release her breasts. He runs his fingers over the skin in slow, tantalising circles, before moving in light strokes down her abdomen. He teases and moves his hand upwards again. Finally it goes down between her thighs and he finds the band in her knickers and goes inside before pulling them off down her legs.

She starts undressing him. He kicks off his shoes and they fall back onto the sofa.

He slips inside her and everything about him is familiar. They move together, his thrusts getting stronger until he groans in climax and her body contracts in waves.

They lie beside each other panting. He is stroking the skin of her shoulder.

"I've really missed you." He brings her in closer towards him. "It's been awful without you, Rachel."

"I've missed you too, Marcus."

"Being with you here today – it's like we've never been apart –"

"That's what makes it worse."

The ferocity of their earlier passion has now ebbed away leaving Rachel with a feeling closer to deflation. Her head is resting in the crook of his arm and he is running his fingers lightly over the skin on her shoulder.

"So what happens now?" Marcus asks eventually.

"I don't know but we're right back where we were and we both know how it ends."

Chapter 45

Ella is standing in the small corner shop, which smells of old linoleum and sweets. She promised the girls a treat. They are busy trying to decide whether to have crisps or chocolate. She takes a two-litre carton of milk from the fridge and walks over to the counter to pay.

"Girls, are you ready?"

They are agonising over their choices. They make up their minds, then change at the last minute and put the bars down and pick something else.

"Come on, it's hardly a life or death decision whether you pick a Twirl or an Aero!"

The shop man is elderly and smiles at the girls, showing perfectly even dentures. "It's hard to choose, isn't it?"

"Yes," they giggle.

"Well, take your time – it's important to get it right." He smiles with twinkling blue eyes. "I would hate for you two to go away from here and feel you had made the wrong choice."

Ella imagines he's a grandfather.

She glances over at the newsstand while they dither and a photo of herself catches her eye. It was taken at the National Broadcasting Awards around this time last year – she had been pregnant with Maisie at the time. She reads the headline beside it: "**TV Presenter Faces June Court Date for Theft Case.**" She picks up the newspaper and reads the text underneath: '**Disgraced TV Presenter Ella Wilde faces sentencing for the shoplifting of a designer bracelet valued at 35,000. Wilde (39), who earned a six-figure salary presenting Channel 2's** *The Evening Review* **was axed from her job following the theft . . .**' She puts the paper back down on the stand again.

"Girls, are you ready? Come on, I'm sure the man hasn't got all day now."

"Ah sure, there's no rush on them! It's turned into a grand day out there now."

"It has, it's lovely."

Celeste finally picks a Galaxy Caramel while Dot opts for a plastic *Hello Kitty* container which Ella knows will be full of neon-coloured balls of sugar.

The girls hand him their sweets and she hands him the milk. He puts on his glasses, which hang from a string around his neck and peers down at the price stickers before punching in the prices on his cash register.

"That'll be 4.19, please."

Ella roots in her pocket and takes out a ten-euro note and gives it to him. He opens the till to put in her money. The girls are busy opening the wrappers of their sweets. No one is looking at her. She picks up a packet of polo mints and feels their weighty drop as they land inside the pocket of her leather jacket.

"There you are now and five and fifty, twenty, ten and one." He is counting out her change. He places the five-euro note in her hand and piles the coins on top of it. "Five eighty-one back. See you now, enjoy your treats, girls."

In Haymarket Books it is quiet for a Friday afternoon. Conor has had a few browsers but no buyers. There were two children at the story time that morning but at least it was two more than last week, he thinks to himself wryly. He is just coming out of the stockroom with a box when she comes rushing in through the door.

"I don't know what to do, Conor – I can't stop it – I just can't help it!"

"What, what are you talking about?"

"Taking things, shoplifting – I can't seem to stop. I know it's the wrong thing to do but I can't stop doing it."

"Where are the children?" He comes out from behind the till and guides her into a chair. He goes over to the door and turns the sign to 'Closed'.

"I dropped them over to Andrea's."

"Do you want to tell me what happened?" he says, coming back over and bending down on his hunkers in front of her.

"I've done it again since the day I got arrested, I can't help myself. I don't know what to do, Conor. I'm frightened by what it's doing to me. I . . . I . . . just don't know. I don't know why I do it . . . I can't seem to stop – I hate it, I hate what it's doing to be me – I don't need to steal things but I just can't seem to help it."

"How long has it been going on for?"

She sighs. "Too long."

"How long?"

"About twenty years."

"*What?*"

"The first time it happened, I was so disgusted with myself. Really, really horrified that I could do something like that, and I swore I would never do it again and I didn't for a long time. And then just after Celeste was born, she was a few weeks old and I don't know if it was the hormones or what but I just kept crying all the time. From the moment I woke up in the morning, I would cry until I went to sleep that night. I'm not exaggerating – people say they run out of tears – well, that never happened to me. I stole something then too. It was just a magazine. I knew I was doing it. Then after I had Maisie it just seemed to get out of control. I would get these urges and it was like as if I had no control over myself. It was like watching myself from up above. I knew it was wrong, I knew I didn't need the stuff that I was taking, I knew I could afford to buy it if I really wanted it that badly, but I couldn't stop myself from picking it up and hiding it in Maisie's buggy or my handbag or wherever I could get away with."

"How have you kept it such a secret for all these years?"

"I suppose I just never got caught. I hate myself so much. I hate the way I do this. The way I can't control myself, the buzz I feel straight away after I do it and then the sinking and sickening guilt and hatred I feel about myself for days afterwards. So I do it again to make myself feel better and then I feel good for a little while but end up feeling even worse after the buzz wears off, and on and on it goes and I can't seem to break the cycle. I know it sounds crazy – if I was listening to me I would think 'that woman is bat-shit crazy' – it doesn't even make any sense. I don't know why I do it; I know it's wrong. One time when Dot was small, we came home from the supermarket and I discovered she had taken a packet of jelly tots and stuffed them into her coat pocket. I was horrified because I was worried that whatever it is that is wrong with me, I had now passed it on to her. I marched her back to the shop and explained what had happened to the manager and made Dot apologise and the manager laughed and said it happens all the time and that I was very good to bring her back in with it, to teach her that stealing wasn't okay. And I was nodding and agreeing with him while he told me what a great mother I was teaching my children that it isn't okay to steal, and there I was stuffing things in my own pockets all the time." She pauses for a minute. "I only did it maybe twice after that but then, after Maisie was born, I don't know . . . It's like a compulsion and I can't stop it. It's like there is something horrible inside me and it has to come out and that is how it gets out. It's awful. I hate it, it frightens me.

I think if I can do that and have no control over myself then what else can I do? What else am I capable of?"

"It must be stress-related," Conor says. "You said after Celeste was born that you couldn't stop crying – but what happened the first time to make you do it?"

She shifts her feet on the floor in front of him and won't meet his gaze. She is feeding the chain on her watch through her fingers again.

"Something happened, didn't it – something must have happened to trigger all of this?"

"Stop, Conor please, I'm not able . . . "

"What happened, Ella?"

"I said *stop*!" she screeches.

He sits back on the floor, taken aback by her outburst.

"Okay, Ella, here's the way I see it – you're in a spot of bother right now – potentially you could serve a prison sentence if the judge decides to make an example of you. You've been doing this for years – there is an underlying issue here – you said yourself it happens whenever you're stressed. Look, I'm worried about you. Ever since the shoplifting incident and losing your job you've been fading away. I thought it was just going to take time for you to readjust but there's more to it, isn't there?"

She remains infuriatingly silent.

"Look, Ella, I'm trying to help you here but there's something you're not telling me which is fine but you need to tell someone or else you're never going to break the cycle here. I can't do any more for you, it's up to you now."

"If I tell you, will you promise not to judge me?" she says in a small voice.

"I promise."

Chapter 46

November 1993

"Litre bottles of vodka, flagons of cider, crates of beer . . ."

They pile it all into the trolley and go to the checkout. They roll their eyes when asked for ID, like people who don't have the time or patience for this. There is a party in Conor's house and everyone is going.

They reach his house and he lets them in. They follow him into the living room where bodies are strewn around the floor.

Later she is sitting on the sinky sofa, wedged between a guy snoring beside her and Eric Keogh who has been pestering her all night by flashing quiz questions at her and then making an irritating buzzing sound when she gets the answer wrong: 'ZZZZZZHH – too bad but the answer is Chaucer' or 'ZZZZZZHH – too bad but the answer is chimera' or 'ZZZZZZHH – too bad but the answer is Saturn'.

She catches Conor's eye and pleads for him to rescue her. He reads her signal and comes over. "Here, Ella, I need to talk to you for a sec."

She jumps up off the sofa and a small splash of her vodka hits her jeans, leaving a dark stain. "In the kitchen," she orders him. She can feel Eric's eyes boring into her back as she walks. "That fella is such a stalker," she says as soon as they are on the other side of the door.

"Who?"

"Stalky Eric. If he was any more of a stalker, he'd have the head of a daffodil on him!"

"Ah, he's all right."

"Ah, I know he's harmless but, God, he's irritating – he won't leave me alone. He keeps firing questions at me. I know we're all trying out for the quiz team but I just want to be on TV. I don't give a shit about it otherwise!"

"He's a nerd." He takes a gulp of beer. "You know what they're like – they're not good on the old social skills."

"Any sign of zee Germans?" she says then.

Conor really likes this German exchange student and is gutted because she hasn't shown up yet. She sees the disappointment on his face every time the bell goes and he opens the door to find she is not standing outside.

"Not yet but she said she'd definitely come."

Conor's flatmate comes in then and pours them both an electric-blue-coloured shot. "Everyone is doing it – come on, you have to!" he says.

She takes it from him and knocks it back. It burns the whole way down but she starts to feel nicely woozy afterwards.

The door opens again and a guy comes in and takes a beer from the fridge and, through the open door, Conor can see the two girls have just arrived.

"Oh my God, she's here! I didn't think she was going to come!" Conor says excitedly to Ella.

Ella turns to look at them. One is tall and has long blonde wavy hair down to her waist. She is wearing a long gypsy skirt with ragged ends and layers of beads. She has a free-spirited, bohemian look about her. This is the girl that Conor has been telling her about. Her friend is darker-skinned with black-cropped dark hair and a strong nose.

"Well, go on, go over there and talk to her!" she orders.

"What am I going to say?" he says anxiously.

"*I don't know, ask her does she want a drink or something!*" *Ella laughs.*

Conor does as he is told and Ella watches him for a minute. She can tell by his exaggerated hand actions and the way that he is laughing at something that the girls are saying, that he is nervous. She pours herself another vodka, mixes it with 7Up and goes back into the sitting room.

Immediately Eric comes up beside her.

"*So it looks like your 'friend' has eyes for another girl.*"

She knows from the way he uses the word 'friend' that he thinks he's being smart.

"*Yes, and that is why he's my 'friend',*" *Ella retorts.*

"*Oh, I don't know, I'd say you give it to him whenever you're having a dry spell. I know what you girls are like – you want all the cock you can get yours hands on.*"

Ella looks at him in disgust. "*What are you talking about?*"

"*Girls like you going around in your short dresses, thinking that you're so pretty and popular and then laughing at guys because you think you're too cool to talk to them. You love yourselves – I know you all want it. That's what all you girls want.*"

"*You're disgusting. Your mind is perverted, do you know that?*"

"*Stop acting all pious and pretending to be innocent – everyone knows that you're a big prick-tease, Ella Wilde.*"

"*Do you not have an off-switch? Shut the fuck up, Eric, and leave me alone!*" *she shouts as a few heads look over at them.*

"*Are you okay?*" *Conor asks, coming back over to her.*

"*Yeah, I'm fine – Eric is a freak.*"

She goes into the kitchen with Conor.

"*I know he is into you but I didn't think he was that bad.*"

"*Well, you should have heard what he just said to me!*"

"*Yeah, well, just ignore him. Here, I want you to come*"

over and meet Leni and her friend Heike."

She goes over and Conor introduces her to the girls. They chat for a while and it's clear that the feelings that Conor has for Leni are mutual. Her face is slightly flushed and she keeps twisting her hair around her finger as she talks to him. Ella is happy for him, he deserves it.

"I'll just grab another drink and I'll be back over in a sec," Ella says after Heike excuses herself to go to the toilet. She wants to give them a chance to be alone together for a minute.

She makes her way back over to the table where the drink is in the kitchen and sees her vodka is almost gone, She opens someone else's bottle and pours it generously into her glass. It doesn't taste so strong after a few. She starts chatting to a girl from DramaSoc who is rounding up a crew to head on to a club. They are mainly Conor's friends but she knows a few of them.

"We're heading into town – are you coming?"

She wouldn't mind leaving now and getting away from Eric but she feels bad for Conor. "Nah – you go on, I'll stay here." She hears 'Today' by The Smashing Pumpkins playing on the CD player. "I love this song!" She runs into the living room and starts dancing with Leni and Heike. She grabs their hands and they start twirling to the music.

Out of the corner of her eye she catches Eric staring over at her. He gives her the shivers so she turns away.

She lets go of the girls' hands and Conor spins her around, then she loses her balance and collapses in a heap of laughter on the floor. The room is starting to circle around her head and Conor has to help her back up. When she tries to walk it is like walking through the sea – she wants to go straight but she can't seem to manage it.

She goes up the stairs, past two girls rolling a joint on the bottom step, to use the toilet. The small bathroom is spinning. She pulls herself up, stumbles forward and bangs her head off the towel rail. She raises her hand to rub her forehead and tries to right herself again. She feels dizzy and needs to lie down. She pushes open Conor's bedroom door and climbs on top of the covers on his bed, and closes her eyes to stop the spinning. A while later she is woken by someone taking off her clothes. Conor, it's Conor helping her into bed. His hands are all over her now, going inside her bra. Why is he doing this? She tries to sit up but he pushes her back down again on the bed.

"Conor? What are you doing?"

He is being rough and insistent now and tugging at her belt. He undoes the buckle and fires the belt so it clatters against the MDF wardrobe.

"Stop!" she says firmly but he is holding her wrists above her head. "Stop!" she screams. "Stop it now!"

He takes a pillow and holds it over her face so she can't breathe. She is inhaling the faint smell of men's hair gel on stale bed linen. She tries kicking at him but he is too strong for her. She is pinned against the bed and he is on top of her, pressing her down. She can feel the metal from the buckle on his jeans digging into her thigh. Then he is inside in her and she can't believe it. Her whole insides tense up and pain shoots through her. She is screaming into the pillow but all that comes out is a muffled sound. The music is booming up from downstairs still – she can hear drunken voices roaring along with it. She can barely breathe as she twists from side to side to try and get out from underneath him but he is too strong for her. The more she fights, the more the pillow presses down, smothering her face, so she stops moving. He is moving in and out vigorously, roughly grinding against her. She can't believe that this is happening. She can't believe that this is happening in Conor's bedroom – only upstairs from where everyone else is.

Eventually he quietens and rolls off her. The pressure pushing the pillow against her face finally stops but she doesn't dare to lift it off. She can't bear to look at him – she is afraid of what she will see in his eyes. She lies there catching her breath and hears him buckling his belt and then, in quick footsteps, he walks out of the room and back down the stairs.

Seconds later the front door slams.

It is only then that she dares to lift the pillow off her face and looks around the darkened room. She knows she is going to be sick. The alcohol, lack of oxygen and shock has come together in a potent mix and she vomits all over Conor's bed and then again on top of a pile of his clothes which are strewn around the floor. With shaking hands she manages to put back on her underwear and her jeans and makes her way down the stairs. The girls who were rolling the joint earlier are now gone. She opens the front door and runs out into the night sky.

Conor calls over to her flat the next day but she pretends to be out. She can't face him. She can't face anyone. No doubt he is wondering why she left without saying goodbye. She wonders if he knows that it was her who got sick all over his room. She is sore everywhere. It stings every time she has to go to the toilet or when her underwear rubs against the chafed skin. She has blue-black bruises on her thighs from where he forced her legs apart. Not to mention the pounding headache that she has had ever since. She knows she should probably go to her doctor but she's too embarrassed. What would she say? I drank too much, got the spins, needed to lie down and then someone came into the room while I was passed out and had sex with me? She feels so stupid to have lost control like that. She doesn't cry. She won't give the bastard the satisfaction.

After avoiding Conor for a few weeks, she eventually comes clean to him and tells him that it was her who got sick all over his bedroom. She apologises for walking out and leaving his room in a state like that but she says that she was too drunk to think straight. She doesn't tell him what else happened that night. He doesn't care anyway – things are finally starting to happen between himself and Leni and he is in love. She can't remember ever seeing him so happy.

She withdraws from the quiz team. She can't bear to look at Eric's sneering face. Conor can't understand why, so she just says that she is sick of looking at nerdy Eric, which is true in a way.

Three weeks later she is late and she knows. She buys a cheap pregnancy test in a chemist in Donnybrook and she does it in the toilets of the pub across the street, throwing it into the sanitary bin afterwards. It confirms what she already knows. It is bad enough living with the memories of what had happened that night and how she had let it happen, but now to be carrying his baby is too much to take. She knows what she has to do. There is no doubt in her mind.

That evening as her dad is reading his paper, she sits down on the couch beside him. He lowers it and looks at her over the top and says, "Well, what do you want?" in his usual good-natured way. She asks him for money to go to London to see a friend. "Do you think I'm made of money!" he says in his pretend annoyed groan. He is used to funding her social life. "Bring me in my cheque book – how much is it that you think you'll need?"

After she cashes his cheque she goes into a travel agent's with the cash and books her flight and a hotel, which they recommend near the airport to stay in for the night.

When she gets off the flight she takes a taxi to the address she has written on a sheet of paper. The driver makes no comment on their destination. They pass crescents of beautiful stucco mansions and she can see the BT radio tower in the distance. They keep going until they reach an ordinary-looking high street with shops and offices fronting the pavement. The cab pulls up outside the address and she sees protestors standing on the footpath holding placards with pictures of unborn foetuses. She almost wishes she could tell the driver to take her back to the airport but she doesn't and instead she pays him and climbs out of the car. They shout

"Murderer!" at her as she passes. Tears spring into her eyes and she lowers her head. Even though it is only seconds away, it feels as though she will never reach the revolving door which leads into the clinic. Finally she gets there, pushes it forward and goes inside.

The receptionist greets her and they have some brief chitchat about her journey over. She gives her a clipboard with a medical questionnaire to fill out and a nurse shows her into a small room to go through her medical history. Then she is brought into a different room that looks like a dentist's surgery and she tells herself that this is where she is. It is just like having a tooth out, she tells herself. She is prepped and given a local anaesthetic and then they all start working around her. The noise of the suctioning machine sounds and she squeezes her eyes shut tightly to stop the tears that are getting ready to fall.

She is surprised at how quickly it is over. The nurse in the recovery room is kind but in a manner that tells Ella this kindness is part of her job, this is what she does, day in, day out, and she will do the same for the next girl who has the appointment after Ella.

The same taxi driver picks her up again a few hours later and brings her to the hotel near the airport where she will stay until her flight home in the morning. He knows she doesn't want to talk so he turns up the radio. To this day she can't listen to Gabrielle's 'Dreams' without thinking of that taxi journey. She is sore and aching and bleeding heavily. She feels nauseated and can't stomach food. Even though she smokes herself, now the smell of cigarette smoke coming down the corridor and snaking its way under her door from the other rooms makes her want to heave. She has just thirteen more hours left and she'll be on her flight away from here. She just wants to get home; once she is back at home this whole nightmare will be over.

She sees him from time to time around the campus. She knows it was him, she can see it in his eyes. There is hatred in his eyes.

Chapter 47

Conor clenches and unclenches his fists because he is finding it very hard to stop himself from punching something right now. Anything, any inanimate object will do, he's not choosy.

"That fucking bastard. That absolute sneery scumbag, looking down on everyone else with his fucking superiority complex! Well, fuck him, *fuck* him!" He is shouting now. He stands up and walks around the room with his head in his hands. Then he stops and looks over at her. "I can't believe it, I just can't believe it . . . I always thought when you struggled that that was just you – maybe too many wild nights when you were younger or something – but it makes sense now." He runs his hands through his hair. "Jesus!"

"It was my own fault. I should never have got that drunk."

"But you didn't choose to have *sex* and get pregnant – it wasn't your choice. Your choice was robbed from you." He feels the anger rising within him again.

"He was due on the twenty-sixth of March – I always felt it was a boy, y'know – Celeste was due on the twenty-third – I was so petrified she was going to be born on his due date – I really was. That would have seemed like the worst betrayal. Thank God she was a week early. I think I might have gone round the twist, even worse than I am now." She laughs a hollow laugh. "He would have been eighteen years old today. Imagine, he might be in college or maybe taking a gap year to travel the world or maybe he might be a bum, too lazy to get a job and living off me. He might have played guitar or been an Emo or sports head. I don't know any of that and I'll never know. All that potential and it was sucked out of me like oxygen when you're drowning." She paused. "I saw him recently."

"Who? Eric Keogh? You saw him?"

She nods. "I was at the launch for a new magazine and he was just standing there with a glass of champagne in his hand, staring over at me. His eyes were fixed on me; it was like he was in a trance. It turns out he was one of the investors. He started making his way over to me and I didn't know what to do – I just panicked, so I ran. I wasn't even thinking straight – I had to get away from him . . . " She lets out a heavy sigh.

"Is this around the time that you took that bag?"

She nods. "The launch was the night before."

"Oh no, Ella! It all makes sense now!" he cries. "You should have told someone. I'm sorry that you're having to go through this nightmare after everything else you've been through."

"I deserve it anyway."

"How can you say that? You did nothing wrong!"

"I killed my own baby – that's what I did wrong. It's my own fault. It's Newton's Third Law – 'every action has an equal and opposite reaction' or some people call it Karma but, whatever it is, I killed my baby so everything in my life has to go shit after that. It's what I deserve, it's payback time. I deserve everything I get."

"Ella, you have got to stop thinking like that – that isn't the way life works. You did nothing wrong!"

"But I *did*. I killed my baby – my own baby. I'm a murderer."

"You need to forgive yourself, Ella. This has destroyed

your whole life. Don't let Eric have any more power over you. I wish I had known – I would have gone after that bastard and pulped him with my own bare hands."

Ella starts to laugh.

"What?" he says.

"It's just the image of you – you know – beating someone to a pulp."

"What? You don't think I'd put Jean Claude Van Damme out of a job then?"

"You're too gentle to beat someone up and that's why I love you." She leans forward and kisses him on the slope of his forehead.

"Does Dan know?"

She shakes her head.

"You mean you never told him about any of this? You carried this around on your own for all these years?"

"I couldn't do it. I wanted to, believe me, for years I wanted to. I was going to but I was afraid of how he would react. I was afraid he would think that I was damaged goods or something. And I just couldn't tell him that I got rid of a child, just like one of ours, but through no fault of its own conceived in the wrong circumstances. I was so afraid of what he would think of me. And then we had Celeste and it made everything so much worse. I thought it would help me to move on, y'know, but instead I kept comparing everything she did to my first baby. Would he have looked like her? Or different. Would he have had colic too? Would he only fall asleep if he was lying on my chest? Would he fall asleep when I was feeding him and I'd have to tickle the soft soles of his feet to wake him up? When she started cooing, I wondered if he would have sounded like that. When she first smiled, I kept wondering when he would have smiled. I couldn't see Celeste for Celeste. I couldn't appreciate all her milestones; I kept seeing her as a reminder for my first baby. I just couldn't bond with her. I tried so hard to make it work and make up for what I did but I couldn't seem to do anything right or get close to her. I don't know why. I kept on crying from when I would wake up in the morning until I went to bed at night. Dan thought that I was missing my work and that I had post-natal depression and looking back I probably did but I wasn't able to get help. I felt I didn't deserve help. So I did the only thing that I knew how to do: I begged Mrs Frawley to come and work for me and went back to work when Celeste was only six weeks old. I felt awful – I hated myself even more than I already did, which is saying something. But I felt she was better off with Mrs Frawley – at least she was getting proper care instead of with me who didn't seem to be able to do anything right – and once I was back doing my job again I was able to block it out and continue with the charade as I had been for so long."

"I think you need to tell Dan. You need to let him in."

"I know," she sighs. "I know."

Chapter 48

After their night together at Alex's graduation Rachel and Marcus had both agreed not to make contact with each other again, no matter what the circumstances. It was the only way it could be. Neither of them could expect to move on if there was still contact there – their feelings for each other were still too strong to trust maintaining a closeness.

Their parting that morning had been teary and difficult. Neither one had wanted to go because they both knew how awful the separation had been for each of them the last time. The wound had been reopened fresh and they both knew it was going to be harder to close it this time.

Since then she's been throwing herself into her work, she's had no choice. In her twelve years doing this job, she doesn't remember ever being this busy. She's not sure if it's because of the recession but the pressures on her office seem to be mounting daily and their resources are stretched to dangerous levels.

The court hearing for the guardianship of Jack White is drawing near and Rachel still finds she is unsure of what way her recommendation should go. Obviously Libby's set-up is brilliant and would provide stability for Jack but she doesn't want to deny the right of John-Paul just because financially he isn't in as good a position. She has seen too many fathers denied rights to their children because of society's natural bias towards women as mother figures. She has seen dads who are brilliant with their children, both loving and kind, but because they aren't in the strongest position financially, they are overlooked. But she also knows that John-Paul is an addict, even if he is a recovering one, so she wants to make sure that she gets it right.

She rings the bell to 9 St Dominic's Terrace and Jack answers the door.

"Hi, Jack, pet, can I come in for a minute?"

He says nothing as he holds the door back for her to enter. He shuts it after her and walks back into the kitchen.

"Right then, I'll just go upstairs," she says to his back.

As usual he doesn't hide his contempt for her.

She climbs the stairs and enters Tina's bedroom and sees the cancer nurse is already in the room. "I only want a quick word. I'll go downstairs and you can call me when you're finished," she says to the nurse.

"Not at all. I'm just finishing up here anyway. I'll be back tomorrow, Tina. Try to get some sleep, okay?"

Tina nods as the woman leaves the room and shuts the door gently after her.

"How's the pain today?"

"The same as all the other days, awful. She's upped me dose again so I'm waiting on that to kick in. I must have done something really bad in another life to go out like this. Did you finish your report yet?"

"I'm almost there."

"Well, I thought it should be very easy – I'm telling you Libby is the best option for him. She's very good to Jack and she has a lovely home."

"How is Jack finding it having her here?"

"She's very good to us, we're very lucky to have her. Only for her poor Jack wouldn't be fed. I just haven't the energy to do anything – she's keeping the show on the road."

"Well, you have to remember, Tina, no matter what I put in my report, as I keep telling you it all depends on the judge on the day. Look, now that I'm here would it be okay to get Jack's view on things?"

"Sure, he's only watching TV anyway – do him good to come away from it for a few minutes."

She pulls the door shut and makes her way down to the kitchen. She feels her shoulders tense as she nears the door. She takes a deep breath and opens it up.

"Jack, can I have a word with you for a minute?"

He doesn't move his eyes away from the cartoon on the screen.

"You know your ma is seriously sick now, don't you, Jack?" she presses on.

"Yeah." He still won't look at her. "She can't even get out of bed now."

Rachel nods. "She hasn't much time left and I need to find you somewhere to live after she dies."

She sees him swallow hard.

"How would you feel if the judge said you had to live with Libby?"

"It'd be okay," he says, turning to look at her.

"You'd be happy with that?"

"Well, she's really nice and I like me cousins. They have goalposts in their garden so we can play football."

"And what if he said he wants you to live with your dad?"

"Yeah, Da's all right – in small doses." He starts to laugh at his own joke. "That's what Ma always says."

Rachel laughs. "Okay, pet, but if you had to live with your dad how do you think you'd like it?"

"Well, if he doesn't get mad then I'll be okay."

"All right, Jack. I think I have all that I need."

Chapter 49

The house is finally quiet. The kids are in bed and Dan is cooking some kind of risotto for dinner. Through the window she can see the sun going down over Dublin Bay for another day. She pours herself a glass of wine and tells Dan she is going downstairs to watch the sun set. She walks down the circular stone steps wrapping around the tower in a spiral, taking care not to spill her wine over the side of the glass. She stands on the rocks, black and treacherous, and looks out at the stretch of an empty horizon, the endless calm. Some rocks are sleek like beached seals and some have seaweed draped across their backs. The water laps off them, slurping and sucking, a gentle and soothing movement. The water looks green this time of the evening; it changes colour several times a day. Sometimes it is pinkish, other times grey. She can smell the sea-salted air of the calm evening sea just before nightfall. The twilight paints the first leaves on the nearby trees in gold foil and the red rosebay willow herb that Mrs Frawley sometimes used for stomach upsets sticks up from the headland. She lights a cigarette and inhales deeply before sending a plume of tarry smoke onto the cool evening air. She gave up smoking years ago but recently has found herself going back to them now and again. She finishes her cigarette before extinguishing it on a nearby rock and taking the butt back upstairs with her. It's time.

"I need to talk you, Dan."

"What is it?" he says, lowering his fork down to his plate. He has almost finished eating.

"I know I haven't been myself lately and I want to tell you why."

"Well, I think that's the understatement of the decade," he says sarcastically.

"I know you're angry with me and I deserve it but there's something that I haven't told you."

"What? Please don't tell me you're in more trouble?" His face clouds over.

"What I'm going to tell you now . . . well, afterwards you might not look at me in the same way ever again . . . and, if that's the case, then I want you to know that I'm sorry. I wish I had told you earlier but I just wasn't . . . able to."

"Jesus, Ella, what have you done now? You're freaking me out here!"

"When I was caught shoplifting, it wasn't the first time." She talks in a slow and measured voice, like it doesn't belong to her.

"Well, I know that – that's what has you in this mess in the first place – you might have had some chance of getting off with the bracelet as people would have believed it was a mistake but you being you had to make sure to take a bag as well the day before. You really did it in style, Ella!"

"It's been going on for years before all this."

She watches his expression change from impatience to shock.

"What are you talking about?"

"I've been doing it since ever before you met me."

Shock gives way to disbelief.

"But I don't understand – you don't need to shoplift! Why would you do that?" he says angrily.

"I know. What I'm going to tell you next . . . well, it might help you to understand why I did it."

He takes a long gulp of wine before putting the glass back down on the table. "Okay, I'm listening."

"Back when I was in college, I got very drunk at a party. Stupidly drunk and I passed out in a bedroom upstairs. I came round to a guy undressing me and then he proceeded to have sex with me."

His face whitens and his fingers tighten around the stem of his glass. She watches the expression on his face change from disbelief to horror and back again, like water trying to find its level.

"Say something," she says eventually.

"You, you . . . were *raped*?"

She nods.

"By who? Who was it?"

"It was dark and I didn't see his face but I know it was a guy who was in college with us. Eric Keogh was his name."

"And did you go to the Guards after?"

"No, I was too embarrassed. I was so drunk, Dan, really, really drunk and I'm still ashamed that I let it happen, that I was so out of it that a man was able to come into the room and climb on top of me."

"But you tried to stop him?"

"Yeah, of course I did, but he held me down – he put a pillow over my head. I wasn't able to fight back. Maybe if I was sober I would have been, I don't know . . . "

"Oh God, Ella." He is holding his head in his hands. "Oh God."

"There's more. A few weeks later I found out that I was pregnant. I went to London and had an abortion."

He raises his head to stare at her in shock.

"Do you remember the launch of the magazine that I went to a few weeks ago?"

Dan is nodding.

"Well, I saw him again for the first time in years. He was at the launch, standing under the archway in the Shelbourne. His eyes were burning into me, so I just ran. The next day I stole the handbag."

The disbelief is there again. "Sorry, I just can't take all of this in. First the shoplifting – the rape – and now an abortion as well? I'm sorry, Ella. I just need to get my head around all of this." He stands up abruptly from the table and walks down the stairs to the living room. She hears him continue downstairs and the front door slams shut.

Dan doesn't come home that night. Ella tries ringing his phone but he doesn't answer. It is after two when she finally hears his key in the door. He doesn't meet her eyes as he comes up the stairs and into the living room. She can feels the tension wind its way around the air in the room. She takes a deep breath and sits forward.

"Dan, please, I need to talk to you –"

This is met with a deafening silence.

"Please don't ignore me, Dan, this is horrible – I can't take it any more."

"Well, you should have thought about that first before living a lie with me for all these years." His eyes look glassy and she knows that he has been drinking.

"I thought that by telling you everything now it might help you to understand why I've been acting like I have over the past while."

"Understand? Understand? How can I even try to begin to understand you, Ella? I don't know you any more. You're not the woman I married, and based on what you've told me recently, I don't think I've ever known you."

"I thought it was time to have everything out in the open for once and for all. I was trying to make you see what it's been like for me."

"What do you mean 'what it's been like'? We all have

issues, Ella, but it still doesn't make it okay to go around shoplifting. It was bad enough when I knew it was the bag and the bracelet but to hear that this has been happening for years and I've never known about it, makes me feel like such a fool. Do you realise how much you've humiliated me, Ella?"

"But that's what I'm trying to tell you – I can't seem to help it. It's like a horrible force descends upon me and I have to do it – it's the only way I can stop it. And then I feel good for about five minutes until it hits me what I've done and then the feeling is awful. I hate myself, I disgust myself."

"Stop making excuses for your behaviour – if you were finding it hard to cope why didn't you go and see a doctor afterwards and get yourself sorted out? I don't get why you would let the situation get so out of control for all these years." He is exasperated.

"I don't know either. I just don't know." And she doesn't know. It's all she can think about yet she can't put into words exactly how she is feeling. "I just don't know."

Chapter 50

"So today's the day," Tina says as Libby fixes her hair in front of the mirror in her bedroom.

"It is. I'm nervous."

"What will be will be. There's nothing more you can do now."

"There's no way they could let John-Paul have custody – it would be pure madness."

"Let's hope you're right. How do I look?"

"You look great. You go in there and show that judge!"

"Right, wish me luck." Libby leans in and Tina kisses her forehead.

"Make sure you ring me straight away, all right?"

"Course I will."

"And tell Jack to come up to you as soon as he's finished his breakfast – I don't want him heading off down to that pervert in the bookshop."

Libby meets with their solicitor outside the court and he briefs her on the way the proceedings will take place.

"Are you ready?" he asks when he is finished. "We'd better go inside."

She nods. "Okay, let's go."

She swallows back a lump in her throat and follows him

into the courtroom. Immediately her heart rate quickens as she eyes up the room. John-Paul's legal team are already there seated on the right-hand side. He looks over at her. His eyes are narrowed and she finds herself looking away from him. She sees Rachel and flashes her a nervous smile.

After a few minutes the judge enters and Libby copies the solicitors as they rise and then sit down after he is seated.

"The case of The Child & Family Agency and Ms Martina White and Mr John-Paul Murphy and Ms Libby Kenefick. Can I have the representatives for Ms Martina White, please?"

Libby feels her chest tighten as their solicitor starts to speak.

"My client Martina White is unable to be present today due to end-stage terminal cancer, however it is her wish that her sister Ms Libby Kenefick should have sole guardianship of her son Jack White. The child's father, Mr John Paul Murphy, has been an unstable presence in the child's life since birth and has shown no consistent input in the raising of his son."

Libby sees John-Paul's face cloud over with anger.

"That's bullshit!" he explodes.

"I have to ask you to remain quiet," the judge says, "and kindly ask you refrain from such profanities in my courtroom. Your side will have your chance to speak. Continue."

"He has never paid maintenance for the upbringing of his son. He also is an addict, which certainly supports the mother's claim that he should not have guardianship under any circumstances. Ms Kenefick has a stable home and has been present in the boy's life since birth. For the sake of the child and as per the child's mother's wishes, I strongly recommend that Ms Libby Kenefick be granted custody here today."

"I now call the team of John-Paul."

"My client is one of a growing number of men being held to ransom for the rights of their children by a system that is antiquated and outdated. The legislation is almost fifty years old –" John-Paul's solicitor starts.

"I am aware of the legislation, thank you. Continue, please."

"Sorry, Judge. Fathers in this country do not have a voice because they are not named on the birth certificate. Too often fathers are being denied essential rights, that is the right to raise their offspring, their genetic flesh and blood, because of an unfair and unbalanced system that favours the mother. John-Paul Murphy is another casualty of this system, a man who knows he is trying to turn the tide. He is aware that his previous drug addiction will be seen in poor light but he is in a recovery programme at present. I appeal to you now, your honour, to do the right thing. This child is about to lose his mother, let him not now lose his father too. A father who through no fault of his own, being pushed aside by a controlling and manipulative mother, was unable to be the constant presence that he would have liked to have been in his child's life. I recommend my client John-Paul Murphy be granted custody of his son."

The solicitor sits back down and silence falls on the courtroom. The judge finishes scribbling his notes before slowly looking up at the parties. He pushes his glasses up on his nose, clears his throat and starts to speak.

"I see many cases like this every day and it is claimed time and time again that the rights of the father are not listened to. The team of John-Paul Murphy believe the case of their client is the same. While I do feel for fathers in general in a case like this, notwithstanding that, based on what we have heard today, I would have grave concerns about Mr Murphy's ability to be a fulltime guardian to his child. I also note the recommendation of Ms Rachel McLoughlin under the Section 20 report, which further supports this position."

Libby sees Rachel lower her head when her name is mentioned.

"Therefore, I direct guardianship and custody to Ms Libby

Kenefick. However, I also note the wishes of the father and the fact that the CFA recognises as a strength that Mr Murphy was agreeable and cooperative in all assessments and that his relationship with his son, as detailed in the report, is both loving and affectionate, and accordingly I award supervised access for two hours biweekly to Mr Murphy at a location of choice by the CFA."

"Oh, thank God!" Libby stands up and exhales deeply.

John-Paul stands up and shouts up at the judge. "Yis are all the same! It's a joke! Two hours? Two fucking hours every two weeks! Being a father doesn't mean anything in this country!"

"I will again ask you to refrain or I will hold you in contempt of court," the judge orders.

John-Paul gets up and leaves the room but his eyes do not move from Libby as he storms out of the courtroom. She feels a shiver run through her.

A smiling Rachel comes over to her then, clutching her folder.

"Well done, Libby – Tina will be relieved."

"You can say that again! And I want to say thank you, Rachel, thank you for doing right by Jack."

"Ach, I'm just doing my job. I wouldn't have recommended you if I didn't think you were the right person."

"Well, thank you."

"I'll be in touch again in a few days to finalise things."

Libby nods. It is a stark reminder of the real reason that they are here. They say goodbye and she waits until Rachel is gone before with trembling hands she fishes out her mobile and rings Tina.

"It's going to be okay, Tina! He's coming to live with me. John-Paul is allowed to see him for two hours every fortnight but only under supervision."

"Well, thank God for that!" Tina starts to cry. "Oh, thank God for that, Libby! I can go in peace now that I know he'll be with you."

Chapter 51

"Jack? I'm not sure you're meant to be here."

He shrugs his shoulders. "But I wanted to see you."

"Well, maybe you shouldn't stay. I don't want to get you into trouble."

"But the nurse is in the house with Ma and Libby went off somewhere all dressed up so I came here to see you."

"Was everything okay the other day after Rachel brought you home?"

"Yeah, she just wanted to talk to me about Ma but I don't like talking about it."

"How is she?"

"Still sick and tired. She keeps crying all the time. She tries to hide it and says she just has something in her eye or a pain in her tummy but I'm not stupid."

"Look, Jack, I think you should go now – I don't think Rachel was very happy with you being here the other day so maybe you should head on."

His face looks sad. "You don't want me here?"

"Of course I do, but I just don't want you or me to get in trouble."

"But why? We're only reading books."

"Sometimes people don't like it when grown-ups hang out

with young kids."

"But I hang out with Ma and Da and no one says anything."

"That's different, they're your parents – you're supposed to hang out with them."

"But you're my friend, aren't you?" He seems hurt.

"Of course I am –"

Suddenly the door flies open and his bell rings loudly.

"I fucking knew you'd be in here!" John-Paul roars. "C'mon quick, we have to go!"

"Where are we going, Da?"

"Just come on, Jack, and stop asking stupid bleedin' questions!"

"Now just calm down," Conor says, stepping in. "He's only been here for a few minutes and he's going now, aren't you, Jack?" He rests his hand on the boy's shoulder.

Jack nods.

"Get off him! What d'ya think you're doing?" John-Paul's eyes are blazing and his lips are pulled back to expose his teeth, bared like an animal.

"I . . . I . . . wasn't doing anything." Conor stands back and raises his two hands in the air.

"I know your sort, don't think I don't! Luring young fellas in here, getting friendly with them so you can start fiddling with them, getting your sick thrills from them. I've heard about you!"

"Be careful what you're saying now," Conor says.

"Or what? You're going to do this?" He swings with his right fist and lands Conor squarely in the eye. The pain shoots through his skull. Then another punch lands on his jaw and another and another. "Ya faggot! That'll teach you not be hanging around young boys – ya paedo!"

Conor puts his hands up over his face to protect it. John-Paul is kicking him now, his ribs, his back – the pain sears through them. He can hear Jack screaming somewhere beside him. "Stop, Da, stop! Stop it!" But the blows keep on coming. "Please, Da, leave him alone, please, Da." He can hear the panic in Jack's voice.

Then Conor can hear the door opening and Jack is running out on the street. "Help!" he screams. "Someone help, please!"

This seems to bring his dad to his senses and the beating stops.

Conor catches his breath, which comes as a choking cough. John-Paul is standing over him and moves his face towards him so that he is only inches away. "You stay the fuck away from him, d'you hear me?" Drops of spittle land on Conor's face.

Conor nods and spits out the blood that has filled his mouth. A final kick lands in his groin before John-Paul moves to the door. He is just at the threshold when he turns back to face Conor again and points his finger at him. "I mean it – if I find him back here again, next time you won't get up off that floor, yeh pervert yeh!" He turns to Jack then. "Stop staring at me like a gob daw and come the fuck on!" And with that he is gone.

Conor picks himself up off the floor. Everything hurts, it hurts to breathe, his nose is running blood and his ribcage feels like it is on fire. Someone comes into the shop.

"Jesus! What happened to you – are you okay?" a woman's voice asks.

Conor can't see who it is through his swollen eyes.

"I think I'd better call an ambulance."

Chapter 52

Dublin 2012

The flashing lights throw strobes of blue into the night sky when he arrives outside the hospital. Running from his car, he sees the ambulance doors fly open at the same time and a stretcher with his wife on it running out through them and into A&E. He starts to run behind them. He can see it on their faces, the speed with which they are doing everything. They wouldn't run unless it was an emergency, would they? He is confused because when he got the call to say that there had been an accident, the man said she had just fallen, but this looks serious. He tries to call out after them but they keep running forward with the trolley so he can't catch up. One of the ambulance men is doing a debrief to a woman in green scrubs. He watches, it feels from afar, as a team descends on the stretcher like an F1 team doing a tyre change in the pit stop. Each person is doing a different job while they take over and run off into another room with her like it is a relay race and Leni is the baton.

He wants to tell them that she is pregnant but they are gone too quickly. He goes up to the double doors that have swallowed his wife and stands there. The vinyl signs on the door say 'Do Not Enter' and he knows from watching hospital dramas that protocol says that he cannot enter and *that he must wait outside – but is this really a time for protocol? It is Leni in there.*

Suddenly there is another man standing beside him, looking ashen and anxious. His blonde hair is gelled back in a quiff – people don't really wear their hair like that any more. He knows it's the man who told him to come here and who kept calling him "mate". Brian, he said his name was. He can't remember his surname.

"Are you Conor?" he asks.

Conor nods.

"I'm so sorry, mate. I really am. I did everything that I could do. He just punched her. Out of nowhere. She was on her phone and he came up behind her on his bike and just punched her. He tried to get her phone but he missed and it went one direction and she went in the other. It was her head, y'know – I knew by the way her head bounced over the pavement like that, that it was serious."

Now Conor is really worried. This isn't just a normal mugging, this is much worse. He looks towards the double doors and whispers: "My darling Leni, what has happened to you?"

"I'm so sorry, mate, I tried to get him but he was on a bike and out of there – I couldn't catch up with him. I picked up her phone, mate, y'know, just in case you . . . I don't know . . . you might want it or something . . ." He hands it to Conor.

"Thanks." Conor takes the inanimate object that has caused his wife to be in an operating theatre right now. A phone has caused all of this. One hundred and forty-nine euro is what her life is worth.

He keeps pacing back and forth on the vinyl floor and his shoes squeak every time.

"I rang 999 straight away and then I picked up her phone because I kept thinking what if she was meant to meet someone and then she just doesn't show up? Or what if someone was waiting for her to come home and she never

arrives – I knew someone would be worried so I rang the number she had dialled last and that was you."

Conor nods. *"I'm her partner."*

Brian looks him in the eyes, a chunk of hair has come free from the gel and is sticking up like a backwards C.

"I'm so sorry, mate, I can't imagine how you're feeling right now. I want you to know that I held her hand, mate." His voice starts to choke. *"I held her hand until the ambulance came – so she wouldn't be alone. I held her hand."*

Chapter 53

Rachel is coming out of her estate on her way to Shirley's house when her phone rings. She pulls the car over and turns down the radio to answer it.

"Rachel – it's Libby."

She had told her that she would be in touch in a few days when they parted in the courtroom earlier, so she knows that something must be up. "Hi, Libby, is everything okay?"

"Listen, when I came home from the court Jack wasn't here. I know there's nothing unusual in that so I checked out on the road but none of the other kids have seen him. I looked in his friends' houses too and he wasn't there."

"I'd say he's probably in that bookshop on Haymarket Street again," Rachel sighs. "He seems to like going there for some reason. I'm actually waiting to hear back from the Gardaí about the background check on the owner –"

"I checked there too but it was all closed up," Libby cuts across her.

"Well, what about John-Paul? Have you tried contacting him?"

"I went around by John-Paul's place, y'know, just in case, but he wasn't home. I've been ringing his phone but it's turned off. I'm really worried about Jack . . . it's getting dark out now and he knows he has to be in before it gets dark – he's frightened of the dark. I just have a bad feeling in my bones. You saw the way John-Paul reacted in the courtroom earlier. What if he's run off somewhere with him?"

Rachel feels a shiver make its way up her body. Something about it doesn't sit well with her. "Okay, don't panic, I'm sure he's just lost track of time – but to be on the safe side maybe you should check with your neighbours again and I'll be right over."

When she arrives at the house, before she even has time to press the bell Libby has answered the door to her.

"Still no sign of him?" Rachel asks.

Libby shakes her head. "I'm worried, Rachel."

Rachel follows her in, to the small kitchen table covered with a PVC tablecloth with a repeating blue-and-brown teapot design.

"Where's Tina?"

"She's still asleep upstairs – she doesn't even know that he is missing."

"Okay, maybe under the circumstances we should call the Gardaí. Usually they won't respond to a missing persons case until a certain time period has elapsed but, in this case, considering today's events, I think it warrants getting them involved sooner."

"Oh God!" Libby's hands fly up towards her mouth.

A short while later Garda Gerry McCartney is standing in the small kitchen with his back resting against the cupboards, taking notes. Rachel has briefed him on Jack's history and the day's events in the district court.

"And you've checked in all his friends' houses?" the Garda asks.

Libby nods. "I've checked every house on the street and even the street behind this one but no one has seen him."

"And what about this bookshop that you mentioned?"

"Well, he likes to go there, y'know, after school, but I checked it and it's closed."

"And still no word from his father?"

"I can't get him. I just tried him again there a few minutes ago. I checked the pub too because he spends a lot of time there but they said there was no sign of him all day, which believe me is strange in itself."

"He might have taken Jack off somewhere and lost track of time," the Garda says.

Libby shakes her head vigorously. "John-Paul knows to ask Tina first if he wants to take Jack somewhere."

"Okay, well, I'll go make a few calls and see if I can track down this bookshop owner and also John-Paul, to see if either of them can shed any light on the matter."

"Thanks, Garda."

Libby sees him out and comes back in and slumps down at the table. She rests her elbows on the table and holds her head in her hands. "I'm so frightened." Her voice is trembling. "What am I meant to tell Tina when she wakes up? She'll be asking where he is."

Rachel puts an arm around her shoulders. "He'll be okay. I bet he just got distracted by something and lost track of time – you know what he's like."

"But what if that fella in the bookshop has taken him somewhere – God knows he could be doing anything to him!"

"Well, let's not jump to conclusions," Rachel says measuredly, even though the same worries have been going around her head since she got the call about Jack's disappearance. She has had her own suspicions about Conor's intentions all along. "For all you know, John-Paul could have taken Jack off somewhere after school like the cinema or someplace and forgot to tell you."

"I'm telling you, he would never take Jack anywhere without asking me or Tina first. I'm going to go up and check on her in case she's awake."

Rachel stays sitting at the table while Libby goes upstairs. She looks up at the light fitting – it doesn't have a shade, just the bare bulb hanging down from the ceiling.

Upstairs, Libby pushes the door open gently, with a soft creak, before sticking her head around it. She sees the pale face of her sister, her hair with its grown-out blonde highlights spread around her on the pillow.

"How are you doing?" she whispers, coming into the room. "Would you like a drink of water?"

She walks over to the bedside locker and fills the glass with water from the jug left on top and holds it up to her sister's lips.

Tina leans forward to take a few feeble sips. Water is all she's able for these days.

"Thanks, Lib, is Jack home yet?"

Libby is torn about whether she should lie to save her from worrying or come clean and risk making things worse for her dying sister. She brushes a stray rib of hair that is trailing across Tina's eye back off her forehead. She stares at the beautiful face of her sister. It's a bit more lined now, of course, but it's still the same face that she remembers smiling up at her through the gap between the wall and their bunk beds, glowing orange in the torchlight when they were meant to be asleep as children.

"Is Jack home yet?"

She can't lie to her. "No."

"Well, where is he?" Tina's eyes widen. "I told him to be back in time for dinner." She looks over to the drawn curtains. "It's dark out – he knows that he has to be home before it's dark."

"I've checked out on the road but there's no sign of him so I checked in all the houses on the street too but no one has seen him."

"I bet you he's down in that bloody bookshop again! I'll kill him!"

"I checked there."

"And he wasn't there?"

Libby nods. "No, it was closed. We think he might be with John-Paul. I tried his place but there's no one home."

"Who's we?" Tina says, trying to sit up in the bed. Libby rushes forward to ease her up against the pillows.

"Rachel and I."

"C'mere and give me my phone and I'll give John-Paul a call. If he's off gallivanting with Jack without telling me, he'll have me to answer to!"

"I've been trying to ring him but there's no answer. I don't want you to panic, I'm sure he's just in one of his friend's houses, but I called the Gardaí just in case."

"The *Gardaí*?"

"Just to be on the safe side . . . I think John-Paul's reaction in the court earlier has us a bit anxious, that's all. Anyway they're going to try find the bookshop owner and John-Paul to see if either of them know anything or have seen him."

"I've had my suspicions about that fella in the bookshop but, God, if he has so much as laid a finger on my son, cancer or no cancer, I'll get up off this bed and make sure he'll never do that to another young fella again!"

After a while Rachel comes into the room and hands Libby her phone. "Sorry, I hope I'm not interrupting, but your phone was ringing downstairs so I answered it just in case it was important – it's Garda McCartney for you, Libby."

"Hello?" Libby says, answering it quickly.

Tina points at her to pass it to her so she puts it up to her ear.

"Sorry, Garda, this is Tina White, Jack's ma. Did you find him yet?"

"Not yet. I tried the address your sister gave me for John-Paul but as she said there is no one home. I did manage to track down the bookshop owner Conor Fahy. I'm not sure if it's related but he is in hospital after being assaulted. The man who owns the newsagent's up the street saw him being carried out of the shop on a stretcher and put into the back of an ambulance just after half past four. He didn't know what had happened. I've been in contact with the hospital and they confirmed that he was admitted there following an assault. His condition isn't serious but he did sustain fractured ribs and severe cuts and bruising."

"Right, and you think this has something got to do with Jack going missing?" Tina asks impatiently.

"Well, I'm not sure but I have a feeling that these things are related. I'm going to go and speak to him to see if he knows anything about Jack's last known whereabouts. I'll update you straight away once I have spoken to him. Any word from John-Paul in the meantime?"

"No, he's not answering his phone."

"Okay, well, I'll update you soon, Tina, and if you hear anything or learn anything new you have my number."

"Okay," she says, hanging up. She feels desolate and helpless.

She tries to get up out of the bed.

"Where do you think you're going?" Libby asks, standing over her.

"I can't sit here and wait for news. I need to be out looking for him."

"But you can't go anywhere, Tina love, you won't be able for it. You heard what the doctor said the last day – you need to conserve what little energy you have left. Even the stairs is off limits for now. Lie back down there, love – they're doing all that they can."

"I feel so useless – God, anything could have happened to him! They need to find him now!"

"They'll find him soon and we'll have him back home with us before you know it."

"Come on, Jack, hurry up!"

They are passing St James' Gate and the earthy scent of hops hangs on the air. The Liffey looks oily and thick in the street lights.

"I'm frightened, Da, I don't want to go. Can't we just go home? Ma's going to be cross. Please, Da?"

"I told you to come on! We have to go."

"But I'm worried about Conor – you hurt him really bad, Da!"

"He'll be grand, Jack. Look I know I probably shouldn't have done what I did back there but it was for your own good. Now hurry on, come on!"

"But Conor is my friend!"

"He's too old to be your friend – trust me."

"But why are we running, Da? My legs are tired."

"Because they won't let me see you ever again and you want to see me, don't you? You want to live with me, don't you?

Jack nods because he is afraid not to.

"Well, then, come on, we have to hurry on before they find us. You don't want to be living in the back of beyond because that's where they'll send you if you don't come on now."

"But where are we going?"

"It's an adventure, Jack, a big adventure." There is a glint in his eyes that frightens Jack.

"Are we going to go on a plane? I've always wanted go on one."

"Maybe, Jack, in a while – yeah, that's a good idea but first we need to hurry on and get on the train."

"Why are we not getting the DART?"

"Because the DART doesn't go where we're going – you're asking too many questions, Jack."

"But where are we going?"

"I told you, I don't know yet!"

"Then how do you know which way to go?"

"Come on, stop asking questions. We're nearly there."

They half walk, half run down the quays until they reach Heuston Station. Once inside the ticket hall, John-Paul goes up to the counter.

"Which train is leaving next?"

"Well, we have the 17.20 to Galway – that'll be leaving shortly – or we have the 17.35 to Cork."

"Galway, please, an adult and child."

He pays the fare and she directs him to the platform. "You'd want to run, it's a long way down."

They run down to the platform and see the door close on their train. A conductor runs up and lets them on before it pulls out of the station. They make their way through the carriages until they find a seat.

"This is exciting, isn't it?" John-Paul says, sitting back into the seat.

"Where are we going, Da?"

"Galway."

"Where's that?"

"In the wild west somewhere. I've never been myself but people go there on their holliers all the time."

"So is that what we're doing, Da, going on our holidays?"

"That's it, Jack. Good fella – we're off on our holliers."

"But we've no holiday clothes. I don't have any swimming stuff with me. "

"We can get stuff down there."

"Does Ma know I'm going? I've never ever been away from her for a night."

"Your ma doesn't want to come – it's just going to be us lads."

"Where are we going to stay?"

"I've a mate somewhere down there and he might put us up. Don't worry, Jack, we'll find somewhere."

"Will I have me own bed or will I have to share with you?"

"We'll see."

"I just remembered – I don't have my toothbrush with me!"

"Don't be stressing. I'll buy you one when we get there. Here's the tea lady now – do you a want a coke or some crisps to eat?"

"But we forgot to have dinner!"

"A packet of crisps will keep you going for a while."

"But Ma will murder me – I'm not allowed eat crisps before me dinner."

"Never mind your ma – if I say you can have crisps you can have them."

"It's okay, Da. I don't feel very hungry anyway."

Chapter 54

Dublin 2012

Sometime later he is sitting on the plastic chairs outside the theatre where Leni is. Brian has gone to get them both coffees. It will be the third one he has drunk in the two hours that they have been there. Brian keeps drinking one after the next and Conor does too because he keeps getting him one as well. The doors flap open and a doctor in green scrubs with a mask hanging around his neck is walking towards him.

Conor is begging inside for good news. His heart is screaming so loudly at this man to deliver good news. The doctor gets closer to him. His eyes won't meet his.

"You are the next of kin?"

Conor nods. "I'm her partner, Conor."

"I'm so sorry to have to tell you this, Conor, but she sustained a massive head injury in the fall. At the moment she is on life support but that is just keeping her organs alive. I'm afraid she's not going to pull through this. I'm so sorry."

"Are you saying she's . . . " he gulps before he says the word, "dead?"

"Well, without the machine to keep her alive, yes, she would be dead. We will need her next-of-kin to make the decision about whether to keep the machine on or not. Again, I am truly sorry. If you would like, you can go in and sit with

her. Have you anyone we can call to come in to support you?"

He immediately thinks of Leni. She's the person he would call to come and support him. She is his go-to person for everything.

"She is eight weeks pregnant," is all that he can think of to say.

The doctor nods. "I see. Again, I am truly sorry." He smiles a sad smile that Conor knows is probably because he has done this so often before. He probably sees cases like this every day. He will go home tonight, sit down to dinner with his wife and children, chat about their day – he might mention this or he might not. He will go to bed and sleep that night and tomorrow will be another day. Some people make it, some people don't.

And that was when his world had ended, when he shut a part of himself off from everyone.

He starts to cry then. "No, no, no. I can't do this without her. I just can't do it."

Chapter 55

Ella gets a fright when she sees Conor in the hospital bed. His face is a mess. There is a bandage covering the bridge of his nose, another over his left eye. The threads of spidery black stitches peep out from underneath.

"Two broken ribs, a broken nose, a fractured eye-socket – you were lucky he didn't kill you!" She takes up a newspaper left on the chair beside his bed and sits down at his bedside where he is being kept in overnight for observation. He has told her on the phone all about what happened in the store. "I hope you're going to press charges?"

He takes a breath in and the pain sears through his ribcage. He grimaces. "I'm not sure . . . "

"What?"

"I don't want to do anything that will upset Jack any more."

"How will that upset Jack? His father is a monster. He'd be better off if he was in prison!"

"His mother is dying, Ella – I don't want to cause him any more trauma no matter how much of a scumbag his dad is. Anyway the doctors said I'll be fine again in a few weeks."

"Well, I hope so – you gave me such a fright." She is holding his hand. "If anything had happened to you, I don't know what

282

I would have done. I'm just so glad that you're going to be okay. I hope if Jack ever shows up again, you're going to tell him not to come any more? You don't need this trouble."

Conor knows she is right. John-Paul had threatened to kill him if he ever saw Jack in his shop again. "Yeah, I know," he sighs. "I'll miss him though."

"Really?"

"Yeah, I've got to know him over the last few weeks and he's a good kid."

"Well, I don't know how he managed to turn out like that with a father like he has!"

"True. By the way, thanks for getting Liam in to look after the shop."

"Don't mention it. He was delighted to get a few hours' work." Liam is a student who sometimes used to cover for Conor before Leni died whenever they were on holidays or had something on, although he hasn't been able to afford to give him any hours lately.

"Who's minding the girls?"

"Andrea said she'd take them for a few hours so I could come in to see you."

"How are things with Dan?"

"Not great."

Suddenly the broad frame of a man in a Garda's uniform is shadowing the doorway. "Sorry to interrupt you. I'm Garda Gerry McCartney. I hope you don't mind if I talk to you for a few minutes?"

Ella stands up to leave. "I'd better go – I have to get the girls anyway but I'll ring you later, okay? You get well soon." She leans over him and kisses him on the forehead.

Garda McCartney removes his hat and sits down in the chair that Ella has just vacated.

"They are some pretty savage-looking wounds you got there. Can you tell me some more about how you sustained those injuries?"

Conor squirms in the bed before him. "It was just a fight, that's all. I'll be all right in a few weeks." He is staring up at the fluorescent lights hanging from the roof.

"And who was the fight with?"

Silence. His eyes flick up again. The lights aren't parallel with the grid of the ceiling tiles and Conor feels the urge to straighten them.

"It is really important that you tell me what happened, Conor. I believe you know Jack White – he sometimes likes to visit your shop?"

That gets his attention.

"You probably aren't aware but Jack hasn't been seen since around four o'clock this afternoon. His mother is very worried for his wellbeing."

"He was in the shop earlier and then his dad came in and went ballistic!"

"Did John-Paul Murphy do this to you?"

He nods.

"And why would John-Paul want to assault you?"

"Jack comes to the shop most days after school. He eats a sandwich, we have a chat, he reads a few pages of a book and then he goes home for his tea. I'm not sure how it started and I don't even know why he comes. I can understand how it must look from the outside, an introverted bookshop owner hanging out with a young boy. I know it's an unusual friendship – if you can even call it that – but, honestly, hand on heart, it is completely innocent."

"But John-Paul doesn't see it like that, does he?"

"No. Jack's dad has always been suspicious of it. He threatened me before and I had to tell Jack not to come any more because I knew it would just incense John-Paul further but he still insisted on coming back. I couldn't talk him out of it."

"So what happened earlier, Conor?"

"I was inside the shop, head stuck into my paperwork, Jack

284

was in the shop chatting to me and the next thing the door opens and before I know it I am on the floor and John-Paul is kicking and punching the living daylights out of me. Jack was screaming in the background but there was nothing I could do to stop it – he took me completely by surprise."

"And do you know where John-Paul and Jack went next?"

He shakes his head. "I assumed they went home – with all due respect I wasn't in any state to get up and look out the door after them."

"Of course not. So they left your shop and you don't know where they went then, is that correct?"

"I just assumed he took him home."

"Okay, Conor, I think I am starting to piece things together. I'll go now and leave you to get some rest and see if I can track down John-Paul."

"I hope Jack's all right."

"Well, thanks for your help, Conor, and I hope you get well soon." He places his cap back on his head and leaves the room.

Jack looks around the concrete walls of the empty shop unit that his dad had led him to, to shelter in for the night. He had to pick the lock on the rear door to let them in. Plywood covers the square where the window should be and the unit isn't yet wired for electricity. It smells dusty and damp and Jack can't remember ever being so cold in his life.

"I'm scared, Da, it's very dark in here."

"Look, I told you, it's just for one night – we'll get somewhere better tomorrow."

"But it's freezin'!"

"Here, put my coat over you." He takes it off and puts it over his son's legs.

"I don't like it here – can we just go home now?"

"It'll be grand, Jack, you'll like it tomorrow, all right?"

"But I'm hungry."

"Well, you shouldha eaten something on the train like I told you to – there's nowhere open now at this time of night."

"I miss Ma – she's going to be worried about me."

"She's grand, all right? I cleared it with her first."

"What about Conor? He looked bad, I hope he's okay."

"Don't worry about that fucker, he's fine."

"He's me friend, Da!"

"He's not your friend – trust me, son."

"I need to go to the toilet."

"There's no jax here – you can go over there in the corner."

"I can't do that!"

"Nobody is using the place, Jack, so it doesn't matter where you do it."

"I can't wee on the floor."

"Well, here, do it into this empty Coke bottle so if that'll keep you quiet."

"I'll just hold it."

"Suit yerself."

"It's so cold, Da, I'm freezing!"

"Stop giving out, Jack! I told you we'll go somewhere better tomorrow."

"But this doesn't seem like a holiday."

"Tomorrow it will – we'll have a great time tomorrow, son."

Garda McCartney leaves the hospital and straight away sets about tracking down John-Paul. His parks up on the path outside the address he was given by Libby. He can tell from the darkness inside the window that the house is empty, just as Libby said. He knocks on the door anyway just in case but there is no answer.

He goes back to the station to make a few calls before calling back to 9 St Dominic's Terrace.

Libby answers the door.

"No sign of him?" he asks. "Or news of his father?"

She shakes her head.

"I just wanted to give you an update and tell you where we're at now. Is Tina awake yet?"

"I'll bring you up to her."

He follows her up the stairs to Tina's bedroom door.

"Is she asleep?"

"She can't sleep and that's saying something with all the drugs she's on."

He goes in and sits down at Tina's bedside.

"How are you doing, Tina? I had a chat with the bookshop owner in the hospital."

"And?"

"And it appears that John-Paul assaulted him following an altercation in the bookshop earlier on."

"Jesus, well, he must have beat the shite out of him for him to wind up in hospital! That's John-Paul all right – he lets his fists do the talking. He always has."

"Indeed, it was a pretty serious assault – he has two broken ribs, a broken nose, a fractured eye-socket –"

"And does he know where Jack is?" Tina is holding her head in her hands.

"Well, according to him Jack was in the bookshop earlier at about four o'clock. John-Paul saw him there, felt enraged and attacked him, and then he left quickly afterwards with Jack. Conor assumed they were going home but as we know Jack never made it back here."

"So it's John-Paul then?" Tina says. "John-Paul has taken him? Well, if he harms Jack I swear to God I will kill him with my own two hands."

"Here's what I think happened. John-Paul was obviously distressed about the court hearing earlier on and he went to find Jack who was in the bookshop as you've told me he likes to do. John-Paul found him there and flipped out. He assaulted Conor and then ran off with Jack."

"But where would he go?"

"Well, that's what we're trying to find out."

"But what if he does something stupid – you never know with John-Paul what he's going to do next. That's why I broke up with him – he's unstable!"

"I have alerts out with every station across the country. And I've left messages for him to say it's okay just to bring Jack home and nothing else will happen but I haven't heard from him yet."

Tina nods. "That's all I want. I just want Jack home here where he belongs. I need him to be here. I don't have the energy for this."

Chapter 56

Ella lies on the sofa watching a rerun of *Mad Men* before eventually falling asleep at some stage. She wakes up to feel someone putting a blanket over her. She opens her eyes. It is Dan.

"I didn't mean to wake you." He sits down on the ottoman in front of her. His blue eyes look red and Ella isn't sure if he has been crying or if it's just tiredness.

She looks around her, adjusting her eyes to the light.

"I've been thinking it all over and over. I can't get it out of my head. I keep having these mental images and one minute I'm raging and the next minute I'm a crying mess." He pauses for a moment before continuing. "I'm so sorry for how I've been acting since you told me. I just couldn't get my head around it all – I'm still struggling, to be honest."

He falls quiet for a moment before leaning forward and taking her two hands in his. "I'm so sorry you had to go through that, Ella."

He is crying into her hair. She can count on one hand the number of times she has ever seen him cry. It is unnerving.

"I'm so sorry, love. I'm sorry that you felt you weren't able to tell me for all these years. But I'm here for you now, do you hear me? We're going to get you help – whatever it is that you need, we'll do it, okay? We're going to get you better again."

She feels relief course through her body. Finally he understands and is going to try to mend her. A song is on the TV with a husky-voiced singer strumming on a guitar. He pulls her off the couch and takes her in his arms.

"Dance with me, Ella, it's been so long since we've danced together." His voiced is croaky, choked with tears.

She feels a bit silly as first but then she presses her head against his chest and it feels good there. It feels as though she has been running for miles and miles and she has finally just sat down.

Dan starts singing softly with the song, *"You and me, honey, it's always you and me. You and me, honey."* They move in slow circles and she can feel the dampness of his tears in her hair. She lets her body move with the sway of the music. He is going to get her through it.

Chapter 57

"Any update?" Rachel asks when she calls in the next morning.

Libby shakes her head.

"I'm so worried about him, Rachel. I'm trying to play it down to Tina – God knows this is the last thing that she needs. What if something terrible has happened to him? Or what if John-Paul has done something to him? He could have him wandering the streets – you never know what sorts he'd bump into. I just am so worried . . . "

"I know you are but you need to be strong for Tina right now. Is she sleeping?"

"She was awake most of the night so she's only after dozing off there just before you came – she's exhausted, the poor thing."

"I know you mightn't like him but, I have to say, from talking to John-Paul I could see that he does love Jack – so we just have to hope that common sense reigns and he lets him come home."

"That fella and common sense don't even belong in the same sentence! What if Tina passes away in the meantime? What then? You saw what she's like, she hasn't long left. She's asleep most of the time. How can he be so selfish? How can he do that to her when he knows she only has a few days left? What if she dies not knowing where Jack is?" Her voice breaks.

"Look, I don't know what's going on inside his head but the Gardaí are doing all that they can – they're making contact with everyone he knows who might have seen him. Let's just hope they get him soon."

"She should be able to go in peace instead of that fella causing more drama. All he has done is bring her trouble since she first met him as a teenager – she broke my poor mother's heart. All she wanted was drugs – I don't think she even liked John-Paul that much – he was just a source of what she wanted. I wish Mam could have seen the woman she turned into though, after Jack was born, and what a great mother she is to him. That's the only thing keeping me going – that I know Mam and Tina will be together very soon. They'll have each other then." Libby yawns, searching out the air in the room. "Sorry – I'm exhausted – it's been a long day."

"Why don't you go upstairs and lie down for a while and if there's any news or update from the Gardaí, I promise I'll wake you straight away."

"You shouldn't even be here, Rachel, it's not your job."

"I want to be here, I want to see Jack safe where he belongs just like you. Now go up and put your head down for a bit. "

"Thanks, Rachel, I really appreciate this and I know Tina does too."

Garda McCartney calls in after ten.

He shakes his head. "No news," he says.

Rachel goes upstairs to wake Libby.

"Is there any news?" she says quickly.

"No – no news apparently."

"I better wake her up – she made me promise I'd wake her when he came. Will you bring him up?"

Libby goes into Tina's bedroom and opens the curtains to

let in the morning before she gently starts to rouse her sister.

"Please tell me he's home, Libby?"

"Garda McCartney's here now – he's on his way up the stairs."

"Have you have something for me, Guard?" Tina says as soon as he appears at her door.

"I'm sorry to say that we still have no sightings of either of them and no new leads," he says, walking into the room.

"Why can't you find him?" She has had enough. No one seems to be treating this as urgently as it needs to be treated. "Surely you have to be able to track them down! I don't know what you're at at all!" Her voice is raised but her throat feels dry and scratchy.

"I assure you we're doing all we can but I wanted to talk to you about something. I think at this stage it would be advisable to put out an appeal through the media."

"What do you mean?"

"It would involve issuing an Amber Alert whereby we would circulate a photo of John-Paul and Jack along with an appeal to the media asking the public to notify us if they have any sightings of them. We would also use social media and road signs to get the message out there. We have had good success using appeals in previous cases but you need to be aware of the risks associated with doing a media appeal. If the abductor knows he is being hunted," he pauses, "he may panic and do something to harm the child."

"Jesus!" Tina voices breaks and she starts to sob. "I just want my baby home, that's all I want!"

"I know, love," Libby says, rubbing her hand, "but I don't think we've many options left at this stage – we need to find him."

Tina nods. "You're right . . . okay . . . do it."

"I'll get you the photos," Libby says to the Garda.

One o'clock goes to two, two to three and three to four. The day passes with no new information from Garda McCartney. Libby watches the news bulletins and her stomach knots every time the photo flashes up with the photo of Jack that she had taken on Christmas Day last year. They watch every hour on the clock. They are waiting for a knock on the door and for Jack to run inside the kitchen but it doesn't come.

Darkness falls on the terraced house but still Jack doesn't come home.

Chapter 58

"Dot Devlin, what are you doing up there dangling out of that window? Come down here this minute!"

She has climbed up onto the radiator and is lying backwards across the stone windowsill so that her head is outside the window and her hair is hanging out over the ledge. She straightens up when she hears Ella's voice.

"I'm just trying to see how long my hair is."

"And that explains why you need to hang out of the window how?"

"Because I want to see if it's touching the ground. I have to check every day to see how much it has grown." She says it as if it is the most obvious thing in the world.

"It would take hundreds of years for your hair to grow long enough to touch the ground, Dot."

"Well, it didn't take Rapunzel that long."

"No, it didn't, but that was a fairytale."

"Oh Mummy," she sighs. "Don't you know that fairytales are real? Sometimes I feel so sorry for you."

She shakes her little head in despair and Ella has to fight to keep the smile off her face.

Ella climbs the stairs to the top of the tower. The kitchen is like a glasshouse – it is always unnaturally warm on sunny days. She searches amongst the cereal boxes left out from breakfast to find the remote to open up the windows and let some air in.

Dan is sitting at the table, feeding Maisie in her high chair. Ever since their conversation the other night, she feels as though a weight has been lifted off her shoulders. The tension that had been dividing them over the last few weeks has finally lifted. She knows he is on her side and that, together, they can get through it. She has her first psychotherapy session that evening and she feels a knot of anxiety every time that she thinks about it but she knows that she needs professional help to get through this. It's the only way.

"We need to start thinking about Celeste's birthday party," she says. "It's only two weeks away now."

"Well, what were you thinking of?"

"I think we should have it here."

"But where are we going to fit them all?"

"It doesn't matter – we'll manage. We could have one of those makeover parties or maybe a cupcake-making class – what do you think Celeste would prefer?"

"But you always said that you hated those things. Didn't you call them over-commercialised and tacky?" Dan says, laughing.

"Yeah, I do hate them, but it's not about *me*. I'm going to give that child the best party – there is no way I'm going to let her down after everything she has been through over the last few weeks."

"Are you sure you're not trying to win back her friends for her?"

"And so what if I am? Do you know how guilty I feel at the backlash she is getting because of me? I just think if she has a brilliant party then maybe they'll forget about the whole thing and can all go back to being friends again."

"I don't know . . . " he says warily.

"Well, I'm doing it." She feels an excitement that she hasn't felt in months. She takes the spiral staircase down to the living room two steps at a time. Celeste is sitting cross-legged in front of the TV.

"I thought we might have a party here in the house for your birthday – what do you think?"

"Really? In the house? But you never let us have birthday parties in the house because you said it's too much hassle – you always go out somewhere because it's easier." Her tone is unmistakably doubtful.

"Yeah, well, I've changed my mind and I actually think it would be nice to have a party here for a change."

"Well, nobody is going to come. You know that, don't you, Mum?"

"Of course they will." She grabs her iPad and starts jotting down names and ideas. "Oh, and we need a theme, Celeste."

Dan has brought Maisie down. "Now let's not get too carried away here," he interjects.

"What does a theme mean, Mum?" Dot is asking Ella.

"You know at parties when it's all about pirates or cupcakes or whatever you want?"

"How about princesses?" she suggests helpfully. "I could be Rapunzel."

Celeste looks at her. "Eh . . . I'm going to be nine," she says in her best little-girl-trying-to-be-grown-up sarcastic voice. "Maybe mermaids because we live beside the sea," she says cagily.

"Great idea. Okay, mermaids it is then. We should get caterers too."

"But they're eight-going-on-nine-year-olds – they don't care about food once there are a few Rice Krispie buns going," Dan protests.

"Eh . . . we won't be having Rice Krispie buns at this party! Besides, the parents will expect food."

"But can't we just stick a few cocktails sausages into the oven?"

She shakes her head despairingly at him. "I hate to break it to you, love, but parties have come a long way since 1983."

"Well, I hope this isn't some kind of crusade to make yourself popular with the other mothers again."

She shoots him a look and he knows that he probably should shut up now.

Chapter 59

John-Paul has checked them into a B&B on the outskirts of the city. It is situated in a seventies housing estate beside an industrial park. The owner, a rotund, motherly lady is fussing over Jack.

"This is a lovely treat. I don't get many young boys here – usually just grumpy old businessmen and older couples. I bet you'll eat a big breakfast for me in the morning, won't you, love?"

Jack grins up at her shyly.

"Do you like sausages?" she continues. "Because if you do I'll put on the jumbo ones especially for you."

Jack nods eagerly. "I love sausages but I don't like it when the beans touch off them."

"Well, how about I put the beans on a separate plate for you – would you like that?"

"Yes, please."

"And such lovely manners too! Are ye just down for the one night?"

John-Paul nods. "Yeah, just a short break away."

"Well, isn't that lovely – well, I'll let you off up to your room and you can get settled. Will I show you up to it?"

"Ah, you're grand – we'll go on up ourselves."

"Well, it's number five, up the stairs and it's the second door on your left-hand side."

"That's great thanks, love," John-Paul says, taking the key from her.

"Here, take a few more of those up to the room with you." She presses a packet of bourbon biscuits into his hand.

"This is weird, Da – it's like staying in someone's house," Jack says as they climb the stairs.

"That's because it is someone's house."

"But why does she want people staying in her house? Does she get lonely?"

"No, we have to pay her – it's not for free, yeh big ninny!"

"Ma should make our house a B&B because we have a spare bedroom and then we'd have more money to buy things."

"I'm surprised she hasn't done it already – your ma's always looking for a way to squeeze a few extra bob out of people."

John-Paul unlocks the door and they go inside the room.

"This is cool!" Jack says. "But there's only one bed – I bagsy it." He says jumping on it. "Can I turn on the TV?"

"Yeah, go on."

"It's a bit small, though, isn't it?"

"You're never happy!"

Jack sits up on the bed with the remote control and flicks through the channels while John-Paul takes a shower.

John-Paul is just coming out of the bathroom, towelling himself off when Jack says, "Look, Da, that's me!"

"What are you saying?" He stops drying himself and looks up at the screen and sure enough there is a photo of Jack with his front tooth missing. It was taken last Christmas standing in front of the Christmas tree.

"Cool! How did I get on TV?" Jack asks excitedly. Then it flashes to a photo of John-Paul. "Look, Da, it's you now!" He starts laughing. "Look at the state of your hair." It's an old one, taken about five years ago. His mother was in the photo too but they must have cut her out of it. "Why are we on TV, Da?"

"I don't believe it, I don't fucking believe it!" John-Paul rubs his hands down over his face and starts pacing the room.

"What's wrong, Da? Why are we on TV?"

"We have to get out of here, Jack, we have to go." He pushes his feet back inside his trainers.

"But Mrs Walsh promised me a lovely breakfast in the morning – she said she'd put on the jumbo sausages especially for me!"

"I'll get you a sausage roll in a deli – now come on, Jack, we have to go fast."

"But it's not the same!" he protests. "I like it here! It's nice and warm and Mrs Walsh is nice!"

"Come on, we're going, but you have to be really quiet."

They tiptoe out of the room and creep quietly down the stairs. John-Paul unlatches the front door and beckons Jack silently outside. He starts running until they reach the top of the estate, Jack behind him trying to keep up.

"Where are we going now, Da? I hate this. I'm tired, Da, I just want to go home."

"Stop it, Jack!" he shouts at him. "I can't hear meself think!"

Jack is taken aback and starts to cry. "I want to go home to Ma!"

"Look, I'll get you sweets in the shop, all right?"

They go into a shop and the woman behind the counter is looking at them. She watches them as Jack picks up a packet of crisps and some Giant Jawbreakers and hands them to her to scan.

"Da, can I get a drink as well?"

"Go on then."

"Ye're down from Dublin?" she asks, hearing the accents. John-Paul looks at her and she looks at him.

"Come on, Jack, we're going.'

"But what about my stuff?"

"Come on quick!"

They are running down the street and Jack can't keep up but John-Paul keeps roaring at him to hurry on. They round a corner onto a darkened cobbled lane and take a left off it down a back alley full of cardboard boxes left out the back doors of the businesses on the other side. Shadows loom dark and threatening.

"I'm scared, Da – I don't like this any more."

"They're after us, do you understand?"

"Who is?"

"The Gardaí – we're on the news. If they get me, that's it, Jack – I won't get to see you again."

Jack starts to cry.

"Why are you crying, Jack?"

"Because I'm scared, Da. I miss Ma and I know she misses me too. I don't like it here – it's no fun. I just want to go home."

"But like I said – if I bring you home, Jack, that's it – they won't let me see you again. You know that, don't you?"

"But why, Da?"

"Look, Jack, it's hard to explain but I did something stupid. I wasn't thinking and I lashed out but now we're too far gone. I'm sorry I didn't fight to see you more when you were little and all. I shouldha' tried harder. I know your ma is sick and I'm sad because, believe it or not, there was a time when me and your ma got on all right, you know? We had some good times back in the day and no matter what's gone on between us, she's been a good ma to you and I can't take that away from her. But I love you, Jack – you're me son, me flesh and blood, and I don't want to be without you but sometimes they don't give fathers a chance and then we end up doing something stupid like this and then they say they were right all along but they weren't. We just get desperate. Do you understand, Jack?"

Jack won't meet his eyes.

"Of course you don't, sure you're only a child. I'm sorry, Jack." He is melancholic. "Two hours every second week, sitting in an office with people watching you, that's all they agreed to give us but this is probably going to be it for you and me now. I know I'm not the sharpest tool in the shed but I know they won't let me see you after beating the head off that queer in the bookshop and then running off with you here. I know that's it, son. Do you understand what I'm trying to say to you? I wish I could just hold onto you here forever myself, just you and me without any of the rest of them sticking their beaks in. Do you know what that means, Jack?"

He shakes his head. His small body is shivering, his teeth chattering.

"It means that no matter what happens next I want you to remember that your da loves you very much. I'm not the best da in the world, nowhere near it, and I've made a lot of mistakes but it won't change how much I love you, son, do you hear me?"

Jack doesn't answer.

"Come on, son."

They get up and walk down the cobbled street. They keep walking until they are standing at the water's edge. They stand and stare as moonlight glints off it in blue-grey and silver.

"Where are we going, Da?" Jack asks eventually.

"Back where you belong."

Chapter 60

"Oh thank God, thank God!" Warm tears spring from Libby's eyes and course down her face. She turns to Tina. "They have him, love, he's in Galway. John-Paul's turned himself in." She continues on the phone, "Thank you so much, I can't thank you enough. Here, Tina, do you want to talk to Jack?"

She passes the phone to her.

"Hi, Ma." The sound of Jack's small voice on the other end is the best sound she has ever heard.

"Hiya, Jack love – you don't know how good it feels to hear your voice. It is the sweetest voice I have ever heard. Thank God you're all right. We've all been so worried about you. Are you okay?"

"Yeah, I'm in the back of a police car and they've turned on the lights and we're speeding through the city."

"Well, they'll have you home to us soon. God, I can't wait to squeeze the bones of you, my little man!"

A little over two hours later an exhausted Jack comes through the door. Libby hugs him tightly before leading him upstairs to see Tina.

He runs into the room and throws both his arms around her.

"I didn't want to go, Ma! Am I going to be in trouble?"

"You're not in trouble, don't worry, pet. It wasn't your fault."

"I never want to go away from you again. I didn't like it – we stayed in a place with no glass in the windows, just wood – it was freezing. It wasn't finished being builded."

"I know, love, I know."

"Why are you crying, Ma?"

"Because I'm so happy you're home, so, so happy."

"Are you feeling any better?"

"Well, now that you're home I'm feeling on top of the world. Was everything okay – your da didn't hurt you or anything?"

"No, he didn't get mad or anything, but I think he is a bit sad though. He kept saying they weren't going to let me see him any more but that's stupid because he only lives around the corner."

"He's home, Rachel, he's home!" Libby is laughing down the phone to her. "He's home!"

"Oh, thank God! Is he all right? He wasn't harmed in any way, was he?"

"No – he's good, he's in good form – just hungry so I made him some dinner, gave him a bath and put him to bed. He was asleep before his head hit the pillow."

"I'm so glad he's okay. I'll call over to see him in the morning, I want to talk to him anyway."

"Sure, Rachel, we'll see you then. And thank you so much, you've been brilliant over the last few days."

"Ach, not at all, I'm just glad he's all right."

She hangs up and does a little dance around her living room. She feels amazing. The relief of knowing that Jack is okay is rushing around her body. It's only now that she realises just how worried about his welfare she was.

The next morning she calls over to the house and Jack is

already up eating breakfast at the table. Libby is sitting with him, clasping a cup of tea.

"How're are you doing, buster? You gave us all an awful fright."

"I hope it's not too hot in here for you, Rachel," says Libby. "I've the heating up high to stop Jack getting a chill."

"It's fine."

"I'm just going up to see if Tina can stomach anything this morning. I'll be down in a minute." She winks at Rachel and she knows it is her cue to talk to Jack.

She waits until he has finished his cereal. He lifts the bowl to his mouth and drains the last of the milk before putting it down on the table again.

"Jack, love, would you be able to tell me what happened in Galway?"

Silence.

"You have to tell me – I just want to help you. It's really important that I know everything that has happened over the last few days."

He shakes his head.

She is getting used to Jack's stubbornness.

"Look, Jack, sweetheart, this isn't your fault – whatever it is, it isn't your fault, okay?"

"It is." He takes his eyes away from the light fitting and looks directly at her.

"Please tell me what happened."

"I can't. He's going to get in trouble."

"Who is, Jack?"

"Da."

"Look, I'm not concerned about your da – anything that he has done is a matter for the Gardaí. Now I'm not going to lie to you, what he did was very serious, but it's not my business – my concern is you, so that's why I need you to tell me what happened."

It did the trick as Rachel knew it would.

"Da beat Conor up in the bookshop and there was blood all over his face and clothes. I was so scared."

"I see. Do you know why your da attacked Conor, Jack?"

"Because I was in the bookshop again – it's all my fault," he says in a small voice.

"No, Jack, it's not your fault."

"I don't know if he's okay." He starts crying. "Da hurted him really bad and I can't stop worrying if he's okay but I don't want Da to go to jail."

"That's okay, Jack, you don't need to worry about that just now. Thank you for telling me – it was really brave of you, do you know that? I just want to check what you and Conor were doing at the time when your da came in – just before the fight started?"

"I was in the bookshop and Conor was doing work on his computer. Then Da just came flying through the door and starts punching and kicking Conor."

"That's all right, that's all I wanted to know.

"I don't want to go to Galway again. I didn't like it there."

"What your da did, Jack, is very serious – he isn't allowed to take you anywhere without telling your ma first. I'm sure it was very frightening for you – but don't worry, no one will be taking you away anywhere like that again, I promise. How about if I find out how Conor is doing and I'll let you know – would that be one less worry for you?"

He nods. "I really hope he's all right because there was a lot of blood and Da kept on hitting him."

As soon as she sees him standing behind the till in the bookshop, she realises why Jack was so traumatised. His face is darkened with blue-black bruising and he has a gauze-padded bandage above his left eye.

"Hi, Conor, I'm Rachel McLoughlin. You may recall meeting me before. I'm the social worker assigned to Jack White's case?"

"I know who you are," he says stiffly. "Have they found Jack?"

"Yes, thankfully he's home."

"Thank God." He lets out a huge sigh of relief. "Where was he?"

"John-Paul had taken him to Galway."

"He's okay?"

"He got an awful fright, which is only natural, but he's doing okay. I have to hand it to him, he's a tough little cookie!"

"He is."

She pauses for a moment before continuing. "Jack told me what happened, before his dad ran off with him – you must have been so frightened."

"I was – I've never been in a fight in my life. Call me lily-livered or whatever you want but I'm not a fighter."

"I wish more men were like you – it would make my job a lot easier for a start." She smiles. "Look, Conor, as you know, Jack's mum Tina is very sick. She has only a short time to live – doctors reckon it's probably only another few days now at this stage."

Conor sucks in a sharp intake of breath through his teeth. "The poor kid."

Rachel nods in agreement. "It is so sad. That's why it is such a relief that he has come home – imagine if she had passed away not knowing whether her son was safe or Jack didn't get a chance to say goodbye to her?"

Conor nods.

She continues, "I'm not sure how much Jack has already told you but, strictly between us, as Tina is terminally ill, I was appointed to do a Section 20 report to recommend a guardian to take care of him for when she passes away. Because Tina and John-Paul were never married, he wasn't an automatic guardian to Jack and he never went down the legal route to be appointed as one either. Tina didn't want John-

Paul to have guardianship of Jack at all and after everything that has happened over the last few days, I can't say that I blame her. Jack's grandfather has Alzheimer's and is in a nursing home and not in a position to take on Jack, and his other grandparents are dead. It was Tina's wish that her sister Libby would be appointed as his sole and primary guardian after she passes away. I've met Libby and her family myself and visited her house. They live in the County Wicklow countryside so it will be a big change for a city boy like Jack but she has a nice set-up, a lovely home and three other boys who Jack gets on very well with by all accounts. It is a stable and loving family life, which is what Jack is going to need when Tina goes. Thankfully the court went with my recommendation and Libby is now Jack's legal guardian but John-Paul was very upset about this in the court. I think he panicked and that's why he went to snatch Jack but obviously he happened to come across you in the meantime and unfortunately you ended up being dragged into it."

"I see, so I guess I was just in the wrong place at the wrong time."

"I guess so."

"Well, I'm glad his dad didn't get custody. From what I know of Jack, just from him coming into my shop, he's a really great kid, he has a big heart and is soft. It's going to be very hard on him when Tina passes away and he needs someone who can mother him and give him stability, and the fact that his cousins would be there too would be really good for him."

"I think so too, Conor. Look, the real reason that I am here is because a certain wee man is worried about you."

"Jack, I'm assuming?"

She nods. "I promised him that I'd find out how you're doing."

"I'm fine – you can tell Jack that I'm going to be okay. Look, Rachel, I've only known Jack for a short time but Tina should be very proud of him."

"Ach, she is, Conor, she dotes on that boy." She takes a deep breath. "That's what makes this case even sadder." She brushes a stray rib of hair from in front of her eye. "Okay, well, I've taken up enough of your time anyway. I'd better go." She is back to formal Rachel again.

"Okay, well, will you tell Jack I said not to worry, that I'm doing fine?"

"I will of course. Okay, thanks, Conor, and I hope you're back in full health again very soon."

She is just coming out of Haymarket Books and is just getting back into her car. She sees him hurrying towards her and she stops dead on the path. Everything, all her thoughts leave her head like she doesn't have room inside to take in what she is seeing.

"Rachel – I wasn't sure if it was you or not –" He is breathless. "So how've you been? You look great?" He leans in to kiss her on the cheek.

There is a faint brush of stubble against her skin. She feels a tingling run through her body. She takes a second to breathe in his scent. He is wearing the aftershave that she bought him last Christmas. She still loves how it smells on him.

"I've been good. You look well, Marcus."

"I'm on a bit of a health buzz. I've taken up cycling. I'm trying to keep busy, you know?" He knows he is speaking too quickly between the surprise and excitement of seeing her.

She nods. "How's work?"

"Busy but, yeah, it's good. There is a problem with the due diligence for the Francine buyout so everything is up in the air until that gets resolved. I've been working crazy doors but I've cut back on the travel a bit. I'm trying to do more through Skype and video conferencing. After we broke up I had to do a bit of an assessment of things in my life and that was one thing I needed to change – so no more sitting in hotel rooms eating dodgy room service and drinking the mini-bar dry."

"Well, I'm glad for you, Marcus."

"But enough about me, how've you been? Still solving the world's problems one case at a time?"

She nods. "Trying my best," she smiles.

"That's what makes you so good at your job, Rachel, it's because you care." He takes her in his arms and then steps backwards to look at her fully. "God, it's so good to see you."

"How are Eli and Alex and of course Jules, Brian and baby Leo?"

"They're all good . . . they miss you though . . . " His tone is bittersweet.

"Well, tell them I said hi."

"I will, of course I will – they'd love to see you, some time, you know . . . maybe when we're both a bit further down the line . . . "

"I'd really like that, Marcus."

Chapter 61

Ella drives down the hill and along the promenade past people jogging and power-walking, and mothers with a coffee-to-go in one hand, pushing three-wheeled buggies with the other, chatting as they walk. She pulls up at the school gate.

Celeste runs across the school car park and over to where Ella is waiting at the gate. It has been so long since she has seen Celeste like this. "I gave out my invitations and everyone says they're coming, Mummy!"

They have invited the whole class of twenty-four so that no one feels excluded.

"Really?" She tries not to sound too surprised. "Everyone?"

"Uh-huh!" Celeste nods her head enthusiastically.

Ella had expected most people to politely refuse. "Well, isn't that great!"

"And I've been thinking about it some more – can we have a mermaid makeover party, please?"

"That's a great idea – I like that one!"

"Thanks, Mum, I'm so excited!" Celeste exclaims happily.

"And I ordered your cake this morning – you're going to love it!"

"What's it like?"

"It's a surprise."

No matter what Dan says about her trying to woo back the other mothers, she doesn't care. She is buzzing: Celeste is finally letting her in. Once the kids come to the party, she's going to make sure they have so much fun that they'll forget all about excluding her.

Chapter 62

Rachel drives to St Dominic's Terrace. She rings the bell but there is no answer so she knocks gently on the glass in case Tina is sleeping. Finally the door opens and Jack is standing there.

"How are you doing, Jack?"

"I'm okay."

"Is your ma here?"

"She's asleep."

"Where's Libby?"

"She's gone home for a few hours to get a few things and to see the boys."

"Okay, well, do you mind if I come in for a few minutes? I need to talk to you about something anyway."

He groans audibly but Rachel ignores it. She follows him down the narrow hall with its shelves of ornaments and figurines. She sits down at the kitchen table but Jack bounces a ball up and down on the kitchen floor.

"I went to visit Conor."

That gets his attention. "Is he in his shop?"

"He is."

"Is he okay?"

"He's doing fine. He wanted me to tell you that he's doing well and not to worry about him."

Jack looks relieved. "Is Da going to go to jail?"

"Look, wee man, I can't tell you, that's going to be up to the judge – but try not to worry – none of this is your fault. Your dad shouldn't have done what he did. Is your mam awake?"

He nods. "She's upstairs in her room."

Rachel climbs the stairs and knocks on the door to Tina's bedroom.

"I thought I heard you downstairs all right," Tina says as Rachel comes into the room.

Rachel notices that she has got noticeably thinner over the last few weeks. Her skin clings to her bones and darkness shadows her face. Her breath comes in shallow beats.

Jack follows them in and lies up on the bed and cuddles into his mother.

"Hi, Tina, how are you feeling?"

"Sure can you not tell by the look of me?" she says in her usual sarcastic tone.

Rachel sits down on the chair beside her bed.

"Jack, love," Tina says, "would you mind getting me another pillow from the hot press – this headboard is too hard for my back."

Obediently he hops up and goes to do as Tina asks.

"I called into the bookshop earlier."

"Oh yeah? Did you ask that Conor fella what the fascination is with Jack?"

"Well, it seems Jack just started coming into the shop to have a chat and read a book and then it just became a habit. For what it's worth, from talking to Conor today and from what Jack has been saying, I don't think there is anything untoward going on. I actually think that perhaps Jack looks at Conor as a sort of father figure."

"Well, that wouldn't be hard, would it? When he has a father like John-Paul!"

"Did you tell Jack about going to live with Libby."

315

"I did."

"How did it go?"

"He was okay about it actually – he kept going on about goal-posts and bunk-beds and computer games. I think he's excited actually."

"Well, that's good anyway."

Tina grows quiet and Rachel knows what she is thinking.

"Obviously no one can give him as much as you can, Tina, we all know that. Unfortunately life isn't being very fair to you right now."

Tina nods. "I know," she says, her voice breaking.

"Are you okay?" Rachel reaches for her hand.

"I'm all right, I'm just sad, you know?"

"I think you're entitled to be."

Tina pulls back her hand. "Where has that fella got to with me pillow?"

The door opens and when Conor looks up from his paperwork Jack is standing in the middle of the shop floor.

"Jack – no way!" He rushes out from behind the till. "You cannot be serious – you have got to get out of here!"

Jack goes to move backwards and Conor feels bad for him.

"I'm sorry, Jack, but you just can't come back here any more – it's too dangerous. I'm not risking having your da finish me off for good this time – go on, go!" He points towards the door.

"I know I cause trouble but I just wanted to say that I'm sorry about the fight and all your broken bones and all the blood on your clothes and all the books that fell off the shelves and everything."

Conor is stunned. "I appreciate that, Jack, but you should go now."

"I don't like fighting even though all the boys in school love it. There was one time when Seán Brady beat the head off Kev Higgins and everyone thought it was great and they were roaring 'Fight! Fight! Fight!' but I didn't because poor Kev Higgins was lying on the ground with his two hands over his face and Seán kept on kicking him even though Kev wasn't even fighting back. Then when Seán stopped, Kev got up and ran home crying because Seán hurted him really bad and everyone started laughing at him and telling him to 'run home to his mammy for a cuddle' but I didn't."

"I don't like fighting myself, never have. But what happened to me wasn't your fault, okay? You know that I don't blame you, don't you?"

Jack nods. "Okay, well, I'm going to go now and, don't worry, I won't come back here again even though I like you, and your sandwiches, and your books."

"I think it's probably for the best, Jack."

Jack walks to the door with his shoulders dropped and Conor feels bad.

"How's everything at home?" he calls after him.

"It's all right. Libby did the shopping yesterday and she bought all the wrong things. She bought the spaghetti that I don't like – I only like the hoops not the ones that look like snakes. Ma said that I hadta eat it and stop being such a fusspot but it was all slimy and gross and I nearly got sick."

"You're a hard man to please, Jack White."

"That's what Ma says too. Well, I better go now in case Da comes back and tries to beat you up again."

"I think that would be a good move."

"Okay, bye."

"Bye."

He watches Jack as his small, skinny body makes his way along the road until soon he is out of sight.

Chapter 63

It is the morning of Celeste's birthday party and Ella has set her alarm for six, but she is already awake before it goes off. She throws on her tracksuit bottoms and Dan's hoody and goes up to the kitchen. She looks out the window and sees daylight is just starting to break across the bay. Making herself a black coffee, she takes her mug outside where the heat of the mug meets the cool air in rising steam. She sits up onto her usual rock. She likes this one because it is flat for the most part with a groove beneath where she can tuck in her feet. There is an intense pinky-orange sun rising on the horizon. A ferry is gliding majestically out of Dublin Port, leaving a silvery trail of backwashed water behind it as it traverses the Irish Sea. When she sits out here in the morning stillness on the very edge of Ireland with its sheer cliff faces behind her, it reminds her that her and her problems are only a minute dot in this whole universe. There is no one standing between her and the horizon. No one shouting abuse or crying for her attention. In days gone past, she has stood on this headland and imagined stepping off it and plunging straight down into the deep water lapping at its edge. She has lain in bed and thought about how the water would feel as it washed over her and brought her down as she sank into its darkness. She knows she would never do it though – the kids stop her from doing something like that.

She thinks back to how this time nine years ago, a screaming, angry Celeste had just been placed into her arms and how bruised and battered and exhausted she had felt after forty-eight hours of labour which ended in an emergency Caesarean section. Celeste has never come easily to her. Nothing about her relationship with her eldest daughter has ever been easy. She wavers on the balance of an almost primeval, smothering love for her and yet sadness and guilt at why she can never seem to get close to her. That is why she wants today to be perfect. She wants Celeste to look back on this day when she is older and remember the party with fondness. This will be the day she remembers when she is backpacking around Asia and is feeling homesick or when she has a bad day in whatever her chosen path is and longs to be back in childhood again. She wants this to be the memory that she goes to in her mind. A kind of synthetic, go-to memory.

She brings the mug to her lips and drinks back the last of her coffee. She has a lot to do. She had always been too busy before to have a proper party, but today she is determined to make up for it. Although she has had the cake professionally made and the caterers are taking care of the food, she wants to add her own touches. There are decorations to be hung, cocktails to be prepped for the parents and she wants to bake some buns herself. As well as Celeste's classmates, she has invited both her and Dan's families. It's a Saturday so Conor has to work. She gets off the rock and picks her path back up to the stone steps of the tower.

She rolls the icing, watching the white mass spread larger, then she lifts it up with the rolling-pin, just like the book told her to do, but it breaks. So she brings it all back together again into a ball and spreads yet more icing sugar onto the table and rolls . . . but the same thing happens again.

"Damn it, I can't get this to work at all. I think I've used too much icing sugar!"

"But I don't understand why you need to do that when we already have a cake?" Dan says, coming into the kitchen and pointing over to the mermaid-shaped cake lying along the crest of an azure-blue wave, which sits in pride of place on the table.

"I told you – I want to add my own touches – I want Celeste to be able to say that her mum baked her something for once in her life even if it tastes disgusting."

"You put too much pressure on yourself." He lifts a marshmallow-and-strawberry kebab and brings it up to his lips.

"Will you please stop eating them, Dan – we'll have none left for the kids!"

"No one is coming, Mummy!" Celeste comes up into the kitchen with her arms folded.

"They will, don't worry."

"But it's nearly two o'clock and no one is here yet."

"We're going to have a great party, Celeste," she says determinedly, trying again to pick up the icing but it falls apart. "Oh here, I give up!" she says, throwing it back down on the table.

"She has a point," Dan says, looking at the clock.

"Look, I keep telling you, it's going to be great."

"So you keep saying."

Ella has made bunting out of old dresses and tops that she doesn't wear any more and it hangs from wall to wall, crisscrossing the ceiling. Balloons tied with long tails of ribbons are weighted down around the walls. Shells she picked up along the cove decorate every surface, as do cardboard anchors. She has ordered gold glittery mermaid tails from eBay with elasticated waistbands for the children to wear. The pamper girls are setting up in the sitting room and the caterers are already working away doing the finishing touches. Everything is ready to go.

Dan comes over and puts his arms around her. "You've gone all Cath Kidson and I like it," he says, fingering a piece of bunting hanging on the wall near them. "Where's your floral apron?"

"Very funny! I just want to get it right, y'know – give Celeste a birthday party that she will remember instead of the last-minute Tesco job like I usually do."

"You've done a great job. I'm really proud of you."

"Well, let's wait and see if people turn up first," she says, nervously looking up at the clock again.

Her phone vibrates in her pocket. She takes it out and answers it.

"Hi, Ella, it's Katie's mother Wendy here."

Katie had only started in Celeste's class last month after moving to the area from New York after her dad was transferred to Ireland with his company. She is probably the only person who isn't aware of Ella's scandal and gladly accepted the invitation and even offered to come over early to help her out.

"Oh hi, Wendy, I hope you're not lost?" She'd had directions to the house printed on the back of the invitations.

"No, but my little guy Tyler, Katie's brother, has just woken up covered in chicken-pox welts."

"Oh no, poor little guy!" Ella's heart sinks.

"I know, talk about bad timing! He's scratching like mad and really cranky. And Ed is working so I have no one to mind him . . . we won't be able to make it unfortunately. Katie is so upset – she's so mad with her little brother and I keep trying to explain to her that it's not his fault. It's at times like this I sure miss having my family around, I can tell you."

"That is such a pity." Ella tries to mask the disappointment in her voice. At least she knows for definite that at least one of the children in Celeste's class will come because she goes to everything. Her mother has eight children and is only too glad to off-load one of them for three hours – she isn't fussy about who the hosts are.

"Mum, there's still no one here and it's after two o'clock."

"Look, here's someone now," she says, looking out the kitchen window to the car coming over the headland.

Celeste rolls her eyes. "That's Granddad."

"Yeah, well, I'm sure they'll all be here soon."

She hurries downstairs. "Hi, Dad," she says as she opens the door to him.

"Hello, my love."

Celeste hurtles down the stairs and runs straight into his arms.

"And how's my favourite birthday girl?"

Her sister Andrea arrives with her kids soon after so that keeps Celeste occupied and she stops reminding Ella of the lack of guests. Celeste, Dot and Andrea's two daughters sit up on high stools and the pamper girls start transforming them into mermaids and they giggle as they put hair bands around their heads and start applying lots of sparkly eye shadow.

Finally a car belonging to a non-family member pulls up outside.

"Louisa is here, Mum!" Celeste squeals, pulling open the heavy door and running down the steps to her. The two girls run back inside past Ella.

Then more cars arrive and soon there are seventeen girls from Celeste's class running around inside the tower. The pamper ladies are working hard on making over the girls.

"They're having a great time. Celeste is having a ball. You've done a great job," Dan says, putting his arm around her as they watch her father, who is pretending to be a pirate, chasing a group of squealing girls around the kitchen.

Ella is starting to wonder if the mermaid tails were a good idea after all. "Slow down, girls – we don't want anyone to trip now!" she chides gently.

They cut the cake and sing happy birthday to a beaming Celeste. Ella feels a huge surge of pride looking at her daughter's excited face. She wraps her into a big hug, kissing her forehead over and over again and for once Celeste doesn't push her away.

After a while one of the pamper girls comes up the stairs. "The kids are all done. We're going to head on now, if that's okay?"

"Sure, of course." She takes the envelope with the money to pay them out of the drawer where she had left it earlier. "Thanks for all your hard work."

She sees them down the stairs. Andrea's bag is sitting on the hall table where she left it when she came in the door. Ella closes the door after them and walks over and opens the bag. Andrea's Orla Kiely wallet is sticking out and inside there are sheets of paper folded in half, the lid of a lipstick, a box of raisins, a few loose coins. She lifts up the wallet and moves the zip back across the teeth with difficulty. When she opens it, she sees there is a twenty-euro note, bank cards and loyalty cards for supermarkets and coffee shops. She lifts the twenty out and holds it between her thumb and forefinger. It is so tempting, it is almost unbearable the rush that calls to her. She folds the note in two and is about to slip it inside the pocket of her jeans. She is wrestling the feeling, the need to do this. If she does it now then she has crossed a line and gone back to that dark place again and she is afraid of what lies in wait for her over that line. For the first time in her life she is going to say no to it, she isn't going to let it control her life any more. She finally feels strong enough to resist the urge. She puts the money back in the wallet and the wallet back down inside the bag and goes back upstairs.

Chapter 64

"Conor?" a woman's voice says at the other end of the phone.

"Yes?"

"It's Rachel here – Rachel McLoughlin – I'm the social worker working with Jack White?"

"Oh hi, Rachel."

"I wanted to let you know that Jack's mother passed away this morning –"

"Jesus . . . so soon . . . how is he . . . is he okay?"

"It's hard to say, to be honest – he's a bit stunned – it's like he keeps forgetting and then he asks for her and remembers. He hasn't cried yet though, which is worrying. Libby and her family are all here but the reason I'm calling you is because he's been asking for you."

"Really?"

"I thought maybe you might come over to him? Don't worry, John-Paul isn't here – he is still in Garda custody."

"Sure, of course, if it's okay with everyone else?"

"Yes, it is. The address is 9 St Dominic's Terrace."

"Okay, well then, I'll be right over."

Conor gets a taxi to the address Rachel has given him.

He walks down the hallway and enters the kitchen. He sees

Jack sitting beside a woman with similar features to him. He presumes this is Libby. From looking at the photos of Jack and Tina on the wall, she looks like her but Tina's face was more weathered. There are three boys sitting in a row on stools and he guesses these must be Libby's sons, the cousins that Jack is always talking about. There is a pot of tea on the table and he instantly feels awkward, like he is intruding. He stands in the doorway, waiting for someone to notice him. Jack looks up, jumps up and runs towards him. He wraps his arms around him tightly and Conor, feeling all eyes on him, does the same.

"Ma die-ded."

"I'm sorry, Jack . . . I'm so, so sorry."

"I don't like the people being here. They keep looking at me." He is trembling. "They tell me to go in and see Ma but I don't want to see her. She doesn't look like me ma."

"It's okay, love," Libby says, coming up beside him, "it's all right – everyone just wants to help you, pet."

"It's going to be okay, Jack," says Conor, "do you hear me?"

Jack nods. "I miss her, Conor, it's all weird."

"I'm not going to lie to you, Jack – you're going to miss her a lot and it's going to be weird for a long time but you've got to remember what we said happens when people die."

"They're still with us but we can't see them?"

"That's it."

"Do you think ma is watching me now?"

"Oh, I think so, in fact I'm sure she is."

Libby brings Conor over and introduces him to her family. He offers his condolences and then sits down beside Mrs Morton while Jack and his cousins play on the X-box in the corner of the room.

"I'm tired," Jack says after a while.

"I bet you are – you've had a tough day," Conor says.

"Maybe I should take you up to bed, buddy?" Libby says, stroking his hair.

"Can Conor take me?"

"I don't know – I –" He hesitates, looking around him.

Libby looks at Conor. "Do you mind?"

"Of course not."

"Thanks, Conor."

He takes Jack up to bed and sits on the chair at the side of the bed as Jack starts pulling off his tracksuit bottoms and hoody and putting his legs into his pyjama bottoms.

"Do you not want to wear a top?" Conor asks.

"I don't like wearing tops because I always get too hot." He jumps in under the duvet. "I don't like all these people being in my house. I want them all to go home. I miss Ma, Conor."

"I know, Jack, but they just want to help you."

"Libby says she's gone to a better place but she's wrong because there is no better place than with us. She always said you can give her fancy holidays but her favourite place in the world was with me." He looks pale and exhausted.

"Remember what we said about her being still with you?"

"Yeah?"

"Well, your ma is with you right now and she wouldn't like to see you sad, would she?"

"I guess not. She'd say 'Take that puss off you, sure you haven't got a care in the world'."

"Exactly."

"I'm so sleepy."

"Why don't you close your eyes?" He remembers that after Leni died the exhaustion from the emotional grief was incredible but he couldn't sleep. Jack is probably feeling the same.

"Promise you'll stay with me?"

"I'll be right here."

Conor watches as Jack's lids grow heavier, droop and fall until they finally close.

Conor wakes up sometime and light is creeping in around the curtains. He sits up and checks his watch. He notices someone has draped a blanket over him. Jack is still sound asleep and Conor watches the soft rise and fall of his chest. He hopes he is in the middle of a happy dream far away from here.

When Jack wakes, he leaves him to get dressed while he goes downstairs. Libby is sitting at the kitchen table clasping a mug and her eyes are red-rimmed. She starts when she sees him.

"Sorry, Conor – I didn't hear you come in – is Jack awake yet?"

"He is, he's just getting dressed, and he'll be down in a minute."

"Thanks for sitting in with him last night – I peeped in and you were fast asleep in the chair."

"Was it you who put the blanket over me?"

She smiles. "I did."

"Well, thank you. Did you manage to get any sleep at all yourself?"

She shakes her head. "I just couldn't, you know." She starts to choke up. "I'm sorry – I'm just finding this all very hard," she whispers. "I mean, I knew she was dying but now that she's left us – I just don't know how I'm going to do this." Her voice breaks with tears. "I miss her so much already."

"I know what you're going through – my partner Leni died last year."

"So you know what it's like then. I'm sorry you had to go through this too, Conor."

He nods. "What time did everyone go home?"

"Most went around midnight. My husband took my three boys off home before eleven – they were exhausted – yesterday was a long day."

"I can imagine."

"I'm sure they'll all be over again soon anyway."

"Any word on John-Paul?"

"They're not releasing him on bail as they reckon he poses a risk to Jack. Garda Maguire reckons he's looking at a hefty sentence, first for assaulting you and then for the abduction of a minor. He said the judge might be lenient because of the mitigating circumstances such as the court ruling earlier on that day but still they're very serious charges."

Jack comes in then.

"Jack, pet, how did you sleep?" She forces brightness into her voice.

"I dreamt me and Ma were on an airplane and Ma didn't like it because we had no pilot so we couldn't take off and she said 'What kind of a shower is this at all?'"

Libby laughs. "That's exactly what she would say, Jack. Would you two like some breakfast?" She turns to Conor. "One of the neighbours left stuff for a fry-up in the fridge."

"Well, okay . . . I mean, if it's not too much trouble."

"No bother, we've a long day ahead – we need to get a good breakfast into us. What would you like?"

"Can I have Coco Pops?"

"Go on then –"

Jack gets up and pours his own cereal. They all sit around chatting while Libby starts the fry. Conor phones Liam to ask him to open up the shop for him so he can stay on with Jack.

"Would you like to go to the cinema for a few hours, Jack?" Conor hopes it will help take his mind off things and also give Libby a chance to organise things for the funeral.

"Okay – but only if I can get a supersize popcorn?"

"Are you trying to blackmail me, Jack White?" Conor asks in mock indignation.

When they get back, Jack sees his cousins playing on the road and runs to join them. Conor goes on into the house and sees Rachel is in the kitchen talking to Libby. Mrs Morton and a few other ladies that he doesn't know are making sandwiches.

"How's he doing?" Libby asks.

"It's hard to know – one minute he's okay and then at other times he just looks so lost."

Libby nods. "He is lost, poor fella." Her voice threatens to break again.

"What's going to happen to him?" Conor asks, sitting down with them at the table.

"Well, as you know the court have granted me full guardianship as per Tina's wishes, so when he's ready, Jack will be coming to live with me and my family. I don't want to uproot him straight away, I want to give him time to make the adjustment – he's had a tough couple of weeks, God love him."

"You live in Wicklow, right?"

"Yeah, we're out in the heart of the countryside. Jack loves it there – we've a big garden and any amount of trees for boys like that to climb. And he loves his cousins. There is a good school where mine all go and the principal has him down to start in a couple of weeks, when he's feeling up to it, you know?"

"I suppose it's the best outcome for him."

"I'm going to do my best by him for Tina."

"I know you will. Look, I need to go back to the shop and sort a few things out with Liam, the guy I have covering for me, and I want to grab a shower and a change of clothes but I'll be back in a couple of hours."

"Sure – you don't have to be here, you know – if you have stuff you need to do –"

"No, no, I want to be here – I'll just be a couple of hours."

"Well, take your time – Jack is occupied playing at the moment."

"I'll walk out with you," Rachel says.

They go out the front door and walk down the path to where Rachel has parked her car.

"Want a lift?"

"Nah, I'm only a few streets away."

"Look, I just want to say thanks for all that you're doing for Jack right now."

"There's no need – he means a lot to me."

"There's more. I want to say that I'm sorry for misjudging you – you know, when we first met?"

"You don't have to apologise – I understand why you might have thought that my motives . . . weren't entirely good . . ."

"It's just sometimes doing this job makes me very cynical – I tend to see the worst in things because that's what I'm so used to seeing, if that makes sense?"

"It does."

"Well, I'd better go – I've an appointment but I'll be over tomorrow morning before the funeral just to make sure that Libby is getting on okay."

"I think she's going to be good for Jack, you know – it's a stable setting and he gets on really well with his cousins. Obviously it'll never compare to having his own mother alive but he's lucky he has her."

"He is lucky – it makes my job a hell of a lot easier too, I can tell you, when I know someone like Libby is there to step in. Right, I'll see you tomorrow, Conor. And thanks again. For everything."

Chapter 65

Conor is sitting in a pew a few rows behind Jack who is sitting in the first pew with Libby and her family. He watches as people go up and shake their hands before taking a seat. The coffin stands lonely in the centre of the aisle, surrounded by wreaths of flowers. There are also photos of Tina at different stages of her life. There is one of her holding Jack as a baby and Conor finds himself looking away from it. It's just too heartbreaking.

Jack turns around and catches his eye. Conor puts a half smile on his face and Jack does the same.

"How is he?" Rachel whispers as she slides into the pew beside Conor.

"He's all right. I don't think it has hit him yet, to be honest. John-Paul isn't here?" he says, turning around to do a quick scan of the church.

"Well, even if they let him come here on compassionate grounds, I don't think he'd dare show his face."

"Good – it's better that way."

"Well, the last thing Jack needs right now is more drama with his dad."

Conor nods. The priest clears his throat before starting his homily.

When the service is over, they all walk heavily back out into the morning sunlight. Rachel and Conor stand on the steps where the sun is glinting off the white marble. "I'm driving to the crematorium if you want a lift?"

"That'd be great, thanks."

Conor gets into Rachel's car and puts on his seatbelt. He notices that it smells of her perfume. She takes off her heels to drive in her stocking-feet.

At the crematorium Jack is on the seat in front of them and Conor notices from behind how he tenses up as the coffin is retracted mechanically behind the curtain. Libby has one arm around his shoulders, while she uses her right hand to dab at her eyes with a tissue.

They all head back to St Dominic's Terrace when it is over. Mrs Morton and a few of the other neighbours are dishing out sandwiches and serving cups of tea.

"Are you feeling okay, mate?" Conor says, coming up beside Jack who is pouring himself a glass of Coke.

"Yeah, but I wish Ma was here." He is pulling at the collar of his shirt.

"I know you do," Conor says. "Here, let me open the top button for you."

After a while Jack gets changed out of the trousers and shirt that Libby had dressed him in for the funeral and goes out on the green to play football with his cousins.

That evening, after most people have cleared out of the house, Libby's husband takes the boys home.

"That must have been some game of football – your hair is all sweaty," Conor says as they climb the stairs.

"Yeah, and Stephen said I could be Ronaldo even though Eoghan wanted to be as well."

"Cool."

"Libby didn't tell me to put back on my glasses. Ma always makes me wear my glasses even when I'm playing football."

He sounds sad.

"She has a lot on her mind at the moment, Jack."

"I like having Libby here and you and my cousins – it's lots of fun – but I miss Ma – I wish she was here too because it's like we're having a party and she loved parties."

"Of course you do, Jack . . . but just remember what I said? I bet she's here with us, having a great time too – it's just that we can't see her.

"Ma wanted to be burn-ded because she said she didn't want the worms eating her up and spiders crawling all over her in the ground. Ma hates spiders."

"Yeah, some people hate the thought of being buried in the soil. My girlfriend Leni was the same."

"She got burn-ded as well?"

"She did."

"I don't think I'd like to be burn-ded."

"Me neither. I think I'll take my chances with the worms."

When Jack dozes off, Conor goes downstairs. The only ones left are Libby and Rachel. They are sitting chatting at the table.

"Did he go off all right?"

"He did. The boys have him exhausted. You look tired yourself, Libby."

"I am, but even if I went to bed I don't think I'd sleep."

Conor nods. "Well, I guess I'd better be off home now," he says.

"Thank you so much for coming, Conor – I'm really grateful for the support and it's meant so much to Jack."

"I'm glad, Libby."

"And I think I'll head off myself," Rachel says. She stands up and starts to put on her coat.

"Thanks for coming, Rachel," Libby says. "I'm sure it's not part of the job to go to funerals and we really appreciate you being here today."

"I wanted to come to pay my respects to Tina – and Jack too, y'know."

"Well, thanks, we appreciate it."

"I'll call around again in the morning. Try and get some sleep, Libby, you've had a long day." She puts her hand over the other woman's.

"I'll go up in a while."

"Right, I'll see you tomorrow."

"See you then."

Conor and Rachel walk out to where her car is parked on the street.

"Do you want a lift?" she offers.

"Nah, I could use the walk to clear my head, to be honest."

They both fall silent for a moment until Conor speaks again. "Will Jack be all right?"

"I think so, I hope so. I'm doing this job for over twelve years now and, believe me, I've seen a lot. I've seen people whose love for alcohol and drugs will always be stronger than their love for their children – it's sad and it's hard to watch and we're all programmed to believe that Mother Nature will kick in and be the strongest force – maybe it's Hollywood – but unfortunately it isn't that way for everyone. It's a sad fact but that's life. But Tina was one where Mother Nature did kick in and she turned her life around all because of her love for Jack. People like her are the reason that I do this job. The hope and belief in humanity that people can change. Otherwise why would anyone do it?"

"I understand what you're saying. Hope is what keeps us all afloat, isn't it?"

She nods. "It's like that Emily Dickinson poem – '*Hope is the thing with feathers that perches in the soul –*'"

"'*And sings the tune without the words and never stops at all*,'" he finishes it for her.

Their eyes meet and she looks away quickly. "God, sorry, listen to me yakking on! Sorry, I don't usually lose the run of myself like that . . . " She can feel the heat rise in her cheeks. She stuffs her hands down inside the pockets of her coat.

"My girlfriend is mad about that poem," he says eventually. He still hates using the word 'was' about Leni because it makes him feel he is being disloyal to her. You would use the word 'was' if you broke up with someone but he and Leni never broke up.

"The photo in your shop – the one beside the till – is that her?"

"It is –"

"She's very pretty."

"She is." He feels awkward keeping up the present tense. "She died last year."

"Oh my goodness, I'm so sorry!" Her hands fly to her mouth. "Why do I always do things like this?"

"Here, I can see if there's a shovel out the back if you want to dig yourself out of the hole?" He is smiling at her.

"How did she die?"

"She was mugged for her phone but the guy who did it pushed her backwards and she fell and banged her head against the pavement and that was it. She was on life support and myself and her family had to make the decision to turn off the machine because the Leni that I knew and loved wasn't coming back again."

"God, that must have been so awful for you."

"It was – it still is to be honest –"

"I can't imagine . . . so that's why you understand what Jack is going through. And there's me crying a river over a break-up when what you have to deal with is so much worse."

"It's all perspective – I'm sure whatever you're going through is a pretty big deal for you."

"I just wish I could find a way of moving on, you know? Because I know in my heart and soul that it was never going to work out between us. God, listen to me banging on! What is wrong with me?" She laughs.

Rachel always appeared uptight and aloof every time that

he had met her but here he was getting a glimpse of a different Rachel, the Rachel that her friends and family saw presumably.

"Did you ever try lighting a paper lantern?"

"Huh?"

"You know, the Chinese paper lanterns that you see at weddings and things. Well, please don't think I'm nuts – it was Leni who got me into them actually. Sometimes I light them with messages inside them for her. I tell her things from my day or I tell her how I'm feeling, how much I miss her. Or other times they're just angry rants about how cheated by life and fate I feel."

"So you think I should write a message to Marcus?"

"Well, not so much a message to him but a letter about how you're feeling about it all – it really helps to straighten your head out when you put the words down on paper. You'd be amazed – it's quite therapeutic."

"I don't think I'm really the writing kind – I'd feel a bit silly doing that –"

"Well, I didn't think I was either but Leni used to love lighting them and I found after she died it really helped me to reconnect with her. I don't know how or why but maybe it was because I knew it was something that she would do, if you know what I mean?"

Rachel nods. "I get what you're saying."

"And now I find myself doing it automatically – whenever I'm missing her or if I have a bad day."

"Well, maybe I'll try it sometime . . . "

"It doesn't make the pain go away but it helps for some reason."

"Okay, I'll take your word for it," she laughs.

"You think I'm for the birds, don't you?"

"No, I don't honestly,"

They stay talking for a while before Rachel says. "I'd better go – it's been a long day."

Chapter 66

Conor is cutting some sellotape to gift-wrap a book for a customer when he sees the white van pull up on the path outside. He watches as the driver unloads more equipment and carries it into the shell of the unit next door. They have been working on it all week and a sign has gone up this morning to say that a new coffee shop will be opening there soon. It will be good for Haymarket Books to have a coffee shop beside it. There was an item on the news that morning where an economist reckoned the recession was over. Maybe things are finally on the up. He hopes so – it's been a long time coming. He puts the book in a bag and then says goodbye to the customer.

The door opens shortly after and in walks Rachel.

"Rachel, nice to see you! Is everything okay with Jack? I was going to call over to see him later on."

"He's fine but I just wanted to let you know that he's going to live with Libby tomorrow. We both felt it was time that he got into a routine and had some normality back in his life – well, as normal as things can get for a boy who has just lost his mother."

Conor gulps. "I see, it's for the best, I'm sure."

"It is. I . . . eh . . . thought you might like to say goodbye

337

to him before he goes?"

"Oh God – I don't know, Rachel – I don't think I could do that –"

"Really?"

"I'm sorry, I realise that sounds really selfish but I'm not good at goodbyes." He hates himself for being so weak.

"Oh . . . I see . . . I thought it would be good for Jack . . . "

"I'm sorry, Rachel, I can't do it – I'm sorry – I just can't."

"He thinks a lot of you, y'know! Can't you at least come and say goodbye to him and wish him well?"

"No, I'm sorry." He is brusque.

"So that's it, you're going to let him go out of your life just like that?"

"It's for the best."

"But he's always going to wonder why you didn't come!"

"I said I can't do it, all right?" His tone is sharp and final.

"Right . . . well, it's up to you." She looks disappointed in him.

"I'm sorry, Rachel, but it's better this way."

"Is it? For you or for Jack?" Then she turns and walks away from him.

Chapter 67

Dublin, 2012

The room is white. Leni looks like an angel. Her hair is the only thing that is different. He can see the part where they had to shave it in the theatre. She is fast asleep, her skin is pale, her full lips are not as pink as usual. The doctors have talked them all through it in hushed solemn tones – him, her parents and her brother. They have explained to them exactly what is going to happen. They all nodded to say that they understood. They gather around her bed where they are supposed to be saying goodbye to her and holding her hand for the last time before the organ-donor guys take what they need, scavenge her body to give life to another and the ventilator is turned off.

It is then that he realises that he can't do it, he can't do this. Beads of sweat break out across his forehead and neck. He stands up from the chair and rushes out the door. He can hear them calling after him but he keeps running down the corridor past trolleys and IV machines. Nurses and visitors clear out of his way and he keeps on running, down the granite hospital steps, weaving his way through the rush-hour traffic and away from goodbyes.

Chapter 68

"Sorry for dropping in unannounced," Conor says.

"You don't need an invitation to come to see me, you know that. Come in."

"Where are the girls?"

"Dan has brought them to drama so myself and Maisie have the house to ourselves for an hour."

After she has made him a coffee, they sit at the table.

"How are you doing?" he asks.

"Things are a lot better, a lot, lot better. Dan is being brilliant. You were right about telling him. I already feel like a huge weight has lifted just having it out in the open like that and, guess what, after the first shock he wasn't horrified that his wife is a shoplifter or got too drunk at a party and ended up having to get an abortion – he was just really sad that I didn't feel I was able to tell him all of this before now. I had my first psychotherapy session last week – God, I hate that word, it makes me sound like a lunatic."

"How did it go?"

"It went well actually. I've been diagnosed with kleptomania. It's is a type of impulse-control disorder where you can't resist the temptation or drive to perform an act. It can be triggered by stress. I won't lie, it was tough going back

340

there and I've a long road ahead of me. It's not going to be easy but I wish I had done it years ago. I felt so much lighter even after the first session. She also thinks I may have had undiagnosed post-natal depression after all three pregnancies which makes complete sense so I've been to my GP about that and I've started on some meds which seem to be helping. I'm not crying every day now. I think the weight of darkness is finally starting to lift. Even with the girls it's like I can see them properly for the first time without guilt beating me up."

"I'm so glad for you, Ella. I really am. I don't know how you suffered for that long."

"I also called into the store –"

"Really?"

"I had a chat with the manager. I wanted to say sorry in person."

"How did it go?"

"Well, I apologised and I told him what had happened and why I did it. I told him that I'm getting help for it. He was very nice actually and then he said that as both items have been recovered that perhaps they could withdraw the charges, providing I make a donation to charity and on condition that I never engage in theft in their store again. He said that because of my public persona I've already suffered enough."

"Oh my goodness, that's brilliant news! I'm very proud of you. I'm so glad you're finally getting the second chance that you deserve."

She is beaming. "It's such a relief, I can tell you. So how's everything with you?"

"Jack's mother died."

"Oh no, I'm sorry. How is he?"

"He's doing okay. He's lucky his aunt is great and she's going to take good care of him. He's going to live with her tomorrow. Rachel – that's the social worker – she wants me to go over there to say goodbye to him."

"And you're going to go, aren't you?"

"I can't – I feel awful but I can't do it."

"Conor!"

"I know I feel awful but I just can't do it."

"Is it because of Leni?"

He nods. "I never told you this but, when we were all called in to say goodbye to her, I ran. I ran out of the hospital. I couldn't do it. I never said goodbye to her."

"I never knew that, Conor."

"Well, I'm not exactly proud of it! I'm going to miss Jack a lot. When I look at him, I can't help thinking if Leni had had a boy that he might have been like Jack."

"I know this is hard for you, Conor, but think of Jack. What is he going to think if you don't show up to say goodbye to him? He's going to think you don't care at all for him!"

"He knows that's not true."

"Does he? He's eight years old! You owe it to him to go over there and say goodbye to him. You were the one who told me it was time to face up to the past and to stop running away from my demons. Well, I think I could say the same thing to you."

Chapter 69

The winter is over. It is an unusually warm April day as Conor walks down past the railings of St Dominic's Terrace. He notices that a few children have bravely donned summer clothes. He stands outside Number 9, takes a deep breath and rings the bell,

"Conor, you came!" Rachel answers the door.

He nods. "I want to give him something before he goes."

"He's upstairs in his room, packing up the last of his things, if you want to go up to him? Libby is sorting a few things out in the kitchen."

He climbs the stairs and, from the landing through the open door to his bedroom, he sees Jack sitting on his bed staring off into space.

"That doesn't look like packing to me!"

"Conor!" Jack runs to him and throws his arms around him and Conor knows he made the right decision to come.

"How are you feeling?"

"I'm okay, I'm a little bit nervous."

"That's normal. It's going to be a big change at first but remember what we said about change?"

"You can't have something good happen without first having some change?"

343

"Exactly! So you do listen to me!"

Jack grins up at him with his gappy smile, having recently lost his other front tooth. "Libby said I get to sleep in a bunk-bed!"

"Cool. I want to give you this." He hands him a copy of *Tom's Midnight Garden*. "It's a first edition – that means it's really old – it's the first version of the book that ever came out, so you have to mind it, yeah? Put it in a safe place with all your football autographs."

"I don't want it." He hands it back to Conor.

"But why? You love that book and you still have four more chapters to go!"

"But if you give me the book I won't be able to come back and read in your shop."

"Hey, it's okay – of course you can come back to read in my shop. And maybe I can come and see you too sometimes if Libby says it's okay."

"You promise?"

"I promise."

"Cross your heart and hope to die?"

"Cross my heart and hope to die."

"Stick a needle in your eye?"

"Stick a needle in my eye."

When Jack has finished packing, Conor helps him to carry his case down the stairs.

They walk out the front to where Libby is packing things into her boot. The sunlight glints on the paint on the car and hits Jack's eyes in a thousand shiny particles. Libby smiles warmly as she turns towards Conor and Jack, and Rachel who is following behind them.

"Are you ready, little man?" Libby asks. "Your cousins are all waiting for you – they're all so excited. I think they have lots of fun in store for you. I have bunk beds ordered and I thought you and Eoghan might share? You can take turns to sleep in the top one. The only thing is our dog Freddy likes to sleep in Eoghan's room at night so I hope that will be okay with you?

Jacks face lights up. "Can he sleep on my bed?"

"Sure," she says, laughing. "Now we were thinking of having a barbecue for our tea later because it's so nice out and it's not often we get the chance to have our tea outside in Ireland. You do like burgers, don't you, Jack?"

He nods enthusiastically. "But I don't like tomatoes," he adds as a caveat.

"Sure haven't I known you since you were a baby? Of course I know that." She rubs his hair. "We'd better go – the boys are waiting for you to play football – they need you to even up the teams. They're so excited because now they'll be able to play two a side."

He walks over towards the car before turning back around and running smack into Conor's chest full force and throwing both arms around his waist.

Conor bends and puts his arms around the boy. He clings tightly to him and breathes in the smell of his clammy head. This boy who has become such a huge part of his life, who gave him a purpose when he thought he had nothing to live for – this boy who means the world to him. Conor can see the tears in his eyes. He grips him close. "God, I'm going to miss you." He stands back and bends down on his hunkers. "I love you, Jack White – you know that, don't you?"

Jack nods. "I love you too."

"You're going to be good for Libby, yeah?"

Jack nods. Conor swallows back a lump in his throat and stands up.

"Okay, you'd better go now. Libby is waiting for you."

She walks over to him and Jack looks up at her, sadness filling his eyes. She bends down and whispers in his ear. "It's all going to be okay, Jack, I promise you. I promised your mother that I would take good care of you and that's exactly what I'm going to do. We're going to be a team. I know I'll never be able to replace your mam but I'm going to do my very best for you, okay, buddy?"

"Okay."

He places his hand in hers and they walk towards the car. Jack climbs into the back seat, Libby into the front.

Rachel, who had been standing back, comes up beside him now. "Are you okay?"

He nods, not trusting himself to speak. He is working very hard at keeping back the tears.

They watch as Libby checks her mirrors carefully and then waves. They pull out and drive off down Haymarket Road.

"You did the right thing, you know, coming here today," Rachel says, reaching out to squeeze his hand tightly. "I'm glad you came."

And he finds himself squeezing hers back even tighter.

Chapter 70

They stand on the sand of Dollymount Strand. Smoothened pebbles stick out like jewels on the flattened sand. Waves break in a foamy arc at their feet before creeping up towards them. The clouds leave wispy trails across the sky like a stretched and pulled fleece.

"Am I holding it right?" Rachel asks him.

"Maybe turn it this way slightly."

"Like this?"

He comes behind her and adjusts the position of her arms. He pulls back the match and cups his other hand around the flame to protect it from the wind before holding it up to the lighting strip of the lantern. They both watch it come to life.

"Will I let it go?"

He nods. They watch as its orange glow soars up, caught on the wind.

"For Jack."

"For Jack."

THE END

ACKNOWLEDGEMENTS

When I was writing this book and whenever anybody asked me what it was called, I referred to it as *Into the Night Sky* also known as 'The Book That Nearly Killed Me'. I'm not being facetious; I really struggled at several points to finish it. There were many times where I felt it wasn't going anywhere and I questioned whether I might be better off scrapping it and starting something new. That's why to be at this stage, where I get to write my acknowledgements, is a bit like when you climb to the top of a mountain and are finally rewarded with the view.

In writing *Into The Night Sky* I am majorly indebted to so many people but special thanks must go to the following:

Firstly, to everyone in Poolbeg thank you. To Paula Campbell for your faith in me, especially in difficult times. I am really excited to be working with you, going forward in a new direction. Ailbhe, for all your hard work. To my editor Gaye Shortland for pushing me when you know I can do better. I really find your critical eye invaluable. You are always able to pinpoint the things that I know aren't working but can't quite figure out why. Your insight has definitely made this a better book.

My agent Sallyanne Sweeney for being warm and kind, and

most importantly, for your encouragement. We're only starting out but I'm looking forward to working with you on lots more books!

I am also hugely grateful to Niamh Maher who spent a lot of time helping me with the research for Rachel and Jack's storylines in this book when, yet again, I felt as though I was banging my head up against a wall. Thank you for sharing with me some insight into the role of a social worker in this country. I hope I have done it justice. I don't doubt there are errors within but I take full responsibility. I also want to take this opportunity to acknowledge, though often vilified by the media, the huge and great work that social workers do every day in the most challenging of situations.

A special mention also for Paul FitzSimons who put me in touch with Eva-Maria Oberauer who helped me with my rusty German and also for pointing out a few things that I had missed! Thank you so much!

For my little farfalles Lila, Tom & Bea: you three amaze me every day and I am blessed to have you as my children. I am really enjoying watching your individual personalities develop and the bond of friendship grow between the three of you. You give me and your daddy lots to smile about when you are tucked up in bed and I think I can speak for both of us when I say we couldn't be any prouder of you.

To Simon, to whom this book is dedicated and who is also the co-creator of the aforementioned children. It definitely isn't easy being married to a writer, or more specifically, me. Thank you for allowing me to dream big. I love you.

My wonderful parents for always going above and beyond for me when I was a child and for still doing it today. For just being there at the drop of a hat, for your understanding and always being ready to jump in my corner. I love you so much and more. You also do more than your fair share of baby-sitting to allow me to write. And also Niall and Nita, Tom and DeeDee, I know how fortunate I am to have a family like you. From the bottom of my heart I love and thank you.

All the van Lonkhuyzens for their support and for being brilliant grandparents to my three children. Even though you have seen your grandparenting duties literally multiply over the last five years, thank you so much for all that you do for us.

To my friends: I don't want to mention names because I will leave somebody out but you know who you are. Thank you for the laughs (and sometimes inspiration)! A few of you have some exciting things happening this year and I'm looking forward to sharing them with you. Love you all x

A special mention has to go to Margaret Scott who I've only come to know through writing but I think I can safely say that our friendship transcends just writing. Thank you for being an amazing support through the ups and downs and for always being at the end of the phone for the reassurance. Especially your encouragement when I struggled at several stages of writing this book.

To the booksellers who are fighting the good fight. I will never tire of walking into a bookshop and seeing a book with my name on the cover on the shelves. It still feels as good as the first time and I realise how privileged I am to experience this. To the book-bloggers and reviewers who have been so supportive of me to date and also to Vanessa at www.writing.ie who is a fabulous support of Irish authors and emerging writers.

Lastly, to all my readers who pick up my book from the shelves and especially the people who take the time out from their lives to get in touch with me about my books. It never ceases to amaze, humble and make me pinch myself how lucky I am to be doing this.

With much love,
Caroline x

BOOKCLUB QUESTIONS

1. Did you feel empathy for Ella's situation initially? What about afterwards?

2. There is strong use of imagery of the sea in Ella's story, specifically her Martello Tower home situated on the rocks in Dublin Bay. Do you think that was intentional and does it add to the story?

3. Conor and Ella have been friends for a long time and share a close bond. Do you think friendships between men and women can ever be truly platonic?

4. Rachel and Marcus have a seemingly perfect relationship except for the fact that he doesn't want to have any more children. He is adamant that it is unfair to bring a child into the world when he doesn't want it. Do you agree with this belief? Do you think he should have relented so he could hold on to Rachel?

5. What did you think of John-Paul's relationship with his son?

6. Do you agree with John-Paul's solicitor when he argues in court that society is unfair to fathers, especially unmarried fathers, and has a natural bias towards women as mother figures?

7. Ella and her sister Andrea have very different attitudes to their mother's desertion of their family as children. Why do you think this is?

8. Do you agree with Ella's assertion that 'every action has an equal and opposite reaction' i.e. that we must suffer the consequences of our actions?

9. Rachel mentions that you wouldn't do her job if you didn't have hope that people can change. How important is it to have this attitude in our everyday lives?

10. Who saves whom in this novel?

11. Which character do you think grew the most over the course of the story and why?

12. What do you think the future holds for Jack?

AUTHOR INTERVIEW

Where did the idea for the storyline come from?

A question that writers get asked a lot is 'where do your ideas come from?' and sometimes it can be hard to pinpoint exactly where they originate. In general, I think writers are always switched on. We are intuitively soaking up ideas all the time. With *Into The Night Sky*, I heard a piece on the Ray Darcy Radio Show about a woman who had found a Chinese paper lantern in her garden one night and inside it there was a love letter. The woman was trying to trace the person who wrote it, as it was obviously very personal to them, which was why she contacted the show. This story stayed in my head and I had an image of this beautiful lantern, glowing orange and sailing majestically up over a background of a navy-blue sky and at the same time I imagined this grieving man and the story came from there.

For Jack I had this image of a precocious boy from a disadvantaged area in my head for a while. Initially Conor jumps to the conclusion that Jack is going to be another troublemaker like the other children who live near Haymarket Books. Then as a friendship develops between them people automatically jump to conclusions that there is something untoward going on. With Jack's storyline I wanted to explore further how we prejudge people every day and form often incorrect preconceptions about them. In a day and age where people are fearful of predators it is too easy to automatically assume the worst about everyone. As a mother myself, I am guilty of prejudging people when I hear of an adult befriending an unrelated child, especially if that adult is male. I wanted to turn the preconceptions on their head and show that theirs is a story of true friendship. What is special about Conor and Jack's friendship is that as much as Conor helps Jack come to terms with his mother's imminent death, Jack helps Conor to accept what has happened to Leni and he provides a chink of light in a very dark period in Conor's life. They both help each other without realising it.

As I was exploring the theme of friendship further between Conor and Jack I wanted to contrast it with a very different kind of friendship, namely the friendship between Conor and Ella.

I initially hadn't intended on Ella being such a big character in the story but I kept having this image of a woman undergoing intense personal suffering and not being able to cope and it wouldn't leave me. I read about a woman in a magazine who was very well off but she was addicted to shoplifting. Financially, she obviously didn't need to shoplift but it was an impulse that she couldn't control. I think there is very little awareness of this problem and the reasons aren't properly understood. Even when I was doing my research I kept finding conflicting information on it. With Ella I wanted to explore the very fine link between good mental health and instability, the knock-on impact it can have in other areas of our lives.

Regarding the custody battle between John-Paul and Tina, there has been a lot of media coverage in recent times of the rights of unmarried fathers in Ireland. In Ireland at present if a parent isn't married then the father has no automatic guardianship rights unless he specifically applies to the courts to become a legal guardian which is the situation that John-Paul finds himself in. Originally when I started writing the story, the role of the social worker was only meant to be a sideline character. I didn't intend to have Rachel being so prominent in the book but as often is the case when you start writing, characters take on a life of their own and she was one of those. I realised that by giving Rachel a storyline of her own it was an opportunity to show the brave and important work that social workers do and how difficult it must be to do that job every day.

Your novels all have a 'what would you do?' moral dilemma at their heart. Did you set out to be an issue-led writer?

No, I didn't actually, but I can certainly see this is the route that I am going down and I'm happy with that as these are the books I like to read myself. Both *In a Moment* and *The Last Goodbye* and now *Into the Night Sky* have big issues at their heart. My plots usually come to me with a central issue or theme and then the characters usually come after. I think there are lots of situations in life where there are no easy answers. As a fiction writer I have the benefit of being able to explore both sides of a dilemma. Sometimes when I am writing, I ask myself 'What would I do in that situation?' but then when I think about it from the other point of view, I can often empathise with that viewpoint too.

In general I am interested in back-story, the childhoods that shape the people we are today and family relationships.

Addiction features prominently in the book both with John-Paul and Tina who are recovering drug addicts and then also with Ella's kleptomania. Why did you choose this theme to explore?

I think addiction is a very worthy theme in its own right. It is a personal tragedy. It is horrifying to watch someone lose everything they care about because they are overpowered by a synthetic substance or a damaging behaviour. The addiction is always the master to which all other things come second place. Some people can be strong enough to overcome its calling, such as Tina because of her love for her unborn son Jack. However, it also destroys so many lives such as in both Ella's and John-Paul's storyline.

Did you have a favourite character when writing *Into The Night Sky*?

I actually fell in love with the character of Jack. I loved his spirit and tenacity. As I was writing the story I often found myself thinking of him as if he was a real child in my life. For example, I was in a department store one day and I saw something about the footballer Cristiano Ronaldo, who, as you know if you've read the book, Jack is a big fan of. I found myself thinking 'Oh, Jack would love that!' and I had to remind myself that he was fictional. So he was very real to me and I will definitely miss him but who knows, I may revisit him as an adult down the line in a future book to see how his life has turned out.

Do you plan carefully or just see where the writing takes you?

I really, really wish that I were a better planner. It catches me out on every book and I always say next time I will plan more first but I just can't do it no matter how much I try. I've come to accept that my brain just isn't wired that way for some reason. I will usually start with a rough plot outline and the main characters. I usually have the title as well which for me seems to be crucial to forming the story in my head. Personally speaking, I don't really get to know the story until I get to the end of the first draft and then I go back over it again several times to bring it all together.

Do you have your own writing rituals?

Not really. I tend to write whenever I can grab a few minutes between family life or when my children are in bed, so I don't have the luxury of being choosy. Often I write in coffee shops at weekends and I quite like that. Sometimes it's nice to be immersed amongst other people – the background noise can be soothing for a change as writing can often be a lonely experience.

Caroline Finnerty
What are you working on at the moment?

I'm in the middle of my fourth book, which at the moment I have entitled *My Sister's Child*. It is the story of the relationship between two sisters Jo and Isla. Fourteen years before Isla donated eggs to her older sister Jo who was undergoing fertility problems. Two embryos were made, one of which was implanted into Jo resulting in her daughter Realtín, and the other was frozen in storage.

Fast forward to the present day where Isla is experiencing infertility problems too, and with no options left to conceive a biological child of her own, she decides to ask Jo if she can have her last remaining embryo from storage.

The story deals the dilemma faced by Jo, who doesn't want Isla to have the embryo even though genetically it was conceived using Isla's egg. It focuses on the tension between Jo and Isla and the ethical dilemmas surrounding egg donation. The central theme is 'nature versus nurture'. I must say I have really enjoyed writing it so far and it will be published in 2015.